BETWEEN WORLDS

BOOKS 1-3

LORI WOLF-HEFFNER

Consulting editing by Heather Wright

Editing by Susan Fish

Cover design by Fresh Design

All photographs from Shutterstock

Head in the Ground Publishing

Waterloo, Ontario, Canada

www.headintheground.com

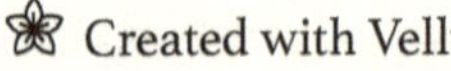 Created with Vellum

BETWEEN WORLDS 1

THE MOVE

This book is dedicated to my grandparents:

John & Mary Heffner
Theresia Heffner
Martin & Magdalena Wolf
Sebastian & Katharina Zimmermann

who dared to leave everything they knew behind to
immigrate to Canada to give their families a better life

PROLOGUE

Juliana watched in the bathroom mirror as she whipped her long, board-straight hair into a ponytail.

"I hope this new brand of elastic holds for a change," she muttered to herself.

Already dressed in her leggings and crop top, she threw on her warm-up suit.

"Juliana! Come on! You're going to be late!"

Juliana sighed. "I know, Mom!"

She quickly tapped the baking soda out of her jazz shoes and into the sink, dropped them on top of her ballet shoes, pointe shoes, tap shoes, and hip-hop shoes in her dance bag, and tossed her bag over her shoulder.

"Don't yell at me like that!" Mom shouted back.

Juliana stopped at her door and checked the date on her

phone, hoping that she maybe had the wrong day in her head. But she didn't: it was her last practice with the dance team she'd grown up with and the last time she'd see her friends before she and her family moved across the country to some dipstick city in Ontario.

She wiped away a tear as she ran downstairs.

Elisabeth stared into the looking glass in the front room as she completed the braid that began at the nape of her neck, folding it back upon itself so its end was over the top of her head. She dug a comb into her hair, against the end of the braid, to fasten it down.

"I had better add in a few of these," she muttered to herself as she stuck in several hairpins.

Already dressed in her four underskirts and long-sleeved white blouse, Elisabeth slipped her white pleated outer skirt over her head, settled it on her hips, and closed it.

"Elisabeth! Where are you, child? We'll be late!"

Elisabeth sighed. "I know, Mammi!"

"Do not speak to your mother like that!" Mammi replied from the kitchen.

Elisabeth quietly asked Jesus for forgiveness, gave her leather boots a quick wipe with a rag, and tossed two clean handkerchiefs into her tiny purse—one never knew where one might need them.

Before she left the front room, she glanced up at the crucifix that hung above the doorway. It was the first Sunday of Advent, the last year her town, Semlak, would belong to Hungary, and the day before her father left for America.

Knowing Mammi would scold her for crying, she swallowed her sadness, picked up her boots, and tip-toed into the kitchen so she wouldn't get her stockings dirty.

Juliana entered the front door, kicked the snow off her boots at the entrance, hung her coat with all the other coats on the rack, and tiptoed through the slush and water left behind by other boots until she reached the carpet of the main hallway. Mom followed.

They passed the door to the first studio, on their right, and Juliana stopped.

"Where's the music?" she asked. Normally, junior jazz took place at this time in Studio 1, but Juliana couldn't hear anything.

"Maybe they're watching the seniors in Studio 2," Mom offered.

But even from there, Juliana heard no music. Maybe

everyone was getting in trouble for something. That had happened several weeks ago when students started complaining about shoes going missing from their bags, and it had turned out to be a joke carried out by a few junior and intermediate dancers.

Juliana entered the tiny change room, took off her warm-up suit, and slipped on her hip-hop shoes. Still no noise.

"Okay, something's going on," she said to Mom, who just shrugged.

Juliana opened the door to the second studio. Old fluorescent lights flickered on and voices yelled, "Surprise!"

Juliana jumped. The intermediate dance team squeezed through the door and came running at her. Within moments, she was engulfed in friends. As everyone tried to hug her and she tried to hug everyone, Juliana fought back tears, but her friends couldn't.

Miss Kasia, her long black hair pulled into a pony-tail, walked up from behind the group. "We've got a little party for you," she said.

Juliana looked up, and only then did she notice that the studio was packed with students, at least sixty or seventy of them, almost half of the entire dance school.

"Finally!" a five-year-old girl with black pigtails exclaimed. "I've been waiting for hours to hug you!"

Juliana laughed as the girl wrapped her arms around Juliana's hips. Shortly afterwards, all the young kids hugged Juliana in turn on their way through the hall and the tiny change room into Studio 1. She followed their movement with her gaze and saw that a bunch of different activity stations had been set up for them.

Miss Kasia smiled at Juliana as she helped an assistant teacher herd the children. "So you can enjoy some time away from your adoring fans and be with your friends."

Juliana was the studio's biggest cheerleader, cheering on the dancers at every competition, helping the younger students practice before they went on stage, doing their hair as they got ready, giving novice competitive dancers pep talks... And that was in addition to starting as an assistant dance teacher this year, a new role in her life she was absolutely loving.

If only this move hadn't gotten in the way, this school year would have been absolutely perfect.

"Oh my god, Juliana!" Rachel said. "I'm so going to miss you!" Friends since their first class ten years before, the girls squeezed one another until they could hardly breathe.

Miss Kasia guided the older students back into Studio 2, which was decorated with streamers and balloons in purple and gold, the studio's colours.

Messages written in window markers were scrawled across the wall of mirrors.

"I'm going to miss you! Matilda"

"Remember when you tripped me at Dance Olympia last year? LOL I'll never forget! Linda"

"You're an awesome partner! Declan"

Juliana walked slowly along the reflective expanse, reading each message and taking as many pictures as she could. One mirror had lots of little-kid scribbled printing on it.

"You teached me how to point my feet! Liliana"

"You're too tall, but I'll still miss you. Farah"

"You'll be famous someday! Jason"

With each message Juliana read, she laughed or sniffled or both. There must have been at least a hundred messages and it took her a little time to read them. She barely noticed her friends holding up their phones to record it all. By the time she got to the end of the line of mirrors, Juliana had tears streaming down her face.

Declan came up to her and hugged her. "You look a mess," he said, smiling. Juliana wiped her eyes. "I hate surprises," she said.

Rachel piped up. "Just for once I wanted to see what would happen if something unexpected happened to you."

"This was your idea?" Juliana asked. "You're my best

friend!" She playfully punched Rachel in the shoulder and then hugged her again.

"Come over here, Juliana," Miss Kasia said and pointed her toward a plastic chair decorated with purple and gold balloons reaching up toward the ceiling on long, matching ribbons. Juliana glanced over at her mom quickly, and her eyes, too, were a little wet.

The young kids were brought back in from their activities, and one by one they handed Juliana a picture they had drawn. Nateesha, one of the dancers from the pipsqueak classes, gave Juliana a huge hug. Juliana had watched their competitive jazz number every time it was up at competition and had always cheered them on from the audience. It was something she tried to do for every dance the studio had entered.

"I'm going to miss you." Nateesha started crying. "You're a fun teacher." Juliana cried, too. She had just begun the teacher training program this year and had already fallen in love with it. Why did she have to leave all these amazing people behind?

Miss Kasia headed over to the studio computer and clicked a few keys as someone turned off the lights. A video started playing on the white wall opposite the mirrors. Nateesha sat herself on Juliana's lap.

Rachel leaned over to her best friend and whispered, "I don't want you to go."

"I know. But Mom and Dad say we're the only ones who can look after my grandfather."

"Can't they just put him in a home?"

The opening slides in the video showed pictures of Juliana growing up, from her pipsqueak days to her intermediate classes.

"I asked that, too. Mom says it's too expensive and he doesn't have the money for it."

Juliana loved her life in Calgary: she had amazing friends, was in her last year of junior high school, and had just begun learning how to teach dance. Moving now, at Christmas no less, meant she'd have to leave her friends behind, miss her graduation, and hold off on apprenticing as a dance teacher until at least next year. Aunt Anne lived around the corner from Opa, and Uncle Peter didn't have any kids. Couldn't they look after Opa? Why was it Juliana's family who had to move half-way across the country to live with a man she hardly knew?

JULIANA SWITCHED OUT HER HIP-HOP SHOES FOR HER TAP shoes.

"One last time?" Matilda asked. Juliana nodded.

The entire group, all eleven intermediate tap dancers, took up formation in the studio while everyone else sat along the walls, the little kids in the laps of the big ones. The music came on. Juliana, standing sideways, her head bent down and her right hand grabbing the rim of an invisible hat, dropped her heel in time with the beat, a simple rhythm to start the number. Then, one by one, each dancer heel-dropped to their own rhythm, creating a percussion foreground for the music. On a loud cymbal crash, they turned front, their heads down, waited eight counts, and then jumped into the opening riff sequence.

As Juliana's feet slammed onto, slid along, and grazed the floor, she thought of the conversation she'd had with Mom in the car on the way to the studio.

"This isn't fair," Juliana had said.

"I know you're scared—"

"No, I'm not." The last thing Juliana wanted was a heart-to-heart with Mom. "I have my friends here, my dance team, the teacher training program."

"Your new studio also has one."

"But when I emailed them, they said they'd have to see me first and that I'd have to spend at least a year with them before I could be considered."

"You'll need time to adjust to things, anyway," Mom said. "If you started teaching at the same time as you started at your new studio and your new school, you'd be too overwhelmed. I know you, sweetheart. If you can't stay on top of things, you fall apart. As it is, we're lucky they accepted videos of your dancing and agreed you can join the competitive program this late in the game."

Lucky? To leave the studio where she had danced since she was four? To leave all these friends?

Now, as the rhythms flowed through her body, her anger grew. She slammed harder and slid farther than usual. Her hands flew into the air on command and stopped, sharp, as though they had hit a wall. She kept looking out the corner of her eyes to stay in line with the others, but the more she looked, the angrier she became. She had travelled to Vancouver and Edmonton with this group, even to Seattle, to compete. They didn't always win, and sometimes they lost horribly, but no matter what happened, Juliana's dance team was always there for her.

How could it possibly be the same in Kitchener, Ontario?

Cramp roll, cramp roll, da-da de-de, da-da de-de. Prepare, wait, double pirouette, land.

Juliana remembered that time two years before when she'd swung her leg into the high kick that led into the climax of the jazz group, right where the music began its crescendo and the rest of the group had frozen into different positions, waiting for her to land her kick so they could burst into the final counts of the routine.

They were at a national championship and had a good shot at diamond, the highest ranking.

But the stage had been too slippery and Juliana had lost her footing, landing on her bum and hands. The fall had shocked her so much that she hadn't been able to move. Normally, the other dancers would have continued dancing around her, finishing the number. And she wouldn't have been angry at them had they done that! But everyone had stopped and immediately rushed to her aid. Miss Kasia had run onstage and conducted a short examination, and doctors had later confirmed her suspicions: Juliana had sprained the ankle of her supporting leg and broken a wrist.

All during her healing and therapy, her friends hung out with her, encouraged her—almost forced her—to come to the studio to watch from the side and to continue learning, and they were there for her when she could finally return to class, her technique weaker than it had been before. Their frequent texts to keep up her physio, not to push too hard...all of that had kept her going and brought her back stronger than before.

Juliana's feet became louder, her arms sharper, her anger channelling itself into the floor. *Flap ball-change across, pose, hold for 32...jump up, chaîné turn in, continue.*

She caught her anger in the mirror, the intensity of her face startling even her.

Chaîné turn out, continue.

Fast flaps, kick, dig, arms, hat.

The music stopped and the room broke out in applause. Juliana, huffing and puffing, looked around at her fellow dance mates, and everyone's face was covered in tears. They ran together for a massive group hug.

Juliana didn't want to let go.

It was November 30, 1919: the first Sunday of Advent and the second Christmas after the war. Each of the four Schuhmacher children scurried out of the house to avoid Mammi's hurry-it-up tap on the bum, and then Tata closed the house door behind them.

As everyone stood under the overhang in the blustery winter wind, Mammi inspected each child one last time, from oldest to youngest, as she always did: She pulled up the collar on Elisabeth's blouse, tightened Anna's white kerchief, wiped a smudge off Luki's face, and straightened Rosina's apron.

"I will not have my family attending church looking like pigs," Mammi said, and Elisabeth's father gave an approving nod.

Elisabeth tugged at the cuffs on her blouse so they covered her wrists. Although she hadn't grown in a year or two, some of her clothing just never seemed to fit, and she hated a cold breeze blowing through her sleeves. She slipped her hands into the knitted mittens she'd received last Christmas and pulled her thick shawl tighter over her shoulders. Sometimes she envied the men: their coats looked so warm. However, they were nowhere near as beautiful or as precious as the meticulously embroidered, thick shawls the women wore over their Sunday clothes.

It hadn't snowed in a few days, and the wind had blown much of it off the trees, exposing their grey, dried branches. The ground crunched underneath Elisabeth's feet as the family of six walked down the street to the Lutheran church. Why they had all had to polish their boots, she didn't know.

"It's been a year," Tata said, "and I still miss the church bells."

"Churches have bells?" Rosina asked, her eyes wide open. At only six years old, Rosina was too young to remember life before the war. Elisabeth laughed. If only she could see life so innocently, but the war had showed her a side of the world she hadn't known existed and wished she could forget.

"Two years ago," Tata said, "the big church bell was

taken so it could be melted to make cannons for the war. A year later, the small one, too."

Luki, only eight, and named after their father, chimed in. "You don't remember the loud noises they made before church began? I covered my ears whenever we got close!"

Rosina shook her head.

The nearer they came to the church, the more families they saw. Elisabeth waved to several of her friends. Her best friend, Maria, was walking just ahead of them.

"Maria!" she shouted, smiling.

"Elisabeth!" Mammi scolded. "No need to look stupid by smiling so much."

Elisabeth tried hard to suppress her reply; she knew it would only bring her some kind of punishment, especially because it was Advent service they were attending today. But before Elisabeth could close the lid on her anger, her retort escaped her thoughts and flew out her mouth.

"I'm certain Jesus smiled, too," Elisabeth said.

Tata grabbed her wrist, and through clenched teeth said, "Nowhere in the Bible does it say that."

Elisabeth said nothing further, and it wasn't because she was giving in to her father's statement; it was because Tata was leaving for America tomorrow, and she didn't want to quarrel with him on his last day. She would miss him. At fourteen, Elisabeth had already finished her schooling two years ago, and her father had taken it upon himself to continue to teach her. Elisabeth loved nothing more than to sit with Tata after supper, with several gas lamps placed on the kitchen table, and read from the Bible, Martin Luther's teachings, and their family's encyclopedia, which had been left to her Otata, her grandfather, by a family friend a long time ago. She wanted Tata to remember her for how hard she studied, not how quick her mouth was. She took a deep breath, silently asked Jesus for forgiveness, and changed the topic.

"Why can't you find work in Temeswar?" Elisabeth asked Tata. "You could work in a store that has electricity and more customers, and earn more in a day than you would here with farming and shoemaking." Temeswar was a city that lay about ninety kilometres away. Although her father would have to board there during the week, at least he could come home on some weekends.

"Elisabeth," Anna interrupted, "stop asking so many questions. We're almost at church." Only a year older than Luki, Anna attended school with her brother. Her teachers had always praised her abilities and she was among the top students in the school, but Anna knew the unspoken rule: just like everyone else born in the village, her schooling would stop after grade six.

Tata patted his eldest daughter on her kerchief. "I'll

miss you, too, Lissika. But I can't earn enough money here."

Rosina pushed her way in front of Luki to talk to her father. "But you're a shoemaker. Don't people in Temeswar wear shoes?"

Tata and Elisabeth laughed.

"Of course they do," Tata answered. "But now that the war is over, our little village and many, many others like Semlak are being taken from Hungary and given to Romania. People are scared about that. It means they'll try harder to save money and they won't buy new shoes. After only a year's work in America, I can buy us more land to farm when I return."

"Get out of my way!" Luki shouted at Rosina as he pushed her.

"Mammi!" Rosina cried. "I was just talking to Tata—"

"You were standing in front of me on purpose!"

"Was not!"

"Was, too!"

Mammi grabbed both their wrists and dragged each child to either side of her. She then let go and spanked each one once. "God is watching," she said.

"We always need to make money," Tata continued, "and farming is always certain: the land here is fertile, and people will always want food. If I could earn money just from making and repairing shoes and save you all so much hard work, I would."

"But why can't we all go?"

"Why would you want to leave your *heimat*?" Tata asked. "This is where your heart is. Semlak is more than just your home, my sweetheart. It is who you are and where you come from. Your ancestors arrived here a hundred years ago. You know everyone, can speak with them all, and you can celebrate our festivities with them. When I arrive in America, even though I'll be among friends of friends, it will be different. Very, very different."

Before Elisabeth could say anything, a voice shouted through the crowds of people.

"There you are, Herr and Frau Schuhmacher. We haven't seen you all week! Have you finished packing?"

Elisabeth shuddered. If there was one person in this village she disliked—and may Jesus forgive her—it was Meier Josef. Every Sunday, he moved from one family to the next, asking what was new when he was really trying to learn what was wrong so he could tell others.

Tata shook his hand and Mammi nodded slightly.

"I'm almost done, Herr Meier," Tata said politely. "My wife will bake me some fresh bread tomorrow. My last loaf of fresh bread from her."

"Nobody bakes like a good housewife, I always say," Meier Josef said. Ordinarily, Mammi would show a small smile after such a compliment, but with Meier Josef she barely nodded an acknowledgement.

"Do you have the list I wrote out for you?" Meier Josef asked.

"It's in my travel bag. I can't thank you enough for it."

Meier Josef tipped his hat. "Then I will pick you up tomorrow morning at seven."

Tata nodded in acknowledgement before Meier Josef saw another family, waved to them, and headed in their direction. Elisabeth sighed with relief. At the service last week, Meier Josef had wanted to know if Mammi had fully prepared all the food Tata would need, as if suggesting she would neglect her familial duties. It was an impertinent question and Mammi wouldn't stop complaining about it for the rest of the day.

The Schuhmachers finally reached the church. The yellow-painted, single-steeple structure stood on the east side of the village, like a bright sun in the dead of winter. An Advent wreath adorned each of the two doors of the main entrance. Normally, Elisabeth loved every sight, sound, and smell of Christmas. But this time, she dreaded it: Tata was to leave tomorrow, just as Christmas preparations began.

She wiped a tear from her eye as she entered the church.

AS THE FAMILY WALKED DOWN THE AISLE, TATA AND LUKI split to the left to sit with the other men, and Mammi and the three sisters went to the right. Omama, Elisabeth's grandmother—and only grandparent—sat up at the front with the other older women of the congregation, and Elisabeth could also see many of her parents' siblings, nieces, and nephews sprinkled throughout the church.

This was one of few situations in her life where Elisabeth truly appreciated all her skirts: where her brother frequently squirmed on the hard pews through the service, and she even occasionally caught Tata shifting around, Elisabeth, her sisters, and their mother could sit relatively comfortably because of the extra cushioning those layers provided.

It was frowned upon to talk in church, but lately, people had given in to temptation, discussing Semlak's future before the service started. Today was no different.

"Maybe the laws will change back," a woman sitting behind Elisabeth said.

"They won't," another replied. "The war has destroyed Hungary. My husband says we will do better under the Romanian king."

The pipe organ silenced everyone with the opening

chords of a hymn, and the congregation stood up. The choir began to sing, and the harmonies of the voices with those of the pipe organ filled Elisabeth's soul.

Pastor Fröhlich entered through a side door in the nave, dressed in his black robes. His face stern, his hands folded in prayer, he walked toward the altar like a soldier of Jesus.

Jesus is about to be born, and yet we all look so sad, Elisabeth thought. No one knew what it would mean to belong to Romania, and she didn't know what it would mean to not have her father at home.

She pulled out one of the handkerchiefs from her black purse, dried her tears, and wiped her nose. Mammi threw her an angry look, which Elisabeth ignored.

Even Jesus had a father on earth, she thought.

Juliana slumped into the backseat of the SUV they had rented for the cross-country trip. They'd been on the road for four days now and were about to leave Winnipeg. That was four days of being cramped into a vehicle with her parents, their luggage, and vain attempts at trying to make her feel better.

And that was four days without any dance to *actually* make her feel better.

"Would've been more fun in your truck," she complained. Dad had been a transport truck driver all of Juliana's life. When she was younger, she'd even joined him on day trips. They would eat at truck stops, and she got to blast the horn at stupid drivers.

Compared to the spaciousness and rumbling of a

transport truck on the Trans-Canada Highway, an SUV felt like a twenty-year-old car that couldn't drive over sixty.

Dad took a deep breath, a sure sign he was losing his patience. "I've told you time and again that I sold it because I no longer want to own one, and flying would've been a waste of money. Besides, this way we can bring more along while we wait for the rest of our belongings." He threw their suitcases into the trunk and a few bags into the backseat beside Juliana before sliding into the driver's seat. Mom was still inside at the hotel, checking out.

"I can't believe I have to spend another two days in the car with you," Juliana said. The harshness of her words surprised even her. She mumbled an apology, but it was too late.

Dad slammed his door shut and whipped his head around.

"Sometimes you have to make sacrifices for the people you love," he growled.

"I don't even know Opa!" Juliana shouted back.

Dad sighed one of those loud "now I'm fed up with you" sighs and turned back to the front. Through the rearview mirror, Juliana could see him roll his eyes in exasperation.

"I saw that," she said.

"Think of it this way," Dad said. "You won't have had to wash lettuce for almost a week."

Juliana couldn't stand kitchen work. It involved a lot of tiny actions to create something that would disappear an hour or two later. But washing lettuce took the cake: cold water, little bugs, and the monotony of tearing leaves left a bitter taste in her mouth every time she had to do it. And somehow her parents found her dislike amusing and wouldn't let her out of the task.

Mom got in, passed the receipt to Dad so he could double-check it, stuck it back in her wallet after he okayed it, and buckled up.

"Got your seatbelt on?" she asked Juliana, oblivious to the fight that had just taken place.

"Mhmm."

Dad turned on the ignition, and off they drove. After a few moments of silence, Mom looked at both of them.

"What? Another fight?" she asked.

"Mhmm," Dad replied.

Four days of not dancing, talking and laughing with her friends, or evening playing in Calgary snow. Juliana had looked up recent photos of Kitchener. Her new home, if you could call it that, looked dreary and plain, not alive and magical.

She was angry, alone, and stuck in a car with her parents, who were making her leave everything she loved behind.

Which left her with one question: Who was cheering for Juliana?

Juliana tapped out a beat to her music with her hand on the car-door handle. Day number five was three-quarters done, and she could barely sit still anymore.

"Juliana, can you stop that, please?" Mom asked.

Juliana moved her hand to tap in her lap.

"That, too."

Juliana grumbled under her breath and flipped through her phone to find something to distract her. Her parents had cancelled her phone number back in Calgary so she would have a Kitchener area code: 519 or 226 instead of 403. Seeing those new numbers made her skin crawl. There was something unnatural about them.

But without a connection, she couldn't access any of her cloud services and could only scroll through photos and videos from the last three months, the limit she had set ages ago so her photos stayed organized.

"Juliana," Mom said, "you know why we're doing this, right?"

"Uh-huh."

"To look after Opa."

"Yup." She scrolled through her photos and found

the video Miss Kasia had taken of the party at her studio.

"He can't live alone anymore."

"There's always old-age homes." Juliana tapped on play and watched the tap routine from her going-away party.

"Can you take out your earbuds, please?"

Juliana did as requested but still kept her eyes focussed on the screen.

"And shut off your phone?" Mom asked. "Please?"

Juliana sighed and just turned her phone over, which seemed to satisfy Mom.

"Opa can't afford an old-age home, sweetie. They cost upwards of $2,300 a month. And when Oma was in care, it was awful."

"That was ten years ago. I'm sure things have gotten better." Did this conversation have to continue? They were already on the road, they had sold their house in Calgary, Mom had already found a job managing a grocery store in Kitchener, and Dad had found work with a trucking company. It was a done deal. There was no point in talking about it anymore. "Can I put my earbuds back in now?"

"No. I need you to understand. This is my father we're talking about. He's alone, has early signs of dementia, and never learned how to cook except for boxed cereal, cold cuts, and toast. We're worried an accident will happen."

Juliana made eye contact with Mom through the sideview mirror. "You have a brother and sister in Kitchener. They could check in on him while Meals on Wheels drops by everyday with his food. I don't get why we have to move."

Juliana knew she was trying her parents' patience, but they were trying hers, too. With Dad always on the road in his transport truck, often gone for a week or two at a time, and Mom always early at the grocery store and staying easily an hour after closing, Juliana sometimes had the feeling she was raising herself. What right did they have to tell her what to do? They were hardly home as it was.

Mom took a deep breath. In contrast to Dad, who took deep breaths when he was getting angry, Mom took deep breaths after she was angry and needed to calm herself. "I just feel you still don't understand everything. Your Uncle Peter's job takes him away from home for days—sometimes weeks—at a time, and Aunt Anne has to look after six children, the youngest of whom is only eight. Neither of them can look after Opa, and both my job and your father's can be done anywhere in the country."

Juliana slammed her hand on her lap. "I get all that!

But my life can't just happen somewhere else in the country!"

"You're a student," her father replied dryly. "There are thousands of schools in Canada, most with hundreds of students for you to choose your friends from. Same with dance studios. Your 'life' can very well be done anywhere in the country."

Juliana propped her elbow on the door handle and looked outside. Why did Mom have to bring this all up again? Juliana needed to get out...being cooped up in a vehicle with her parents was driving her insane. As the forests of Ontario rushed by, she had to admit that the snow on them did look beautiful, almost like out of a storybook or a cheesy Christmas movie. If Kitchener looked like this, it might have made things a little easier. But she had searched lots of images of Kitchener online again this morning, and she saw the same as every other morning this week: a dreary, grey city.

"In a few hours we'll be in Kapuskasing, where we'll stop for the night," Mom said.

Juliana looked at the clock on her phone: 5:32 PM. They'd been in the car since eight that morning, stopping only for bathroom breaks and lunch. Supper would be in the car so they could get to their hotel and sleep.

"Yay," Juliana mumbled to herself.

VAUGHAN

That's what the sign said. Juliana's legs were bouncing in the car, but at least her parents had let her sleep in this morning and spend some time in the hotel's pool. If they hadn't, she didn't know how she would've handled these last two hours before they would arrive in Kitchener: she already felt like a trapped animal dying to get out of its cage.

But the city name seemed familiar to her.

"Why do I know that name?" she asked.

"It's home to the university that goes on strike all the time," her father said. He always supported the Conservatives, so it was no surprise to Juliana that he would make that comment.

"But it has a world-renowned dance program," her mother added from the driver's seat.

"Ah, okay. That's where you went, right, Mom?"

"Mhmm. Did my master's in dance there."

"What's that again?"

"A lot of research. I investigated representations of the feminine body in Busby Berkley's musicals, looking at how the images of unified women helped create a new discourse on the ideal body of a woman."

Juliana had no idea what her mother had just said, but she was used to it by now. Anytime discussion of her mom's dance education came up, so did the topic of her research. And anytime Juliana asked Mom to bring it down to her level, as hard as she tried, Mom couldn't. After three minutes of listening to Mom explain it to her, Juliana would just ask her to stop. Juliana of course knew Busby Berkley, the long-dead Hollywood producer responsible for all those incredible chorus-line shots taken from above. But representations? Discourse? Not Juliana's language. Dance was her language: no matter what happened anywhere in her life or at any time, she could always turn on music and free her emotions from her body. Whether she was happy, sad, frustrated...it didn't matter. That was part of the reason she felt so caged right now: she couldn't let loose while trapped in the SUV with her parents. Even tapping out a rhythm annoyed them. Dance was not something to be contained and analyzed in the mind— it was meant to live in and be expressed through the body.

"Listen," Dad said, and Juliana braced herself. Anytime he said "listen" she knew she was about to get a lecture of some kind. "I know it's been really tough sitting in a car this entire time, especially with us. And I know your whole life has been uprooted." He paused.

"Okay...?" Juliana answered, not sure of where he was going: it didn't sound like an on-coming lecture.

"We celebrate Christmas Eve tomorrow with Mom's

family, then Christmas Day with the Morgan side. Then it's Boxing Day. On the 27th, I have to check in with my new employer, and the moving truck should arrive then, too, but that evening we'll head over to the mall and get you a new SIM card, okay?"

Juliana's eyes popped out of her head.

"I have to wait another four days?"

"Sorry, sweetie," Mom said. "We thought that would be good news. It's just because of all the timing and the holidays. If we try and get you a SIM card on Boxing Day, we'll be in line for hours."

"So?" Juliana asked. Then an idea came to her and her mood lifted immediately. "Oh, all right. I'll just log in to Opa's network."

Dad looked at her through the sideview mirror, "Your *opa* doesn't own a computer. We've arranged for the Internet to be installed on the 27th, too."

"What?"

"Don't worry—we're only talking a few days here. We'll be so busy with Christmas you'll hardly notice." Dad tried to elicit a smile from Juliana through the rearview mirror, but she just stared back at him.

Her hope so quickly deflated, Juliana stared out the window again at the grey and brown buildings flying by.

"One of the things I hope we can afford when I return is a shingle roof," Tata said. "Herr Meier couldn't stop talking about his after church yesterday. Not a single leak."

Why was a shingle roof so important that her father had to leave the family on a dangerous journey to America? Yes, their straw roof leaked in the spring melt, but they could always repair it. She'd rather deal with that than not have Tata around.

"You can ask him more about it as you drive to the station," Mammi said.

The whole family was waiting outside their home, by the sidewalk, for Meier Josef to come by in his sleigh. He'd offered to drop Tata off at the train station in a neighbouring town, and Elisabeth worried about what family matters would turn into church gossip.

"It'll be nice not to have the roof leaking all the time," Mammi said, and Elisabeth frowned. "Lukas, do you have everything in your luggage now?"

Tata patted his trunk. "I have my tools—though I left some important ones with you so you can work while I'm gone. Clothing, shoes, my coat..."

All the children—Elisabeth, Anna, Luki, and Rosina—had tears in their eyes, and their parents didn't seem to notice.

"And your food?"

Tata opened the heavy bag he had hung across his body. "Your bread, sauerkraut, sausage, plum jam, and cheese."

"Three loaves should last you the trip so you shouldn't have to buy anything," Mammi said.

Tata nodded. "Saving money is what matters so I'm prepared for whatever happens in America. I have the addresses of Meier Josef's friends in Pennsylvania. He said he's written them all to let them know I may be calling. Hopefully I can stay with one of them until I can find boarding."

Many Semlakers had travelled to America over the years, and many had done very well for themselves, sometimes even staying there and bringing their families afterwards. Although Elisabeth wasn't aware of anyone in her family who had made the long and fearful journey there, a cousin of Maria's grandmother had moved there maybe twenty years before. Elisabeth had never heard any bad news, but that didn't mean nothing had happened.

"When are you coming back?" Rosina asked through her sniffles.

"Hopefully in a year," Tata replied. "Fewer people died in America because of the war than here. That means more people need shoes."

"But just go to Arad," Anna said, referring to the central city of their region. She wiped her eyes and nose with the back of her mittened hand. "There are more people there than in Semlak."

"Anna!" Mammi scolded. "Use your handkerchief!"

"I don't have one," Anna replied.

Mammi slapped the back of her hand. "You can wash those when we get inside."

Anna's shoulders drooped.

"I expect you to remember your manners while I'm gone," Tata said. "Once I have a place to live, I'll write you all immediately with my address, and then your mother will tell me all about how you've behaved." His face was stern. "God is still watching you, even when I am not."

The children nodded.

"And your tickets?" Mammi asked, as though nothing had just happened.

Tata unbuttoned his coat to show travel tickets poking out of the pocket inside and then buttoned it back up again.

Elisabeth shivered. The sun hadn't come up yet, and with only an undershirt and blouse underneath her shawl, the morning cold had reached her bones. A quick glimpse at her sisters told her they felt the same. Little Rosina was shivering, so Elisabeth bade her to come closer and then lifted part of her skirt to the side and extended it around her baby sister. Rosina pulled it tight around her.

"I'm cold, too!" Anna snuggled into Elisabeth, but Elisabeth had no more free fabric to help her.

"Anna," Tata said, again in his stern voice, "we do not complain of such things. Jesus endured forty days in the desert. A little time in the cold is nothing compared to that."

"I'm fine," Luki said.

"Because you have a coat!" Anna shot back.

"And you have mittens!"

"Enough!" Tata commanded.

Everyone stood in silence and said not a word for a few moments.

Then something dawned on Elisabeth. "I almost forgot!" she said, unwrapping herself from her sisters and running back inside the house. She unlaced her boots at the door in the kitchen so as not to wet the loam-and-straw floor, darted into the front room, grabbed a folded piece of paper and an extra two blankets, rushed back to the kitchen, slipped into her boots, leaving the laces undone, and appeared back outside in a matter of moments. She handed each of her sisters a blanket, ignoring the frown on her parents' faces. Then she passed the paper to Tata.

"Here," she said. "It's your Christmas card. It's from the last page in my drawing book."

On the card's cover was a drawing of Jesus lying in a manger, with Maria and Josef kneeling on either side. Yellow and brown pencil crayon showed the straw that lay on the ground. Above the manger was a yellow star that shone brightly, and the face of an angel peered in from the corner of the page.

Tata's jaw dropped. "Elisabeth..." He showed the card to everyone. The children gasped, and even Mammi nodded approvingly. "You've never drawn anything this lovely," Tata said. He opened up the card and read aloud what Elisabeth had written: "Dear Tata —I promise to keep reading the Bible, the teachings of Martin Luther, and your encyclopedia while you are away. I will do my best to help Mammi, and I will not complain this spring when I must whiten the walls again. I pray that you arrive safely in Pennsylvania and that many friends will be there to help you. Love, Your Elisabeth."

"My golden one," he said, "thank you. I will keep this in my coat pocket always."

Luki piped up. "I want to give you a hug!"

Tata smiled as Luki wrapped his short, skinny arms around Tata's middle. Anna and Rosina joined in. All the children began to cry again, and Elisabeth's anger rose up.

"It's not fair!" she said. "We want you to stay! I don't care if the roof leaks! I don't care how much land we have! I want you to stay!"

Mammi slapped her cheek. "You do not speak like that to your father!"

"I'll hand you the belt when we're back inside," Elisabeth said defiantly. "You didn't die in the war or disappear. You returned. It's not fair that you're leaving us again!"

"Hold your tongue," Tata said. "This is not how I want to remember you, Elisabeth. You are a kind, obedient, pious child, not an angry one possessed by the Devil." Elisabeth hung her head in shame. "We must all make sacrifices to survive. Remember that God made the ultimate sacrifice: think of Him before you speak like that again."

He sacrificed His only son, Elisabeth thought, daring not to speak her mind again. *What father does that?* Then she immediately vowed to ask God for forgiveness before bed tonight because of her thoughts.

The *clip-clop* of horses approached the house. Elisabeth wrapped her shawl tighter around her, not against the cold but to comfort herself with an embrace she needed. Meier Josef pulled up, tipped his hat, and climbed down from his wagon. He shook Tata's hand and nodded to Mammi and then shook little Luki's hand and nodded to the girls. He looked down at Elisabeth's untied boots. She knew at least one thing he'd tell everyone about after he returned.

Meier Josef and Tata hoisted the trunk onto the sleigh, and the former took his seat again at the front. The younger Schuhmacher children cried as they hugged their father one last time. Elisabeth at first held back—if she embraced him, she feared she would break apart. But when Tata opened his arms to her, she couldn't resist. She rushed in and squeezed him so tightly it was as though her body were trying to anchor him here, to keep him from taking that step onto the sleigh and driving off to a new world, one that was so far away it would be weeks before they knew he had even arrived.

"My golden one, your Tata can't breathe," he said. Embarrassed, Elisabeth pulled away. He lifted her chin with his finger and looked in her eyes the way he did after she had correctly answered all the questions to one of his quizzes.

"You are the oldest," he said. "Be strong. Jesus can help you."

She swallowed and nodded.

Tata and Mammi looked at each other, their faces serious, but Elisabeth caught a glimpse of love in their eyes that she had seen only once before: not in the wedding photo that hung in the back room, but in one that had been stuffed in a drawer. They embraced—tightly—then separated. Tata climbed onto Meier Josef's sleigh and took one last look around.

"By the time I return, I am certain the treaty will be signed, and this will all be Romania." He let out a heavy sigh, Meier Josef shook the reins, and the horses trotted off.

"I want to be the golden one," Luki pouted as the sound of the horses' hooves grew distant, taking their father from them. "When do I get to be the golden one? I'm the only boy."

No one answered Luki's question as Mammi pushed everyone back inside.

"Elisabeth and Rosina, you clean the breakfast

dishes. Luki, I'll help you feed the animals. Anna, wash those filthy mittens."

Anna and Rosina clung to Elisabeth, and Elisabeth didn't know what to do. Like them, her world had just changed. Unlike them, Tata had asked her to be strong.

I don't know if I can, she thought as she looked in the direction the sleigh had gone.

ad rang the doorbell at the side door of the little bungalow, and after a few moments, Opa opened up. He was tall but slouched over, the winter sun reflecting off his shiny head. He wore a plaid shirt, a tan sweater, brown slacks, and brown leather slippers. *The quintessential grandfather*, Juliana thought. Despite her anger at her parents, she would do her best to be polite right now.

A huge smile lit up his face.

"Katy!" he said as he saw his daughter. Mom smiled back. They clamped onto each other in a tight embrace, leaving Juliana to hope she wouldn't be stuck in a hug like that. It wasn't that she didn't like Opa—he always sent her cards for her birthday, Christmas, and Easter, and even put money in them—but she only hugged friends. Hugging anyone else, especially adults, was...weird.

"How are you holding up, Tata?" Mom asked.

"I'm doing fine," he said in his mild German accent. Opa shook Dad's hand and their hug was less intense, which gave Juliana a little hope.

"Oh my goodness," Opa said, his smile growing even bigger. "This isn't Yulika, is it?"

She could never figure out why he called her that. She didn't like it, but she didn't have the heart to tell him.

"It is," Mom said, smiling. She didn't correct him, even though she knew Juliana's feelings about the name. Was Juliana going to have to answer to that all the time now?

Be polite, she thought. *Soon you can find room to dance.*

Opa opened up his arms and Juliana wrapped hers around him loosely. He had the old-man smell, so she tried to turn her nose away.

Thankfully, the hug didn't last very long.

"I know young people don't like to hug," Opa said, "but I haven't seen you since you were this big," and he held his arms as though cradling a baby.

He stepped back from the door, and Juliana could see inside: the door opened on a landing, with a full staircase leading into the basement and two stairs up to the main floor. Each member of the family had to take off their shoes on the tiny landing before going all the way in, and Juliana shivered. This damp, snowless cold in Kitchener was so uncomfortable.

"Come in, come in!" Opa said as he gestured to the small, round table in the kitchen. "What can I get everyone to drink?"

"You sit, Tata. I'll look after us," Mom said.

But Opa would have none of it. "Your mother would not allow it, and neither will I."

The kitchen had two small windows, one that looked out over the driveway, and one that looked out to the front. Just to the right of the front window was a dishwasher in '70s green. To its left came lower cupboards and the kitchen sink, a tiny area for preparing food, then the oven, with some cupboards above it, the fridge, and finally a cupboard under the side window.

"Yuliana?" Opa asked. He also never said her full name with a *j*. "Would you like some pop?"

Juliana shook her head. "Just water, please, Opa."

"I have juice and milk, too."

"No, thank you. Just water."

Opa gave Mom a confused look and Mom smiled back at him. "She's really into dance, Tata. Now that we're in town, you'll hopefully be able to see her. She's wonderful." She smiled at Juliana and Juliana let the corners of her mouth turn up.

Opa beamed and then reached for a glass out of a cupboard above the dishwasher.

Juliana had to admit that his exuberance was kind of sweet.

To the right of the dishwasher was the house's front door. Now it made sense to Juliana why they had come in the side door: who'd want slushy boots in the kitchen? Beside the door, as part of the next wall, was an opening to the living room, followed by cupboards—glass ones up top and solid-wood ones below—then another opening to the living room, and then, extending from the kitchen's back wall, a small hallway, likely where the bedrooms and bathroom were. Beside the hallway was a small wall unit with an old telephone hanging beside it, whose numbers were arranged in a circle, and the fattest TV Juliana had ever seen: it almost seemed to be deeper than it was wide.

Opa placed her glass of water in front of her on the table.

"Thank you, Opa," she said.

"So, Peter," Dad said, "the moving truck will be here on the 27th, and we're getting Internet installed. It'll be a really busy day, but it shouldn't be too bad."

Opa nodded. "I remember, and I have it written down on my calendar." He walked over to the phone and pointed to a small calendar hanging beside it. "Rebecca and Tony moved my things to the basement room a few weeks ago, so my bedroom is ready for the two of you." So far as Juliana could remember, Rebecca and Tony were the oldest children of Aunt Anne and Uncle Phillip and had already finished high school. "And Yuliana, you'll have your mom and aunt's old room. The third bedroom is for guests."

"Good," Dad said.

"All written down," Opa said. "See? There's nothing wrong with me."

Juliana was beginning to wonder the same thing. Opa seemed perfectly happy and wasn't forgetting anything. Why did they have to come here? Not only was she thousands of kilometres from her friends, but she was in a tiny house with only two bathrooms—her parents had warned her about that—meaning she wouldn't have her own ensuite anymore. She knew her bedroom was going to be small, too.

"Where can I practise?" Juliana asked. It was the one question her parents kept saying they wouldn't know until they'd arrived.

Well, now they'd arrived.

"How's the rec room in the basement, Tata?" Mom asked.

Opa wrinkled his nose. "I'm sorry...I haven't had time to clean it."

Didn't have time to clean it? What did he do all day? Watch TV on that really old set?

"We'll have to clean the basement first," Mom said, "and then you can try it out. But it'll be a few days before we get to it."

Juliana didn't want to imagine what the rec room—or the entire basement for that matter—looked like. With any luck, her bedroom would at least be big enough for her to stretch and maybe do a little ballet barre in the middle. At this point, she'd settle for almost anything.

IT WAS TEN AT NIGHT, AND JULIANA SAT ON HER BED, IN her room that was thankfully long enough for her to stretch in. But it had no desk or bookshelves. Once the rest of her furniture arrived, she'd have to stretch elsewhere in the house.

"Hopefully the basement will have more space," she said to herself.

The closet in her bedroom was about a quarter of the size of the one back in Calgary, maybe even smaller, and Juliana had no idea how all her clothing would fit. And where would she keep all her books?

She pulled her portable speakers out of her suitcase and placed them on the night table. She plugged in her phone, opened her music app, and then grunted in frustration.

"'No connection to the Internet,'" she read aloud. "Of course not. Why are we even here? Opa seems just fine, this house is way too small for us, I've had to leave all my friends at home...this city is the ugliest I've ever seen, and all there is around here is farmland." She missed the Rockies and the permanent blanket of snow that stayed on the ground from mid-fall to mid-spring. Outside in Kitchener was dismal: the temperature had hovered just above freezing all day, which explained why the grey sleep of winter that snow always covered in Calgary had been uncovered in Kitchener.

She took a book from one of her suitcases, pulled back the covers on her bed, and shrieked: a spider scurried away, apparently terrified that someone had interrupted its slumber.

"Honey, you okay?" Dad called from his and Mom's room, which was next to hers. The walls were so thin you didn't need to open any doors to shout through the house to someone.

"Spider!"

Within a few moments, Dad came in, and once they had located the spider in a dark corner on the floor, he squashed it with a tissue. Dad inspected the rest of the room to make sure there weren't any more.

"We've hired cleaners to start in January," he said. "That doesn't guarantee there'll never be spiders in here, but it should help keep them down."

Juliana and Dad stared at each other for a few moments, and Dad put his hand on her shoulder.

"I know you're going through a lot, but we'll make it. In the end, you'll find this move to be really good for you."

He gave her a quick good-night hug and returned to his and Mom's room.

"What does he know?" Juliana said to herself. She turned on the lamp on her night table, flicked off the overhead light to her room, climbed into bed, and opened the book to where she'd last left off. As she read, a rumbling sound from the basement traveled through the floor.

It was Opa snoring.

"Yeah, it'll be really good for me."

CHAPTER SIX

Elisabeth wiped her hands on her apron, an old one that tied around her waist—like all aprons did—and had fraying embroidery along the bottom. It had once been her great-grandmother's Sunday apron, but over the years, it had become damaged and worn. With a little trimming and repairing, Mammi had turned it into a work apron for Elisabeth.

"Anna," Elisabeth said, chopping carrots at the kitchen table, "get me two jars of sauerkraut." Anna nodded, slipped on her boots and ran around the house to the cellar. "And Rosina, sweep under the table again —I can still see some crumbs."

Rosina dutifully wet a cloth and dampened the floor underneath the table to avoid kicking up dust. She then picked up the straw broom from the corner of the kitchen and began sweeping, the long broom handle threatening to bump her in the nose from time to time as she tried to manoeuvre it like an adult.

"Don't forget the corners, by the legs," Elisabeth said. "Jesus will be born tonight and Mammi's family is coming tomorrow: the house needs to be clean as though Jesus were joining us." And Rosina swept harder.

Mammi was in the yard tending to the poultry live-stock and had instructed Elisabeth to manage the kitchen. There was still so much to do before Christmas Eve celebrations could begin: prepare vegetables for a dumpling soup, wash potatoes for peeling and cutting tomorrow, prepare the dressing for the goose for tomor-row, keep the oven hot...the list of tasks never ended, and they had just washed up the morning's breakfast dishes. Tata had been gone for nearly four weeks now, and although men didn't help with household chores or most Christmas preparations, with him gone, it still seemed like there was more work to be done.

"Cornstalks!"

Luki—who was playing in the front room—and Rosina stopped to look at her.

"I have to remember to get cornstalks," she explained and promised herself to get them after she was done with the carrots. She still had time.

The oven! She needed to wipe down the oven before Mammi returned. Made of brick and covered in a white lime mixture, dirt showed on it easily.

"Luki, take that cloth in the bucket and wipe down the oven. I want to make sure it's perfectly white."

A mischievous smile crossed Luki's lips. "That's your job."

Elisabeth sighed. Why did he have to be like that today of all days? Couldn't he wait until after Christmas to be a boy again?

Anna returned, placed the two jars of sauerkraut on the kitchen table, and immediately set to work, helping Elisabeth chop.

"Luki," Elisabeth said, "the *stornickels* will give you coal tonight instead of a gift. Go wipe down the oven."

"No."

Luki sat defiantly on the ground.

"You're going to make your pants dirty!"

If Tata were here, he'd be teaching him *skat*, the popular card game, or otherwise keeping him occupied, maybe even collecting the bare cornstalks for the oven directly from the cows' stalls.

"You have to wash them, anyway, so it doesn't matter," Luki said, standing up with a devilish grin on his face, and Elisabeth wanted nothing more now than to pull out that box of dried corn kernels herself and watch him kneel in it for five minutes.

"Elisabeth!"

Elisabeth jumped. She had been so busy with Luki that she hadn't even heard Mammi come in. When she turned around, she could feel herself shrinking on the inside: Mammi was carrying a bushel of cornstalks in her arms. Elisabeth was one more transgression away from the belt.

Forgive me, Jesus: I'm just trying to prepare our meal for You quickly. I was going to get the stalks. You know I was, right?

Elisabeth wiped her hands on her apron and rushed over to take the bushel out of her mother's hands. "Mammi, Luki won't wipe down the oven like I've asked him to."

Mammi slipped out of her boots and into her house shoes and folded her shawl as she took it to the back room to put away.

"You've asked your brother to do your chore? Really, Elisabeth. Your brother will never need to wipe down the oven, so there's no point in making him do it now."

Luki's grin couldn't have been more triumphant, nor Elisabeth's scowl any angrier. She opened the door to the oven, shoved the glowing coals to the side with the poker, and then stuffed the bare cornstalks in.

"Do I have to sweep that, too?" Rosina asked, looking at the tiny scraps and peelings from the stalks that had fallen onto the floor.

"Of course you do," Mammi answered as she headed to the kitchen table to chop vegetables. "A woman's work is never done."

"But I didn't make that mess!"

Mammi banged the handle of her knife on the table, and everyone jumped. "We are a family. That means we help each other, no matter who did what. We're celebrating Christmas Eve tonight, that means the birth of Jesus, our saviour. Do not complain about something as meaningless as sweeping."

Sulking, Rosina dragged her feet over to the oven door and swept up all the tiny pieces—while kicking up some dust from the floor with the broom—and threw them into the oven, too. She then joined Mammi and Anna at the kitchen table.

Elisabeth stopped for a moment to see what still needed to be done: the other three certainly didn't need her help, and she had no desire to wipe down the oven right now. All sixteen underskirts were starched and pressed and Luki's vest and pants as well—she had taken care of that over the past few days. She couldn't start on the goose until the vegetables were done. Baking had been done over the past month and was in the cellar at the back of the house.

"I'll polish everyone's shoes," she said. She laid out a rag rug in the front room, in front of her bed, found everyone's dress shoes, placed them on the rug, took her father's black polish and a cloth from a drawer in the dresser, and stopped.

Mammi's shoes were the biggest now. Elisabeth had momentarily forgotten about her father's absence, but now the memory returned, ramming into her with the force of a farmer's wagon piled high with harvested wheat. Elisabeth began to cry. She stood up to retrieve a handkerchief from her drawer, and Tata's encyclopedia set caught her eye. Elisabeth pulled down one volume and looked up America. She sat on her bed and stared at the map. Even though she had practically memorized it, every time she saw it, she wished it was somehow closer to Hungary, or Romania, whatever country she lived in now. But the map hadn't changed and Tata was still gone.

"Elisabeth?" Mammi's footsteps pounded into the room. Mammi grabbed the book out of her hand, slammed it shut, and returned it to the shelf. Elisabeth expected the belt.

"You don't have time for this anymore," Mammi said through gritted teeth.

Elisabeth dropped her chin and wiped her eyes and nose with her handkerchief. "I know. I'm sorry. These next few days will be very busy."

"That's not what I mean," Mammi said. Elisabeth looked up. "You no longer have time for this. With your father gone, I'll need to run his business after Christmas. You're almost a woman now, Elisabeth. It's time you acted like one."

Elisabeth furrowed her eyebrows. "What?"

"You will be in charge of the household: the cleaning, cooking, looking after Rosina. And you'll also be helping Luki and Anna with their schoolwork."

"But..." Elisabeth didn't want to believe what she was hearing and quickly sought another answer. "I can read after they've gone to sleep."

Mammi shook her head. "Not any longer. After the younger ones are in bed, you'll be busy sewing with me. You may have stopped growing, but your siblings haven't."

Elisabeth's jaw dropped.

"You're almost a woman now," Mammi repeated. "You only have a year or two left before we find you a husband, and you're still not fast enough or good enough in your duties."

"I am very good..." Elisabeth began to defend herself.

"If you're polishing shoes, then where are the boots?"

With that, Mammi returned to the kitchen.

Elisabeth stamped out of the front room and into the kitchen and scooped up everyone's boots.

"Be nice," Luki said. "Jesus is coming."

Elisabeth threw her brother a look that frightened

even him and returned to the front room. She wiped her cloth in the small canister of polish and began rubbing Mammi's shoes, her hand going faster and faster, until her muscles became too sore. Then she switched hands. And so she continued, rubbing until one arm hurt and then the other, until the pain in her arms matched the anger in her heart.

CHAPTER SEVEN

Uncle Peter. Aunt Anne. Uncle Phillip. Rebecca. Tony. Charlie. Dean. Sophie. Scott. Opa. Mom. Dad.

In a tiny house.

Christmas music blaring out of some crappy old radio.

And Juliana.

In her bedroom.

The door closed.

Unsuccessfully trying to drown out the noise with her earbuds.

With her younger cousins running up and down the squeaky, short hallway, and boy jokes farting out of every boy mouth in the house, the safest place for Juliana was in her tiny, thin-walled bedroom, on a bed with a mattress so old she was scared she wasn't the only one in her room.

"Oh, sorry!"

Juliana startled.

"Not used to someone being in here!" Scott slammed the door behind him.

"How did Mom get one daughter and her sister four boys?" she grumbled to herself as she returned her focus to the video of her and her old dance team at her goodbye party. Aunt Anne and Uncle Phillip had two daughters, too. Rebecca was way older, out of high school. Sophie, although only two years younger than Juliana, was going blind, and that made Juliana nervous. What would she talk to her about?

"Besides, Mom said she's into skiing. I hate skiing," she said to herself.

In all honesty, it wasn't so much that Juliana hated skiing, but she was scared of any sport that could possibly sideline her for dance. She didn't mind jogging or swimming, for example, but anything more daring than that and she stayed away. Her gym marks were the only ones below an A-.

She hit pause, got off her bed, and walked around her room, feeling too antsy to sit still much longer. Without her own practice studio in the house, she had nowhere to release all her pent-up energy. She jumped up and down, trying to shake things out, but the floor creaked, and the full-length mirror on her closet door shook. Juliana worried she'd break a hole in the floor as the mirror slipped out of its ancient, plastic brackets. She couldn't dance in here if she stood still and just moved her arms.

Looking at herself in the mirror, Juliana smoothed the A-line skirt of her favourite red dress, which was fitted in the bodice and had broad straps that curved over her shoulders. Mom always said she looked lovely in that dress and that it highlighted her brown hair.

The noise from outside quieted down for a moment, and Juliana wondered what was going on. Maybe she should join them. It was Christmas after all, she was here, and there was nothing that could be done about it. But the last thing she wanted right now was everyone's attention, and the only thing she wanted was time with her parents. Alone.

A knock interrupted her thoughts. Mom entered, and she looked concerned as she closed the door behind her and sat down on Juliana's bed. Juliana joined her but sat far enough away that Mom couldn't touch her. Juliana wasn't in the mood for hugs tonight. She wanted to spend time with her parents, not sit glued to them.

"It's a lot, isn't it?" Mom said.

Juliana nodded. She could feel tears starting to well up and she tried to push them back.

"Not only have we dragged you across the country, but you're now in a family with a lot of boys." Mom smiled, as though she'd hoped that last comment would also make Juliana smile.

It didn't. "I miss our Christmas Eve at home, with just you and me and Dad. It was one of the few days in the year when I knew we'd all be together."

Mom reached her hand out and placed it between them on the bed. "You know this is how I celebrated Christmas, right?"

Juliana nodded.

"And how your Opa celebrated? And all the way back through my ancestors?"

"But that doesn't mean it has to be this way now."

"No, of course not. We know things change. Just look at your name: We named you Juliana to break with tradition."

What was Mom talking about? Juliana had never heard that before. Evidently, her confusion registered on her face, and Mom continued.

"Every child in your Opa's family is named after a family member or close friend. In your case, you should've probably been named Katherina, Rosina, or Anne. Or Irmgard, after your grandmother."

Juliana laughed at her grandmother's name. She couldn't picture herself as an Irmgard.

"I love my name," Mom continued, "and I love you,

but I wouldn't have wanted two of us in the house with the same name."

"And Paul, if I was a boy?"

"Possibly. Or Peter, after Opa, or Lukas, after his uncle or grandfather." Mom smiled.

A huge explosion of laughter sounded from the kitchen and family room, and both Mom and Juliana looked in its direction.

"Your Uncle Peter must've just told another one of his travel stories." She paused. "When are you coming to join us?"

Juliana shrugged. "Whenever." Could she tell her mom she'd rather wait until they were all gone?

"I know you're going through a lot," Mom said, "and that there's nothing you can take control of right now. But everyone's asking where my daughter is, and it's..." She hesitated again and Juliana felt her lighter mood evaporate. "It's quite frankly embarrassing that you're in here."

Seriously? That was why Mom had come in here? To tell Juliana that she was being rude when it was Mom who was expecting Juliana to do an about-face and pretend like everything was fine?

She shoved her earbuds back into her ears. "You and Dad had all the time before you told me about the move to get used to the idea." Her voice got louder. "I had three months! I can't contact my friends, and I don't have access to the Internet. What I need right now is a place to dance to just…to just get a grip on myself! And now you want me to put on a happy face and perform the 'good little daughter' out there for everyone? Dream on."

Mom's jaw dropped and her eyes opened wide. "I have never heard such words from your mouth!"

"And I've never been dragged across the country and forced to live with people I don't know!"

"Of course you know your *opa*!"

"Hardly! He sends me nice cards and money in the mail and says a few words to me over the phone!"

Mom stood up and drilled her gaze into Juliana's eyes. "As your dad and I have said, you're not the only one going through a transition here. Now, there's an entire family out there dying to get to know you. Dean is exactly your age, Charlie's just…" Mom counted for a moment. "Charlie's just three years older. Sophie is a wonderful young lady and is two years younger than you. That's three cousins right now you could talk to. I get that Scott might be too young for you—he's only eight—and Tony's in university and Rebecca, too—but you could at least make an effort."

Mom let out an angry sigh and Juliana returned her attention to her phone.

"And if you do talk to Sophie," Mom said, her lips

tight, "leave your phone out of your grasp. She can't see that you're ignoring her."

Then she left, leaving the door open behind her. All the boisterous sounds from the kitchen flooded into Juliana's room.

Furious, Juliana slammed the door shut—the noise from the kitchen was so loud she was certain no one would hear her—and dropped onto her infested-with-God-knows-what bed.

She continued watching the video. Even just a quick phone call with Rachel would make her feel so much better. But she didn't know how to use Opa's phone and she also didn't know how long distance worked on a landline: Mom, Dad, and Juliana all had their own cell phones and Juliana could vaguely remember a conversation where Mom kept telling Opa that long distance for them was really cheap and that she was happy to call him. Was it the landline that was so expensive? Or Ontario?

Juliana's door opened, startling her again.

"Oh, is someone in here?" It was Sophie.

"Um, yeah, just me," Juliana replied.

Sophie looked puzzled for a moment and then her face relaxed. "Juliana, right? Sorry. Stupid question. Who else would it be? I can't see all of your face, and I've just never heard your voice before, that's all."

"That's okay," Juliana said, and glanced at her

phone. The frame she'd paused at held her frozen in the worst imaginable position: just after take-off into a grand jété, when she looked more like a bug flying through the air than a graceful human.

Then she remembered what Mom had said and looked up again.

"Are you going to join us? We've never met but I think we might have talked once over Skype a few years back."

Juliana looked down at her phone and then snapped her gaze away from it again.

"Um, yeah, I think you're right. I'll be out soon."

"Okay. Sorry again! Not used to someone being in here."

"No worries."

Sophie closed the door and Juliana let out the breath she didn't know she'd been holding. Sophie was really nice, and really normal. Of course she was normal. What else would she be?

Stop it, Juliana told herself. *Would you want people talking about you that way?*

She hit play on the video and watched herself finish the grand jété across the studio, her legs straight but still not in a full split.

"I really need to work on that this year," she said. Then her thoughts went back to Mom and Sophie.

She stood up and looked at herself in the mirror

again. She couldn't spend the rest of Christmas in her bedroom. Maybe this was no different than being on stage. Flash the happy smile, do the routine, bow, exit. Miss Kasia had told them all the time to just "go out and have fun, no matter what happens." Did she mean situations like this, too?

Juliana straightened out her dress, pushed a few hairs back into place, pulled her shoulders back and lifted her chin.

"Just go out and have fun," she told herself. She took a deep breath. "No matter what happens."

"Juliana," Mom called from the hallway, "I need your help in the kitchen. Now."

The kitchen? Juliana's most despised room in any house?

"Yes, Mom," Juliana said. Then one more time to herself in the mirror, "Just go out and have fun."

CHAPTER EIGHT

lisabeth rushed out of the cellar, across the back of the house and then along the side, under the overhang. She stamped the snow off her shoes before entering, passed the sausages she'd retrieved to Anna, and then returned to the cellar.

Christmas Eve service would be at seven o'clock, which meant supper and gifts at about five and getting herself and her sisters ready starting sometime after three.

And it was already after one.

Elisabeth's heart was racing in panic. Moreover, they had to prepare for Christmas Day, because it was her mother's turn to host her family. Each of the Braun siblings took turns, and with seven of them before the war, the full Braun family hadn't visited the Schuhmachers for Christmas since 1912. Elisabeth tried to count in her head how many would be coming.

*Resi-Néni has had four children since then, but two died. Gretchen-Néni had twins, but one had died, like Anna's had...*She continued counting, adding and subtracting as she rhymed off her mother's siblings, remembering though, too, that Adam-Bátschi and Andreas-Bátschi had died in the war, so their families would be celebrating with their other side of the family on Christmas Day. Although Elisabeth still missed her aunts and cousins at family Christmas, it had been two years since Andreas-Bátschi's death and four since Adam-Bátschi's. The new traditions had already taken hold.

But another tradition needed to be created: who would sit at the head of the table and carve the goose in Tata's absence?

She retrieved several small rounds of cheese and darted back around the house and into the kitchen.

Twenty-five people, she'd finally calculated.

Elisabeth held out the cheeses to her mother.

"I wanted the freshly smoked meat from the attic," Mammi said, her voice firm and angry. "And you were to get the cheese later. I don't have space in the kitchen for it yet." Elisabeth ran back around to the cellar and lay the rounds back on their shelves. She then lifted her skirts with one hand and began ascending the rickety stairs into the attic.

"This would've been Tata's responsibility," she said. "Luki should be doing this." Even though Luki was now the "man" of the house, at only eight years old, he was spared from carrying things up and down those old stairs.

And he's certainly too young to sit at the head of the table, she thought.

The smoke from the oven in the kitchen below floated up the chimney, some of it escaping through the opening in the flue where Tata—and recently Mammi—would hang meat for smoking. The loam-and-straw floor always scared Elisabeth: even though it was thick and supported by rafters, she still feared it would one day soften and she'd fall through.

She tiptoed through the smoke to the hooks where meats were hung to air out a little before being carried down to the cellar. She pulled several links down, hung them around her neck and headed back down the ladder. She then grabbed a basket of potatoes from the cellar—she knew Mammi would appreciate having those in the kitchen already, and the basket could sit out of the way, under the table—and hobbled to the front door, laden as she was with all the food.

"Rosina," Elisabeth called to her sister, and her youngest sibling ran over and carried some of the smoked sausages.

"Is that all for now, Mammi?" Elisabeth asked.

Mammi nodded, and Elisabeth switched out her boots for her house shoes and quickly washed her hands in the water bowl by the door.

"Now, get the back room ready," Luki commanded, and Elisabeth scowled at him.

"What are you waiting for?" Mammi said. "He's right."

Elisabeth grabbed a clean cloth from the basket of cloths in the kitchen and began polishing—for the third time in a week—all the furniture.

"And remember to place all your Sunday clothing to the front room!" Mammi shouted through the kitchen door.

As much as Elisabeth wanted to clean the house so that God and Jesus would be proud of her, her patience was wearing thin. "That's the fifth time she's told me today," she grumbled to herself. Elisabeth would have carried the family's best clothing to the front room earlier, but flour had covered much of the kitchen from Mammi's bread baking that morning, and Mammi insisted Elisabeth wait until the kitchen had been cleaned. But by then, Elisabeth had been sent on her first cellar chases, after which Mammi had begun chopping vegetables for Christmas Day.

"Did you hear me?" Mammi was getting angrier by the moment.

"Yes!" Elisabeth replied, louder than was needed.

Within moments, Mammi appeared in the doorway.

"Do not shout at me like that! Remember the commandment: honour thy father and thy mother!"

Elisabeth shot a look of defiance at her mother. "It would be easier if Tata were here instead of in America just to earn money!"

Mammi's mouth and eyes opened wide. "At least you know where your father is! Have you forgotten your uncles? And what about the Kaisers? They still haven't found Kaiser Hans or young Markus yet! You should be grateful Tata returned from the war!"

"And what if he doesn't return from America?" Elisabeth surprised even herself with her question.

Mammi's face turned red, and Elisabeth knew a storm was coming her way. Even her siblings, just past Mammi in the kitchen, had their eyes glued to the argument.

But nothing happened. Or rather, Mammi did nothing. Her face suddenly became pale again and her lips thinned into the tight line she normally held them in.

"He will be back." Her voice was almost a whisper. "Because I will not have another man raising my children."

With that, Mammi turned on her heel and marched into the kitchen.

"Back to work," she barked at everyone.

ELISABETH HAD FINISHED POLISHING ALL THE FURNITURE in the back room and was now carrying everyone's Sunday clothes through the kitchen and to the front room.

She felt guilty about what she'd said to Mammi there. Elisabeth already knew the answer to the question, and she knew that asking it would hurt Mammi. Why had she asked it?

Returning to the back room, Elisabeth looked up at the crucifix over the doorway.

Did You ever yell at Your father or mother like that?

Elisabeth knew the answer to that, too: no. But with everything Jesus wanted to do, how did He make His wishes clear to His parents?

She pulled Anna's underskirts and outer skirt out of the wardrobe.

Elisabeth knew that no wife wanted to think about the death of her husband anymore than a child wanted to think about the death of her father. For a wife, it meant having to marry again quickly. For children, it meant having to learn how to be around a man who wasn't their father but who now stood in that role. After the war, there had been a rash of weddings for many of the widows, and from what Anna and Luki sometimes heard at school, those marriages didn't always work well for the children.

But at least they had someone, Elisabeth thought. Often, wives—like Frau Kaiser—who didn't know if their husbands were alive or dead were forced to wait for some kind of confirmation before marrying again. Even though brothers and older sons helped, these families still toiled harder than the others without the head of their family.

Was Elisabeth's situation now any different from theirs? Once Tata had returned from the war, she could take comfort knowing he was alive when she fell asleep at night, and his presence greeted her every morning. She no longer had that certainty.

The Schuhmachers were by no means a rich family, but they also weren't destitute. They had a house, some farmland, enough money for food they couldn't grow, and Tata's shoemaking business meant he could earn money through the winter, too. Yes, their roof was made of chaff and wire, but Hungarian Germans had lived like that for over a century, many at least two. Her father's life was worth more to her than a roof or more land.

Elisabeth felt Jesus's eyes looking down on her again. *But no matter what I was feeling, I was still wrong to yell at Mammi like that.*

Anna's skirts in her arms, Elisabeth stopped in the

kitchen, where Mammi was cleaning up the last of the cooking dishes.

"Keep moving," Mammi said. "There's no time for idling."

But Elisabeth stayed put, her arms overbrimming with the white skirts. "I'm sorry," she said. "I don't want you to be angry with me, and I don't want Jesus to be angry with me, either. I just miss Tata."

Mammi nodded, acknowledging she'd heard, and then waved Elisabeth off.

"Can you forgive me?" Elisabeth asked before leaving.

Mammi nodded again, and Elisabeth knew Mammi wasn't going to do or say any more than that.

She placed Anna's skirts on her bed, laying each one out separately. Then she scurried through the kitchen again to get everyone's blouses and the women's *tschu-raks*—light, fitted, formal jackets that cinched at the waist before expanding several centimetres over the skirts and apron—but as she ran out the back-room door, the crucifix stopped her again. Although His hands each had a nail piercing through it, Jesus's open arms seemed to invite her somehow to embrace Him. And although He had died long ago, His message to turn the other cheek when one had been struck still wrapped around her heart.

Elisabeth resolved to do better, to treat Mammi as

she would like to be treated. She passed through the kitchen and to the front room, lay the clothing on her bed, sorted it out, and then recited the Lord's Prayer three times before returning to her duties.

TWO HOURS LATER, WITH SUPPER JUST BEING SET ON THE kitchen table, Elisabeth found herself standing in front of the looking glass in the front room, her four under-skirts and outer skirt already tied on, and her blouse tucked in. Her hair hung in waves to below her waist; it had become messy from all the running around, so she needed to redo it. Everyone else was ready, but she wasn't going to show her face to her mother with hair that looked like it had been through the biblical Flood.

"Can I do it?" Anna asked as she entered the room.

"You may braid it, but I'll pin it," Elisabeth replied.

Rosina and Mammi were busy setting out the last embroidered table cloths, cushions, and table runners in the back room for tomorrow's afternoon dinner while Luki was given the Bible and told to practise his reading. All the kids would eat in the kitchen, so chairs from the front room would be carried into the back room first thing in the morning. But other than that, most of the food was finally prepared, ready to be cooked up the following day. Only the potatoes were left, because they would turn grey if they weren't cooked soon after being cut.

Anna pulled over a chair and stood on it, and Elisabeth handed her a brush. As Anna pulled the brush through Elisabeth's blonde hair, Elisabeth couldn't help but wonder how her younger siblings felt now that Tata was gone. With all the time spent preparing for Christmas Eve and Christmas Day, they had never spoken about it. She asked Anna now.

"I miss him a lot," Anna replied and said nothing further. She reached the brush back around to Elisabeth and then pulled the sides of Elisabeth's hair to the back and began to braid.

"But you've never said anything," Elisabeth remarked.

"I don't want to get in trouble like you."

Elisabeth could feel Anna tug lightly as she braided her hair. Truth be told, she loved it when one of her sisters did her hair because of the gentle tickling feeling on her scalp.

"I won't get you in trouble," Elisabeth said. "You can talk to me about it."

Anna stepped down from the chair now that the braid was getting longer, pushed the chair out of the way, and stood directly behind Elisabeth, but not before Elisabeth caught a glimpse of her sister's eyes in the looking glass: they were turning red. Elisabeth regretted raising the topic right before the family sat down for a modest Christmas Eve dinner.

"Listen, Anna. I don't want to make you sad on Christmas Eve. I just want you to know that if you need to talk to someone, you can talk to me."

Anna finished the braid and passed its end to Elisabeth.

"If I talk to Jesus, then no one will know and I won't get into trouble," Anna said.

Elisabeth had to smile: a logical answer to an emotional problem, exactly what she would expect from Anna.

"Well, if you need someone who answers you back in a way that you can hear, you can talk to me. Now, you'd better get going. No need for both of us to be late to the table."

Anna left, and Elisabeth folded the braid to the top of her head, stuck a comb in against it, and then inserted hairpins to keep it all in place.

"Oh, there you are!" Uncle Peter called, flashing a big grin. Every picture Juliana had ever seen of Uncle Peter, right down to some teen ones in one of Mom's old photo albums, showed him with that grin. He looked so happy, Juliana couldn't help but smile back at him.

"Has Juliana joined us?" Sophie asked.

"She has," Aunt Anne replied.

Sophie beamed.

Mom called Juliana over to the stove and passed her a pot to carry to the table. So far so good. If all Mom needed help with was carrying things, Juliana could do it. It wasn't fun, but it wasn't horrid. Carrying things was neutral.

The normally round kitchen table that was barely

big enough for four had been lengthened with an insert and extended by adding a small table Dad had carried up from the laundry room earlier. A bunch of old wooden chairs had been brought in from the garage, and when Juliana placed the pot on a hot plate on the table, she bumped one of them and it rocked sideways. She made a mental note not to sit on that chair.

"Juliana, can you quickly wash that head of lettuce?"

"Seriously? Shouldn't that have been done before?" Juliana immediately regretted what she'd said.

Mom narrowed her eyes. "Yes, it should have, but you were too busy moping in your room."

An awkward silence filled the kitchen and adjoining living room. Out of the corner of her eyes, Juliana could see everyone looking into their drinks or at the floor, or exchanging glances. She tucked her chin in and headed for the sink, avoiding all eye contact.

"I think the salad spinner is in here," said Rebecca, one of the older cousins, bending to rummage through dishes stacked in a cupboard in the wall unit.

"How are your studies going?" Dad asked her, clearly trying to ease the mood. "I hear you've started your master's in mathematics now?"

Rebecca handed an old, orange salad spinner to Juliana and nodded. "I love it, but it's really challenging. I'm just glad I finished this semester. But I still have five more to go."

Juliana stared at the massive head of romaine lettuce in the sink. Really? Now? On Christmas Eve?

Mom leaned over to her. "We're eating in thirty minutes. All the other vegetables for the salad are done, thanks to your Aunt Anne."

Juliana removed the strainer from the spinner bowl, set it on the counter, and waited for it to fill with cold water. Of all the tasks Mom could've asked help for! Was Mom trying to embarrass her on purpose? Torture her somehow? One by one, Juliana ripped each outer leaf off. She could hear her mom sigh at Juliana's slow pace.

"Does Opa have a green cart?" Juliana asked.

"That green bin over there." Mom pointed to a brown bin tucked back in the corner of the counter.

She couldn't even get the name of the local composting program right without being corrected. She let out a heavy sigh and continued washing and ripping. After she'd removed the outer leaves, she began pulling off the remaining leaves, again, slowly. She remembered how Rachel had laughed when she had found out how long it took Juliana to rip lettuce.

"Just do it and be done with it," she'd said.

"I hate it," Juliana had replied. "And if I go slow enough, Mom will stop asking me to do it someday."

But even in front of the entire family, Juliana's protest didn't work. Everyone else continued on with their conversations, talking about the Rangers, the LRT, some new development on King Street, wherever that was...none of it interested Juliana. When she finished, she said so and immediately returned to her room. She picked up her phone again and saw the time: she'd completed the entire head of lettuce in ten minutes.

"Seriously?" she said to herself. It had felt like longer. So much for her protest.

She looked at herself in the mirror again. Sometimes trying to have fun just didn't work—it was like dancing your hardest in front of a really tough judge who'd already decided your mark before the music started.

She dropped onto her bed and pulled out her phone. Only three more days until she'd have Internet and a SIM card again.

"Where's my Yulika?" Opa said from the hallway in a voice louder than was needed.

"She's moping in her room," Dad said.

Juliana's eyes began to well up.

"Well, I hope she gets better soon," Opa said. The hallway floor creaked as Opa walked down it, and Juliana was scared he'd open up her door and come in.

He wasn't the reason for her anger. If anything, he'd been nice to her this entire time, even patient with her, though she had heard him yell at Mom that morning about getting lunchtime meals delivered. Mom had insisted he had to get used to it because no one would be here to cook him lunch once her job started, and he had lost too much weight in the past year.

"She's always telling people what to do," Juliana said out loud.

She double-tapped on a photo from her first class back after summer last dance competition. She, Declan, Rachel, Matilda, Linda, and the rest of the competition team were posed in front of the competition's big sign, their purple-and-gold studio warm-up suits on, hair back in curled ponytails (except for Declan's), faces made up (except for Declan's) with bright red lipstick, pink blush, heavy eyeliner, and purple eyeshadow to match the tap-line costumes they were about to change into.

"All thirty of us don't even smile enough to equal Uncle Peter's smile," she said and giggled at her own remark. Her uncle did seem really friendly, too, like Opa, but in a dorky way, as opposed to a grandfatherly way. He had a mullet to go with the huge grin.

Her door slammed open and Juliana jumped. Both her parents now stood at the foot of her bed. She had never seen them this angry before.

"What is wrong with you?" Dad asked. "You have an entire, loving family out there who wants to meet you, and you're hiding here in your room, sulking like a little kid."

Juliana was scared she'd start to cry if she said anything.

"Well?" Mom asked. "You just disappeared after the lettuce. My family is asking why. You owe us and them an explanation."

Juliana stared at her phone, praying that her parents would leave her alone if she just ignored them. Instead, Dad ripped her phone out of her hands.

"Why the attitude, Juliana Elizabeth?"

The middle name. Juliana knew she was in trouble. She remained silent.

"You're not the only one going through a transition here," Mom said.

Juliana couldn't hold it inside anymore. "But I'm the only one who doesn't know anyone!" she shouted. "I have no friends. This is not my bedroom. This is not my home. And I don't even know how to use the freaking phone to call Rachel!"

Dad's face tightened up, the way it always did when he got angry, and he sighed. The angry sigh. "You're the one whose attitude is affecting everyone else."

"Then just leave me alone and go on with your little Christmas party!" Juliana jumped off her bed, pushed past her parents, and stormed out of her room. She entered the kitchen and felt like she had stepped into a scene from a Hollywood movie, where everyone was frozen in place, glasses halfway to their mouths, and all eyes on the embarrassed main character.

"I'm sorry," she mumbled and stormed down the stairs and straight ahead into the rec room. She slammed the door behind her and flicked on the light in time to see a cloud of dust rise from her entrance.

"Oh my god," she said and then sneezed once, twice, three times. The rec room looked like it had never been cleaned. Cream-coloured wallpaper was peeling off all around the room. Cobwebs hung from the ceiling and fly carcasses were trapped in ancient webs stuck between the bars on the windows. The furniture looked at least fifty years old and was brown and orange, but if it was faded because of age or dust, she couldn't tell. To her left was another door and beside it a drink bar with...one side of her upper lip curled in disgust... orange vinyl with black dots across the front.

She sneezed again and wiped her nose on the back of her hand. The door to her left stood partway open, and Juliana didn't know if she should peek inside or stay where she was. All she knew was that she couldn't go back upstairs but she shuddered at the thought of sitting on that furniture. What was she going to do? Stand in one place?

She tiptoed through the dust-laden shag carpet, its polyester fibres scratching at her bare feet. She gripped the door handle and paused. What if a dead animal was back there? Didn't Mom say her parents used to have cats? When had the last one died? She didn't see a light switch on the wall, so she'd have to open the door all the way to see anything inside.

Juliana held her breath as the door squeaked on its hinges. Ahead of her, she saw a lightbulb with a chain hanging from it. She lowered her gaze to the cement floor to look for anything gross. Seeing only dust, she stepped in on demi-pointe, the cold of the floor traveling through the balls of her feet up her legs and into her core. She reached for the chain, closed her eyes and pulled.

CHAPTER TEN

lisabeth buttoned up Luki's overcoat, brushed
a few pieces of lint from his sleeves, and
pulled her own shawl tightly around her. In the absence
of the church bells, neighbours began ringing cowbells,
but for Elisabeth, the higher-pitched, frantic ringing of
the smaller bells couldn't replace the loud clanging of
the big and small church bells that announced it was
almost time for evening service.

Elisabeth's duty was to help the other children dress
and get them out the door so Mammi could set up the
Christmas tree on the table in the front room.

It was as though Tata was away at war again.

"Do you know your prayers off by heart?" Elisabeth
asked. "You must be ready for when the *Christkind*
comes."

Luki and Anna nodded, but Rosina looked nervous.

"I was busy helping! I forgot to practise!" she said.

Elisabeth gave her sister a stern look, the kind of look she'd expect Mammi to give them. "You can pray while you clean, Rosina," she said.

"But that's hard!" Rosina protested.

Elisabeth waved her siblings away from the door, mindful to keep their gaze away from the front windows so they wouldn't catch Mammi setting up the tree. As Elisabeth led them down their property to the front gate, she tried to think of something to keep the kids' minds off their mother. While Tata was in the war, they had sung Christmas carols. Not wanting to relive those years again, she thought of something else.

"Let's practise our prayers," she suggested.

"But when Tata was in the war," Anna said, "we sang carols on the way to church."

Inwardly, Elisabeth grumbled, but she resolved to stay strong.

"But prayers are something different," she countered.

"Can't we sing?" Luki asked.

"And where's Mammi?" Rosina asked. She looked toward the house, and Elisabeth jumped in her way.

"Fine," Elisabeth said. "We can sing. What will we sing?"

"'Silent Night!' 'Silent Night!'" Rosina shouted.

How could Rosina remember what they had sung in those years? Elisabeth felt a lump forming in her throat, but she started the carol. By the time they'd finished the second verse, they were halfway down the street, and Elisabeth was fighting hard to hold back tears. She had promised to be a better daughter to Mammi. *Mammi didn't cry in front of the children, and neither will I*, Elisabeth thought to herself.

The closer they got to the church, the more friends and acquaintances they saw, and the easier it became for Elisabeth to take her mind off her father. Rosina wanted to run off to see a friend, but Elisabeth grabbed her by the collar of her *tschurak* and kept her with the family. At the stairs to the church stood Pastor Fröhlich, his usual black robes covered in a black coat. He was ringing a hand bell and greeting everyone as they entered. Mammi came rushing up behind them.

Dressed in her black Sunday attire, Mammi's black outer skirt puffed out in a beautiful, smooth circle over her underskirts. Her blouse was hidden under her black *tschurak*. Her navy-blue apron, which Elisabeth had pressed herself, hung effortlessly against all the black. And on her head, Mammi wore a stiffened, black kerchief that tied under her chin and hung down to the base of her neck in the back. Elisabeth couldn't wait to wear clothes like that when she got married someday.

"What did you forget?" Luki asked her.

"What do you mean?"

Elisabeth gave Mammi a knowing look. "I told the children you'd forgotten something and that's why we left ahead of you."

"Ah, yes, of course," Mammi said, somewhat too unnaturally for Elisabeth's liking, though the other children didn't seem to notice. "Just my handkerchiefs. But no more chit-chat now. We're at church."

Pastor Fröhlich wished each family member a Merry Christmas as they passed by him and through the main door.

The smell of burning candles greeted Elisabeth's nose. Their simple church, with its two columns of pews, small pulpit, and high nave on the ground level, and its organ and balcony above, was lit with hundreds of candles. Pastor Fröhlich always preached that the light of God was everywhere, and at Christmastime, Elisabeth believed it. A helper passed Elisabeth and each family member a small candle in a glass holder and Elisabeth felt like she was holding Jesus in her hands.

The small church glowed with hundreds of little halos throughout. Once inside, Mammi spotted Peter-Bátschi with his children on the men's side of the church and nudged Luki in their direction. The remaining Schuhmachers slid into a pew, with Elisabeth pushing all the way to the outer edge. She turned around and looked up at the choir, members of their congregation who had offered to lead the church on this special night in song. Usually, the children sat up there, but tonight they could sit with their families. Elisabeth couldn't wait until they began singing. The organist, sitting at the small pipe organ, played quietly as everyone entered. Elisabeth turned back around and, for a moment, took in her family. Her mother's usually earnest face had relaxed beneath its black, stiffened kerchief. Anna and Rosina, in their white kerchiefs, couldn't have looked more angelic as they, too, stared in awe at all the candles in the church. Over by the men, Luki wrinkled his nose. He never liked the smell of so many burning candles.

"I don't know why Pastor Fröhlich won't let us join the synod in Siebenbürgen," a woman behind Elisabeth whispered.

Siebenbürgen was a large area in Romania's Carpathian Mountains where more Germans lived.

Another woman answered, "I know. We're a German community, but he still insists we worship in Hungarian."

As much as Elisabeth loved her German language, if the language of church had been changed this Christmas, she knew it would have been too much for her. She folded her hands in her lap, bowed her head, and prayed to Jesus for strength to sit quietly and not say anything.

"But we are no longer part of Hungary," said the first woman.

"My husband says the pastor is angry because the Romanian king—who is actually German—wants all our children taught in Romanian, even though we're German."

It was Christmas Eve. Couldn't these women just stop for a moment and be thankful? The last thing Elisabeth wanted was for this evening to be ruined by gossip and political talk. She turned around in her pew.

"Can you please stop talking?" she whispered. "We've gathered here to celebrate Jesus's birth, not criticize our church or pastor. We sing in German, we worship in Hungarian. Whereas the tower of Babel was a punishment, we have turned our languages into a blessing. We should be grateful for that."

The women, who were dressed in black like Mammi and every other married woman in the church, looked indignant.

"Frau Schuhmacher," the first one whispered to Mammi, "surely you can raise your daughter better than this."

Mammi turned around. "With all due respect, Frau Krehling and Frau Müller, I have raised her just fine. Now, if you will allow us to enjoy this solemn evening, I am certain Jesus will forgive your transgression if you ask Him."

Not wasting another word, Mammi turned back around, but not without quickly glancing at Elisabeth and giving her a nod so imperceptible, Elisabeth wasn't entirely sure she'd actually seen it. But if Mammi was allowing Elisabeth to speak up, it meant she thought her oldest daughter really had become almost a woman now. Elisabeth only had to marry now to complete this journey in her life. After her confirmation on Palm Sunday, she would be allowed to start dancing with boys.

Elisabeth's thoughts were interrupted when the organist stopped, the silence signalling to those below that Christmas Eve service was about to begin. He then played the opening notes to "Oh, How Joyfully" and everyone stood. As each note rang through the candle-lit stillness that engulfed the church, they unveiled to Elisabeth the miracle of Jesus's virgin birth. A shiver ran through her spine.

No one needed to open their hymnals; they all knew the words by heart:

> Oh, how joyfully; oh, how merrily
> Christmas comes with its grace divine.
> Grace again is beaming; Christ the world
> redeeming.

> Hail, ye Christians, hail the joyous
> Christmastime!

With the harmonious melodies of their modest pipe organ, and the voices singing, Elisabeth was certain she could feel Jesus entering her heart.

LUKI AND ROSINA COULDN'T GET THEIR BOOTS OFF FAST enough. Mammi even slapped Rosina on the cheek for dropping her shawl on the floor instead of carrying it to the back room, folding it, and laying it in a drawer in the wardrobe.

"I made that shawl for Elisabeth and it has been passed down to Anna and now you. You show respect to your family by taking care of the gifts they have given you," she admonished her youngest child.

Rosina crying, but Luki and Anna laughing in anticipation of what was about to come, all three siblings ran into the front room. Elisabeth took Mammi's shawl and hers, folded them and lay them on top of those of her sisters, and walked back through the kitchen and into the front room, almost skipping as she went. Mammi hadn't said a word on the way home about what Elisabeth had said to Krehling Susi and Müller Lissa, so that nod must have meant she'd approved.

The Christmas tree was perhaps one metre tall, a majestic height, and it stood on the table in the middle of the front room. Several paper ornaments hung all around it, and a gentle light shone from the small candles perched on its branches. Small packages were laid around it.

"Elisabeth, go make the tea. The water is already in the pot on the kitchen table," Mammi instructed. "Anna, you may get a tray of cookies."

Anna jumped in the air and clapped her hands. Too young to remember much of life before the war, Anna had grown up in a time when cookies only came out at Christmas, Easter, christenings, and funerals. Elisabeth, though, remembered an earlier time, when cookies came out every Sunday to entertain any families who dropped by to visit.

Elisabeth placed the pot on the stove, fed the oven another bushel of cornstalks that had been brought in this afternoon, and closed the pot with a lid, while Luki begged her to hurry up. She glanced up at the crucifix over the house door and again prayed, this time asking for patience.

"Come on, Elisabeth!"

She took a breath before answering. "Luki, it takes time to boil the water." She pulled out six teacups from the cupboard at the other end of the kitchen. Only after she set the teacups down did she notice she'd miscounted. Her heart ached as she placed one teacup back and then grabbed the canister of dried chamomile flowers.

"Elisabeth!" Luki whined.

"Stop it!" she yelled back at her brother. *Why does it come out so fast?* she thought to herself, again regretting her reaction.

Mammi shouted from behind the Christmas tree, as though Mother Maria herself were now speaking: "Show your brother some patience: he's six years younger than you!"

Elisabeth clenched her jaw and sighed.

"Don't you have something to say?" Mammi asked.

Elisabeth sighed again. "I'm sorry," she murmured.

"And?" Mammi prodded.

Her cheeks burned as the question rose from her throat. "Will you forgive me, Luki?"

"I'll think about it," came the response. Elisabeth heard a swat and Luki began to cry.

Jesus, I pray You, please grant me one miracle: please boil this water faster.

Elisabeth's prayer was left unanswered.

CHAPTER ELEVEN

*J*uliana peeked through barely open eyes the way a child does after a jack-in-the-box has frightened them. Still standing on demi-pointe and holding the chain, she looked around.

The lightbulb shone an eerie yellow hue Juliana had only seen in old movies. In front of her was an old green fridge with the doors taken off but its shelves stacked with old dishes, small kitchen appliances, and folded fabric that looked like it was from the '70s. Two tall wooden shelves stood next to it, filled with empty mason jars and a box containing all the lids. As she turned her head to the right, she saw that boxes upon boxes were piled up against the wall, many with their flaps open. She let go of the chain and lowered her heels. She crept over to the boxes, sneezed again, and lifted the flap of a box that almost seemed to teeter at the top of the pile, like a boulder nearing its tipping point.

In the box lay numerous leather-bound books with gold-embossed writing and decorations on brown spines. The script was fancy, like something out of an old movie. She wiped her nose and then reached into the box and pulled out a book. Its cover was navy blue and had no title, just little black triangles at the top and bottom right-hand corners. She inspected the spine again. The script of the title was too elaborate for her to make out the letters, but below the title was an embossed creature of some kind: it had a lion's body and tail, a hawk's wings, and a bird's face. One paw rested on some kind of shield that had more elaborate letters and the numbers 1805. The shield itself rested on two books. Below the image was the number 16, but then more letters.

The book's binding cracked as she gently opened the cover. Juliana felt like her eyes were crossing as she stared at the ornate script. She blinked, partly hoping her eyes would somehow figure out the strange letters and partly because they were beginning to itch from all the dust. A sneeze formed again in her nose and she turned her head just in time to miss the book and instead blowing more dust into the air.

She looked back at the title page. The black ink on paper made the script a little easier to read.

"That looks like 'conversations' but with a k," she said to herself. The word above started with *B...r...o...c...* maybe a lowercase *b*? The last letter was an *s*. But was that an *n* or a *u* before the *s*?

She turned the page and saw more illegible writing. However, at the bottom, it said in clear type 1889.

If that was a date—she paused for a moment as she did the math in her head—this book was over 125 years old. No wonder its condition was this bad. She paged through a little. Near the middle she found something folded up but attached to the book. She opened it to reveal a world map, printed in colour. At the top, in regular font, it said,

ÜBERSICHTSKARTE DES WELTVERKEHRS.

Canada was in its normal spot at the top left of the map. Across its expanse were the words "BRIT. NORD-AMERIKA." Through all of the world's oceans were curved lines connecting the continents. She held the book right under the lightbulb so she could better see the tiny print along each of the lines: "Rotterdam—N. York," "Liverpool—Halifax," and "Liverp—Para—Ceara" were just a few.

"I guess this is where ships travelled," she said to herself.

She folded up the map, closed the book, and slid it back into the box. Her curiosity piqued, she gingerly opened another box.

"Ahh!" she cried out and jumped back. Several dried-up insect carcasses lay on top of one of the books. She aimed her mouth in their direction, closed her eyes, and blew, trying really hard to ignore the sound of their shells hitting the side of the box. When she opened her eyes again, the bugs were gone.

The cover of that book looked identical to the one she'd just opened. In fact, all the books in the box seemed to be identical except for the number and combination of letters at the bottom.

"Like that encyclopedia set Mrs. Palubeski showed us back in grade seven," she said. But, for the life of her, Juliana couldn't make out the words on the spines.

The old-fashioned script reminded her of tap: to anyone who didn't study it, tap looked like a bunch of blurred movements making crisp sounds. But to anyone who knew tap, each step had a name, a sound, and a volume level, and together, they worked like letters, making up words and then stories, depending on how they were combined. If she could read these letters, she could type them into an online translator and figure out what the book said.

"Fat chance of that happening anytime soon," she said. Even if she had Internet, with their belongings finally arriving in a few days, she'd be busy with getting organized again until school started.

She moved the box of encyclopedias out of the way so she could inspect more boxes.

Now I feel like a real snoop, she thought, but she couldn't help herself. The next box had more modern books, and as she lifted them out, saw that many had to do with a hostage situation in Iran. Their dust covers were sometimes torn, sometimes not, but they interested her less than that old encyclopedia set. As she was about to place the books back into the box, she saw another leather-bound book. This one was smaller than the encyclopedias, much smaller, and had no writing on the spine. Juliana pulled it out and opened it. Another dead bug welcomed her, its legs crinkled against its body. She almost dropped the book, but her fingers seemed to understand and held onto it as though it was something precious.

The first page was written in handwriting, but again she couldn't make out what it said. Deciding it would be best to sit down instead of risking dropping it, Juliana went back to the rec room, but it was too disgusting. She thought of Opa's room and headed there. Now feeling like a complete intruder, she flicked on the light and went in.

Opa's room was small, with more of that shag carpeting, but Juliana could see that the carpet had been visited by a vacuum. The same peeling wallpaper from the rec room covered the walls in Opa's room, and he only had a single, tiny window letting light in. With the bars in front of it, it reminded Juliana of a jail cell. A single bed made of dark wood lay against the wall. A doily covered the surface of the night table. Juliana fingered it and guessed it was made of yarn or something similar. Along the opposite wall was a wardrobe with large doors for anything Opa needed to hang up and then a chest for anything that could be stored folded. Both matched the bed and the night table.

I hope he doesn't get angry at me, she thought as she sat on his neatly made bed. She placed the book on the bedspread and, barely touching it, opened the cover and then turned to the page after the handwriting. There she saw a pencil drawing, somewhat smudged, of a room.

The artist had apparently stood in a corner and looked into the room. In the middle of the page but higher up was a doorway with a crucifix hanging above it. Through it could be seen part of a window on the far wall. In the foreground and to the right were part of a table and a few chairs that looked like they were made of wood. To the left, next to that doorway, she saw a cube of some kind sticking out of the wall, but she couldn't figure out what it was. It had a darkened door in the middle of it. A table stood next to it with long stalks or sticks of some kind in a basket.

Juliana carefully flipped through one page after another. These were likely from Opa's country, from Romania. Did he draw them? But Mom had never mentioned that Opa drew. Would he be angry if Juliana took the book into her room to look at it some more?

Scratching sounds from above signalled that everyone was sitting down to eat supper.

"Dang it," she said. She'd have to put the book back for now; the last thing she wanted was to have everyone see her with it, especially if she wasn't supposed to be rummaging in the cellar to begin with.

She closed the book, stood up, and smoothed out the bed. She'd be sure to tell Opa that she had gone in there, but later, when she had time to talk to him alone. She turned off the light and tiptoed back into the rec room.

"Oh, god," she said as she noticed even more dust and cobwebs than she had seen the first time. The ceiling vent caught her attention, and she noticed it was closed. *Opening that should help with the air down here,* she thought. She reached up and pushed hard with her thumb against the tiny lever in the vent to open it. A dead spider fell out when the flaps shifted and she shrieked and danced as though she were on hot coals.

"Oh my god, oh my god, oh my god! Where'd it go?" she said as she inspected her dress and the floor. She didn't know what she'd dread more: not finding the spider and therefore not knowing where it was or finding it on herself. She'd have to check herself over in Opa's bathroom.

She tiptoed over the scratchy carpet to the cellar to return the collection of drawings, but a loud, shrill sound startled her and she jumped, almost dropping the book. She heard the ringing again: it was Opa's phone upstairs. She put the book on a box.

"Juliana!" Dad called down the stairs. "Rachel's on the phone!"

The butter cookies Elisabeth had baked were passed around on an heirloom silver platter. She had cut the dough into stars, hearts, and Christmas trees with cookie cutters, and later had decorated them with icing made from icing sugar and water, squeezing out the most exquisite patterns from a piping bag she had sewn herself last year. She bit into one now and let it melt in her mouth, while her siblings shovelled cookies into their mouths so fast that Mammi ripped the platter out of their hands and lectured them about the seven deadly sins.

The chamomile tea wasn't black tea, but at least it was warm. It reminded her a little too much of flus and stomach pains, but she drank it anyway.

Once everyone had had a sip of tea and several

cookies, Mammi passed out the gifts. First came the oranges, the only time in the whole year that the children got to eat one. Rosina almost broke her nose as she pressed it against her orange to smell its sweet scent. Anna rubbed her hands all over hers and then sniffed them. Luki licked his orange and his face squished into a raisin.

Elisabeth giggled. "You have to cut it open before you eat it."

Mammi then passed around four small packages wrapped in brown paper. Elisabeth's felt partly like a book, and her heart began to race. The last few Christmases, they had usually received either embroidered handkerchiefs or new mittens.

Rosina began to tear at hers and Mammi admonished her for being so greedy. Rosina sulked after the punishment was doled out: she had to wait until last to finish opening hers.

Anna gingerly opened hers and gave a little yelp. "My own pair of mittens!" she cried out. Elisabeth was happy for her sister, who always had to wear Elisabeth's old clothes. To add to the difficulties, Elisabeth preferred pink, but Anna liked red.

Luki opened his package next. "A man's pair of mittens!" he said. Instead of the brightly coloured hand-me-down mittens he'd had to wear from Anna (and therefore from Elisabeth), he now had a pair of his very own black ones. "Black! Just like Tata's gloves!"

Just then, there was a knock at the door. Mammi stood up, brushed the crumbs off her apron, and answered. The younger children all ran up behind her, knowing exactly who it was going to be.

Standing outside the door were several older children dressed in costume. The *Christkind* wore a white dress and carried in her arms a little baby doll. Next to her stood another girl about Elisabeth's age, dressed in a white gown and holding a whip made of twine. Three other children were dressed as *stornickels*, wearing oversized felt caps and masks with fringe hanging around the long horns that protruded from the top. Luki and Rosina charged back into the front room and hid behind the table and tree.

"Can the *Christkind* come in?" the older children asked.

"Yes." Mammi smiled slightly and stood back from the door, welcoming them in. Elisabeth immediately recognized them as former classmates but knew that it was her job now to keep their secret.

The *Christkind* group stood inside the door so Mammi could close it.

"Lukas," one of the *stornickels* called in a gruff voice.

"Anna," called another.

"Rosina," called the third.

One by one, the young children crept back out into the kitchen and faced the kindly smile of the *Christkind*, the harsh expression of the angel with her whip, and the non-human faces of the three *stornickels*.

"Can you say a prayer for me?" the *Christkind* asked, and all three nodded, though Elisabeth noticed beads of sweat forming on Rosina's temples. Luki and Anna began and Rosina joined in, watching their lips and listening to every word, always a half-word behind them. She wrung her hands, her eyes shifting between the angel's whip and the three *stornickels*. Once the children had finished, they received each two walnuts. Everyone wished each other a Merry Christmas, and the *Christkind* group moved on to the next home with little kids. Rosina beamed.

Elisabeth gave her siblings a hug, and Mammi gave them an approving nod.

"Can we get back to our gifts?" Elisabeth asked eagerly. The moment she finished the question, though, she knew she shouldn't have asked it.

"Elisabeth," Mammi scolded. "Did Maria or Josef ask for their gifts?"

Sheepishly, Elisabeth shook her head.

"You can wait until tomorrow morning now."

Elisabeth glared at Mammi. "That's not fair! Tata's—"

"You're not the only one who misses your father,"

Mammi retorted, "and yet the rest of us are coping fine."

An uncomfortable silence fell over the family as everyone walked back into the front room. Elisabeth was boiling mad. How little did Mammi know about her own children? But if she said what Anna had told her, she'd be betraying her sister's trust. She couldn't do that.

Once they all took their seats, Rosina spoke up. "Mammi, it is Christmas Eve. Jesus says we should forgive."

Mammi's eyes widened in anger. "You can both wait until tomorrow. I will not be told by my children how they should be raised." She stood up and took the platter of cookies into the kitchen.

"Girls, you come out here and help me prepare for tomorrow while Luki changes into his night clothes."

With drooping shoulders, Rosina and Elisabeth followed their mother, Anna behind them. Luki closed the door to the front room.

"CHILDREN, OBEY YOUR PARENTS IN THE LORD; FOR THIS IS right. Honour thy father and mother; which is the first commandment with promise: that it may be well with thee, and thou mayest live long on the earth." Elisabeth paused. She tried to create saliva in her mouth, but after whispering Ephesians 6: 1-3 thirty-three times, her mouth had dried out. What she really needed was water, but that would mean going into the kitchen to find some.

The entire family lay asleep in their beds in the front room. It was pitch black. Mammi snored. Anna made hardly a sound. Rosina mumbled a few incomprehensible words now and then. Luki barely lay still for long, leaving Elisabeth to wonder whether he was actually asleep.

All Elisabeth could do was lay there and try to figure out why she couldn't behave the way Jesus asked her to. She had only wanted a moment of joy, to see what she would get, and she couldn't keep quiet. Tomorrow was the happiest day of the year after Christmas Eve, a day when her mother's siblings and their families would come by, and Elisabeth was still thinking about her present.

Elisabeth sat up. Her bed was at the back of the room, next to one of the windows facing the street, so reaching the kitchen meant navigating around the other furniture. She pulled a blanket over her shoulders —the oven had also fallen into its cold nighttime slumber by now—and tiptoed through the room.

"Owa!"

She managed to keep her voice down but her knee

had bumped a chair and pushed it into the table. Mammi stopped snoring and Elisabeth stood perfectly still. Within a few moments, though, Mammi's snoring began again, and Elisabeth felt her way around the table and chairs. She reached out one arm and worked her way toward the door, one small step after another. She overshot her angle and touched the protruding back side of the oven, but now she knew she was close. She felt along the oven to the wall, and then found the handle and opened the door.

Once in the kitchen, she breathed a sigh of relief. The moon shone through the single window, making it easy for her to find a lantern and box of matches.

Holding the lit lantern ahead of her, she immediately saw her gift sitting square in the middle of the kitchen table, calling to her to open it. She set the lantern on the table and sat down. Her thirst could wait.

She reached out a hand to touch the gift but she yanked it back. Wasn't it moments like these that Luther always spoke of? Ones where the Devil was trying his hand? She had to fight it.

But she only received one big gift a year, and this one was by far the largest: perhaps ten or twelve centimetres wide by twenty-five centimetres or so tall. She knew it was at least a book. But what kind of book? Surely not a drawing book: her family couldn't afford that yet. There was also something of the same shape under the book and then three long bumps under that.

Elisabeth reached out for it again.

"No, I mustn't," she said and abruptly stood up.

She picked up the lantern, searched for a jug of drinking water and found it on the washing table in the far right corner. A few scoops into her mouth quenched her thirst. She dared not return to the kitchen table so she headed into the back room. Maybe some reading would take her mind off her temptation. She pulled down a book of Martin Luther's sermons that she always read when she felt her soul needed help.

The back room's dirt floor was covered in large woven carpets, while the sofa and benches were draped in the Schuhmachers' best crocheted blankets. A table runner that had been crocheted by Elisabeth's great-grandmother, one of the original Lutheran settlers in Semlak, lay across the dining table, and one embroidered serviette lay folded on each placemat. Elisabeth was scared she might mess up the handsomely decorated room, but if she took the book into the kitchen, she risked getting it dirty, the punishment for which would likely be more severe.

She set the lantern down at the edge of the dining table and placed the book next to it, careful not to disturb the table setting. She searched for the sermon she preferred in times of temptation: "Our Conduct Toward God: Rejoice in Him."

She whispered as she read, making Luther's words feel more real than if she just read them silently. After she finished the first page, she turned it and continued reading. Then, one passage jumped out at her:

Hence the expression, "Rejoice in the Lord"; not rejoice in silver or gold, not in eating or drinking, not in pleasure or mechanical chanting, not in strength or health, not in skill or wisdom, not in power or honour, not in friendship or favour, nay, not in good works or holiness even. For these are deceptive joys, false joys, which never stir the depths of the heart. They are never even felt.

Elisabeth glanced out into the kitchen. Was she rejoicing in her gift instead of in God? She continued reading.

When they are present we may well say the individual rejoices superficially, and without a heart experience. To rejoice in the Lord—to trust, confide, glory and have pride in the Lord as in a gracious Father—this is a joy which rejects all else but the Lord, including that self-righteousness whereof Jeremiah speaks (ch. 9, 23-24): "Let not the wise man glory in his wisdom, neither let the mighty man glory in his might, let not the rich man glory in his riches; but let him that glorieth glory in this, that he hath understanding, and knoweth me." Again, Paul enjoins (2 Cor 10, 17), "He that glorieth, let him glory in the Lord."

Elisabeth now looked up at the crucifix over the doorway and began to feel guilty about wanting her gift. She read further:

The apostle further commands in our text to rejoice "always." Thus he rebukes those who rejoice in God —who praise and thank him—only a portion of the time. These rejoice when it is well with them; when not, rejoicing ceases.

Which is what I've been doing because of Tata's departure, she thought to herself. *I only thought of me, but Tata is thinking of all of us.*

Surviving the war had been hard on everyone: food had become scarce, families had lost their husbands and sons, and now with her village's transfer to Romania, everyone was nervous, and here was Elisabeth, only thinking of herself.

"I promise to do better," she said to Jesus, but in her heart, she didn't know if she could keep her promise.

CHAPTER THIRTEEN

How did Rachel know to call her here? Hopefully everything was okay? Whatever it was, Juliana couldn't have been more relieved right now.

But when she climbed up the creaking stairs and appeared in the kitchen, her mother was aghast.

"Where in God's name have you been?" she asked.

That everyone was seated at the table didn't help.

"What's going on?" Sophie whispered to Scott.

"Juliana's dress is full of dust," he replied, not taking care to lower his voice. Several in the room tried to stifle giggles.

Now that Juliana was standing under full lights, she could see smudges on her shins and streaks of dust down her arms and across her beautiful red dress. Her cheeks turned almost the same colour.

"Never mind," Mom said. "Here." She handed Juliana the phone.

"Hello?" Juliana said.

"Hey, Juliana! It's Rachel! Merry Christmas! How are you doing?"

Juliana looked around and caught some stares and side glances. She chose to avoid the question so no one would hear her answer. "How'd you get my grandfather's number?" She moved around the corner and leaned against the wall. The cord didn't even stretch a metre.

"Your mom gave it to my mom. I only found out today that you don't have a SIM card. No wonder I couldn't reach you. Sorry I'm only calling now! You know how parents are."

"Yeah, I know."

"So? How's it going? How's your grandfather?"

Juliana tried to brush off some of the dust on her dress. "Fine," she said. She wanted to say more, but not in public like this.

"You okay?" Rachel asked.

"Sure."

Mom carried the bowl of salad to the table. Scott shouted, "I don't want salad tonight!"

"It's a bit loud," Rachel said. "Can you go somewhere else?"

"No. It's one of those old-fashioned phones. I'm attached to the wall."

"Ooooh. That's why you can't talk."

"Mhmm."

"Everyone can hear you."

"Yup."

"Can you use Skype?"

"No Internet."

"Not even a wireless network?"

"Nope."

"Oh, man. That's gotta be brutal."

"Yup."

"That's why wireless access is a human right."

"Tell me about it."

Dean came over to Juliana and reached into her hair. Juliana was about to swat him away when she saw what he now held between his thumb and finger: the spider that had fallen out of the vent. Juliana squealed, jerking the receiver away and lifting the phone off its screw on the wall. It crashed on to the ground, its shrill ringer announcing its impact with the floor.

"Ask me next time first!"

"But you were on the phone!"

Opa shuffled over and patted her on the shoulder.

"It's all right, Yulika," he said. "See if your friend is still there."

As Juliana lifted the receiver to her ear, he bent down, picked up the phone, and hung it back on its screw.

"Rachel?"

"Juliana? You still there?"

Juliana sighed. "Yeah."

"What happened?"

But all eyes were still on her. "Listen, can I call you in a few days? I'll have my new SIM card by then."

"Um, sure." Rachel paused and then asked, "You're not okay, are you?"

Juliana brushed back the tears that had begun to form. "No," was also she could say, fearing she'd break.

"It's too much?"

Juliana tried not to pay attention to everyone in the room, but she could feel their gaze fixated on her like some kind of privacy-sucking vampires.

"Can you just all stop it!" she shouted. "I know I look like an idiot! I don't need you staring at me to rub it in!"

"Juliana?" Rachel said. "Ignore them. What's going on?"

"Nothing. I'll call you back. Merry Christmas. Thanks for calling." Juliana hung up.

Her father jumped out of his chair and stuck his

face into hers. "I've had it with this show. Everyone here is trying to enjoy Christmas, your best friend even called, I imagine to say she misses you and to see how you're doing, and you're acting like a self-absorbed little child. Go back to your room."

For Juliana, dance was more than "just for fun." When things got tough at school—a hard test was coming up, she and a friend were having an argument —or at home—like when she missed her parents—she could dance it out in the basement, where her practice studio was. It was her way of coping with the world. She couldn't just think her problems away like some people seemed to be able to. Of course, she'd talk to her friends, too, when she could, but dance was her private way of dealing with life.

And now, after not dancing for over a week, all the anger Juliana had bottled up exploded.

"No!"

Within a split second, she was down the stairs. She shot into the rec room, yanked the cellar door open, pulled on the light bulb chain, and slammed the door behind her. She didn't care anymore how many decomposing insects there were—it was better than being upstairs with all those staring strangers.

She stood barefoot on the cold cement floor, though her feet, and actually her whole body, felt numb. Christmas couldn't get any worse than this.

"It's just not fair," she said, tears freely flowing. She really needed Rachel right now. The two had started at the dance studio in the same year, had duets together, and even when they competed against each other in their solos, hugged each other regardless of who got the higher mark. Rachel's parents had divorced just two years before, and Juliana had spent many nights with Rachel as she cried about it. They had a bond that was now being stretched thousands of kilometres across the country.

"I can't dance," she said to herself. "I can't call Rachel. I can't even talk to my parents. Who do I have left?"

She reached for the book of drawings and opened it. The picture of the empty kitchen looked like a dream to her right now. She could imagine herself sitting in there, all alone, with no one staring at her. Then at least she could talk to Rachel on the phone.

Juliana turned the page and stopped at another drawing.

"Beds, a sofa, a table, chairs...all in the same room." But what caught her eye was the small Christmas tree perched in the middle of the table. Candles stood on many of its sparse branches. "Must be a poor family," she said.

Juliana closed the book. Her feet were starting to get cold. She had to go upstairs and face everyone: she had no choice. Even if she chose to stay down here until they all left, one of her parents would certainly come searching for her.

Juliana had to admit that the house did smell nice, especially the scent of warmed sauerkraut, which surprised her.

"It can't get any worse," she told herself. "I'm separated from my friends, my school, my studio, my entire life, and I've humiliated myself in front of people I hardly know. At Christmas. It can*not* get worse than this." As she took a deep breath, her resolve strengthened to just get through today. She had stretched in her bedroom: that had helped a little. And Mom had said they would clean the basement, though Juliana didn't know how she would dance on shag carpet.

But she would find a way. Dance was too important in her life to just stop.

Juliana tugged on the chain to turn off the light and headed to the bathroom in the basement to freshen up.

The bathroom walls, though devoid of the peeling wallpaper that decorated the rest of the basement, were covered with cracked and sometimes mouldy beige tiles around the sink. The shower stall was made of white metal, and in front of it and opposite the sink, where Juliana stood, were the water heater and furnace.

She searched around the bathroom for a clean washcloth but only found a stack of dry, crusty ones behind the water heater on a shelf. She would have preferred to re-apply her make-up, but what she saw in the mirror would have to do.

"Juliana!" Dad called down.

"I just need one minute!" she replied, honestly trying to sound friendly.

She wet the least-crusty cloth, washed her face, arms, and legs, and then gently brushed at the bits of dust on her dress.

"Juliana!" Dad called again.

"I know! Really, Dad, I'll just be a minute!" She wiped faster but to her dismay the water left marks on the nylon fabric. She opened the cupboard doors under the sink, hoping for but not expecting to find a hair dryer, but saw none. She removed her bobby pins and redid her hair, opting for a quick French braid across the back, wrapping the tail of the braid back on itself, and sticking the pins back in.

"Just have fun, right?" she said to herself in the mirror. If her ten years of dance had taught her anything, it was to find a way to keep going.

She took a deep breath and headed upstairs.

CHAPTER FOURTEEN

"How can Pastor Fröhlich keep ranting on like that about leaving Hungary?" Peter-Bátschi slammed his fist on the table.

"Don't tell me you're happy about it?" Krehling-Bátschi, Susi-Néni's husband, said. Krehling-Bátschi's first name was Adam, so, to avoid confusion with Mammi's deceased brother Adam, all his nieces and nephews called him by his last name.

"Of course not. But it's been said and done. Let's move on!"

Elisabeth could hear the men as they slammed their fists on the table in the front room, drinking schnapps and conversing about the pastor's Christmas morning sermon. She enjoyed listening in on their conversations; they were much livelier and about bigger things in this world than what the women gossiped about. But one voice was missing in all the discussion: her father's. He was always one to "move on," as Peter-Bátschi was arguing, and for the same reasons, even if moving on saddened him.

"But what about our children? They're having difficulties with Romanian, and many parents can't help them," Krehling-Bátschi said.

"That's my point!" Peter-Bátschi said. "Instead of going on and on like that and getting everyone angry about the changes, he could be focusing on helping our church's two schools make the necessary changes."

As much as Elisabeth wanted to agree with both her father and her uncle, she also felt the fear that Krehling-Bátschi was talking about. What changes would happen in their town? They had wanted to celebrate the 100th anniversary of their ancestors' arrival in Semlak this year, but the war and the destruction of the Austro-Hungarian Empire had left everyone feeling less than festive. Did the people in power know their decisions affected everyday people like the Schuhmachers and Brauns?

"But that he even dared speak about it this morning! We're celebrating the birth of our saviour and he's going on about Hungary!" Peter-Bátschi said again.

Krehling-Bátschi shook his head. "When Lukas returns, everything will be different for him. Poor man.

He'll take it all in stride of course, but the Semlak he loves will no longer be Hungarian."

The mention of her father caught Elisabeth off guard.

"I don't understand," Luki piped up. "I'm right here."

The men all roared with laughter while Elisabeth swallowed a sob and continued on with her work. While the men enjoyed their drinks in the front room, she, her sisters, Mammi, and several female cousins were hustling about in the kitchen finishing preparations for a full Christmas dinner for lunchtime with only a work apron protecting their Sunday clothes.

Omama, still alive at 61, sat at the kitchen table and peeled potatoes over the slop pail. Her many underskirts bubbled up on her lap as her black pleated outer skirt tried to contain them all. Her *tschurak* was a little faded after washing it for so many years and hanging it outside to dry. Her black, stiffened kerchief enclosed her face like a triangle, the ties sticking out sideways under her chin. The expression on her face looked as stiff as her kerchief.

"Your mother tells me you're taking over the household," Omama said to Elisabeth, who was slicing a fresh loaf of bread. "It's about time." Potato peels dropped into the pail, splashing into the dirty water that sat above the morning's breakfast waste. All of it would be carried out later and fed to the pigs.

Elisabeth tried not to frown as she carried a loaf of bread past Omama and set it on the dining table. When she returned, Omama continued.

"You're old enough to take on that work. Martin Luther taught us that work will bring us closer to God."

Elisabeth knew what was coming next. She forced a smile as she sliced another loaf.

"And all that reading you do is not bringing you closer to God," Omama said.

"I read the Bible and Martin Luther's teachings, Omama." Elisabeth then quoted from what she'd read last night: "Luther says, 'Until the heart believes in God, it is impossible for it to rejoice in Him. When faith is lacking, man is filled with fear and gloom and is disposed to flee at the very mention, the mere thought, of God.'"

"And God judges favourably those who study His words. But if it were up to me, I would have your father's books burned: they will only tempt you to ignore your responsibilities."

Elisabeth shuddered at the comment. Mammi took some of the peeled potatoes and began cutting them up. "She'll no longer have time, Modr." "Modr" was what Mammi called her mother. "There's much too much work to do around here." Omama gave an affirming nod.

Elisabeth opened the iron door in the wall to the oven and checked the goose she had butchered the other day. The skin was browning up nicely, and the rich aroma from the dripping fat made Elisabeth's stomach growl. She closed the oven door.

"I think the goose will be done within the hour," Elisabeth announced, hoping to change the subject.

"Then help Omama with the potatoes," Mammi directed, wiping her hands on her apron. "Anna, take a pot outside and fill it with water."

"Do I have to?" Anna complained. "It's bitterly cold!" Mammi raised a hand to indicate she was about to hit her daughter, and Anna dropped her chin, apologized quietly, switched her house shoes for boots, asked Elisabeth to pass her a cooking pot, and headed out back to the well.

"Lissa," Omama said to Mammi, "you should have slapped her. That's no way to raise a child."

Mammi sighed. "I know, Modr, but I'm far too busy right now to deal with her tears."

"Then you insist she not cry. They'll never learn without discipline."

Mammi carried the second loaf of sliced bread to the back room, got a damp cloth and wiped up the bread crumbs on the kitchen table. She then took the cutting board over to the washing table.

Elisabeth was dying to ask if she could open her gift from last night, but she tried to heed Luther's words, to rejoice only in God and not in silver or gold.

Another hand banged on the table in the front room.

"There's no point on lamenting about Empress Sisi: She died—when was it? Over twenty years ago now," Peter-Bátschi said.

"Empress Sisi?" Omama's face softened. "She was practically as old as I am now when that horrid Italian man stabbed her."

Peter-Bátschi, who was sitting with his back to the kitchen, turned around. "And you're just as lovely as she was, Modr."

Omama flapped her hand at him and smiled, her face turning into a raisin. "Now you're being dishonest."

Elisabeth had finished peeling three potatoes with her knife and was about to start on the fourth one when she couldn't hold it in anymore: she had to ask. As the conversation about the late empress of the former Austro-Hungarian empire continued through the kitchen, she crept over to her mother. Part of her was screaming inside, telling her to stop and stay on task, but a bigger, stronger part was pulling her toward Mammi.

Elisabeth spoke in a low voice. "I'm really sorry about last night. I was just so excited about my gift. I saw what the others had got but noticed that mine had a different shape and weight. I just couldn't wait to open it."

Mammi's eyes flashed with anger at Elisabeth. "Is that still on your mind?"

Elisabeth shrank into her blouse and *tschurak*.

"Do you really believe God wants you to focus on gifts instead of your family and your behaviour?"

Elisabeth shook her head.

"Good. If you mention it one more time, you can pull out the box of corn kernels yourself."

Elisabeth bit her lip to stop it from quivering. She wanted to run to her bed and hide under her blanket, but so long as the men were in the front room and so long as it was Christmas Day, she had nowhere to run.

She wiped her tears with the back of her hand, returned to the kitchen table, and kept peeling. If Omama had noticed anything, she didn't say.

THE MEN WERE ONCE AGAIN IN THE FRONT ROOM, NOW divided into groups of three and playing *skat* and drinking more schnapps and getting even louder. Luki was sitting under the table and flipping around his own deck of cards. The women were in the kitchen, cleaning up.

Stacks upon stacks of dishes sat piled on the table next to three washing bowls, and three of Elisabeth's cousins had lined up, each one in charge of one bowl: one for the first rinse, one to wash and scrub, and a third for a final rinse. Mammi and Rosina stood at the end of the line to dry the dishes and put them away. Omama now sat on a chair in the back room facing into the kitchen: she had broken an ankle a year before and could no longer stand for any long period of time.

Elisabeth was in charge of making a light soup for supper, so she started the broth that would simmer on the stove the rest of the day. She stood at the kitchen table and snapped the bones from the goose apart. Anna helped her.

"You asked me about Tata," Anna whispered. Elisabeth stopped breaking the bones and listened. "I couldn't hear him sing at Christmas service this morning." Anna sniffled. "He always sings so loud."

"Elisabeth," Omama called over, "idle hands are the work of the Devil."

Elisabeth continued pulling the goose apart, but slowly, so she could hear her sister's quiet voice.

"And he didn't cut the goose this year," Anna went on. "Krehling-Bátschi did it."

Elisabeth understood what her sister meant, and she also knew that everyone else had noticed it. The silence as everyone looked around the table to see who was next in line to cut the goose had filled their home. Normally, it would be the next man in the household, but Luki was far too young to use a knife that large. Krehling-Bátschi was the eldest man at the table and so was given the honour.

Elisabeth wiped a hand on her apron and then lay it on Rosina's shoulder. Rosina, walking a plate to the kitchen cupboard, stopped by her sisters, and judging by her red eyes, had also been crying.

"I miss Tata," Rosina whispered, and Elisabeth rubbed her back to show she understood.

"Mammi," Elisabeth said, "may Rosina help us with the soup?"

Rosina placed the clean plate in the proper pile on its shelf and looked at their mother hopefully. Mammi nodded. "You're too young to move fast enough here, anyway," she said.

"Here," Elisabeth said and pulled out a chair for Rosina to kneel on. She passed her the uneaten potatoes and a paring knife and asked her to cut the potatoes smaller while Elisabeth continued with the goose carcass. Anna squeezed past Omama to retrieve the last of the uneaten food, and came back with a serving bowl of sliced carrots and sauerkraut.

"Throw them in," Elisabeth instructed, and Anna did.

"I'm going to get more water," Elisabeth said. "Keep adding to the pot." She picked up the slop pail on her way to take it out back to the animals. Elisabeth knew the girls needed to get their minds off their father's absence, and so did she. Her gift could wait: Elisabeth needed to help her sisters right now.

"Good. You're making yourself useful," Omama said as she watched from her chair while Elisabeth switched her shoes, and Elisabeth scowled, her face turned away so no one could see.

CHAPTER FIFTEEN

Juliana sat on her bed in her green circle skirt and simple, cream blouse, having just returned from morning Christmas service at a Lutheran church with her parents and Opa. Now she had an hour or so to rest, though church had been boring enough that she'd almost fallen asleep there. She was flipping through the book of drawings, trying to piece together the life the artist had led, when someone knocked at her door. She quickly—but cautiously—shoved the book under her pillow before her parents entered the room.

"Hey, sweetie," Mom said.

Juliana responded with a weak smile. The next stop on the Christmas celebration train was Aunt Anne's house so they could celebrate with Uncle Phillip's family. The last thing Juliana wanted right now was to spend more time with all the people she'd humiliated herself in front of last night and then meet a bunch more she didn't know: Uncle Phillip was one of eight siblings, and he and Aunt Anne had a home that was apparently large enough to hold them all, their families included.

Hence the weak smile.

Dad sat down at the edge of her bed and brought out a large, flat package wrapped in cheesy snowmen and topped with a red bow. He lay it on the bed. "Your mom and I had a talk about you last night."

"I know," Juliana said. "I could hear my name through our doors."

Her parents looked surprised.

"But I couldn't hear what you were talking about," Juliana admitted. "Listen, about last night." She stared at her hands. As a teen, apologizing to her parents wasn't something she did easily. It came with the territory of growing up. "I got overwhelmed. I'm sorry."

She didn't look up.

Dad scratched the back of his neck. He was either about to drop a bomb on her or apologize. One of the two. Hopefully the latter.

"We also wanted to apologize for yesterday evening."

Juliana breathed a sigh of relief.

"When Aunt Anne left last night," Mom said, "she mentioned that maybe we'd overdone it. Just because we're your parents doesn't..."

...mean we're perfect.

"...mean we're perfect."

Juliana nodded. As much as she appreciated that her parents apologized—she knew not everyone's did—she wanted to know what was inside the gift. Was that a bad thing?

"Are you listening?" Mom asked, and only then did Juliana realize she'd actually been staring at the gift.

She repeated Mom's last words: "Just because you're my parents doesn't mean you're perfect."

"Right," Mom confirmed. "And we wanted to give you this."

Dad slid the gift over to Juliana. "We were going to give it to you for New Year's, but we know not being able to—"

"Paul," Mom interrupted, "just let her open it."

Juliana tore away the wrapping paper. Strip by strip, her anticipation grew. She thought she knew what it was, but she didn't want to get her hopes up until she had unwrapped all of it.

"Well?" Mom said.

Juliana's jaw dropped. It was exactly what she thought it was: a wooden tap board with foam cushioning underneath. Although only about one metre by one and a half metres, it was big enough to practice on without killing her shins or sliding on carpet.

"We know not being able to dance since we left Calgary has been hard on you," Dad said. "And we don't know if we'll be able to turn the rec room downstairs into any kind of practice studio for you. Aside from the fact that it's not our house, the ceiling is low, the floor underneath the carpet is cement, and we may need to use the room for entertaining."

Juliana nodded. "It was pretty crowded in the kitchen last night."

Mom walked over to Juliana and lay a hand on her shoulder. "Tomorrow morning, you and I can take a vacuum cleaner and duster to the basement. No need for you to be tapping while you're sneezing your brains out."

Juliana had to help clean that disgusting room? Suddenly, washing lettuce didn't seem so bad.

"But when we get home this evening," Dad said, "I'll show you how to use the phone. We ordered a long-distance plan for Opa, and it's already active, so you can call Rachel whenever you want and it won't cost very much." He patted Juliana's back and then stood up. "Oh. And I found an extension cord for the phone when I was cleaning the garage a little this morning. You already know the phone comes off the wall..."

"Paul!"

"What?" Dad said playfully. "Just trying to make light of the situation." He adjusted his tie. "Sorry. Anyways, just make sure the cord stays along the wall so Opa doesn't trip. But then you can have your private conversation with her until we get you a new number in two days."

Juliana let out another sigh of relief. Her parents headed for the door.

"Juliana," Dad said. "Can you forgive us?"

That question always made Juliana uncomfortable, though she could never figure out why.

"Yeah, sure, of course," she said and smiled the best daughter smile she could.

Her parents seemed satisfied. "We love you," Mom said.

Ugh, more mush. "Yup!"

Her parents nodded, smiled again, and left.

JULIANA PULLED THE BOOK BACK OUT FROM UNDER HER pillow. Her parents said they were going to lie down for a half hour, so it was a good time to talk with Opa.

The hallway floor creaked under her feet, a sound she was finally getting used to.

Wonder if I could turn that into a dance someday? she thought and filed the idea in the back of her mind.

She peeked into the living room, and Opa was sitting there, staring at the wall.

"Opa?"

He snapped to, took a moment to see who'd called him, and a big grin appeared on his face. "My Yulika," he said. "You look lovely."

Juliana blushed.

"You take after your mother that way. Not so much your father."

Juliana giggled. "Well, Dad does spend most of his time sitting in a truck." She smoothed out her skirt with one hand, holding the book in her other behind her back. "Opa? Can I ask you something?"

"Of course." He patted the spot beside him on the couch.

She sat down and pulled out the book. "Who did this belong to?"

Opa took the book in his hands and opened the cover. He read the writing on the front page and his eyes lit up, his sagging cheeks plumped out, and his smile appeared again. He closed the cover, turned the book over in his hands, opened it again, and leafed through some of the pages.

"Where did you find this?"

Juliana's cheeks burned: she felt like she'd been caught. "Last night...when I went into the cellar."

"Ah, when you were angry with everyone."

"Well, not everyone. Just Mom and Dad."

"For a child, that is everyone."

He turned over more pages and seemed to be studying the drawings. His fingers came close to touching the pages but he held them back. Was it out of some kind of fear?

"I hope you didn't touch the pages," he said.

Juliana's neck disappeared as her head shrunk into her shoulders. "I did. I'm sorry. But I was really careful!"

He patted her on the knee. "It's all right. But please don't ever again. These are pencil drawings, and the oils in your fingers will smear them."

Juliana nodded fervently. "Who made them?"

But Opa didn't seem to hear her question. He opened the book to the front again and stopped at the first drawing.

"That's the kitchen she grew up in," he said.

"Who?"

He pointed to the cube with the dark door on the left of the drawing. "Over here is the stove and *backofa*."

"And what?"

"*Backofa*."

He'd heard her, so she asked her first question again. "Who did the drawings?"

"And look at that...she even included part of the kitchen table and chairs."

"Opa, who?"

"They used to heat that *backofa* with cornstalks. See? They're in the basket."

Juliana was beginning to lose her patience. Why wasn't he listening to her?

He looked at the drawing some more, then chuckled to himself. "I remember her telling me about that Christmas: it was the first one after Opa had left for America. She had tried so hard to please Oma. Oma was always strict, but she was even stricter then. She didn't even let her open her Christmas gift on Christmas Eve. It was only many years later that Mammi realized it was Oma's way of just getting through that Christmas."

His *opa*? His *oma*? Mommy? Juliana thought for a moment. So, this drawing, and all the rest in the book were made by...his mother.

"My great-grandmother," she said, but Opa didn't react.

"Look at that. No phone back then." Then his face changed, as though he was suddenly remembering something else.

"I have to call Karl. I have to wish him Merry Christmas."

Karl? Juliana didn't recognize the name.

Opa set the book on the coffee table and headed for the phone.

Juliana picked up the book and studied that first

drawing again. Her great-grandmother. Mom had never talked about her.

Mom almost never talked about her family, Juliana thought. *Why?*

She studied the drawing again. That a phone was missing didn't stand out to her—it could've been around the corner or in another room. Juliana glanced out the doorway and into the kitchen, where Opa was dialling. She knew, too, that their house in Calgary, an older one, had had only one phone jack, and it had been in the kitchen. It was the main reason each of them in the family just had a smartphone: Mom and Dad needed them for work, anyway, and once their cordless phone system had died, they figured getting Juliana a phone plan would cost the same as their monthly phone bill for the landline.

Now that I think of it, some of my friends had the same issue in their homes, she thought. At some point in time, phones seemed to be in the kitchen.

"Karl?" Opa said, and then began to speak in German. He laughed, then a minute later turned serious only to laugh again. He listened and then banged his fist against the wall. She had no idea what he was saying, but he seemed happy.

No phone. Juliana had learned about early Canadian settlers. She had also learned about ancient civilizations and all that. But it had never really occurred to her what life might have been like without a phone.

I would've had to write letters to Rachel, she thought. Suddenly, not having been able to talk to her best friend for a week didn't seem so bad.

She headed back to her room, checked the time on her phone, and figured a quick nap before the next Christmas festivities wouldn't actually be a bad idea. Opa obviously remembered the book, so she'd just have to ask him more about it later.

"Can't we get undressed?" Elisabeth asked. After all the food from the afternoon, her multiple underskirts were beginning to hurt against her stomach. She wasn't sure if she'd have space for the soup she and her sisters had made.

"The first Christmas Day is not over yet," Mammi admonished. "We may still get visitors."

The sun was already at the horizon, it was mid-afternoon, and all Elisabeth could think of was sleep and comfortable clothes. Unable to change the situation, though, she headed to the front room, where it was nice and warm, and pulled down an encyclopedia. The house was clean, her sisters were joyfully playing with the dolls they'd received from Mammi's family, and Luki was occupied with the rubber ball and jacks that had been his gift. Mammi occupied herself in the back room, reading the Bible.

Elisabeth lit a few gas lamps, placed them on the table, and then opened up the encyclopedia to an entry on *Weltverkehr*, international transportation. Across the top it said,

ÜBERSICHTSKARTE DES WELTVERKEHRS.

The map showed the routes that ships took to travel through the oceans and those that trains took to carry passengers through countries. Although the set had been published thirty years before, Elisabeth guessed that these routes hadn't changed: She couldn't imagine railways laying tracks and then ripping them up again or shipping companies changing routes that already looked quite direct. There might be more transportation now, especially with the war over and life returning back to normal, but certainly not less.

Tata had been gone for almost a month. She traced a rail line with her finger, passing through empires that no longer existed: the Holy German Empire and the Austro-Hungarian Empire. Then she followed the shipping line from Bremen to New York. She didn't know how he had arrived in Pennsylvania, though: the map was too small to show her those rail lines.

"Elisabeth!" Rosina came running in, her face all aglow. "Maria is here!"

Elisabeth's heart immediately lit up. "She is?" Finally, someone she could actually talk to about Tata!

Rosina nodded so fast that Elisabeth worried her head would fall off. But before Elisabeth could close the book, Rosina came over for a peek.

"What are you reading?"

Elisabeth showed where they were and then where Tata hopefully was, in Pennsylvania.

"That's not too far," Rosina said, and Elisabeth knew better than to correct her youngest sibling about this. Better that she should believe that Tata was close.

"Elisabeth!" Luki called. "Maria's here!"

"I know, Luki!" Elisabeth laughed, delighted at the surprise visit. "I'm coming!" She closed the encyclopedia, placed it back up on the shelf, and headed into the kitchen. Mammi carried the guests' winter attire into the back room, and the parents, Haibach Adam and Haibach Anna, greeted Elisabeth quickly and then followed Mammi inside. Maria's brother and Luki climbed under the kitchen table and played with Luki's rubber ball and jacks. Rosina and Anna stole away to the table in the front room.

"Merry Christmas!" Maria said as she hugged Elisabeth. Elisabeth embraced her best friend. They hadn't spent time together during Advent, and seeing her now in their home was the blessing Elisabeth sorely needed.

Maria was a year older, which Elisabeth knew didn't always mean a year wiser. She had somehow survived falling through the ice on the Marosch River, being hit by a bicycle when she ran across the street to greet Elisabeth, and lighting the tips of her hair when she had had her back turned to the stove. But if Elisabeth ever needed to talk to someone, Maria was the one who would listen. Now, Elisabeth sniffled as all the feelings she'd tried so hard to suppress began pouring out and into her embrace.

Maria gently pushed Elisabeth back and Elisabeth wiped her eyes.

"What's wrong?" Maria offered Elisabeth her handkerchief.

Elisabeth shook her head as though to say "Nothing," but Maria obviously knew better.

"It's your father, isn't it?"

Elisabeth nodded as she dabbed her eyes, and Maria led her to the large sofa. They sat down, and Maria took Elisabeth's hand in hers.

"Tell me about it," she said, and Elisabeth began to cry.

"I can't stop missing him," Elisabeth said. "I'm trying so hard to take care of my chores, but I can't seem to control my feelings the way Mammi wants me to."

Rosina and Anna peeked out from under the table and eventually crawled out. Anna, usually nervous around too much emotion, stayed back, but Rosina gave Elisabeth a hug.

Everything Elisabeth had experienced came out: Tata's voice missing from Christmas service, Krehling-Bátschi serving the goose, Elisabeth now having to take over the household so Mammi could make shoes. The only thing she left out was her gift: she didn't want Mammi to hear her complain about still not having opened it. Even Rosina had been allowed to open hers that morning—also a new pair of mittens Mammi had knit.

"Elisabeth!" Mammi called through the house.

"Yes?" Elisabeth dried her eyes and blew her nose.

"Bring us some cookies and tea!"

"Yes, Mammi." She looked at the three girls surrounding her. "Thank you." Their sad eyes gave her little comfort, though; she knew she had just shown her sisters that she wasn't strong enough to deal with Tata being away. She glanced up at the crucifix above their door. How often had she prayed to Him, only to receive silence as her answer?

You wouldn't understand, anyway. Josef was on earth, always with You.

Elisabeth grabbed a pot, tied on her boots, and headed outside to fetch water. She grasped the handle on the well and turned it as fast as she could, lowering the bucket deep into the ground.

You could turn water into wine, and feed thousands. What do You know of my existence? she asked Jesus. *What can You possibly understand of it?*

The bucket hit the water and she reversed her movements, pulling the now heavy bucket back up. *All the miracles You performed and I can't even get a pot of water to boil fast. But You did it all in the name of—*

The answer came to her. Was it Jesus talking to her? Or was it her own thoughts? She couldn't tell. But she had an answer.

Josef was Your father here on earth, because Your real father lived in Heaven. You never saw Your real father, but You knew Him. In Your heart, You knew Him.

Despite the cold weather, a warm feeling grew within Elisabeth. Even though she didn't know when Tata would return—or, she admitted to herself, if he ever would—she knew in her heart that he was with her. She could pray for his safety and well-being, and once he mailed them back his address, she would write him every week. It wasn't going to be easy, and it wasn't the same as having him home, but it was enough to get through this.

I will somehow make it, she thought to herself. *I don't know how, but somehow I will.*

Elisabeth carried the pot back inside.

BACK IN THE FRONT ROOM WITH MARIA, HER MOOD MUCH uplifted, Elisabeth nibbled on another cookie and sipped on some chamomile tea.

"Your mother's cookies are astounding," Maria said after she finished her sixth one.

"Actually, I made these."

Maria's eyebrows jumped up. "Only fourteen and you can bake like this already? The decorations you made with the icing are exquisite. Your husband will be so very happy!"

Elisabeth's cheeks turned red and she nodded. "Mammi taught me last year, showed me again this year, and then left me on my own to do it while she packed Tata's belongings. You have to make sure the butter stays cold in your hands, so I opened the window in the kitchen and pushed the table over."

Both girls giggled.

"Didn't it get cold in the house?" Maria asked.

"I closed both doors to the other rooms and just worked fast. Even Tata was impressed. Last year, it took me four hours to get batches ready for the oven, and this year I did it in maybe an hour."

Elisabeth could now say "Tata" without wanting to cry. She knew where he really was, and for now at least, she could accept it.

"But I had to scrub the floor that much harder on the weekend—pushing the table had created grooves all along it."

"Next time just get your brother to help you carry it."

The girls giggled again.

Mammi appeared in the doorway and produced Elisabeth's gift. Her usually stern face looked surprisingly relaxed.

"Jesus would approve of your behaviour today, Lissika. I trust you've learned your lesson?"

Elisabeth nodded. "I know I have much to learn still, but I am trying, Mammi."

And yet, Elisabeth couldn't deny that every bone in her body was screaming for her to jump up and snatch the brown-paper-wrapped package out of Mammi's hands. Ignoring her racing heart, Elisabeth slowly stood up, approached her mother, and extended her hand. Mammi placed the gift in it and waited while Elisabeth untied the twine and then carefully unwrapped the package. She gasped.

In her hands she held a blank leather-bound drawing book, three pencils of different thicknesses, a sharpener, and a thick pad of paper.

"Patience is a virtue," Mammi said. "Never forget that. In fact, your father bought this months ago, when he last travelled to Arad, knowing you would soon be running out of paper in your old book. He also knew you would also want to write him while he was away. He wanted to give you the gift as soon as he returned, but I told him to wait and leave it for Christmas."

Elisabeth's smile stretched from ear to ear, and tears of happiness welled in her eyes.

"I regret you won't have much time to use the book," Mammi said. "Housework is much more important. It's a shame God gave you such a useless gift, but he gave it to you nonetheless. You will need to use it from time to time to honour him."

So much happiness flowed through Elisabeth that she ignored Mammi's hurtful words.

"Now I must get back to our guests," Mammi said and returned to the back room, her black skirt brushing through the doorway.

"Elisabeth, it's beautiful," Maria said. "What are you going to draw first?"

Elisabeth opened the front cover and saw a note from Tata.

My Golden One,

You have a gift from God, and you must use it. I regret that I will not be able to see your drawings while I am gone, but I do expect to see them when I return. Keep them safe. I do not know what plans God has for your gift, but you have a duty to use it.

Take care of your family, and write me often.
Tata

"Well?" Maria asked, just as a rubber ball rolled into the room.

"Maybe I'll start with the most important room in the house," Elisabeth said as she picked up the ball and shot Luki a look.

"Which is?"

Elisabeth walked into the kitchen, rolled the ball under the table to the two boys, and then stood to the left of the door and leaned against the washing table.

"What are you doing?" Luki asked, peering out from under the table.

"Drawing," Elisabeth replied. She changed her angle slightly so she wouldn't get Luki and Maria's brother in the picture.

"Why here?" Maria asked.

"We spend time in all the rooms in the house, but this is where we cook," Elisabeth replied. "Just as Jesus fed thousands with bread and fish, we fed dozens today with bread, one bird, and vegetables. Because we don't go hungry, our family exists."

Elisabeth began sketching the crucifix above the doorway.

CHAPTER SEVENTEEN

It was Boxing Day. Finally. Juliana had survived her first Christmas in Ontario. She'd helped Mom clean the rec room that morning and when they'd finished, she was ecstatic to see that it was retro décor, from the popcorn ceiling to the—vacuumed—shag carpet and peeling cream wallpaper. Even the furniture, in its fabrics of browns, oranges, and puke greens (what else could she call it?) practically sparkled.

Now, with Dad in the garage cleaning it up for the moving truck tomorrow, and Mom with Opa at Opa's old friend Karl's house, Juliana could finally enjoy some time to herself.

Down in the basement, standing on the tap board, her tap shoes already on, she stood in complete silence. No parents to please, no strange family to make conversation with, just her new tap board, her shoes, and whatever rhythm she wanted to start with. Music was not an option today, not so much because she only had the poor speakers on her smartphone, but because she wanted to fill the silence with only her taps.

She outlined the tap board with her feet, her taps scraping along its surface.

Looks like a piece of paper, she thought to herself. She took a moment to remember the drawing of the kitchen and then began copying it with her feet, scraping her taps along the board in long lines and short lines, squiggling and shimmying her feet where her great-grandmother had filled in some shading. The partial chairs and table, the doorway, the window behind it, the cross above it, and then the oven.

What did Opa call it? She thought for a moment and the word came to her. *Backofa.* Even though the white cube with the small dark door didn't look anything like an oven to Juliana, she figured maybe back then—whenever that was—they didn't have regular ovens.

"*BACKofa.*" Emphasis on the first syllable. ONE and two.

Juliana created a basic combo to the rhythm of the word.

BACKofa—ONE and two, *BACKofa*—THREE and four.

BACKofa—STOMP heel stamp, BACKofa—STOMP heel heel.

And so Juliana continued, the simple rhythm relaxing her muscles—from her feet all the way through her legs, torso, arms, and up to her head—as her body sank into the repetitive steps.

She'd wanted to ask Opa more questions today, but he seemed a little out of sorts. Even Mom and Dad had noticed it, so Juliana had left the book in her night-table drawer.

BACKofa—STOMP heel stamp, BACKofa—STOMP heel heel.

But, also that morning, Mom had gotten a phone call from Juliana's new studio, the Kitchener Dance Academy. The school offered more than just dance, despite its name, and was easily four times the size of Juliana's old studio back home. Judging by videos from last year, her new dance team alone had almost thirty members, massive compared to her old team of ten.

BACKofa—STOMP heel stamp, BACKofa—STOMP heel heel.

To say that the sheer size of the new team made Juliana nervous was an understatement. But when she had looked up the studio online back home, she saw that they offered everything: singing, drama, guitar, tap, jazz, ballet, contemporary, acro...the whole works!

Juliana switched up her little combo.

ONE and two, THREE and four became and ONE and two, and three and four.

Heel STOMP ball-change, flap ball-change.

But Mom had registered her only for dance, worrying Juliana would get overwhelmed if she took on too much. Even pulling out all her report cards to show Mom the steady stream of A's, Excellents, and Well Dones she had earned couldn't sway Mom.

"You have to write your exams in January, and you're going to be busy meeting new friends and wanting to join half the extra-curricular groups at school. I know you, Juliana," she'd said.

And Dad had agreed.

"Once your mom and I start working, we're not going to be here all the time to help you with your responsibilities."

Juliana began a series of running flaps, though she had nowhere to go. The peeling wallpaper blurred her vision as the sounds from her feet filled her ears. Her heart racing, her body sweating, her feet moved faster and faster.

But when had her parents last helped her with her homework? She loved learning: science excited her as much as English and French, math as much as history and geography. She was always on top of her work, always striving for the best marks.

But only through dance could she let out every

emotion, every happy, sad, frustrating, angry, and ecstatic moment of her life. She needed it as much to get through school as she needed air to breathe while studying.

Juliana's muscles started to hurt, but she kept pushing as her body shunted its energy to her feet, and the flaps gave way to a barrage of triple taps, pull-backs, cramp rolls, shuffles, flams...whatever they felt like doing. Juliana no longer had any control over them.

And only through dance could she begin to express what was storming through her with this upheaval she'd just endured. The loneliness, the shock, the confusion, the embarrassment.

But also the discovery: What was her great-grandmother like? How would this new studio be? And what would school be like?

Her feet started to slow down, her body tiring from the exertion.

Flap, flap, flap, flap, cramp-roll, cramp-roll...

Whatever happens, I can get through it.

Shuffle, heel, pull-back, step...

I can do this.

Heel stomp, ball-change, flap, ball-change...

I know I can.

Stomp.

Silence.

"I can do this."

SETTING THE RECORD STRAIGHT

Between Worlds tells a contemporary fictional story together with a story that is historical fiction. In both parts of the book, I've taken facts about life in the time period in which the story is set and included them in a fictional story. In writing novels, the story always comes first (because otherwise this would be a history text-book), so this section explains any important facts that may have been changed to fit the story and adds more background to the story. If you have any questions about what you've read in this or any of the other books in the series, ask away! Email me at author@loriwolfheffner.com.

SEMLAK, ROMANIA

Semlak, today spelled Semlac, is indeed a village in Romania, though very few Germans live there anymore. It's in Arad County, in a valley along the Marosch River ("Mureș" in Romanian), and is 4 km long from end to end. Arad, the central city of the county, is about 37 km away, and Temeswar (Timișoara), in neighbouring Timiș County, is about 90 km away. Although not "in the middle of nowhere" for North Americans, it certainly was for the people of the day: The nearest train station was 3 km away, but across the river. It could only be reached by cable ferry. Semlak has its own train station today.

Thanks to the online genealogy group Donauschwaben Villages Helping Hands and the German non-profit Heimatortsgemeinschaft Semlak, I was able to reconstruct much of the living situation in Semlak at the time, though I also had to invent various details.

For example, the typical farmer's house in Semlak did have only three rooms, and the family did sleep all in the same one. You can visit www.dvhh.org and www.semlak.de for more information.

However, I don't know for sure what books a family like Elisabeth's would have had, if any at all. Day-to-day living and conforming to the community's unspoken rules dictated everyday behaviour. The Lutheran church congregation supported two to three schools, depending on finances, and these schools only went to grade 6. Grade 7 was necessary to attend secondary school, so if anyone did seek further education, they would have had to travel out of the village for it. (It would be another several years before grade 7 was introduced to these church-funded schools, despite post-war Romanian law requiring that it happen sooner.)

The story about the bells is true: as World War I progressed, church bells were taken down and melted to make cannons. However, I don't know if the German villagers would have used other bells on an occasion as special as Christmas to replace such a beautiful sound. A new large bell for the village's Lutheran church was purchased in 1920.

THE SCHUHMACHERS

A great-grandfather of mine, Mathias Heffner, was a shoemaker and lived in a Danube Swabian town in Hungary, so I took inspiration from him for Tata's trade and the family's name.

Elisabeth is inspired by—but is not—my great-grandmother Katharina Wolf. My Omama Wolf was born in Semlak, attended the Lutheran church, and cherished her family, but she also had a sharp tongue, meaning she wasn't the gentle, innocent "village girl" one often romanticizes in historical fiction. However, in postcards she wrote to her granddaughters in Canada years later, you can hear her sadness: the Iron Curtain the Communist dictatorships had drawn around their countries prevented her from ever seeing her son after World War II or his children in Canada. Some of the postcards were indeed meant for her granddaughters when they were old enough, but the messages in them were delivered decades after her passing. My mother told me that they had actually completed all the paperwork for Omama Wolf to immigrate, but she died before she could travel.

But what Katharina Wolf thought about the changes that affected her village and way of life, I'll never know. And that's where Katharina Wolf ends and Elisabeth Schuhmacher begins. I had to free myself from the pressure of trying to accurately represent an ancestor whose memory still lived in others, even if only faintly.

You may have noticed that Elisabeth does a lot of housework, and that she hopes to marry one day. This was normal for her time and culture. World War I had just begun to shake things up, but there was still a strong desire to maintain the community's way of life as it had existed for generations.

You may have also noticed that the parents used corporal punishment to discipline their children. This was, unfortunately, commonplace, and erasing it from the story doesn't erase it from history. My grandfather John Heffner Sr., Mathias Heffner's son, is 14 years younger than Elisabeth and comes from a different town. He writes in his memoir that, if he got into any mischief on his way home from school, the telephone-free communication system worked so efficiently that his mother was often already standing at the door with the stick when he walked in.

Naming conventions in Semlak and other German villages in Eastern Europe differed from ours. For example, it was normal to refer to people by their last name first, e.g., Meier Josef, or Haibach Anna. This helped villagers differentiate between all the people with the same first name. In the book *Semlak*, for example, from 1819-2000, the top 10 girls' names accounted for 87% of all 4,092 girls's names in the village, and the top 10 boys' names 82% of all 4,205 boys' names. Nicknames abounded to help separate people. These could have been based on someone's occupation or a noticeable (usually unflattering) characteristic of some kind, or they could have been a short form.

One naming convention I strayed from was addressing acquaintances and friends. I believe that writing about this culture in English means losing some of the context that would have signalled to a person living in that village and at that time what form of address to use. For example, the added words *Bátschi* for *uncle* and *Néni* for *aunt* were used not only for actual relatives but also for anyone who was at least half a generation older than the speaker. You, a reader of this book, are at a disadvantage, because you obviously don't know the entire congregation and you can't see each character to judge their age unless I break from the story to give you a description. I don't know about you, but I would find that tedious very quickly! A third factor is linguistic: Just as French and Spanish have multiple pronouns you can use when addressing someone directly, so does German. Having multiple forms of address would also have helped the inhabitants of Semlak and other villages like it to keep everyone straight. However, English has simplified to only one form: *you*. Therefore, I stayed with the more standard German *Herr* for *Mr.* and *Frau* for *Mrs.*, even though historically in these towns these forms of address were reserved for educated professionals, e.g., clergymen, doctors, teachers, etc.

The repetition of first names within a family is historically accurate. To me, this shows just how important the family, both nuclear and extended, was in the lives of Danube Swabians. For example, one ancestor of mine had given birth to 14-16 children. (The church records differ from family accounts.) Of those, only four grew up to become adults. Of the children who had died in childhood, four were girls named Elisabeth, after this ancestor. It's in her honour and in theirs that I named Elisabeth in this series.

OTHER SEMLAKERS

The only real person in the novel is Pastor Fröhlich, who, I have read, was very much against Semlak's transfer to Romania and strongly supported Semlak's connection to Hungary, its culture, and its language. He was apparently responsible for several controversies within the church and its schools, and I can't wait to explore them further.

It was common for Germans in Eastern Europe to travel to the US to earn money, and in the case of the villagers of Semlak, Pennsylvania seemed to be a preferred destination. I believe an ancestor of mine made the trip twice, though he returned home, living out the rest of his life in his home village, his *heimat*.

MARTIN LUTHER IN ENGLISH

I had a difficult time selecting how best to represent Luther's original teachings, because in the research I had conducted, there were no contemporary (or close to contemporary) English translations of his work, and as it was, English back then differed considerably from our English today. (Think of it this way: Martin Luther died 18 years before Shakespeare was born.) So, for the English translations of Luther's sermons, I referred to the links published at www.martinluthersermons.com.

THE ROTHS AND KITCHENER, ONTARIO

All characters in the present-day timeline are fictional, though the city of Kitchener is very real. (And I don't think of it as a dipstick city!) Kitchener does have a size-able German population, but the younger generations rarely speak German anymore.

(If you're interested in learning more about German culture in Kitchener, visit www.lib.uwaterloo.ca and search for "Lori Heffner" to find my thesis. It's called "Heritage languages and the case of German in Kitch-ener-Waterloo." I interviewed three generations of three families of German heritage and discussed how German was or wasn't passed on through the genera-tions. Warning: it makes for dry reading and not the best writing, but it shows how the German language gradually disappeared in the three families I inter-viewed. On the upside, all interview transcripts are included. It's free to download.)

ABOUT THE 2ND EDITION

This is the second edition of *Between Worlds 1: The Move.* The difficult part about this series is that I will always be researching. Although I won't be able to backtrack through the series to always correct errors—that would be far too expensive!—I felt it important to at least straighten up a few facts and correct typos in the series opener to lay a stronger foundation for the series itself.

Some were minor typos, but others were important enough that I wanted to correct them here so the series remains as historically accurate as I can make it. (There will always be differences between what I write and what the historical documents show, due to time, lack of language knowledge, and the limitations of what research I can access without traveling to archives.) If you're curious about exactly what was changed, head over to my blog at www.loriwolfheffner.com.

ACKNOWLEDGEMENTS

I'd like to thank the following people for their help with this book:

My mom, Gerda Wolf, and dad, John Heffner, for not only enrolling me in dance but also for supporting my writing all these years, from pencil-and-paper, to typewriter, to computer.

My sister, Kristin Werner, for updating me with insights into the studio scene today.

Deardra King-Leslie, my tap and jazz teacher, for teaching me for over 15 years and for tolerating all the times I was reading when I wasn't supposed to be.

Heather Wright, my consulting editor and writing coach, for advice on the early concept of the novel and the series.

Susan Fish of Storywell, my editor, who saw missed opportunities, wasted sentences, flattened characters, and more, and then helped me fix it all. (Any errors remaining are mine.)

Michelle Fairbanks of Fresh Design, my graphics designer, whose patience was greatly appreciated as we shuffled through dozens of photos to find the perfect ones for this cover.

Ali MacGee, who has unknowingly (unwittingly?) become my mentor.

Nick Tullius, for filling in a few details so I could make the second edition more accurate.

Tom Harding and Helena Calogeridis, librarians at the Dana Porter Library at the University of Waterloo, for helping me with my research and finding me an old encyclopedia I could actually use in the series. (A book that old feels electrical to a writer.)

The Heimatortsgemeinschaft Semlak and member Georg Schmidt for supplying me with much of the information I used to recreate Semlak in 1919.

The membership of Donauschwaben Villages Helping Hands, who patiently answered many of my detailed questions about day-to-day life back then.

And finally, the Straus Haus: my husband, Corey, and two boys, Khristopher and Jonnathan, who have supported my writing and had to deal with Mommy slipping away into her office every evening and often on weekends so she could finish the first book of a project she'd been dreaming of for years.

BETWEEN WORLDS 2

THE DISTANCE

This book is dedicated to my mentor, Carol McCuaig, whose encouragement to write about my history helped create this series. Carol passed away February 22, 2018.

CHAPTER ONE

"Remember that time we put on fake tattoos and took photos?" Juliana asked.

Rachel's face, spread out on the screen of Juliana's laptop, lit up in a smile. It was a thing best friends would always remember. Even if they lived in different cities now. "Our parents were not happy about that!"

Juliana smiled, too, but then her cheeks turned red. "I'm just glad the tattoos washed off. I honestly didn't realize that one was a cross. I honestly thought it was a 't' and I wanted something for 'tap.' I don't know why they don't make tap tattoos."

"You and me both," Rachel agreed.

Juliana had forgotten about the whole mess until she began reorganizing her photos just before Rachel called from Calgary. She remembered the awkwardness of the lecture from both of their parents. The girls had thought tattoos would be cool and had wet them and put them on their wrists. The pictures they'd taken weren't for anyone in particular; they had just wanted to have some fun. But their parents had panicked, thinking the tattoos were permanent.

"I miss having you around," Rachel said.

"I miss you, too," Juliana replied.

It had only been a week since Juliana and her parents had driven halfway across the country to move in with and look after Juliana's grandfather, who was in the early stages of dementia. Only a week since she had had friends to laugh or be embarrassed with: all her dance and school friends were back in Calgary. Although she had no family there—Dad didn't have any at all, and Mom's was here in Kitchener—Calgary was still her home.

"Show me your room," Rachel said.

Juliana rolled her eyes at the idea of carrying her laptop around her tiny bedroom.

"No, really," Rachel insisted. "I can't be there in person, so give me the tour."

Juliana unplugged her laptop and lifted it up. "This is my bed," Juliana said, pointing the camera towards her single bed, tucked against the wall, with her duvet smoothed out and pillow set properly on top.

"Beautifully made, of course," Rachel said. "Here's mine."

Juliana saw a pile of blankets at the foot of Rachel's bed threatening to teeter over at any moment. "I wouldn't expect any less!" she said. "And these are my bookshelves—"

"Let me guess: organized alphabetically by author?"

"Aha!" Juliana said, playfully pointing a finger at her best friend as though she'd caught her in a trap. "Nope! By title. I thought I'd try something different."

"Well, Ms. Roth, I'm very impressed," Rachel replied. "You may be thousands of kilometres away, but you're still as organized as ever. I mean, the moving truck just came yesterday! Oh wait! Stop right there!"

Juliana's laptop faced an empty wall. "What?"

"That wallpaper is to die for!"

The girls broke out in a simultaneous giggle. Juliana knew exactly what Rachel meant: the wallpaper had an awful floral design on a cream background, and the pattern was separated by wide stripes of deep green velvet. Or so it felt, anyway: it was fuzzy.

Juliana set the laptop back down on her desk. "Oh!" she said. "There's one thing I haven't shown you yet." She stepped away from her desk, opened up her night-stand drawer, and carefully pulled out her great-grand-mother's book of drawings. "I've told you about it, but you haven't seen it." Juliana opened the book to the first page—its old spine complaining at being disturbed—and held up the drawing of her great-grandmother's kitchen.

"Wow...that's not your work is it?"

Juliana feigned indignation. "How long have we known each other?" She lowered the book so Rachel could see her again and then smiled. "No. This is that book of drawings I told you about. This is the kitchen my great-grandmother grew up in. The floor was made of dirt and chaff—that's the stalk from wheat—and they had no phone. It really looks like they lived in a Third World country, but it was Europe."

"Europe? I thought Europe was rich? Isn't it super expensive to go there? That's why all the famous people live there."

Juliana shrugged.

"What else is in there?" Rachel asked.

"Tons. Take a look."

Juliana held up the book and slowly turned the next pages: a pair of mittens, a party of some sort, and a drawing of an envelope. Then she lowered the book again.

"There are tons of these drawings in here."

"And you found it in a box in the basement?"

"Mmm. And this really old set of encyclopedias. All on Christmas Eve. An otherwise totally embarrassing night for me."

Juliana heard the hallway floor outside her room creak as slow steps made their way along. Opa didn't knock like her parents did, but the rhythm of his walk had the same effect. He entered her room.

"Hi, Opa," Juliana said. "I'm talking to my best friend, Rachel."

Opa paused for a moment, as though he was trying to think, and then his eyes opened wide. "In Calgary?"

"Yeah!" She leaned out of the way so Opa could see the screen.

"*Na, so was!*" he said in German. Juliana didn't understand the words, but his body language showed his amazement.

"Rachel, this is my grandfather."

"Hello!" Rachel smiled and waved.

Opa smiled in return. He brushed his hand over his bald head. "I'm not as attractive as I once was," he said with a sheepish grin.

They laughed.

"I'm showing Rachel your mom's book of drawings."

The book was still open to the drawing of a party: a woman in a simple but formal dress was surrounded by other women in similar dresses, all reaching out to hold a bonnet.

"I haven't seen a wedding ceremony like that in many, many years!" Opa said.

"That's a wedding?" Juliana asked.

Opa nodded. "The bride is getting her *haube*."

"Her what?"

Opa opened his mouth wide and enunciated the word. "*Hau-be*."

Juliana followed his lips' movements. "How-ba?"

Opa nodded.

Although now satisfied that she could say it, Juliana had no idea what the word meant.

Opa pointed to the bonnet. "That's a *haube*. It's what every girl wanted when she grew up. Once the wedding ceremony was over, others at the wedding sang a song and put it on her head. It meant she was married and now a woman. She'd then wear it in the home or under her headscarf outside the home."

On the other side of the screen, Rachel's eyes got wide. "She wasn't a woman until she was married?"

Opa nodded. "That's how it was back then."

"What did boys do to show they were finally men?" Rachel asked.

Opa thought for a moment and then shrugged. "I don't know. I've never thought about it."

Juliana studied the drawing more closely. Her great-grandmother had drawn the scene in a way that she could show the back of the bonnet: it was white and looked like it fit close to the head. Juliana fingered her brown hair, having a hard time imagining tying it up under a bonnet. She loved styling it, sometimes braiding it, other times curling it. She especially loved the elegance straightening her hair gave her.

Opa turned the page back to the image of the mittens: the mittens were worn by one pair of hands with another pair of hands pulling at them.

"Ah, that reminds me," he said. "We had fresh snow this morning. I should check the basement. Maybe I need to switch the blankets."

At Rachel's confused look, Juliana explained. "There's a crack in the foundation, and with the warmer winters here, water sometimes leaks in. So he's got blankets on the floor there just in case."

"I called Annie and told her not to come shovel today," he said.

"That's my aunt," Juliana explained. "They live literally around the corner and she always comes here with one or two of my cousins to shovel Opa's driveway and sidewalk."

"That's so cool," Rachel said. "My family lives all over Calgary, so it's hard to get together that much."

"I'm very lucky like that," Opa said. He patted Juliana on the head. "And now that Yulika has moved here, my life couldn't be better." Without saying another word, he turned around and left the room.

"'Yulika'? Oh my god, Juliana! Your grandfather's so cute! Especially with his accent! My family's been here for so long, we don't have anything cool like an accent."

Juliana nodded. "I know. He's the only grandparent I have, and I'm just getting to know him now. It's sad but also good."

"But your aunt couldn't look after your grandfather? I mean, if they live just around the corner..."

"She's also got six kids, and even though two are already in their twenties, she's still too busy. I think with us moving in, Mom and her sister and brother don't have to worry as much about Opa, because now there's always someone to help him."

Rachel's face became dead serious. "I guess that makes sense. I still have all my grandparents. If I had only one, I'd probably take extra care of them, too."

"Dad never talks about his family, and I'm only starting to get to know Mom's. It's a lot different when you meet them in person."

"You start dance soon, right?" Rachel asked, switching to a different topic.

Juliana's face lit up. "Tomorrow, actually! I can hardly wait."

"Just remember who your best friend is."

Juliana's heart almost broke. "Rachel, how could you think that? You'll always be my best friend, even when we're half a country apart!"

She looked at the screen. Even though they had talked this way forever, it was different when it was the only way they could see each other. In order to look each other in the eyes, they had to look at their screens, which meant they weren't looking each other in the eyes. It felt odd and made Rachel feel farther away or like Juliana was watching Rachel talk to someone else.

"Listen, Rachel, I should probably get going. Opa might need some help, especially if those blankets are wet."

"Best friends forever?"

"Absolutely. Best friends forever."

"I know your dance practice tomorrow will be stellar."

"You think so?"

"I've got a really good feeling about it."

CHAPTER TWO

*E*lisabeth wiped her hands on her apron. It was Sunday, January 11, 1920, in Semlak, Romania, the second Sunday of the new decade. Sadly the new decade was not beginning in peace: Romania was still at war with Hungary. However, as Elisabeth knew, it would be the year that would complete Semlak's transition from being part of Hungary to Romania, as had been officially announced by Romania's king just after Christmas.

Elisabeth didn't have time to think about the bigger world: in the weeks after her father's move to America, she was now in charge of the household.

"That girl never picks up after herself!" she mumbled under her breath. Anna, the second oldest child in the family at nine, had left her new red mittens on the ground again. Knowing her sister was already finding it difficult to continue in their day-to-day lives while Tata was away in America to earn money, Elisabeth picked them up and ran to put them in the back room where the girls' winter shawls lay folded up. She hoped to save Anna from punishment.

Maybe Anna can make a promise to be tidier this year, she thought.

"What is so urgent that you have to run?" Mammi asked from the front room, where she was braiding the younger girls' hair for church.

"Just tidying up!" Elisabeth replied.

"Did Anna leave her mittens on the floor again?"

Elisabeth shot a quick glance up at the crucifix that hung over the doorway between the back room and the kitchen. *Please forgive me*, she prayed. "No," she lied.

She heard a slap and Anna began to whimper. Within moments, Mammi came stomping through the house, from the front room, through the kitchen, and into the back room, her waist-long brown hair swishing as she marched, and her black overskirt and layers of underskirts having a hard time keeping up with her speed. "One more lie like that and you'll be kneeling in the box of corn!" Mammi threatened her oldest child.

Trembling with regret, Elisabeth nodded. "I'm

sorry." She knew Mammi was also finding life without her husband hard, and Elisabeth had promised herself at Christmas that she would do her best to help her family instead of causing them trouble.

Elisabeth gave up the hope that Anna would try to be neater. Instead, she made a mental note to remind Anna to pick up her mittens from now on. If Anna didn't remember after that slap.

Mammi looked Elisabeth up and down, let out a short grunt, and returned to the other girls and Lukas, their only brother.

The family hadn't heard from Tata yet, and it had been six weeks. They had expected him to be underway for about two weeks, give or take a few days, but to write immediately once he'd arrived. How much longer would they have to wait? No one in the Schuhmacher household said anything, but Elisabeth could feel it: they were all worried something had happened to him.

Anna had stopped whimpering, but now she let out little shrieks as Mammi jabbed hairpins into her braids to pin them on her head.

"Now, out, all of you," Mammi ordered. "I have to get myself ready. Lissika, make sure they're ready for church."

Anna, Luki, and their youngest sister, Rosina, scrambled out of the front room and into the kitchen, and Elisabeth knew she had very little time to get her younger siblings dressed and looking impeccable before Mammi finished whipping her own hair into a flat bun on top of her head and covering it with her *haube* and stiff headscarf.

The children rushed into the back room to put on their boots—which Anna had polished—and their clothing for outdoors. Luki pulled on a coat, hat, and new black mittens, while his sisters wrapped themselves in elaborately crafted shawls, simple, white headscarves, and mittens. Anna stared for a moment at the red mittens she had left on the floor earlier and then looked down at the dirt-and-chaff floor.

"Sorry," she mumbled, barely loud enough for Elisabeth to hear.

Every German farmer's household in Semlak had the same floor, and Elisabeth knew other families had messy children, too. Anna certainly wasn't the only one to leave her things lying around. Elisabeth dusted off any bits of dirt from the mittens.

"I'm sorry, too," Elisabeth whispered back. "I'll try to remind you next time."

Anna nodded.

The children put on their leather boots, and Elisabeth helped Rosina, who was only six, to tie hers up.

"Are you all ready?" Mammi asked as she swung open the door and emerged from the front room.

Dressed all in black, from the top of her head to her

feet, Mammi looked almost regal. Her black *tschurak*—a thin, fitted jacket that covered her hips—hugged her bodice, and her skirts gave her an air of authority that no unmarried girl could have. And just sticking out from under her headscarf were the edges of her *haube*. Elisabeth could hardly wait herself to marry in a year or two—if all went well—and to be able to dress as all the married German women in Semlak and other villages in their region, called the Banat, did.

ELISABETH, ANNA, ROSINA, AND MAMMI SAT ON THE right side of the church, and Luki sat with Tata's brother Konrad-Bátschi on the left. Next to Konrad-Bátschi sat his two sons, Georg and Samuel, who were much older than Luki. Georg had fought in the war but had not come home until a month after the big conflicts had ended, in December 1918. Samuel had contracted polio as a child, and his limp left him unfit for war.

Elisabeth looked around the women's side of the church and politely nodded to almost everyone she knew, including her aunt, Konrad-Bátschi's wife, Margarethe-Néni.

Pastor Fröhlich read intently from Martin Luther's Bible. As he read, Elisabeth tried her best to listen to

Luther's words, but all she could think about was how much she longed to read at home again, from both her father's encyclopedia and the family's humble but important collection of Luther's works. But with all her new chores and responsibilities since Mammi had taken over making and repairing shoes in her husband's absence, Elisabeth had no time during the day or evening to read. And now she would be busy helping with wedding preparations: Konrad-Bátschi's youngest daughter, Susanna, would marry Schubkegel Adam in a few weeks. That meant Elisabeth would join a group of girls and young women from Susi's family and friends to cook for several hundred guests and sew whatever the bride and bridal party needed.

Jesus only had to teach, she thought.

Anna poked her in the side, pulling Elisabeth back to the present: everyone was already standing for the next hymn, so Elisabeth jumped up and joined in.

"Welcome, Lissika! Welcome, Anna! It's so good to see you!" Their cousin Gretche, older than Elisabeth by a few years and already married, kissed each girl on the cheek and stepped back into the kitchen so both Schuhmacher siblings could come inside and take off their boots at the door. Six other women and older girls, all of whom Elisabeth and Anna knew, stood around the table and either nodded or waved.

Susanna, the bride-to-be and the youngest of this part of the Schuhmacher family, rushed to the doorway and also kissed each girl on both cheeks. At sixteen, turning seventeen later that year, she was someone Elisabeth looked up to now.

Konrad-Bátschi and Georg were out back in their blacksmith shop. As was customary, Margarethe-Néni was in charge of preparing the food and managing the group of ten or so women and girls at her house today.

"It's wonderful to be here." Elisabeth smiled as she leaned a bag of flour, a wooden rolling pin, and a pastry board against the wall so that she could remove her boots. She appreciated the chance to spend time outside her own home for a few hours, though she dreaded the actual tasks they'd have to do. And the gossip.

Anna laid a basket of eggs and her rolling pin and pastry board against the wall, too, and then set her mittens next to them so she could untie her boots.

Both girls slipped into their house shoes and passed their shawls to Gretche. Elisabeth then gently nudged Anna to remind her about her mittens.

"May I leave my mittens here?" Anna asked,

pointing to a table near the lime-painted brick stove. "Some boys threw snowballs at me on the way here."

Gretche's smile stretched from cheek to cheek. "Oh, those boys can be bad, can't they? Of course, you may. But don't put them too close: you don't want the wool to shrink."

Anna nodded and placed her mittens on the table. Elisabeth nodded approvingly and both girls picked up their tools and ingredients and carried them over to the kitchen table.

The door opened behind them, letting in a blast of cold air. "Ah, Lissika! Anna!" Their aunt came in, carrying a basket of eggs she had retrieved from the cellar out back. The sisters greeted their aunt and kissed her on both cheeks. "It's so nice to have two people from your family join us!"

Margarethe-Néni's comment was not a compliment, and Elisabeth knew it. When Tata had first announced that he was leaving, back in October, his brother and sister-in-law had repeatedly complained that he was needed here. As much as Elisabeth had agreed with them and had even prayed that Tata would listen to them, she now understood that he loved his family with all his heart and that it was his love that took him away. Margarethe-Néni's "compliment" was actually an attempt to quietly insult Elisabeth's family.

"Mammi sends her regrets, but she has to keep an

eye on little Rosina and Luki," Elisabeth said in the politest tone she could manage. She didn't add that her mother needed to rest after all the hours spent making shoes this past week in the cold, dark workshop. But at almost thirty-five years old, Mammi was already halfway through her life, God willing, and had enough on her plate as it was. "But she has promised to bake her famous coffee cake in time for the wedding, and she's also happy to look after any *minor* shoe repairs for the wedding party."

The emphasis on the word minor was Elisabeth's: she knew her aunt would take advantage of Mammi's offer if Elisabeth didn't clearly explain the details.

"That's very kind of her," Margarethe-Néni replied. She handed the eggs to her daughter, who set them on the floor by the table, which was covered with a white, handwoven, linen tablecloth and crowded with pastry boards. "Susi's wedding will have hundreds of guests," she said, "so good shoes will be necessary! No need to give Meier Josef something to gossip about!"

Elisabeth nodded in agreement: her aunt was right about that.

Margarethe-Néni clapped her hands. "To work!"

Elisabeth smiled to keep pushing her real feelings down: of all the cooking chores she had to do, she disdained making special noodles the most. Rolling out the dough so flat you could almost read the Bible through it often left Elisabeth with a sore back.

And now she would be doing that for hours.

"Elisabeth!" Eva emerged from the back room, adjusting her black headscarf. "I'm so sorry I didn't greet you right away! I just had to fold up some tea towels and put them away."

Eva was Georg's second wife, only eighteen years old, young compared to Georg's twenty-nine years. With Eva so young, she could provide him with many children, and because Georg would inherit Konrad-Bátschi's blacksmith shop one day, he could provide stability for their family. Eva wouldn't even have to work the fields except at harvest time, when all children were taken out of school and every available hand was required to bring in the crops for the winter.

"Thank you for coming to help, even though you're not part of the wedding. That's so kind of you!"

Elisabeth again forced a smile, though part of her wanted to roll dough over Eva's mouth. Living with her in-laws had already turned her into one of them, it seemed.

"I'm happy to help out anyway I can, of course," Elisabeth replied, silently asking Jesus to forgive her for lying. And for her bad thoughts.

"Anna!" Eva continued. "It's wonderful to see you! I can't believe how much you've grown!"

Elisabeth tried hard not to roll her eyes. They saw one another at church every week and here was Eva, talking as though they hadn't seen each other in months, something that would rarely happen in Semlak. If anyone left for long periods of time, it was usually for war, America, or Heaven.

Eva helped the other girls and women move their pastry boards over to make room for the two sisters. Elisabeth greeted the others at the table, rolled up her sleeves, and dug her hands into an open bag of flour.

"What do you think about Wagner Anni?" one of the older girls asked.

"Didn't she look just terrible?" another replied. "Her nose is now so crooked after her accident!" Everyone giggled, leaving Elisabeth feeling terrible about the poor girl.

"Jesus says we are to be nice to one another," she said.

The other girls looked at each other uneasily, so Elisabeth tried to change the subject. "What did you think about Pastor Fröhlich's sermon yesterday? I'm certain he was talking about trying to remain with Hungary. Did you hear that, too?"

The only answer she got was more blank stares. Although their reaction was expected, Elisabeth had hoped someone might say something in reply. She couldn't bear an afternoon of mean chatter. But after an awkward silence, Gretche returned to the topic of Wagner Anni, this time disdaining her shoes, and the gossip about the poor girl continued. Elisabeth sighed and wished the men were there so she could listen in on their conversations instead.

Juliana rubbed her eyes, stretched her hands and feet as far away from her core as she could, then grabbed her left leg, straightened it, pulled it as close to her face as she could before letting it go and repeating the stretch with her right leg. Then she rolled over onto her stomach and folded her legs back so that her heels touched her bum. She grabbed her ankles and pulled everything towards the ceiling, bending her body backwards into a dough-nut. Finally awake from her morning stretch, she let herself flop back onto her bed. Her ears now awake, too, she heard the wind howling outside.

Snow piled up in the corners of her small bedroom window. She sat up, rubbed her eyes again, and shivered. She grabbed a sweater off the back of her desk chair and stumbled out to the kitchen.

"*Guten morgen*, Yulika," Opa said, using his nickname for her. He peeled himself a banana, starting from the bottom. He was always up and wide awake before she was even conscious of anything.

"Good morning," she replied. She had assumed that was what those words meant, and since he never looked confused when she replied in English, she had decided to go with it.

"We got thirty centimetres of snow overnight," he said. "Roads are closed, and the city wants no one on the streets so they can plough."

"What?"

Juliana walked past the kitchen table to the front door, which opened into the kitchen, yanked on it to open it, and stared outside.

Their small street, which had houses on this side and apartment buildings on the other, was covered in a thick blanket of snow.

"It looks like packing snow!" Juliana exclaimed.

"You can make a snowman in the backyard," Opa said. "You're not going anywhere today, and no one will bother your snowman back there."

"Not going anywhere?"

Opa bit into his banana and pointed to the bowl of

fruit, suggesting Juliana help herself. She grabbed an apple and washed it in the sink.

"Don't you have dance class today?" he asked.

Juliana was surprised by how much he remembered sometimes. She still wasn't entirely sure if he had dementia: sometimes she was certain he did, but what if his forgetfulness was just because he was getting old? He was already seventy. Even her teachers at school forgot things sometimes, and they were much younger.

"I do." She bit into the apple.

"They'll close it."

"Close it? But it's just snow!"

Juliana set the apple on the table, ran back to her bedroom, clicked her phone on, and called up her email. There was a message from Kitchener Dance Academy, her new studio.

Dear Juliana,

We regret to inform you that classes are cancelled today due to snow.

Regards,

Mrs. D. Laing

Juliana shook her head. Whoever this Mrs. D. Laing was, she didn't sound very friendly. Juliana had exchanged emails with her over the past couple of months, and each email sounded corporate. Hopefully it was just this Mrs. D. Laing who talked like that and not everyone at the studio. She tossed her phone back onto her bed and returned to the kitchen.

"You were right, Opa. I got a message on my phone." She slumped into a chair at the table and bit into her apple. "It's like Kitchener's never dealt with snow before!"

"How does your phone tell you that?" Opa asked as he handed her a plate.

Juliana smiled. "It's not that my phone told me, it's that I got an email."

Opa nodded, but Juliana could tell he didn't understand. "It's like a letter, but instead of getting it from the mailbox, I get it from my phone. Just like you can call someone and leave a message, you can also type something to someone and send it to them."

Opa's eyes lit up and Juliana saw that he understood. She was beginning to learn how to explain things to him: how she bought her music online, or, like yesterday, how she stayed in touch with Rachel. Maybe she could set up an email account for Opa someday.

Juliana finished her apple and got what she needed for a bowl of cereal. "Do you want some, too?"

"Cornflakes, please," he said.

As Juliana retrieved bowls and spoons, Opa continued to talk. "When they served us cornflakes on the boat, we knew we were coming to the new world."

Juliana almost burst out laughing, but not in a mean way. Cornflakes? The new world?

"It's all right," Opa said. "Laugh all you want. But it's true. It meant we didn't have to grow our own food anymore."

Juliana chuckled. "But growing your own food is trendy."

Opa smiled and nodded. "I'll never understand that. Why would you want to spend all that time tending to plants when you could sit down, put your feet up, and watch television?"

Juliana had to agree: gardening wasn't her thing either.

BY MID-MORNING, JULIANA WAS ON THE TAP BOARD HER parents had given her as a Christmas gift, hammering to her own rhythm with her feet. Her parents, finally awake, were eating a leisurely breakfast and chatting away with Opa upstairs.

Juliana let the sounds of her tap shoes roll off her feet and onto the wooden board. If she heard anything uneven, like a cramp roll that went *da-de-de* instead of *da-da-de-de*, she slowed the step to improve her articulation.

A knock at the side door of the house—which was

just up the stairs from where Juliana was in the basement—distracted her. She ran up to answer it.

It was Aunt Anne and Sophie, one of her aunt's numerous children and the one closest in age to Juliana, though two years younger. Sophie was also going blind, a fact that made Juliana nervous. The door opened onto a small landing with the basement below and the kitchen two steps up and to the left. How would Sophie come inside without falling down the stairs?

"We came over to shovel," Aunt Anne said.

Juliana nodded. "We could've looked after it." She stole a glance at Sophie and wondered how she'd shovel. How would she know where to put the snow?

"Katy told me that, but we do this all the time. And since your parents are returning to work in a few days, it made no sense to break the tradition."

"Come on in," Juliana said, trying hard to be friendly. She took a step back onto the top stair to give them room to enter and so she could catch Sophie should she come too close to the edge of the stairs. But they stayed outside.

"Hi, Annie!" Opa called from the kitchen.

Aunt Anne peeked in the door and up to the kitchen. "Hi, Tata! Katy, Paul!"

"You're early," Mom said. "Give us a sec and we'll help."

Aunt Anne waved her hand. "You guys just sit and

enjoy while you can. We'll get this done in no time. If someone can just hand us the keys to the garage…"

"Yulika, top drawer, in the table, under the window," Opa said.

Juliana opened the drawer and found several keys on a ring, all gold with a square top. She held them up to Aunt Anne.

"Oh, I can never tell which one is the right one. Give them to Sophie—she'll figure it out."

Puzzled but not wanting to show it, Juliana handed the key ring to her cousin. Sophie fingered through one key after another and within a few seconds said, "Found it!" She held the apparently correct key in her hand, turned around, and walked back outside towards the detached garage.

"Won't she trip?" Juliana said before she could stop her thoughts from coming out of her mouth.

Aunt Anne's smile drooped and Juliana could feel her own cheeks burn. Too embarrassed to look at her family sitting in the kitchen, but wanting to do something to apologize, Juliana ran up through the kitchen and into the back hallway, where she tore off her dance shoes, jumped into her boots, whipped on her winter jacket, red gloves, beige scarf, and multicoloured tuque, and headed outside.

"I'll help," she said as she stepped into the garage.

"Just watch you don't put out your back," Aunt Anne warned. "This snow is heavy."

Juliana nodded.

"Excuse me." Sophie's voice told Juliana that she'd heard Juliana's question from a few minutes before. "Trippy blind person coming through."

No dance class, and now this. The day that was supposed to be the highlight of her holidays—especially after her failed Christmas Eve—began to feel like an exam where she was being tested on things she didn't know. She'd never talked to a blind person before. Juliana wanted to be nice, but based on Aunt Anne's and Sophie's reactions, her intentions weren't coming across as she intended.

Sophie slowly walked to the end of the driveway and began shovelling as though she could see. Juliana was confused.

"You don't have to stare at her," Aunt Anne whispered, startling Juliana.

"I'm...I'm really sorry," Juliana stammered. "And about before, too. I've never been around someone who's blind."

Aunt Anne's face relaxed. "I forget that sometimes it's new for people. Sophie has what's called juvenile macular degeneration, so she's not as blind as you're probably thinking: she's losing her sight in the middle of her field of vision."

Juliana nodded, though she didn't quite understand.

"Go online later and look it up. You'll find images that'll show you what she sees. But it means she has peripheral vision, so she can see things beside, above, and below her, but nothing in front of her. She can tell, for example, when she's following a wall, but she can't read a normal book."

Now Juliana understood why her cousin was so confident when she walked.

"But it also means she'll continue losing her sight for some time," Aunt Anne continued. "It progressed really fast when she was younger, and the ophthalmologist said it would keep going."

"You're talking about me, aren't you?" Sophie asked.

"Can she hear really far?" Juliana asked.

Aunt Anne chuckled. "No. She just pays more attention to sound: the fact that our voices are lowered and no one's talking to her tells her that we're talking about her." She called out to her daughter, "Just catching your cousin up on things."

Juliana knew she had to change the conversation: it was still morning and her day was already headed for a cliff. She moved over to one side of the single driveway and tried to push the shovel all the way across. By the time she got to the other side, though, she could barely lift it.

"You're right," she said. "This stuff is heavy."

"You don't get this in Calgary?" Sophie called over.

"We do, but my parents always had a service to shovel the driveway and sidewalk, and since Dad has no family, there was no one to shovel for either." Juliana paused for a moment as she thought back. "To be honest, I think the last time I shovelled snow was maybe...in grade four or five."

"Must have been nice!" Sophie said.

"It definitely was!"

Juliana looked over at her aunt and saw a smile on her face.

Can u talk?

No at restaurant but I can text u ok?

Juliana was relieved she could talk to Rachel. Aunt Anne and Sophie had left a couple of hours ago, and Juliana was still mortified about what she'd said. She adjusted the ice pack on her lower back and then kept texting.

Feel like an idiot

U r NOT an idiot! What happened?

Said something stupid to Sophie

???

Too much to text just stupid day so far

There was a pause, and Juliana began to wonder if

Rachel also thought she was stupid. Then her phone rang. It was Rachel.

"I thought you couldn't talk."

"I told Dad you needed me, and we're still waiting for the food—we're having lunch at one of those fancy places—so he let me step out by the foyer, where this place has a nice fire burning."

"That's what my cheeks felt like outside today, in the midst of thirty centimetres of snow."

"Juliana, you have to tell me what happened."

Juliana recounted the entire story to Rachel, including how she was worried Sophie would fall down the stairs.

"And to finish it all off, my back is killing me from all that shovelling." She flipped the ice pack around.

"You're not supposed to use your back," Rachel said.

"Figured that out now, thank you, Einstein. But it's just been a crappy day and I could really use a best friend."

"Listen, Jules, your first dance practice got cancelled and you're still getting used to your mom's family. You've never had to deal with family before. Everything about this situation is totally new for you." She paused for a moment, and Juliana wondered if she was supposed to say something. She looked out the window in her bedroom and sighed. It hadn't even been a week yet, and she was homesick. How long would this last?

"Listen, I've gotta go," Rachel said. "Food's coming. Chin up, eh? And remember what Miss Kasia always said."

"Just go out and have fun."

"No matter what happens."

Juliana hung up. "No matter what happens," Juliana repeated and adjusted the ice pack again. "That's easy for Rachel to say. She doesn't live here."

CHAPTER FOUR

ammi snored, Anna remained silent, Rosina mumbled incoherently in her sleep, and Luki lay as still as an acacia tree. Elisabeth's back ached too much from rolling out so much dough, making it hard for her to get comfortable.

She rolled onto her side and caught a glimpse of the clear night sky. She tried to rub her back to remove the aches and pains from hours of rolling out dough and cutting noodles, but she wasn't having much luck.

Elisabeth rolled onto her back and pulled up her knees, and her back felt momentarily better. She looked out at the stars again and thought back to her afternoon at her aunt's. All the idle gossip that always put other people down. Elisabeth knew she had bad thoughts about people, but she tried hard not to share them with others. Besides, Jesus was watching all of them, wasn't He?

But where does Jesus actually live? she wondered. *Behind the stars? On them?*

Tata's encyclopedia would surely have an answer. It was almost pitch black in the front room, where everyone slept, but she knew the order of the books by heart. She couldn't sleep anyway, so she might as well satisfy her curiosity.

Elisabeth's nervousness grew with each beat of her heart. She couldn't sleep because of her back, but would Mammi let her read? Or would Mammi want Elisabeth to finish up some sewing instead?

But after a day of wedding preparations and endless gossip about others' dresses, shoes, and noses, Elisabeth needed bigger ideas. *If Tata were here, he could answer my questions*, she thought. Since he wasn't here, she would need to find out for herself.

Elisabeth touched the edge of the second row of books, brushed her hand over the first two books on the end and then picked up the third one. It would certainly have something about stars in it. She then tiptoed her way past the table in the middle of the room, touched the back of the now-cooling oven, and followed it to the kitchen door. She retrieved candles from where she'd left them earlier on the washing table and carried them to the back room.

Once she'd lit her candles, she flipped the book open to "Stars." The entry said:

General term for all celestial bodies. One differentiates between stars that emit their own light, planets, comets, moons, or minor planets and shooting stars.

That was it? That was all it could tell her about the lights in the sky? Not even the writers of the encyclopedia knew where Jesus really lived? Or did He maybe not even live in the sky? Feeling disappointed, she pulled the family's Bible down from its shelf in the back room, its weight straining her sore back, and set it on the table. The candles flickered, casting both light and shadow on the thick leather-bound book. But where to start even looking? She glanced at the crucifix above the door. "Jesus," she whispered, "where do I begin?"

The answer came to her like a bolt of lightning. "Begin...of course! The beginning!" she whispered to herself and opened to Genesis, chapter 1:

In the beginning God created the Heaven and the earth. And the earth was without form, and void; and darkness was upon the face of the deep. And the Spirit of God moved upon the face of the waters. And God said, Let there be light: and there was light. And God saw the light, that it was good: and God divided the light from the darkness. And God called the light Day, and the darkness he called Night. And the evening and the morning were the first day. And God said, Let there be a firmament in the midst of the waters, and let it divide the waters from the waters. And God made the firmament, and divided the waters which were under the firmament from the waters which were above the firmament: and it was so. And God called the firmament Heaven. And the evening and the morning were the second day.

Elisabeth read and re-read it, letting the words sink in deeper each time. Her mind was tired and her back hurt, but the more she let the words wash over her, the more certain she became: the sky was indeed Heaven and therefore Jesus' home. She still didn't know *where* in the sky He lived, but He did live up there. She would have to leave it at that for now.

Elisabeth put the Bible back, blew out the candles, and shuffled back to bed. Lying on her side, she again stared out the window into the night sky. Jesus was in the sky and could look down upon them. Did that mean He could see Tata, too? If He could, why didn't He send her a sign that her father was alive and well? Or could Jesus not see him?

If He couldn't, then who was looking out for Tata?

IT WAS MID-MORNING THE NEXT DAY, AND ELISABETH carried a cup of tea in her hands for Mammi, who was hard at work in Tata's workshop. Luki and Anna were at school for the morning, and Rosina was sweeping the kitchen.

Elisabeth still remembered when Tata had added the workshop to the back of the house before Rosina was born. Before that, he had done his work on the table in the front room where there was more daylight from the large windows. But it meant the family went to sleep with the smells of leather and other people's feet lingering in the room every night. Mammi had said that she wouldn't have space to raise her children or teach the daughters their crafts. She had eventually demanded that Tata build the small attached workshop, and so it had happened with some help from friends as well as craftsmen from Semlak's Gypsy settlement at the edge of the village.

Elisabeth walked along the side of the house, careful not to let Mammi's tea drip over the sides of the cup. With the weather as cold as it was, Mammi needed all the warmth she could get.

When she opened the door, Elisabeth breathed shallowly so as not to be overwhelmed by the odour of feet, leather, and stale air.

"Here, Mammi," she said, setting the cup on the

wooden desk that had more nicks and scratches on it than their cutting boards in the kitchen. Tata had made the desk and Elisabeth loved its texture and roughness. Neighbours had donated spare wood they'd had, and he had sawed, hammered, and stained the desk himself. No one threw anything out in Semlak: if you could use it, you did. If you couldn't, you waited until a friend or member of the family asked for it, and you gave it to them.

"Thank you, Lissika," Mammi said.

Mammi had begun making shoes on her own after the New Year, and her first project—just to practice—was a pair of shoes for Anna, who had grown again. Girls' shoes were just a shoe with a strap, easy for Mammi to make.

"Anna's shoes look lovely, Mammi."

Instead of accepting Elisabeth's compliment, Mammi grunted. "The stitching is uneven, and I've had to cut a new strap twice. A waste! Meier Josef will gossip about our family for weeks if he sees these shoes."

Elisabeth needed a moment to think of a good response. "I know I need a new pair, and I would be very happy with the shoes you make, and I'm sure Anna will be, too."

"Don't be stupid, Lissika," Mammi grumbled. "Shoes tell everyone who you are. I can't make your pair until I've made nine pairs for customers, and with this kind of sloppy work, no one will buy from us. Now, get me a small piece of bread and some sausage. I'll be out here a long time."

Elisabeth rushed back around the house and into the kitchen, not bothering to change her boots. She cut a piece of the bread she had baked that morning and a few slices of sausage, put them on a plate, and rushed back to the workshop. Mammi was busy—she didn't have time to wait for a slow daughter.

Once inside the workshop, Elisabeth set the plate down on the desk and surprised herself by yawning.

"Did you not sleep well?" Mammi asked.

Elisabeth shook her head. "My back was sore from yesterday." Before Mammi had a chance to reply, Elisabeth asked if Mammi needed anything else.

"Not for me. But you do need to continue helping with wedding preparations. I also promised we would make a rum roll, yeast *kipfel*, and a pot of goulash."

Elisabeth's eyes popped open. A rum roll? Yeast *kipfel*? Gulasch? Elisabeth had never baked a rum roll before: she wasn't even sure she'd be able to peel the cake off the baking sheet carefully enough to roll it without breaking it! And *kipfel*? Each of the hundred or more triangles of yeasted dough had to be rolled by hand into a crescent shape, brushed with egg yolk, and sprinkled with salt and caraway. The goulash was by far the easiest because it had to sit and simmer on the stove for hours, but it required a lot of meat and peppers and every wife in Semlak had her special way of making it. (Or so they said: Elisabeth could barely tell the difference between them, although this was an observation she kept to herself.)

"You will be helping me, right, Mammi?"

Mammi's eyes flared like bolts of lightning. "Are you saying I haven't taught you well enough to be able to handle this all on your own?"

Elisabeth took a step back. "I-I-I'm sorry," she stammered. "No, not at all, Mammi! I just don't know if I can do it so well that everyone will be proud of our family's contributions to the wedding meal."

Mammi tapped nails into the heels of Anna's shoe, though it sounded louder now to Elisabeth. She didn't mean to anger her mother. Would Jesus forgive her for that, too? She stifled another yawn.

"You've cooked by my side for the past eight years, Elisabeth," Mammi said, her voice stern. "I know you're frightened about peeling the cake off the sheet." Mammi stopped for a moment and made eye contact with her oldest child. "But you are ready to do it by yourself nonetheless."

Elisabeth's heart beat like her mother's hammer had.

"Can I at least try a rum roll on my own once before I bake the real one?"

Mammi slammed the hammer down on her work table. "Are we made of money, Elisabeth? No, of course not! You have time to figure it out. Now go. You have chores to do."

uliana's heart fluttered like a young ballet student bourréeing across the floor, faster and faster as she lost her balance and fought to stay *en pointe*.

Only in Juliana's case, she was standing in her boots outside her new studio.

"Come on!" Dad called out from the main entrance. "You're going to be late!" His smile stretched from one side of his face to the other, and Juliana could tell he was excited for her. After laughing at Kitchener's tiny snow ploughs that were nothing more than dump trucks with big shovels on the front, she was finally about to meet her new team.

Juliana nodded, but her feet were frozen in the snow. Her new team would be composed of incredible dancers, but would they like her? Would she have to practise to catch up to them? Could she even improve enough? Bathed in nervousness, she did the only thing she knew how to do: she took a selfie and posted it on social media, captioning it: *At my new studio! #newbie #nervous #dyinginside*. She zipped her phone back into its pouch in her dance bag and ran across the front lawn and to the main entrance. The red sign—Come In! We're Open!—looked so normal and yet so scary. Couldn't they be closed for one more day? Couldn't more snow fall, like right now, and close everything up? She jumped up and down and shook out her hands.

Dad laughed. "I've never seen you this nervous, not even before you head onstage in a finals competition."

"This is new, that—" Juliana's voice cracked and she giggled. "That isn't. I don't know anyone here. I'm scared I won't be good enough."

Dad looked her straight in the eyes. "You will be fine. I didn't drag my daughter across the country just so she could quit when she got cold feet, okay?"

Juliana nodded.

"Good. I had enough of that in my youth. I'm not letting you repeat those mistakes."

Before Juliana could ask Dad what he was talking about, he opened the door and waved her inside. She stepped in to a little foyer with a table to the left that had copies of December's newsletter on it. Juliana picked one up, folded it into a neat rectangle and slid it into her bag, whereas Dad picked up his own copy, folded it into some geometric shape that had no name, and shoved it into his back pocket.

They stamped the snow off their feet, walked to the end of the foyer and then into the waiting room, which had benches along two walls, with coat hooks above. She saw lots of boots but no outerwear. Had people left their boots over the holidays? Where were the jackets? Was she the first one here? That'd make her look like a real nerd. Or really dedicated, which would be better. Then she saw another sign—No shoes past this point. Juliana let out her breath. She was neither the first one here, nor had everyone left their boots behind over the holidays. Her cheeks burned a little as she realized how silly her assumptions were.

"We should follow the rules," Dad said, and both removed their boots.

"Juliana?" An older woman, perhaps in her sixties, with her gray hair styled in an old-fashioned tight perm, came out from behind her desk.

Juliana nodded, her voice locked in her throat.

"I'm Mrs. Laing. We've emailed a few times."

The friendly older woman who looked like she could be anyone's grandmother didn't fit the image Juliana had in her mind of the Mrs. D. Laing who wrote the cold emails. She blushed when she realized she couldn't have been more wrong about this, too.

"Yeah, we did," Juliana said. "Um, where do I go?"

Mrs. Laing smiled like the grandmothers on television who invited their grandchildren inside for a scoop of ice cream after a hot summer's day of outdoor play. Only instead of offering ice cream, Mrs. Laing was inviting Juliana into a new world of dance. "Follow me."

"I'll be back in two hours, okay?" Dad said. "I'm going to pick up some food for tomorrow night. Your mom's family's coming over again."

Part of Juliana wanted to grab Dad by the arm and drag him inside with her, and another part wanted her to act brave and hold up her chin. *You're not a baby anymore!* she admonished herself and waved to Dad.

Mrs. Laing took Juliana down one hallway, pointed out a few music rooms and washrooms, the junior girls' change room, the boys' change room, and then the intermediate girls' change room.

"You're in here. Why don't you leave your bag there and then we'll finish the tour."

Juliana pushed open the heavy door and was greeted by a room with bags all over the benches, and ten or more winter coats on the hooks. She made a mental note to bring her jacket in here next time.

But did this mean she was she the last one? She swallowed. "Am I late?"

Mrs. Laing smiled her kind smile again and shook her head. "They're just finishing up their acro practice. If I recall, you didn't register for acro this year."

Juliana shook her head. "I've never done it, and Mom and Dad thought it would be too much for me."

"It is very demanding," Mrs. Laing confirmed. "Especially if you haven't done it before."

Juliana's confidence took a nose dive, though it admittedly didn't have very high to dive from. Did that mean all the others in her competition group were human pretzels?

"Come along," Mrs. Laing said, but her urging was gentle, not harsh. She pointed out the senior and adult women's change room, an accessible washroom, a hallway with two small studios for little kids, and then the main hallway with the dance studios.

It seemed to stretch on forever with its high ceilings and white walls.

"There are five studios down that hallway," Mrs. Laing said, "aptly referred to by their numbers."

"Like every other studio, I guess, eh?" Juliana said.

Mrs. Laing responded with her smile. "Get changed, put on your tap shoes, and then go back to Studio 3 in five minutes."

Juliana nodded. She turned around to hurry back and then stopped. "Um, which way?" Her face grew hot and she hadn't even stepped inside a studio yet.

Mrs. Laing's face wrinkled like a raisin as she smiled. She spoke kindly, "You'll be fine, Juliana. Your team is a good team. There's no need to rush. If you walk in one minute late, you walk in one minute late. This is your first day, and I know Miss Denise will be understanding." She pointed Juliana in the right direction.

Was it really this relaxed here? Miss Kasia would positively growl if you walked in a minute late.

Juliana whipped off her warm-up clothes and ripped open her dance bag to find her tap shoes. After a few moments, she began to panic.

"Where…?"

She dumped her bag on the ground and pushed aside hip-hop shoes, jazz shoes, pointe shoes, ballet shoes, toe supplies for her pointe shoes, hair elastics, bobby pins, antiperspirant, leggings, everything. Everything but her tap shoes.

She slapped herself on her forehead. "I left them in the basement!"

Her fingers shaking, she tore open the zipper in her bag with her phone in it. She pressed a button on her phone. "Call Dad" she instructed it. Her hand shook as she waited for her father to answer.

"This is Paul. Sorry I can't talk right now. I'm driving. Leave a message."

Juliana's voice shook. "Dad? Why aren't you picking up? I forgot my tap shoes!"

Realizing yelling at his voicemail was counter-productive, Juliana hung up and dialled home.

"Hello?"

"Opa? Where's Mom?"

"Who is this?"

"Juliana!"

"Oh, of course! You sound like your cousins to my old ears."

Juliana had no time for his grandfathering. "Nice. Where's Mom?"

"Let me think..."

Juliana's heart was ready to break through her rib cage. "She's not home?"

"No, she left to go somewhere, but I don't remember where."

"Okay, I'll try her cell. Thanks—"

"She left it on the table, Yulika. It keeps beeping. Do you know how I turn it off? It annoys me."

Every word Juliana wasn't allowed to use flew into her head and she tried to push them all away. The last thing she needed was for Mrs. Laing to hear her swearing.

"I have to go," Juliana said.

"Is everything okay?"

"I left my tap shoes in the basement. I have to go."

"You'll be fine, Yulika. Don't worry."

"You don't understand! You don't show up to dance class without your shoes!"

"You'll be fine. I can't wait to hear about your first class when you get home." Opa hung up.

Juliana slumped onto the bench. Her first dance class and she didn't have her tap shoes.

"Juliana?" Mrs. Laing knocked on the door. "Is everything okay?"

Juliana could feel tears welling up. You didn't show up for your team unprepared, especially at fourteen. Otherwise it looked like your mom still had to take care of you.

She opened the door. "I left my tap shoes at home." She pressed her hands against her eyes, hoping to keep the tears inside their ducts. Mrs. Laing gently pulled Juliana's hands away from her face.

"It's nothing to be upset up," she said, her voice still kind. "Just tell them they're still in a box somewhere at home."

"But they're not. I have everything all organized." Juliana realized the irony of her statement. "Well, except for my dance bag."

"They don't need to know that. I could show you some of the used shoes, if you'd like. Maybe you could find a pair there?"

The thought of stepping into someone's old, sweaty

tap shoes that probably bent in all the wrong places disgusted Juliana. "I'll put on my jazz shoes."

Mrs. Laing placed an arm around her shoulder. "I'll introduce you to everyone. That should make you feel better."

JULIANA STOOD IN THE ROOM, HER FEET HIDDEN INSIDE silent jazz shoes. It took all her courage to keep her chin up.

Mrs. Laing laid a hand on her shoulder. "This is Juliana," she said.

Juliana scanned the room and counted fifteen dancers, all dressed in black crop tops, shorts, beige tights, and black tap shoes. How was she going to learn all their names?

The teacher came over to shake Juliana's hand. "Hi, Juliana, I'm Miss Denise. We emailed a few times."

"Hi," she said, her voice quiet. She looked down at her feet. "I'm really sorry—"

"Juliana's tap shoes are still in a box at home," Mrs. Laing interrupted.

Miss Denise smiled. Did everyone here just smile? "Totally understandable," she said. "You'll just be learning today anyways, so you'll be fine."

Juliana nodded and then stared at each of the

students. A few gave her a weak smile while others didn't react at all. She could see eyes skip to her feet. Were the others angry at her for forgetting her shoes? For slowing down practice to teach her the routine? For some imperfection on her body? She suddenly worried she might already have sweat marks from all her worrying. No antiperspirant could ever fully keep her from sweating.

"This is Janine," and Miss Denise pointed to a girl with a slicked-back ponytail and properly plucked eyebrows. "This is Isaac…" Miss Denise continued to go around the room, the names blurring into one long one: Jasminmackenziebenangelrileysavannahalenadreand-lotsmoreshecouldnolongerunderstand.

Juliana wiggled her fingers in a wimpy wave. What else was she supposed to do?

"Sit at the front," Miss Denise instructed her, "and we'll run through the dance a few times so you can see it. Did you bring your notebook?"

Notebook? What notebook? Juliana shook her head. "I have my phone…"

"No, not fast enough and it won't let you draw. Here —" Miss Denise walked over to the computer desk in the studio and grabbed some paper and a pencil. "Make some notes on this, whatever strikes you. We'll fill them in as we go along."

"But I could just record it…"

Miss Denise shook her head. "No recording during class time except four weeks before competition, and even then, only I record it. Nobody wants to risk their imperfections getting online."

Juliana nodded. As she walked to the familiar line of mirrors along the front wall of the studio, she snuck a glance at her armpits. They looked fine. One thing she didn't have to worry about. She sat down, her back against the mirrors.

Everyone walked to their opening positions and Miss Denise hit play on the computer.

The entire group began a simultaneous opening sequence, tapping in unison. Juliana scrambled to scribble steps and counts down, but there was no way she could keep up.

Miss Denise noticed. "Just write down what you can," she yelled over the music. "You won't get everything."

Juliana nodded, but she didn't really understand what Miss Denise meant. She'd never taken notes before about a dance she'd never learned. Sure, when she'd broken her wrist and sprained her ankle a couple of years ago, she wrote down errors and corrections, but she had already learned her own dances that year.

The dancers kicked, turned, and tapped in unison like a New York City stage revue chorus. Some arms were out of place, and sometimes heads were at different angles, but otherwise things looked pretty together.

By the time the dance was over three minutes later, Juliana realized she hadn't written anything down. No shoes and no notes. Could this get any worse?

"What did you think?" Miss Denise asked.

It could get worse. What was Juliana supposed to say? That she didn't think she could meet them at their level? That there was no way she'd be as good as them? Maybe forgetting her shoes had been a good thing: that way they'd never know how bad she really was.

"Um, I really liked it," was all she could think of to say.

"What errors did you notice?"

Juliana stared at everyone. Miss Kasia said that if you were going to point out someone's mistake, you'd better perform that step better than they did, otherwise you'd look like a stuck-up snob from some TV dance show. Juliana didn't know if she could live up to any corrections she was about to give. But as all eyes were glued to her, she knew she had to say something.

"I found sometimes the arms weren't always in line."

Miss Denise nodded and then looked at the group. "See? It's not just me."

To Juliana's surprise, everyone nodded. No looks of anger flew in her direction, and several even smiled.

"Let's try it again," Miss Denise said.

"WHY DIDN'T YOU ANSWER YOUR PHONE!" JULIANA shouted at Dad.

"Because I'd forgotten it in the car!" Dad yelled back. "*You* forgot to pack your shoes. Why are you yelling at me?"

"Don't know you how embarrassed I was?"

Dad paused for a moment, took a deep breath, and visibly tried to calm himself down. "I can imagine it would be like me showing up to my new employer without my truck driver's license," he said. "So, yes, I do get it, Juliana. But I wouldn't pick up the phone and start yelling at your mother for not reminding me!"

Juliana's whole body was filled with anger. "I can't show up without my shoes and just expect them to be okay with it!"

"You'll get a second chance to prove yourself!"

"A second chance? You really don't get it, do you, Dad?"

"What? Did they yell at you? Make you do embarrassing initiation games? Kick you out and tell you to never come back?"

"Well, no."

"Then they were fine with it and they're giving you a second chance. For once in your life, be grateful for something. Please!"

"That's not what they were thinking!"

"Oh, so you can read thoughts now, can you?"

Juliana crossed her arms. "These things may not be important to adults, but they're absolutely important to teens!"

Dad banged on the steering wheel. "I've already told you that I understand, Juliana! You're the one who needs to grow up here and take responsibility for your actions! They're obviously giving you a second chance!"

Juliana couldn't wait to get home and talk to Rachel. She'd at least understand.

CHAPTER SIX

A week had passed, and Anna and Elisabeth had just picked up their sewing bags at home, after church, and now stood under the overhang outside Konrad-Bátschi and Margarethe-Néni's house. Elisabeth knocked. Today's task would be embroidering handkerchiefs for the bridesmaids.

The door opened, and Eva, Cousin Georg's wife, stood there, smiling from ear to ear. "Lissika! Little Anna! It's so wonderful to see you both!"

They exchanged kisses on each other's cheeks, and Elisabeth wondered how often she'd have to endure being greeted by members of this family as though they hadn't seen each other in months.

"Come in, let me take your shawls!"

Elisabeth and Anna removed their winter shawls and then their mittens.

"May I?" Anna asked, pointing to the table next to the stove.

Eva gave her an exaggerated expression of disappointment, the kind an adult gives a three-year-old. "Boys again?"

Anna's temples twitched and Elisabeth knew her sister was annoyed. She detested being treated as though she was as young as Rosina. Elisabeth had to speak up but before she could say anything, Gretche interrupted.

"Lissika! Anna! Thank you for coming! I already have tea in the front room for us. The men have left for a while, so we'll be all alone, just like the last time!"

And just like last time, Elisabeth tried not to roll her eyes. She didn't want to spend time gossiping about whatever Meier Josef had been gossiping about at church that day. As far as Elisabeth was concerned, if she had time away from household chores, she'd rather be reading than listening to everyone talk about everyone else. But duty was duty, and as a cousin to the bride, she had to help.

At least this time she wouldn't go home with a sore back.

The front room in Konrad-Bátschi's home was similar to Elisabeth's: a wooden, handmade table that could seat eight or maybe ten stood in the middle, and beds were spread out along the room's walls. In between the two large windows stood a wooden bench with a back, furniture that had been passed down for several generations in the family. To the left of the door was the back of the lime-painted brick oven, which heated the room comfortably. When Elisabeth and Anna were shown in, they nodded hello to Margarethe-Néni and Susi, who smiled back, and then took their seats at the table, between Gretche and Eva. It was only family today, which relieved Elisabeth of the agony of listening to a dozen women gossip.

"Have you heard from Lukas-Bátschi yet?" Eva asked, referring to Elisabeth's and Anna's father. But the question surprised Elisabeth: Eva could have begun their conversation with a happier topic, couldn't she?

"No," Elisabeth replied. "Not yet."

Eva's face turned upside down. "I'm so sorry. I'm certain he's fine."

"I hope so. It's been almost two months. We should have heard from him by now."

Eva nodded, her face openly sad. "It must be hard not know how he's faring."

Elisabeth heard a little sniffle from Anna and knew she had to change the topic. That Eva would purposely begin with such an upsetting subject angered Elisabeth: Eva was a woman now. She should know better.

"How are wedding plans coming along?" Elisabeth asked, trying her best to keep her tone polite.

Margarethe-Néni smiled. "We have so many people helping us that we are much farther along by now than we were with Georg's wedding last year."

"That's wonderful to hear," Elisabeth replied, not sure if she really meant it. But she knew that Margarethe-Néni was only telling half the truth herself: part of the reason for the delays in Georg's wedding were his tremors, during which he would press himself into a corner in the room and fight his body to stop shaking, a difficult and embarrassing habit that had begun after the war. Eva almost hadn't married him but, according to Mammi, she had after she was reminded of the benefits of the union. At the very least, it had meant that Eva's family could pay less of a dowry to Georg's family. Elisabeth hoped that, whoever her husband would be, he would be in good health and not request much of her family. With only one boy and three girls to marry off, Tata and Mammi could find the marriage of their children very expensive.

"May I ask how Georg is doing?" Elisabeth said. "I only see him in church, but he seems to be doing better."

"Thank you," Eva said. "Yes, God has been shining his blessings down on him."

"That's nice to hear, isn't it, Anna?" Elisabeth said,

and her sister nodded. Anna rarely said a word outside the home, and Elisabeth felt that it was part of her duty in helping raise her siblings that she needed to teach shy Anna how to converse. After all, no man would want a silent wife.

THE CLOCK CHIMED THREE, AND IT WAS NEARLY TIME TO leave: Elisabeth needed to cook supper. She looked over to Anna's handiwork to see how far she'd come. Anna had chosen a simple rose pattern for her handkerchief: two roses in each corner, their petals stitched in red thread and their leaves and stem in green. Seven of the eight roses were already finished, and Elisabeth knew Mammi would certainly be upset if her daughters left without finishing.

"That looks lovely," Elisabeth said, and Anna beamed. The other women glanced over at the young girl's work and nodded in approval.

"You'll make a fine wife someday if you keep up with that," said Margarethe-Néni. "And speak a little more. We've hardly heard you say a thing these past several hours."

Anna's temples twitched, but no one seemed to notice. The conversation simply continued about others in the village. Elisabeth had had to stifle yawns several times to prevent herself from drifting off to sleep, stabbing herself with her needle, or thinking about Tata. Why hadn't she heard from him yet? She glanced up at the crucifix that hung over the doorway. Was Tata truly so far away that not even Jesus could see him? Why else wouldn't Jesus give Elisabeth a sign that he was well? She was trying so hard to be a pious girl—surely some good must come of her efforts?

"Anna, finish up," she said to her sister. "We should go: I need to start supper shortly."

She headed through the kitchen into the back room to retrieve their shawls. As she returned, Georg entered through the house door. His short hair was neatly trimmed, his face shaven clean, and his broad chest and thick arms showed no signs of feebleness. He removed his hat and nodded.

"Hello, Elisabeth," he said, though without a smile.

The creases in his face made him look older than he was. If he had been anyone else, Elisabeth would have taken his still face to mean something rude, and indeed, many in the village did view him that way. His shaking, his unfriendly greetings, his quiet demeanour—all these things often embarrassed his family. But he was a tradesman: he would take over his father's blacksmith shop someday, so that—and only that—gave him respect, because there were few tradesmen among the German Lutherans.

"I'm here to pick up Eva to go visit her family."

"We're almost finished, I believe," Elisabeth answered, frozen in her spot.

Georg removed his boots without saying another word, walked into the front room, and nodded to everyone around the table.

"Hello, Georg," Eva said, beaming, but even to such a happy welcome he just nodded and left the room. Elisabeth saw Margarethe-Néni's flash of anger once Georg turned around, while Eva's face fell. Elisabeth wondered if this happened all the time. To Elisabeth's relief, Anna was just tying off her threads.

Elisabeth hung the shawls over the back of a chair and smoothed out her handkerchief on the table: she had two blue birds in each corner, joined by a chain of leaves that travelled along each edge. For an extra blessing, she had embroidered a little star on top of each pair of birds. She had begun the handkerchief earlier in the week, so she finished it today.

"Elisabeth, you truly have a gift from God," Margarethe-Néni said and thanked her.

"I can do one more at home if you'd like," Elisabeth offered. It wasn't as enjoyable as the drawing she loved to do, but it would give her a break from her chores without causing Mammi to complain. Margarethe-Néni happily accepted the offer and handed her another cotton square. Elisabeth and Anna collected their bags and shawls and the others followed them, congregating at the house door, in the kitchen. Georg was sitting at the table, puffing on a cigarette. Judging by his unfocused eyes, he was lost in thought.

"Georg," Eva said, "your cousins are leaving."

Georg nodded to both girls but otherwise said nothing.

Elisabeth and Anna wrapped their shawls around their shoulders, and Gretche reached around Anna to the table beside the oven to pass Anna her red mittens.

"No," Georg said, shaking his head. His cigarette dropped onto the floor and Georg jumped up from his chair, his eyes fixed on the mittens.

"Georg," Eva said, her voice polite but stern. "I just told your cousins that you're doing better. Stop this."

Still staring at the mittens, he wrapped his arms around himself, as though he was trying to stop his body from shaking.

"Don't shoot!" he yelled.

Realizing the mittens had somehow caused his change, Elisabeth turned Anna around, said a hurried round of goodbyes herself, and rushed out.

"No!" she could hear Georg call from inside. "Leave him!"

The girls walked around to the front of the house, where Elisabeth stopped in her tracks as she saw Margarethe-Néni slap Georg in the face. "Stop embarrassing our family!" she screamed, her voice carrying through the several panes of windows. She saw Georg collapse in the doorway.

Anna's eyes and mouth were wide open, and Elisabeth didn't know what to tell her. "We should go," she said and tried to push Anna along.

"But he needs help," Anna replied.

"He has family. They will help him." She looked up to the sky. Jesus saw this, did He not? He must have. If the two girls had seen Georg, then Jesus must have, too. "Jesus will help Georg, too, when He feels it's right."

"Shouldn't Jesus help him right now? Margarethe-Néni isn't."

Elisabeth didn't have an answer.

Anna turned around and began heading back to their aunt's house.

"No," Elisabeth said. "It's none of our business, Anna."

Her younger sister's eyes began to moisten. "But he's hurting."

Elisabeth turned Anna around, back to the sidewalk, and pushed her along. "Jesus will find a way to help him. We can help by praying for him."

ELISABETH HAD MANAGED TO CALM ANNA DOWN BY THE time they got home, even though her own mind swirled in confusion. She remembered Gretche and Susi complaining all the time about their older brother when they were all younger: Georg would pull their hair or poke them in the ear with a wet finger when no one was looking. He loved playing a *storrnickel* at Christmas and frightening all the younger children at every house he visited. Elisabeth remembered those years all too well. Most of her childhood was spent running out of the room every time Georg entered it.

But the more time he had spent with his father in the workshop, the less time he had had to bother his family. With the strength of a mule and the aim of a hummingbird, Georg had become a respected black-smith well before he married his first wife. He carried pride in his chest wherever he walked, acting more and more like a man and not a bothersome brother. Georg could wield a hammer to make almost anything: horse-shoes, hoops for wine barrels, even occasionally ploughs and parts for ploughs.

And now he trembled at the sight of red mittens.

Once both sisters were inside their own house and had removed their shawls and boots, Elisabeth helped herself to a glass of water from the jug that sat next to the washing basin. Luki was in the front room playing with a rubber ball, trying to knock over some dried corn cobs that had been cut in half so they would stand. Sitting at the table, Rosina stuck out her tongue in concentration as she tried to crochet the first row after her chain. Elisabeth remembered having difficulty with those first few rows when she was young: sticking the hook through those often tight loops was frustrating. It was also partly why she had taken to drawing: she didn't have to coordinate her hands so much. Anna sat down next to her sister and resumed a scarf she was crocheting for herself.

Mammi, too, sat at the table, though she was knitting a sock while reading the Bible.

"Mammi?" Elisabeth sat down and pulled out her embroidery ring.

"Mmm," Mammi replied, not looking up from her reading.

Elisabeth separated the ring into its inner and outer parts, placed the fresh square of cotton from Margarethe-Néni in it, closed the outer ring on top, and tightened the screw. "I saw Cousin Georg at Margarethe-Néni's today."

"Couldn't step outside his own home again?"

Elisabeth tried to ignore the tone in Mammi's voice. "He had actually just returned to get Eva so they could visit her family."

"I see." Mammi said no more, her mind clearly

focused on knitting and reading instead of talking with her daughter.

Elisabeth persisted. "Why is he like that?"

Mammi's face didn't move when she answered, and her eyes still followed the words in the Bible. "He has weak nerves, Elisabeth, you know that."

Mammi clearly didn't want to be disturbed, but Elisabeth couldn't let it rest.

"But Eva said today that he was doing better, and all it took was Anna's red mittens to..." She didn't know how to describe what she'd seen.

"He fell onto the floor like a sack of potatoes again, did he?"

Elisabeth nodded.

"He obviously isn't the man everyone thought he was, and the war proved that. He's lucky he found a second wife."

Elisabeth threaded some green into her needle and took a moment to look up at Jesus.

Why can't You help him? she silently asked.

ELISABETH SAT IN THE BACK ROOM, SEVERAL CANDLES LIT, and her book of drawings open to the next page. The rest of the family lay in bed, fast asleep. She could not get Georg out of her mind, the way he had shaken and panicked at the sight of a pair of mittens. The memory kept pounding against her skull like a blacksmith's hammer.

And then Mammi's comment: "He fell onto the floor like a sack of potatoes again, did he?"

Wouldn't Georg stop if he could? Or was this God's punishment for the way Georg had behaved to his family and other children when they were all younger? The snowballs Anna had to deal with from other school kids paled in comparison to the teasing, hair-pulling, and private insults Georg would throw his sisters' way and the fights he would start with his lame brother. She even vaguely recalled him telling her a long time ago that they'd never have money because Tata hadn't been the one to inherit his father's blacksmithing shop.

"But in truth," Elisabeth whispered, "Tata never wanted it. He hated the heat." That was of course something that was simply not said. Tata would never have wanted to insult his father or his father's memory.

But if Georg couldn't shake off these tremors, how terrible must it be to have them? To be trapped in a body that trembled of its own will? At the sight of a simple pair of handmade, woollen mittens?

Ideas flew through Elisabeth's mind and she fervently began with an outline: Georg's hands pulling the mittens off Anna's. Elisabeth believed Georg would've wanted to do that, to rid himself of whatever the red mittens reminded him of. At the same time, Elisabeth believed that something inside him was screaming for help; it just didn't know what to do. Georg was a man who had never asked for help, but how could one be caged in such a body that didn't respond to one's own commands?

She began to shade in his hands.

But how could anyone enter inside such a mind to drive out the affliction? Or would it take a blessing from Jesus to do that? And if so, why wasn't Jesus giving Georg His blessing?

CHAPTER SEVEN

On her bed, Juliana fumbled several times as she tried to text Rachel.

R u there? Need to talk!

"You have to answer!" Juliana yelled at her phone. "Rachel, where are you?"

"Yulika?" Opa asked from outside her room. "Are you all right?" Again he came in without knocking.

Juliana shook her head. "I had a horrible day at the studio."

Opa rubbed the top of his bald head. "Because of your dance shoes?"

"Yeah. And Rachel's not even answering my calls or texts!"

"But how can that make you this upset?"

Juliana threw her phone on her bed and looked up

at him. "I forgot my dance shoes. It was a total embarrassment!"

"Yulika, there are much worse things in the world to be upset about."

Another adult who didn't empathize.

"It's just not something you do when you start with a new dance team," Juliana said. "And then I couldn't get hold of Dad to get them for me. They're going to think I don't care!"

"I can see that you do care, though," he said, "so I think your friends could, too."

He gestured to the chair, and Juliana nodded. He sat down, only to surprise himself as it tipped back a few inches.

"Are you okay?" Juliana asked.

Opa laughed. "You can even hurt yourself in chairs these days."

Juliana got off her bed and adjusted the chair so it would stay still.

"Let me tell you a story," he said.

Inwardly, Juliana rolled her eyes: she really wasn't in the mood for a story right now. And if Rachel texted her back, Juliana would have to wait to reply until Opa finished. "Opa, can you tell me later? I'm hoping Rachel calls me."

"No. Your family comes first, your friend can wait," he replied, taking Juliana somewhat aback with his directness. He didn't wait for any further response from her and began. "Mammi had a cousin," Opa began. "Georg. *He* didn't care."

Juliana couldn't figure out if this story was serious or if Opa was setting her up for a joke. If a joke, it'd be short at least.

"The only reason people respected him was because he was a blacksmith."

Rats. His tone told her this wasn't going to be a joke. She really didn't want a lecture about not caring right now. She knew what it meant to arrive to dance on time and prepared and she needed to be accepted into this team. She loved what the studio had to offer, and now that she'd met Mrs. Laing and Miss Denise, she knew it was where she needed to be. She had wanted to make a good first impression and instead she had screwed up big time! Why could no one understand that? The last thing she needed was to hear about some ancient relative who didn't feel like walking to school, uphill both ways.

But Opa had her cornered. She tucked her knees into her chest and listened. What else was she going to do?

Opa continued. "Almost every day, after Georg worked only a few hours in his blacksmith shop, he'd stop working. Just like that. He didn't care enough about his wife and family to look after them. To *work* so he could look after them. And everyone knew it. He wasn't a man, Yulika. Men look after their families, and Georg did not."

Juliana really had no interest in lessons from the past. All she wanted was to talk to someone who understood what she was going through and how important this was. Opa was a wonderful person, but now was a really bad time. She sighed in a way that suggested she was already bored, hoping he would get the message.

He didn't.

"You act like the world is falling apart because you forgot your shoes once. Georg forgot his wife and children, his family, every day. He was an embarrassment to his family."

Juliana had to admit that that did sound bad. But a nagging feeling told her there was more to this story. "Why was he like that?"

"He was fine before the war. When he came back, he was weak. The whole congregation disliked him because he didn't care about his wife and five children." Opa paused, lost in thought. He shook his head again. "Mammi told me years later that none of his children turned out to be good people. The way he acted didn't teach his children how to behave."

"What? What do you mean?"

Opa waved his hand in the air, dismissing her question. "It doesn't matter. I don't talk to them. They're somewhere in Germany now. Too expensive to call, and Mammi said they're not nice people."

Juliana mulled the story over in her mind. A man goes to war, returns, and changes. "Wait. You're complaining about him because he had PTSD?"

"I don't know anything about the new words you kids use these days." He shook his finger at her. It was a friendly shaking, but a shaking nonetheless. "If you want to know what not caring was, Yulika, it was Georg. Forgetting your shoes once doesn't mean you don't care. Forgetting your family everyday does."

Juliana didn't know how to respond. She knew Opa meant well: he was trying to comfort her, probably trying to connect with her, and yet he was talking about how an entire church had turned its back on a man who'd served in the war. She had to explain. Maybe Opa just didn't know.

"Opa, PTSD is post-traumatic stress disorder. It means that your mind can't handle when you've gone through something really painful and traumatic. It sounds like your mother's cousin had that."

Opa's eyes narrowed. "It doesn't matter what you call it. If you can't provide for your family, you're not a man, and that's how you'll be remembered. There were several other men in Semlak who were fine after the war, including Mammi's father. Georg shouldn't have come back. It would've been easier for everyone that way."

With that, he stood up and left. Juliana watched him go, her jaw practically on the bed. Only once she could hear his steps going down the stairs did she dare to move, one limb at a time, until she was standing. She walked over to her door and closed it, catching a glance of herself in her full-length mirror.

"A man is traumatized by war and he 'doesn't care'?" she said aloud.

Was this dementia? Saying unreasonable things like that? Or was that really her grandfather? But how could he be so uncaring? At the same time, though, his story wasn't some jumbled-up string of sentences. Opa wasn't like those commercials about dementia Juliana had seen when she and Mom had watched sitcoms together back in Calgary, commercials where an old man had left lemons all around the kitchen. And Opa was certainly a lot more mobile than old people who needed bathtubs with doors or used lifts that took them up and down flights of stairs.

No, she was certain: those really were his thoughts. Not only had Dad disappointed her today, but Opa now, too.

JULIANA HAD EVENTUALLY FALLEN ASLEEP AFTER WAITING to hear from Rachel for at least a half hour. Her eyes just opening now, she checked the time on her phone. Supper wouldn't be for a while. Feeling groggy, Juliana packed her tap shoes to make sure she wouldn't forget them for her next practice: she was not going to show up tomorrow, New Year's Eve day, without her shoes again. If her new team was giving her a second chance, she didn't want to screw it up.

After she zipped up her bag, she threw it next to her door, dropped back on to her bed, grabbed her phone, and logged into a social media account. "You really need some friends, Juliana," she said to herself. "You can't change the past, but you can talk to your friends." She saw that several of them had posted pictures from Christmas dance practice. She clicked on hearts, left a few notes to some friends, and then began typing a new status: *Survived 1st day at new studio.* Normally, she'd add another detail or two, maybe describe how awesome it was, or how great she looked...but she had nothing good to write there. "Survived" described exactly how she felt.

"Juliana!" Mom called from the kitchen. "I need your help!"

Juliana sighed. She just needed a few minutes alone to touch base with her friends, so she ignored Mom.

Miss Denise was really cool, and thinking about

Mrs. Laing made Juliana smile. She could write, *Felt warm hearts all around* ♥♥♥. But would her old friends back in Calgary think she liked the new studio better? "Okay, what about 'Great place, miss the old one, though?'" she asked out loud. But if anyone from the new studio was looking for her and saw her post, would they think she preferred her old one? She wanted to let her friends know how she was doing, but she couldn't figure out what to write so she wouldn't make anyone angry or make herself look dumb.

"Juliana!"

"Give me a minute!" Juliana shouted back.

"Now!" her mother replied.

"I said, give me a minute!"

Footsteps immediately pounded down the hallway to her room and Dad stormed in. "That is not how you talk to your mother," he said, his arms crossed. "She asked for your help, and you have nothing to do right now."

Juliana didn't need this, not after how the rest of the day had gone. "Why can't you help her? You have nothing to do!" Why was it always that adults were happy to point fingers at kids, but the same rules didn't apply to them?

"Because I do a lot to help out your mom already. I've cleaned out that entire garage, unpacked boxes, driven you to dance—"

"And weren't available on your phone?" Juliana wasn't going to let this rest. Dad could've helped Mom in the kitchen for the few minutes she needed if it was that important.

"You forgot your shoes, young lady, not me."

"You're my dad! You're supposed to help me!"

"And your mom is trying to help you right now by teaching you how to cook!"

Juliana's parents always found a way to twist things around so problems were her fault. She grunted. "That only helps her."

"Excuse me?" Dad said, pretending not to have heard what she had said.

"You heard me. My helping her cook only helps her."

Dad's face began to turn red. "Do you have any idea how lucky you are to have two parents who want to teach you how to be an adult?"

Juliana fingered through the icons on her phone, more just to annoy Dad than anything else. There was no way she was going to accept being spoken to like this, especially not today. Dad had the audacity to yell at her for how she spoke to Mom, when Mom was the one who had no patience? What gave him that right? She had looked like a loser to her new dance team, then Opa had lectured her about not caring, and now this?

"Nope," she replied, trying to annoy Dad even more.

Dad threw his hands up in the air. "No, of course you don't, because you have two parents."

"Excuse me?" Juliana said. "I have two parents? I've seen the two of you more these past two weeks than I have in my entire life! I don't have parents! I have two adults who spend so much time at work they feel like ghosts to me! If you call that parenting, then I have no idea what manual you read!"

The air in the room buzzed like a swarm of angry wasps.

Dad sighed his trying-to-calm-down sigh, the one that hissed through his nose. "I am not getting into an argument with you about this. One day you're going to move out, and I don't care if you think that's tomorrow or in ten years, but you have to learn how to look after yourself. Trust me, it's not easy learning all that on your own."

"What would you know about that? I'm the one left here by myself all the time!"

He sighed loudly again, sat down in her desk chair, rested his elbows on his knees, and leaned forward.

Another lecture, Juliana thought. *Do I get a loyalty reward when I've heard ten?*

But then she noticed something different about Dad: it was as though a dark cloud had settled over him. She'd never gotten this feeling from him before, but she didn't know if it was because she'd just never been around to see it or because he'd never felt it.

"I'm going to keep this short," he said, "because I know you hate these lectures. There's a reason I hardly speak about my family, Juliana, and it's because I barely had one."

Dad stared at the floor as he spoke. "I didn't always make the best choices because my parents were hardly part of my life. My dad was always at work, trying to support me, and my mother...let's just say she wasn't a part of my life at all."

Juliana's eyes popped out of her head. "I—I'm sorry," she whispered. "I had no idea."

Dad waved her apology away, suggesting though that it wasn't necessary, not that he was ignoring it. He continued. "I got into trucking, because my only other option coming out of high school that offered any kind of future was the military."

He paused, and Juliana had collected herself enough now that she knew not to say anything. After a minute of silence, he spoke again.

"When your mother and I decided to have you, I was faced with two choices: find a local job that would pay less but keep me home or keep doing what I do so you could have all the opportunities you wanted in life. Your mom had had those opportunities. She couldn't imagine a life without them and I wished I'd had a life with them. So we decided that my staying in trucking was the better option."

Dad stopped and looked up again. Juliana thought he wanted to say more, and she was ready to listen. It was as though a rope had formed between them, and if Juliana grabbed hold and her father did the same, then they might create a new connection, one that couldn't be cut.

The idea frightened her. She was a teenager: teens didn't have connections to their parents like babies did. At the same time, though, something was missing inside Juliana and that magical rope could—somehow—replace that emptiness. The best she could do now, she believed, was to ask a question to show she was interested in hearing more, that she was willing to listen.

"Why wasn't your mother around?"

Just then, Mom called from the kitchen.

"Are you coming?"

"Just a moment," Dad replied.

"All right," Mom called, "but the lettuce isn't being washed by itself!"

Juliana sighed and rolled her eyes. "Do I have to wash lettuce?"

She clapped her hand over her mouth and the dark cloud that hovered over Dad turned into a hurricane.

"Did you not hear a word I just said? How ungrateful can you be?"

Juliana wished she could disappear into her phone and slide away deep into the Internet. Her words had come out before she could cut them off and now they had cut that rope.

Dad stood up. "You have no idea how good you have it!" He stormed out of her room.

"I'm sorry," she managed to say, although he was too far down the hallway to hear it.

CHAPTER EIGHT

"He's still burning, Mammi." Elisabeth touched Luki's forehead.

Mammi wiped her hands on her apron even though she wasn't cooking, a signal to Elisabeth that her mother was scared.

Luki had been sent home from school that morning, the sixteenth child since last week. By the time he'd reached the house, his face was whiter than the snow outside, and he could barely walk. It had been a fight just to get a few spoonfuls of chicken broth into him.

"Leave him covered up—he needs to sweat it out. People need new shoes for the wedding. Get me only if it's important." With that, Mammi headed back out to the workshop.

Important? Luki was sweating without blankets on

him and he seemed to be fading in and out of aware-ness. If that wasn't important, what was?

Elisabeth got Luki a glass of water and gave him a few sips with a spoon.

"I'm really hot," he complained, sweat dripping down his temples. His little body convulsed as he coughed, his chest gurgling like rough waters in the Marosch River.

"Then let's get a sleeping gown on you. I don't think it's good to leave your clothes on. Can you get changed?"

Luki rocked his head slowly from side to side, and Elisabeth realized she'd have to do it. She wiped her hands on her apron, took a deep breath, and then rolled back the blanket.

"Do what you can to undress. I'll get you your nightgown."

It took some juggling and jostling, contorting and coughing, but between the two of them, they got Luki changed. Elisabeth gave him more water on the spoon, washed down his forehead, and covered him back up.

"Let me get you a little bread."

"I'm not hungry," Luki groaned.

"But you need something in you to give you strength."

Luki shook his head. His eyes closed and then

opened, closed and then opened. It seemed pointless to Elisabeth to force him to do anything right now.

"Rest," she told him. "See if you can get some sleep."

Luki didn't say another word. His eyes closed and his head tipped to the side.

Elisabeth gently covered him with the blanket and then knelt beside him, placed her elbows on the bed, and clasped her hands together in prayer. She recited the first one that came to her for this kind of situation, though she had to change it a little.

> *Now Luki lays himself down to sleep.*
> *I pray the Lord his soul to keep.*
> *If he should die before he wakes,*
> *I pray the Lord his soul to take.*

Tears ran down her cheeks. There wasn't a winter that would go by without children dying from fevers. This was the only time where Elisabeth was glad that the church bells were gone, melted into ammunition for the war. It meant she couldn't hear the familiar patterns of ringing that announced almost daily that a funeral for a child was about to begin.

If Luki died, would his soul fly with angels to Heaven, in the sky? Elisabeth shook the thought out of her head. Why would God threaten to take Luki? Her little brother had done nothing wrong—his antics, his arguments, they were all because he was a boy. Certainly God wouldn't take away a person because of how He created him, would He?

The house door in the kitchen opened and shut. Elisabeth could tell by the footsteps that it was Mammi. She wiped her eyes and stood up.

Mammi's usually harsh lines in her face softened when she saw Elisabeth's tears.

"Jesus told me to come inside," she whispered. "I know we are thinking the same thing, but we must be strong. You have two sisters and now your mother who need you: the animals must be cared for so we have meat. Meals must be cooked, because you need strength to keep caring for your brother, and I, to keep making shoes. If we fail in our responsibilities, then your brother will die and no one will buy shoes from us, which means we will soon run out of money to pay for whatever we cannot make ourselves. This is our life, Elisabeth. It is hard, but it brings us happiness: we have God, Jesus, our family, our friends, and our purpose in life. We need very little, but we must hold on to what little we have."

Elisabeth's situation seemed hopeless to her now. How was she supposed to take care of Luki, help Anna with her homework, keep Rosina occupied, cook supper, embroider that handkerchief, iron, figure out that rum roll for the wedding...? Mammi was right, but Elisabeth still couldn't figure out how to do it all.

"He's resting for now," Mammi said. "Get to work. Our family needs you." She gave Elisabeth a nod and retreated to the family's workshop.

Elisabeth stifled a yawn. She had been up until at least two o'clock drawing, trying to get that image of Georg's hands on Anna's mittens out of her mind and onto paper where she could see it. She had hoped to sleep while Luki was sleeping, even if only for a few minutes, before getting on with her chores. But that most certainly wouldn't happen now. Jesus was watching.

Luki coughed again, his body shaking. His eyes opened. "I'm hot..."

Elisabeth gave him a few more sips of water from the spoon. He coughed a few more times, and then drifted off again.

ELISABETH HAD A POT OF SOUP ON THE STOVE AND ONE OF Anna's school dresses ready to iron on the kitchen table. She grabbed a cloth to protect her hand as she opened the hot oven door. With her other hand, she used a poker to push the coals to the side. She shoved in corn stalks, spread them out, and closed the oven door. She'd put the chicken in the oven in the next hour or so.

"Anna! Can you get me more cornstalks?"

Anna's quiet shuffle from the back room to the kitchen was the only answer Elisabeth got.

"You could at least say you heard me," Elisabeth said.

Anna put on her boots and headed outside into the blistering cold. "I heard you!" she yelled as the door closed behind her.

Elisabeth wiped her brow with her forearm. Was the entire afternoon going to be like this? She quickly scrubbed two carrots clean.

"Rosina!" she called to her younger sister, who was also sitting in the back room. "Can you chop these carrots?"

"I'm busy stiching!"

Elisabeth crossed her arms and stomped over to her sister, who was casting her first row of stitches onto a knitting needle.

"You mean 'knitting,' and you've hardly knit a thing."

"I'm six!"

"Rosina, I need your help in the kitchen."

"And I want to knit Luki a blanket so he can get better!"

"With any luck, you'll be done by your own wedding."

Rosina's lips began to quiver as her mouth started its slow descent to turn upside down.

Elisabeth threw up her hands. "I'm sorry! I didn't mean to hurt your feelings! We have so much to do here and I need your help!"

Rosina followed Elisabeth to the kitchen, although not happily.

"Peel these two carrots," Elisabeth said, trying to calm her voice, "and let me know when you're done. I'll cut them in half so chopping is easier for you."

Rosina did as she was told, but with a big frown on her face.

Next on Elisabeth's list was to boil some water for linden tea for Luki. Anna stomped back inside just then with cornstalks under her arm and handed them to Elisabeth, who gave her sister a pot in return.

"What if the well's frozen?" Anna asked.

"The well is thirty feet down!" Elisabeth said. "The water will be fine!"

Anna stamped her foot. "Stop yelling at me. You're not Mammi!"

Elisabeth rolled her eyes. "I know that! But I still need water to make Luki tea!"

"Fine!" Anna stomped back out of the house with the pot.

Elisabeth looked up to the crucifix hanging over the door to the front room. "Since you're watching over us, can you please protect Luki? And if you find some time, can you also help me a little?"

"The carrots are ready!"

Elisabeth saw Rosina kneeling on a chair at the kitchen table with a knife in her hands. The peels lay all over the table's surface instead of in the slop pail. Elisabeth let out an exasperated sigh. She split the carrots lengthwise down the centre and then let Rosina continue chopping while she cleaned up the peels.

"All right. What's next?" she asked herself. She'd been so wrapped up in the fights with her sisters that she'd completely forgotten her list of chores. She wiped her hands on her apron. She had to iron, stir the soup simmering on the stove, get the chicken in the oven... but not just yet...first she had to make Luki a tea.

Luki.

She rushed into the front room to check on him. He hadn't coughed—or opened his eyes—in a couple of hours. Elisabeth sat down beside him on the bed.

His forehead still burned, but he'd stopped sweating. His face looked like that of a porcelain doll: his cheeks were bright red, his eyelids mauve, and his lips almost burgundy. But he was breathing.

The bed was so comfortable and warm. Elisabeth yawned.

Only a few minutes' sleep...that's all she would need to freshen up a little. Just a few minutes...

"Elisabeth Schuhmacher!"

Elisabeth jumped out of Luki's bed. Only then did she hear Rosina crying and see Mammi standing in the doorway, her face red.

"Rosina cut herself, the soup has boiled all over the stove, the chicken should have gone in the oven a half-hour ago, and Luki still doesn't have his tea!"

Elisabeth's heart fell to the floor. She saw that Luki was also awake from all the noise. "I'm...I'm sorry," she stammered.

"Why are you sleeping?" Mammi screamed at her. "Your family needs you and you're in bed, sleeping like a lazy drunk from the city!"

Tears streamed down Elisabeth's face.

Mammi touched her forehead. "You're not feverish. Why in God's name are you sleeping?"

"I'm just tired," she said, wiping her eyes. She wondered if Jesus had maybe turned His attention to another family.

Mammi looked her up and down and then drilled her gaze into Elisabeth. "No, you're not 'just tired.'" Her gaze jumped to the rows of books in the room. "Tata always leaves those perfectly lined up. But now one of them is sticking out, as though...as though someone put it back at night." Mammi stormed through the kitchen and into the back room and returned holding a few candles. "I noticed earlier today that these seem shorter than they should be." She set them on the table in the room, right in front of Elisabeth. "Do you call yourself a Christian?"

Elisabeth's lip trembled as she nodded.

"How can you say you're a Christian when you lie to me like this? You've been up reading at night!"

Elisabeth tried to hold her emotions inside, but she could feel them bubbling up. At first she felt sadness and regret as Mammi kept yelling at her about her duties to her family. Then that sadness and regret changed into something else: anger. Elisabeth knew what would happen if her anger took control.

Mammi continued. "No Christian lies! How dare you think you can read at a time like this!"

Elisabeth could see Anna and Rosina huddled under the kitchen table, hugging each other. Luki had pulled the blanket over his head. All the children knew that when Mammi was angry, it was best to stay out of her way.

But Elisabeth wouldn't have it any more.

"I'm trying my best to balance everything! How come you have time to read the Bible on Sundays while

Anna and I are at Margarethe-Néni's, tolerating that family's dislike of us? Jesus read, too, so why can't I?!"

Mammi's face turned crimson. "How dare you compare yourself to the Lord! He had a calling, to save us from our sins! He was to be a teacher of the people! Of course He read! Your calling is to be a wife and a mother! You do *not* need to read!"

She returned to the kitchen and Anna and Rosina huddled even closer together. Mammi opened a cupboard, pulled out a small, flat wooden box with a lid on it, slammed it on the floor, and opened the lid, exposing the dried corn kernels.

"For you!" she commanded Elisabeth.

Elisabeth stared at her siblings.

"Now!" Mammi commanded.

Elisabeth pushed down her knit stockings, lifted her skirt a little, and knelt in the corn.

"Wait," Juliana said to Dad. Staying in the car, she opened her dance bag and double-checked that she had her shoes. Twice.

"If you put this much effort into chores, you'd be done washing lettuce in ten minutes. Honestly, Juliana, that's the millionth time you've checked your bag today. You'll be fine."

"Can you just leave it with the lettuce? I can't make the same mistake twice. I'm not going to have any friends if I show up unprepared."

"But you'll always have family. That's it, isn't it?"

Juliana glowered at him. "Can we drop this? I told you yesterday what I think and I really don't want to start that up again." She checked her bag again.

Dad placed a hand on her shoulder. "You need

some perspective. You're stressing out over nothing, and before you tell me I don't get it, I do."

No, you don't, she thought. But as their argument yesterday replayed in her mind on fast forward, she remembered how little she knew about her dad. Maybe she should be the one to drop it. This time, at least.

Dad shooed her out of the car. "I've gotta grab some stuff still from the trucking company. They close in half an hour. Trust your father: you'll be fine."

Juliana turned her attention back to that front door. She didn't want to go in there; the car was much safer. Would anyone even speak to her?

"They're just shoes," Dad said. "Get going or you're coming with me, which means you'll miss practice, and I'm sure they would kick you out for that."

"It's more than just shoes!"

Dad rolled his eyes. "Think of it this way: being a good teammate also means that you have to give them a second chance."

Juliana hadn't thought of it that way. She nodded, actually thankful for the advice, zipped her bag shut, and got out of the car. Once she was at the studio door, she took a quick look back and watched Dad already turning the corner at the end of the street. She gulped and walked in.

So far, so good. Juliana had made it fully prepared to class. She'd even felt slightly confident when stretching: although everyone on the team already had their splits, and several could even bend their back leg so their foot met their head, Juliana was close: she only had a few centimetres left before she was flat on the ground, and on both sides to boot! It was just a matter of time and practice.

But barely anyone said anything to her. A few friendly glances and hellos here and there, but that was it. And to top it off, there were now twenty-four people in the class; a few hadn't made it yesterday because the storm had cut off the rural roads to their homes and those roads hadn't been cleared in time.

Miss Denise instructed everyone to stand in a circle and say their name again.

"I'm Riley."

"I'm Alex."

"Isaac."

"Janine."

"Jasmine."

Juliana stopped paying attention after Jasmine. Jasmine had a confidence about herself that Juliana found both intimidating and admirable. She was also clearly the best dancer on the team. Jasmine made eye contact with her and Juliana looked away abruptly. She'd been caught staring.

Strike two, she thought to herself.

"I'm Angel."

"Mackenzie."

"Ben."

There was a pause.

Juliana jumped. "Oh, sorry." She hadn't realized that the circle had come around to her. Her cheeks burned. "I'm Juliana."

The circle continued, and Juliana did her best to pay attention. At the end, Miss Denise nodded. "All right. Let's take it from the top, everyone."

The class rushed to their opening positions before Juliana could even take a step.

"Juliana, we're going to put you at the back. It'll be easier for you to learn." Miss Denise pointed to a spot upstage right. "Riley, Alex, shift down...exactly."

The back? Juliana knew many studios placed the weakest students at the back so they'd be less visible to the judges. Miss Kasia, on the contrary, believed everyone deserved a chance to shine. Had Juliana chosen a "bad to the back" studio?

"No debate," Miss Denise said. "It's just because you're new."

Juliana's face burned again. *Strike three*, she thought and stared at the floor as she headed to her new spot.

During the next two minutes, Miss Denise reviewed the first thirty-two counts with everyone and included a few pointers of what the others could do better. She turned on the music. Juliana's heart pounded: Miss Denise taught so fast that Juliana could barely remember the first steps. Staring into the mirror didn't help either: instead of twenty-four strangers, she now saw forty-eight.

Juliana kept her eyes glued to Miss Denise, who was nodding her head in time with the beat during the intro. Then she raised her hands and clapped the last four counts.

"Five, six, seven, eight!"

And within the next four counts, Juliana had to spring to the side to get out of everyone's way.

Miss Denise stopped the music.

"Jasmine, take Juliana into another studio and begin showing her up to here," and Miss Denise demonstrated a part in the dance with her hands, scatting a few syllables, to indicate to Jasmine where in the dance she meant. Jasmine nodded.

Juliana swallowed. *At least I've got the right shoes*, she thought hopelessly as she followed Jasmine out.

JULIANA SLAMMED HER FOOT INTO THE FLOOR. "I JUST can't get this!"

She caught Jasmine rolling her eyes. "You know,

you'd find this easier if you'd stop focusing on not getting it."

"Easy for you to say," Juliana said. "You're incredible."

"I've also had four months to learn it. You've had thirty minutes and a day without shoes so far. Now, do the pirouette."

Who did this girl think she was? God's gift to dance? *Well, actually...*Juliana had to admit that she was. She tendued out to second, did a ronde de jambe to fourth, and placed her foot. Then she stopped. If there was one thing she hated doing in tap shoes, it was pirouettes: she always lost control of her rotation.

"What?" Jasmine asked. "You're getting tripped up on tiny details that don't matter at this point."

"What do you mean they don't matter? If I don't get those tiny details, I'll bring the group down. Right now, I can't get my balance on the stupid pirouette."

"What did you do at your old studio?"

Juliana's chin dropped and she stared at the floor. "We only did doubles, and I could barely hang on there."

Jasmine crossed her arms and dug her gaze into Juliana, and Juliana wondered if this was what books meant when they described fear piercing your heart. "You'll bring the group down today if you don't learn this choreography. No one's going to care if you don't get your triple today, but they are going to care if you're in the wrong spot when they go into the turning riff sequence."

What were the other dancers like? Was Juliana going to have to defend herself like this to all of them?

"Listen," Jasmine said. "I'm not trying to be mean—I'm just being realistic. You're not going to get better if you keep focusing on the wrong stuff. Let's skip the pirouette and move on. You know it comes here, and that's all you need to know today."

And she began to show Juliana the next thirty-two counts, her taps blurring in Juliana's eyes.

"My god, you're amazing," Juliana said. *She looks like she does this in her sleep*, she thought.

"Just takes practice," Jasmine said.

Yeah, probably in a home studio, five hours a day.

"I'll slow it down for you," Jasmine said.

She definitely thinks I'm stupid, Juliana thought.

LATER THAT DAY, JULIANA TOOK ADVANTAGE OF A FEW hours before supper to practice. She stared at the old shag carpet on the basement floor and the low ceiling. The space she had to practice was less than optimal.

But she had to make this work. She knew she had been trying Jasmine's patience, and after dancing with the rest of the group for another hour, Juliana had caught looks and side glances towards her. She had become *that* dancer in only two practices.

Dance for Juliana was like air. Some of her school friends back home loved sports, others their dogs, but for Juliana it was dance, the way the music washed over her body and flooded her pores, electrifying her with energy that filled her with life. Both the time she had broken her wrist and sprained her ankle in competition and then the recent cross-country ride from Alberta to Ontario with her parents proved to her that not dancing equalled prison. She liked most subjects at school, too, but learning didn't give her the feeling of disappearing into something greater than herself that dance did, a feeling she couldn't describe to anyone who didn't share it.

But at Kitchener Dance Academy, she had met twenty-four dancers who were greater than her. She had to reach their level and fast.

"Okay, let's get going," she said to herself. "Getting better doesn't happen on its own."

She stretched for ten minutes, aiming to reach just a little lower in her splits. Next followed several warm-up exercises for her feet in order to loosen up her ankles and activate her thighs and calves. She didn't have the music yet for this tap routine, but she had heard it enough today that she could hear it in her mind. Unfortunately, though, she only had her small tap board as her practice space. It made her attempts at her triple pirouette impossible because no matter how much she tried to convince herself that the tap board was not the edge of a stage, her body insisted that it was and that it risked falling into the non-existent audience if she lost her balance.

Which meant she lost her balance. Every time.

She wiped the sweat off her forehead and Jasmine's words echoed in her mind:

"You're getting tripped up on the tiny details that don't matter at this point."

Juliana's shoulders stiffened. That dancer was getting on her case at the studio, and now she was invading Juliana's mind.

She tried the pirouette again and fell out of it.

"Fine," she said to herself. "I'll just start from the beginning."

Doing the first twenty seconds or so of the dance on the spot was hard, but Juliana began to feel the flow of the steps. And when it came to the pirouette, she just pulled up into retiré and didn't rotate.

"Juliana?"

Why did he have to interrupt her now? Juliana turned around, making sure she had a smile pasted on her face by the time she faced Opa. "I didn't hear you come in," she said.

Opa smiled back. "Your mom was right."

Juliana furrowed her brow.

"When you first arrived here," he said, "Katy said I would see you dance and that it would be wonderful. She's right."

Juliana blushed. His compliment was the last thing she'd expected but also the first good thing about her dancing she'd heard all day.

"Can you keep dancing?" he asked. "I want to see more. We didn't dance like this at home."

Now Juliana's smile turned into a real one: she couldn't be angry at him for that, and, to be honest, her practicing was becoming tense.

"It won't be my best," she said. She didn't want to raise his expectations.

"Why not?"

Juliana was worried about insulting Opa if she told him the truth, that his basement wasn't the best place for dance.

"I'm just tired, that's all," she said.

He studied her face for a moment and then wagged his finger at her. "Your Omama had a habit of saying too much. You don't say enough. Be honest with me, Yulika. You won't kill me."

Juliana felt awkward at having been caught lying to her grandfather, even if her intentions were good, but she remembered his embarrassment at how dirty his basement had been when they had first arrived. She wouldn't share the truth with him, not on this one thing, anyway.

"No, really, Opa, it's been a long day."

Opa sighed. "Omama's mouth sometimes got her into trouble. She even had to kneel in corn because of it. But she always spoke her mind. I think it's healthy."

Opa's comments caught Juliana's attention. "Kneel in corn?"

Opa laughed. "Back then, if you were bad, you kneeled in dry corn kernels. On your bare knees, of course."

Juliana's eyes popped open and Opa nodded. "It made sure you listened to your parents. Nowadays kids scream everywhere and run all over stores touching everything. But not back then." He laughed as his mind traveled back. "You know what? We never danced like what you do. We always danced in partners. And always to live music."

"It sounds like you had fun."

"We did, Yulika!" Suddenly his eyes opened wide in panic. "Music! How could I forget?"

And he shuffled upstairs as fast as his seventy-year-old legs could carry him.

Curious, Juliana followed Opa upstairs.

"What music?" she asked him.

"Radio," he replied curtly. He pulled the radio out of

the living room and set it on the kitchen counter. He plugged it in and flicked the switch on.

The most horrendous music Juliana had ever heard came blaring out of its ancient speakers and she had to cover her ears. A mix of trumpet and accordion and Lord knows whatever other instruments played some kind of noisy tune. A march, maybe?

Upon seeing her reaction, Opa turned the volume down a little.

"I'm sorry," he said. "I still need to get used to you living here."

Juliana lowered her hands, but more out of politeness than desire. "What is that?"

Mom and Dad entered the kitchen.

"German hour?" Mom asked, grabbing a granola bar.

Opa nodded. "Only four hours every weekend now."

"Makes you want to dance, doesn't it?" Mom asked Juliana, and Juliana stared in amazement at the question. She wasn't being serious, was she?

"Yulika was dancing downstairs," Opa said. "I think she should dance for our family tonight! The way she moves her feet, I think it would fit the music!"

Opa looked so happy at his suggestion, Juliana wondered if his dentures would fall out. Thankfully, though, Dad saved her.

"She's not used to that kind of music," he said.

She flashed him a silent thank-you look, and Dad nodded.

A new song played.

"A polka!" Mom exclaimed cheerily. Mom grabbed Opa's hands, and the two automatically took up traditional ballroom positions. The tiny space of the kitchen forced them to just hop back and forth on their feet on the spot.

"Um, I think I should go back and practice," Juliana said, and she slipped back into the basement.

If any good had come out of the past few days, it was that Elisabeth didn't have to help with wedding preparations: everyone understood that with Luki sick she was needed at home. However, that meant Rosina had to accompany Anna to their aunt and uncle's house to help. This worried Elisabeth: Anna was still too young to keep a good eye on her sister, who could get into trouble just for doing things that a six-year-old would do.

Elisabeth paused for a moment and looked out the kitchen window into her neighbour's yard and then ladled some soup into a bowl. One thing Elisabeth missed was a connection to the bigger world. Without Tata here, men from the other families didn't come by in the evening to play *skat* and to debate topics that didn't involve dresses, shoes, or noses. Moreover, she couldn't even leave Luki to go hear the postman when he arrived on his weekly visit to deliver mail and shout out any headlines people wanted to hear. She was caged in.

"But I don't mean it that way!" she whispered to Jesus over the door. Of course she was thankful that Luki had improved somewhat, and she rejoiced for her cousin's wedding. But when did Elisabeth get to matter? When was it her turn to do what she wanted?

She brought the bowl of soup to Luki, who was sitting up in his bed. His cheekbones stuck out after several days of eating nothing. But then this afternoon, after another long sleep, he had asked for something to eat, which almost made Elisabeth cry: it was the first sign that Jesus was indeed watching over them.

"I've been praying for you every day," she told him as she fed him.

Luki swallowed the spoonful and smiled.

"Mammi's been busy making shoes for wedding guests," Elisabeth said. "She's earning money for us."

Luki nodded as he swallowed the next spoonful. "Tata?" he asked. His voice was still weak.

Elisabeth shrugged her shoulders. "I'm sorry, Luki, I don't know. We haven't heard anything at all."

Luki's eyes looked sad.

"But," Elisabeth said, "maybe he's earning so much

money that he hasn't had time to write us yet." She fed him another spoonful.

Luki's eyes lit up. "Do you think so?"

Elisabeth shrugged again. "Why must we always think of the worst? Jesus cured lepers, helped blind men see, and no matter how people treated Him, He always talked about God and Heaven and all the good things that are up there. And He has answered our prayers, because you're doing better! Maybe we should think a little more like Him."

Deep coughs overtook Luki's body, and Elisabeth handed him a handkerchief so he could spit anything out that came up.

"Keep praying for Tata," she said, "but also rest."

He coughed. "And you'll pray for me?"

Elisabeth smiled and nodded. As she finished feeding him the soup, she prayed silently: *Jesus, please continue to watch over us.*

ELISABETH TOOK A MOMENT TO REST IN THE KITCHEN. SHE would not nap, but at least she could rest. Mammi was out in the workshop, and after the other day, Elisabeth dared not again fall asleep until bedtime. She had also stopped staying up late at night, which made it easier for her to stay awake during the day.

The house was eerily quiet, as though everyone had died. The only proof that everyone was still alive was the lack of a coffin in the back room. Her eyes shifted between the crucifix over the door to the front room and Luki on his bed in there.

So far as Elisabeth knew, Mammi had had several children who had died, including Anna's twin sister, Rosina. And because Anna's twin had died shortly after birth, Mammi's next daughter was named Rosina to make sure Mammi's great aunt, Rosina-Néni, was still honoured in their family. Would God allow Mammi to have another child if Luki died from this illness? And would it be a boy so that Tata's name would continue in the family?

Elisabeth slapped herself in the face. "I just told Luki to stop having such thoughts. I should do the same."

She took a drink of water to freshen up and then got to work. First, she would make a strong chamomile tea for Luki when he woke up. She slipped on her boots and brought in water from the well outside. Once back in the house, she put her house shoes on, set the kettle on the stove, and poured water into it and then set the lid on.

"And next?" she said to herself.

Luki's pants and shirts on the table caught her eye, and she removed some hot coals from the oven, put them into the iron, and then placed the iron on the stove while it heated up.

"That's heating up...now what?"

Her voice travelled through their three-room house without receiving an answer. She couldn't start preparing supper until the ironing was done: she needed the kitchen table for both activities, and Mammi would certainly make her kneel in the corn again if Elisabeth got the wash dirty. But would she finish the ironing in time to begin cooking supper? She chose to push the washing bowl to the side so she could use that table to chop vegetables.

The lid on the pot of water began to jiggle, so Elisabeth removed the pot from the burner, pulled down a small canister of dried chamomile flowers from a shelf over the oven, tossed a few tablespoons into the water, and replaced the lid. She then waved her hand underneath it to test the heat.

"Almost," she said, placing it back the stove. In the meantime, she spread out Luki's pants and folded the pant legs so the pleats would be nice and smooth.

"I wonder who's ironing Tata's pants?" she said to Jesus on the crucifix above the door. "Does he have help with that? Or does he have to pay someone to do it? Or maybe he repairs their shoes and they iron his clothes?"

Jesus looked painfully, silently down at her.

As Elisabeth grabbed the iron from the stove, she

glanced out the window and almost jumped for joy: Maria, her best friend in all of Semlak was walking up the side of the house. Maria was a year older than Elisabeth and herself had only one brother. Friends since Elisabeth could remember, it felt like Elisabeth had become Maria's only sister and Maria, Elisabeth's older sister.

Elisabeth swung the door open and was ready to throw herself into Maria's arms. Then she stopped herself: Maria was carrying a large pot in both her hands.

"Careful!" Maria said, her smile as big as Elisabeth's, placing the pot on the stove. "My brother came home from school sick last week. Mammi had heard through Meier Josef that Luki was ill, so we made a big pot of soup and wanted to share some of it with you. We know it's especially hard without your Tata around."

Elisabeth was ready to cry. She wouldn't have to cook so much for supper!

"Oh, thank you, Maria!" she said, giving her best friend a tight hug. Elisabeth wiped her hands on her apron before taking Maria's winter shawl and mittens to the back room. "How is your brother doing now?"

"He's eating again," she said, although her face turned sad despite the good news. "But our neighbour's baby may not make it."

Elisabeth could already hear church bells in her head.

Maria clapped her hands. "Now, how can I help you?"

Elisabeth took a moment to survey the kitchen and decide what needed to be done next: the tea was cooking, she was already ironing...

"Could you start some bread?"

"Get me an apron!"

Elisabeth retrieved an apron from a drawer in the front room. "By the way, do you have any tips for making a rum roll?"

Maria smiled. "Actually, I do."

Three hours later, Elisabeth had ironed Luki's and Mammi's clothing, had taken soup and some of yesterday's bread out to Mammi in the workshop, and had given Luki some tea before he fell asleep again. Maria popped two loaves of risen white bread into the oven.

Maybe Elisabeth would finally have some time to read.

CHAPTER ELEVEN

New Year's Eve, and Mom's family had arrived to celebrate: Uncle Peter, and Aunt Anne and Uncle Phillip with all six kids. Opa had been talking about their celebration all day, including begging Juliana to dance for his family. But now that she knew how weak her dancing was, she refused.

Juliana wore a cream dress that reached mid-thigh and she had put on light make-up. She'd even taken the time to straighten her hair. But in part still embarrassed by the events of Christmas Eve, and in part scared Opa was going to make her dance in front of everyone, Juliana couldn't face her family and instead sat in her room, texting with Rachel.

So practice was better today?
Yeah but still lots to learn

They're that good?

Amazing! Backs like elastics

Wow!

Not sure I can catch up

Of course u can!

U rock but you haven't seen them especially Jasmine

When her phone didn't show blinking dots that let her know Rachel was typing, Juliana scrolled through the conversation to see if she'd said anything wrong. She couldn't find anything, but then the three dots appeared at the bottom. She watched them flicker as Rachel typed from the other side of the country.

Your new friend?

Juliana panicked. Jasmine wasn't her new friend! Jasmine probably didn't even like her! The last thing she'd wanted was to make Rachel worry about their friendship, which reached back years to when they'd first started dance.

Noooo! You're my friend. She's just a crazy awesome dancer. NOT my friend

Rachel sent a smiley emoji through and then continued typing. *I'd be really sad if she was*

No one can replace you Rach!

And she meant it. Juliana and Rachel had been through thick and thin together, from Rachel's parents' divorce to tough judges at dance competitions to Juliana's move out east.

Go they're waiting

I can't

You're finally discovering your family go

The door to Juliana's room reminded her of a drawbridge from some old cartoon that creaked as it opened slowly, and you knew that some dangerous monster was behind it. But instead of monsters the Roths, Morgans, and Schuhmachers waited for her. And Sophie, too, of course.

I hardly know them, she typed to Rachel.

A knock on the door.

It was Dad. "Look, Juliana, we've allowed you to sit in here by yourself for at least half an hour. It's time you joined us."

Juliana's phone vibrated with Rachel's next text. Juliana glanced at it.

I'm always here for u!

Juliana sent her a thumbs-up and a wave goodbye. She threw her phone on to her bed but not before reading Rachel's last message one more time. The text left Juliana wondering if Rachel could truly be there for her.

Always.

JULIANA WALKED DOWN THE SHORT HALLWAY TO THE kitchen.

"Well, howdy stranger!" Uncle Peter said in a not-so-funny cowboy accent. He flashed a big smile that made Juliana wonder if his lips might ever snap from being stretched so much.

But she smiled in return. "Hi, Uncle Peter."

Aunt Anne opened her arms wide and gave Juliana a hug. Afterwards, Juliana worked her way from the kitchen to the living room, where she greeted all her cousins and Uncle Phillip. The only place left for her to sit was next to Sophie. But Juliana didn't just want to drop down onto the couch and scare her. Could Sophie see that Juliana was standing in front of her? Was Juliana supposed to say she was going to sit down? Juliana had a hard time understanding just how much Sophie could and couldn't see. To her, blind had meant seeing nothing at all; she had never thought that blind could mean seeing some things and not others.

"Hi, Juliana," Sophie said. "Did you do anymore shovelling today?"

Juliana smiled and shook her head. After a moment, she realized Sophie hadn't reacted and spoke her answer instead. "Sorry, um, no, nothing today. Dad did it." Now that Juliana knew that Sophie had seen her, she sat down.

A moment of silence passed between the two of them.

"Um, did you shovel anymore at home?"

Sophie shook her head. "Dean looked after it today, and Scott helped."

"Cool."

The two cousins sat in silence for a few minutes while everyone else around them talked.

"Juliana," Mom called from the kitchen, "I need your help: I've got to look after the goulash here."

"Sorry, uh, I have to go," Juliana said, kind of happy to leave the awkwardness of the moment but also a little disappointed: a quick glance around the room told Juliana that everyone else was engrossed in conversation and Juliana had barely said a word to Sophie. Now that she thought of it, when she'd first entered the tiny living room, nobody had been talking to Sophie then either.

"So I heard. Do you want any help?"

Juliana froze. On the one hand, having someone close to her age to talk to would be nice. On the other hand, the tiny kitchen was an absolute chaotic mess. How would Sophie navigate it without hurting herself? And what was she going to do? Chop carrots and slice off her finger?

"Juliana?" Sophie asked.

"Uh..."

Sophie stood up and faced Juliana, her eyes focused on her, which surprised Juliana, because it made Sophie not look blind. "I'm not disabled," she whispered. "I can help."

Juliana's shoulders pulled up and she suddenly wished she were a turtle. Or perhaps a gopher. Just an animal that could somehow hide. Even an ostrich would do, so she wouldn't have to see the others in the room, who were now staring at her again, just like on Christmas Eve.

But Juliana wasn't going to run like she had last week. She had to say something, but it had to be something that wouldn't land her kneeling in a pile of corn kernels either. Metaphorically speaking, anyway. She just didn't want Sophie to hurt herself. She was only twelve and if she couldn't see in front of her, then how could she help in the kitchen? If there was one thing Mom always reminded Juliana about, it was to keep her eyes on the knife.

But she couldn't say those kinds of things, and Sophie seemed independent anyway. Dad had taken that moment yesterday to share a tiny piece of himself with her. Maybe she could try that with Sophie.

"I'm sorry. It's been a tough week for me. I was just worried that, um, you know, you might hurt yourself."

Although Sophie didn't exactly smile, her expression relaxed. "I may not be a celebrity chef, but I can chop a carrot or two."

"Okay, sure. I could use your help."

Sophie smiled, and now Juliana relaxed. "The kitchen's a bit of a mess, though," she warned, "so just be a bit careful."

"Thanks," Sophie said, without any hint of sarcasm or displeasure.

"You can cut the carrots," Mom said to Juliana when they got to the kitchen. "Sophie, could you wash the lettuce?"

Sophie smiled. "That's my favourite job!"

Juliana had to smile in spite of herself and felt instantly happier about Sophie being there.

"Thanks for your help, girls. I haven't made goulash in probably twenty years and I want to get it right. I even hunted down Hungarian paprika at a European foods store."

Mom went back to stand at the stove, dropping bits of beef into a reddish soup Juliana had never seen before. It smelled good. Was this something Mom would have grown up with? Or maybe even Opa? Juliana watched her mom out of the corner of her eye—while still paying attention to her knife—to see what ingredients she used.

"Listen," Juliana said to Sophie. "I should tell you something."

"That you've got a third leg?"

"Uh…"

Sophie stared ahead while she worked, her fingers helping her find the mushy parts on the leaves of lettuce. "It was a joke," she said.

Juliana grinned and then remembered she needed to say what she was feeling. "That's funny. But no, that's not it."

"You've never really met a blind person before?"

"Yeah, I haven't. So, I don't really know how to help or when not to help or…well, all that awkward stuff. There's just a lot I don't know, and I don't like feeling that way."

"Well, ask away!" Sophie said jubilantly. "I'm all ears!"

Juliana didn't have to say what she was feeling. She groaned at the bad joke and then both girls giggled.

CHAPTER TWELVE

A week had passed, and Luki was finally eating full bowls of chicken soup, slices of bread—but only with paprika, no butter—and even little bits of pork. His tiny frame saddened Elisabeth: his collar bones and cheekbones protruded like broom handles and his hair was matted to his head after not having been washed in such a long time.

He crept into the kitchen and paused in the doorway to rest. "Can I have more bread?" he asked, his voice weak.

Elisabeth stopped kneading the bread dough she had been working on and sliced a piece from the morning's loaf.

"Go back to your bed," she instructed him. "I'll bring it to you."

Luki turned around and dragged his bony little body back to bed.

"You are looking down on us," she said to Jesus and sprinkled a little paprika on Luki's slice of bread.

Mammi came in from Tata's workshop out back. "How is he doing?" she asked, wiping her hands on her apron.

"He just asked for more to eat," Elisabeth answered.

Mammi's face relaxed and her hands dropped to her side. "You looked after him well. He'll make it now, that much is for sure. I think you can help with the wedding again." She nodded in approval and then returned to the workshop.

Elisabeth smiled.

It was Saturday, and Elisabeth and Anna were again at their aunt and uncle's home. "You make sure those cookies are perfect, Elisabeth," Konrad-Bátschi commanded.

"Of course," she replied, keeping her eyes focused on her work: baking sweet *mandelkipfel*, from almond meal and flour. Konrad-Bátschi stood as tall as Tata, but because of his trade, had a body twice the size of her father's.

"Every *kipfel* shaped perfectly and the same size."

Again, Elisabeth nodded. She rolled a small amount of almond dough in her hands, making sure the middle stayed fat and the ends thin, lay it on the baking sheet, and formed it into a small crescent.

Margarethe-Néni came out of the back room and immediately got to work alongside Elisabeth, Anna, and Susi. Gretche was at the stove, stirring a broth and chopping vegetables for soup. Georg and Samuel followed her, dressed in their winter coats.

"Margarethe, we're heading over to Meier Josef for a schnapps," Konrad-Bátschi said, and as much as Elisabeth didn't like her uncle, she wished she could join him: no reading, no drawing, and only one visit from a friend throughout Luki's illness had left Elisabeth feeling like she was drowning in a sea of gossip. But when Konrad-Bátschi and his two sons left the house, Elisabeth's chest relaxed and Anna let out an audible sigh.

Does he have any idea how hard it is to make these all so exact? she thought to herself. The answer was obvious: he didn't know, because he'd never made *mandelkipfel* in his life and never would.

"You heard your uncle," Margarethe-Néni said.

Several minutes of silence followed as everyone rolled dough. Once the cookies were baked, they would be wrapped up in cloths and taken to the cold cellar behind the house. The wedding was this coming Tuesday, only a few days away now, and Elisabeth had to somehow juggle Luki's improving health, continue helping with wedding preparations, and run her household.

"Elisabeth," Susi said, "would you mind getting me some cloths? They're in the back room, in the dresser on the top right drawer. Mine are getting too greasy."

Elisabeth dusted off her hands on her apron and headed into the back room. Her aunt and uncle's house didn't differ much from Elisabeth's except that they had more crocheted doilies, knitted blankets, and embroidered pillowcases. But with all three daughters all grown up, that was hardly a surprise.

She opened the drawer and pulled out a few tea towels. When she lifted the last one, she stopped. Underneath it was an envelope addressed to Konrad-Bátschi.

It was from Tata.

Elisabeth's heart stopped. *So he had survived the journey! Thank you, Jesus!*

She checked the postage date on it and gasped: he had written the letter four weeks ago! But did this letter mean Mammi had also heard from Tata? Then why hadn't she said anything? Could she have forgotten?

No, of course not! Elisabeth thought to herself. How could she forget something like this? And as mean as Mammi could be, surely she wouldn't hide something like this from the children? Unless Tata's letter to her contained terrible news. If only she could read the letter...

"Did you find them?" Susi called back.

Elisabeth took a deep breath to calm herself and slid the drawer closed. Each step into the kitchen felt like she was walking through thick mud that tried to hold her in place. Elisabeth couldn't believe that her aunt and uncle were so mean that they wouldn't tell her family about Tata's letter.

"Sorry," she said, her voice deceptively calm, as she came into the room with the cloths. "It took me a moment."

"But my daughter's instructions were clear," Margarethe-Néni said.

Elisabeth could only shrug her shoulders. "I'm sorry."

Susi placed the cloths on the cooking table next to their oven and Elisabeth returned to her baking duties.

Could she ask about the letter? Of course not. She'd have to admit she'd been snooping. But Tata was her father and she the eldest child, now in charge of the household. If something was wrong, shouldn't she find out about it so she could help her family?

"Remember," Margarethe-Néni said, "every *kipfel* must be perfect."

Elisabeth saw an opportunity and decided to milk it.

"I will try but I'm distracted. We still haven't heard from Tata. It's been two months now."

Would Margarethe-Néni admit to the letter?

"I'm certain he's fine," she said.

Elisabeth saw another opportunity. She feigned a surprised look. "You've heard from him, then?"

Her aunt responded with an angry look. "Of course not. Obviously I would tell you if I had."

"I'm sorry," Elisabeth replied, remaining as innocent as she could. "I meant no insult." She returned to her baking.

Why was her aunt like this? Konrad-Bátschi had inherited the blacksmith shop from Otata, Elisabeth's grandfather. At every wedding Elisabeth had ever helped out with, Margarethe-Néni had peppered her brother- and sister-in-law with snide remarks and underhanded insults. Elisabeth was certain she even shared personal stories with Meier Josef, who could spread a rumour he'd heard before church so quickly that Elisabeth would hear it on the way home from service.

Suddenly, Gretchc cried out as the pot of soup crashed onto the dirt-and-chaff floor and the broth spilled out everywhere. Elisabeth immediately rushed into the back room and grabbed more cloths out of the drawer.

"Here!" she said, waving them. If that broth soaked

in, the floor would smell like chicken for weeks.

Gretche grabbed the cloths on the cooking table next to the stove and everyone helped dab up the mess immediately.

"You stupid cow!" Margarethe-Néni yelled at her grown daughter.

"I didn't do it on purpose!" Gretche replied. "The Devil took my arm and pushed the pot!"

"Then pray for Jesus' protection."

Gretche stood up and headed for the front room.

"After we finish cleaning up! Or did the Devil take your mind, too, like he's taken Georg's?" Margarethe-Néni said.

"I am not like my brother!" Gretche shouted. She scrubbed the floor with her dirty towels, retrieved a cloth sack from the front room and collected all the tea towels in it. She then stormed back into the front room, dropped onto her knees next to her bed, and began to pray. But Elisabeth stood close to the door and was certain she could hear her cousin instead asking God to punish Margarethe-Néni.

Margarethe-Néni and Susi returned to the kitchen table to keep baking, not even thanking Elisabeth and Anna for helping clean up the mess. It was as though dropping a pot was so embarrassing that they wanted to pretend like it had never happened.

"Anna," Elisabeth said, "why don't you start chopping vegetables for a fresh soup?"

Anna nodded, appearing grateful that her sister had given her a task. The basket of root vegetables was under the table and hadn't been touched by the spilled broth.

The first sheet of *mandelkipfel* was ready and Susi slid it in the oven. Elisabeth noticed they needed fresh tea towels in the kitchen now to pull things out of the oven, so she offered to get some.

Tata's letter and its envelope were on the floor: they must have fallen out when Elisabeth had ripped the pile of towels out of the drawer. She bent down to pick up both, then glanced back at her family, all of whom had their backs to her, and then up at Jesus, who was looking down at her.

The letter was none of her business; she knew that. But Tata had been gone for so long, and she so desired to hear from him...

She peeked into the kitchen again. Everyone was too engrossed in their feelings and their work to notice that Elisabeth hadn't returned yet.

She opened it.

Dear Konrad,

I arrived safe and am staying with one of Meier Josef's cousins. Please don't tell Lissa that I've written. If she or my family are scared because I haven't written, comfort them. You and I don't always agree on things, but we agree on how important family is. I trust you will do as I ask.

I haven't found a good job yet and I don't want Lissa to know. They don't like to hire people here who don't speak English. I've repaired a few shoes so far, but that's all. I wish to have happier news for her when I send her my first letter.

I hope all is well. Please write me and tell me how my family is doing, especially Elisabeth: I need to know that she's growing up and will soon be ready for a husband.

Your brother,

Lukas

THAT NIGHT, ELISABETH COULDN'T SLEEP. SHE HAD managed to keep the letter's existence a secret for the day, but it was gnawing at her conscience: was the Fourth Commandment not "Honour your father and your mother"? But which parent should she honour in this situation? Her father's wish to not say anything to his wife? Or her mother's wish to hear news of her husband?

She lit a few candles in the back room and pulled down a book of Luther's teachings. Hopefully she would find an answer in there.

"Elisabeth!"

Elisabeth jumped, almost knocking over a candle. Mammi stood in the doorway, her own candle in hand, dressed in her nightgown, her long braid flowing down her back. The shadows from the flame deepened her wrinkles and creases, making her look angrier than usual.

"I told you not to read at night!" she whispered through gritted teeth.

Elisabeth didn't know what to say. Jesus required His followers to be honest at all times, and God required that children honour their parents. But she still had not answered her original question: which parent should she honour?

"Elisabeth, you can kneel in that corn for an hour or you can tell me what you're doing."

Elisabeth saw no way out. *Help me find the words*, she prayed. "Can we please sit down?" she asked. To her surprise, Mammi pulled out a chair.

Under the table, Elisabeth wiped her hands on her nightgown. "I saw something today and...I don't know what to do about it. I was hoping to find an answer in Martin Luther's teachings."

The crease between Mammi's eyebrows grew deeper. "Just what are you talking about?"

Elisabeth rubbed her hands together.

"I saw a letter from Tata at Konrad-Bátschi's." Elisabeth paused to let Mammi speak.

"What did it say?"

"This is why I'm confused, Mammi. God commands that we honour our parents, but your wishes and Tata's wishes are different, and I don't know what to do."

Mammi nodded. "I see. Then let me make it simple for you, Elisabeth. I am here right now, and I ask you to tell me what it said."

Elisabeth glanced up at Jesus and light flickering from their candles made it look like he was nodding to her. She decided to do as Mammi asked.

"The letter was mailed four weeks ago—I don't know when they received it. He said he hadn't found a job yet, that he didn't want to write you until he had good news, and..." Elisabeth could barely bring the last part over her lips. "He didn't want Konrad-Bátschi to tell you so you wouldn't worry even more."

The silence that followed frightened Elisabeth: Mammi always knew what to say. Even if it was something Elisabeth didn't want to hear—like a punishment if she didn't obey her mother—Mammi knew what to say.

This time, Mammi didn't. This time, Mammi sat before Elisabeth frozen, uncertain, scared.

But this time, Elisabeth knew what to do: she held Mammi's hand.

It was several days after New Year's Day, and Juliana was back at the studio. Jasmine sat on the floor in a 180-degree splat.

"What are your New Year's resolutions?" she asked.

The question surprised Juliana, who sat in pigeon pose, with one leg folded in front and the other extended behind her. She had New Year's resolutions, but they were written down in a special notebook, her book of goals for the year. She knew what she had written, though:

✓ *Get my splits*

✓ *Bend my back in half*

✓ *Make and keep 5 new friends in January*

✓ *Maintain 90% average at new school*

✓ *Raise competition average from 85% to 95%*

But she didn't want to share her goals with Jasmine, whose resolutions were probably something like getting 100% in everything she did or winning several $5,000 scholarships at competition. But whatever Jasmine's goals were, Juliana preferred to keep hers secret; she didn't want anyone to know if she failed or gave up on them.

"I don't tell them to anyone," she said.

"Okay, everyone, up and to your positions!" Miss Denise said with a clap.

"If you don't share them, no one can help you achieve them," Jasmine replied.

The thought caught Juliana off guard and she barely heard Miss Denise count the dancers in. But once the music started, Juliana's mind snapped to one immediate goal: not screwing up. This was the third team practice she'd attended and she hadn't yet gotten the choreography perfect. She knew what happened to the weakest dancers on any team: they were ignored, even shunned, as though the team was some religious group. It didn't matter if you did your best; it only mattered if your skill matched everyone else's. Although Juliana believed she was already that dancer, she kept Dad's advice in her heart: to give her team a second chance, too. That meant, at least for today, emptying her mind of her worries.

She began the routine and kept up. When the

chaîné-turn sequence came, though, her heart raced: a chassé followed by three turns, four times, and she had to make it through two lines of dancers and not hit a single one.

"Ow!" a boy yelled.

Juliana pulled her arms in and hit the brakes on her sequence. "Oh my god, I'm so sorry!"

"Juliana, keep going!" Miss Denise commanded, but Juliana had already lost track of where she was. Miss Denise stopped the music.

"Isaac, are you all right?" Miss Denise asked.

Isaac nodded, rubbing his shoulder.

"Sorry," Juliana said in a tiny voice.

"No problem," Isaac said, moving back to his opening position. Others followed, and Juliana followed them. Miss Denise didn't say a word, and Juliana was embarrassed that she had caused the restart.

"From the top," Miss Denise said and hit play.

This time, Juliana made it through the chaîné-turn sequence.

Then she fell out of her triple pirouette.

But this time, she kept going, and once she hit a section she hadn't been shown yet, she deftly jumped out of the way and stood at the side, taking note of the next few steps. When the group finished, Miss Denise said, "And again!" and they all obeyed. Juliana succeeded this time, with only minor mistakes, and even completed the following sixteen counts before she had to step out.

When the group finished, the studio fell quiet, except for the sound of everyone catching their breath.

BY THE END OF THE FIRST HOUR, JULIANA HAD ADDED another thirty-two counts to what she already knew. She still had half the dance to go, but she could feel the choreography finally gelling. Sitting in the change room with the other girls, she was eating an apple and some pumpkin seeds when Jasmine sat next to her and patted Juliana on the back.

"I have to admit," she said, "I didn't think you'd be able to keep up."

Juliana froze, her mouth half open and a handful of seeds on its way to her lips. Why on earth would someone say something like that?

Miss Denise knocked on the door and called everyone back to class. The other girls shoved their snacks back into their bags, grabbed their water bottles, and rushed out before Juliana knew what was happening. However, Jasmine stayed behind to wait as Juliana packed her food away.

"When you showed up without your shoes, I honestly thought you were some lazy dancer."

Juliana didn't know if she should cry out in jubilation because she had been right about what Jasmine thought or to pack her bags and head home whimpering. Apparently, something showed on her face, though, because Jasmine put her hand on Juliana's shoulder. Her voice was gentle.

"I'm sorry. I really don't mean to insult you. I just don't waste time beating around the bush. You really surprised me today, and I think it's awesome. It's the holidays, when all our friends at school are hanging out at home, texting with friends, playing video games, doing all that fun stuff, and we're here. You're here. You just started here several days ago, and you've already got half the dance down."

Juliana calmed down. Jasmine's intent seemed sincere. But what should she say in response? If it was the wrong thing, she'd be on the shunning list again.

They walked down the hall to the studio.

Opening up to Sophie had helped, so maybe trying it here wasn't a bad idea, either. After all, Juliana didn't have to tell Jasmine her life story, just something small that was important to her.

"I just arrived about two weeks ago from Calgary, so I haven't had as much time to practice as I'd like: unpacking, meeting new family, all that stuff."

Jasmine looked surprised. "Really?"

"We arrived three days before Christmas."

"Miss Denise said you had recently moved here, but I had no idea you had *just* moved here. And you came all the way across the country?"

Juliana smiled and nodded. "And we've moved in with my grandfather. The house is smaller and a lot older than ours back home. I don't even have a room to really practice in now."

They entered the studio.

"That's a lot. Then I take it all back: you're doing *a lot* better than I would expect under those circumstances."

Miss Denise clapped her hands again. "Enough chit-chat. But yes, Juliana, you're doing very well."

Juliana smiled at her new teacher. Miss Denise continued. "Successful dancers don't make it just because of great technique but because of tenacity. If you keep this up, you may have what it takes to make a career of this."

Juliana beamed. "Really?"

Miss Denise nodded.

"Jasmine, take her into the next studio and show her the next section."

BACK AT HOME, JULIANA STOOD IN FRONT OF HER CLOSET mirror. Freshly washed, her brown hair hung in long clumps over her shoulders and down her back. She had on a fresh pair of denim leggings, a t-shirt that said, "I dance because I exist," and a fair-trade beaded necklace Rachel had given her.

She had never given much thought to a professional career in dance: no one had ever told her it was possible, but now that Miss Denise had said it...

"What do I want?" she asked herself in the mirror. "What do I really, really want?"

She reached for her book of goals and reviewed her list. If she was going to make dance a career, she'd have to do more than just get her splits and high marks at competition. But she was also a good student. For the most part, she enjoyed school, though tests and exams perhaps not so much. But then, who did? She had thought in the past about being a doctor, maybe a physiotherapist. Maybe she would spend a summer on exchange in Australia or go to a French camp in Quebec before she decided everything.

Working as a doctor or physiotherapist would be a career for life. If she danced professionally, she'd have to start a new career by her late thirties. And her body would likely be very broken. She remembered once taking a master class from a former prima ballerina whose legs were permanently frozen in turnout, and

Juliana had read about other retired dancers who had arthritis in their feet, had to have their hips replaced—or both! What good was dancing professionally if you had to stop at some point and deal with a permanently injured body for the rest of your life?

Juliana set her book of goals down and opened her great-grandmother's book of drawings to the sketch of the wedding. Opa had said the other day that every girl aspired to marry and become a wife and then a mother.

She looked at herself in the mirror again, twirled her hair into a makeshift bun, holding it up with one hand, and tried to picture herself with a bonnet on. Then she let her hair drop.

"I don't know what I want when I grow up, but it's definitely not that."

Juliana closed the book and placed it back in the drawer in her nightstand. She dropped on to her bed and began texting Rachel. She didn't want to tell her about how fantastic practice had gone today. She didn't want Rachel to worry about their friendship again—the two of them were BFFs. But Miss Kasia had never told Juliana that she could ever turn professional. She decided to just text her friend a question.

What do you actually want to be when you grow up?

Knowing it was roughly lunchtime back in Calgary, Juliana didn't expect an answer immediately, so she called up one of her social media accounts and posted the same question to her friends.

Then, exhausted from the day's practice, she nodded off.

JULIANA RUBBED HER EYES, STRETCHED OUT, AND ROLLED over to see Mom standing over her.

"Tired, eh, sweetie?"

Juliana nodded.

"Sorry to wake you, but the snow's really coming down, and I need your help. You can shovel or help in the kitchen. What would you prefer?"

Juliana groaned and stretched. "Shovel," she said.

Mom smiled. "I figured as much. Take your time, but not too much time, okay?"

Juliana nodded, and Mom left the room.

Remembering what she'd texted and posted, she swiped open her phone. Rachel had responded.

Why?

Juliana typed back.

Sorry. Was sleeping. Just curious. Not important.

She then opened her social media account and her eyes popped open.

Start-up CEO

Mechanic

Don't know. Hate school.

Who cares? Live in the now! #carpediem

Astronaut #nasa

Garbage collector—always wanted to ride on the side of those trucks

Travel to #Africa first

ur an idiot dumb question the future is dead

POTUS

Help poor kids

A woman

PM, not POTUS

Freedom fighter for kids

The list went on and on, with answers from more than just her friends. Although marked by a few trolls and some smart remarks, the list was as diverse in ideas as her old school was in students.

"Juliana!" Mom called.

"Coming!" She slipped on some warmer socks and stopped for another moment in front of the mirror.

"How am I ever going to decide what to do with my life?"

$\mathcal{E}$lisabeth stood in front of the looking glass in the front room of Konrad-Bátschi and Margarethe-Néni's house and brushed back a few wisps of her hair. She had on her white dress, which had a lightly ruffled collar, long sleeves, and, as all dresses did, a pressed apron, also white. The front half of her blonde hair was pulled back into two braids that joined the rest of her hair in one long braid that folded over itself and was pinned to the top of her head. To make her hair look more festive than usual, Elisabeth had added a white-beaded hairband.

Outside, she could hear the small marching band coming down the street for the bride and everyone else in the house. She peeked out the window and saw a sizeable crowd of perhaps thirty or so men and a handful of women laughing and joyfully walking along through the snow and slush down the street.

She turned to Susi. No matter what Elisabeth thought of her relatives, a wedding was always cause for celebration, and today was no different. Another girl was about to become a woman.

"So?" she said, her voice full of excitement. "Are you ready?"

The other women and girls in the room—Eva, Gretche, Anna, Rosina, Margarethe-Néni, Mammi, and several young cousins from Margarethe-Néni's side—all stared at Susi, who nodded so much that the white floral wreath on her head almost fell off.

"Careful!" Elisabeth said and helped Susi put it back in place.

Konrad-Bátschi was in the back room, waiting with an open bottle of the wedding wine to share with the crowd of male guests who would arrive any moment.

Mammi tried to smile for her niece, but Elisabeth could tell that her mother was boiling inside: no one had even said a word of comfort as Tata had asked them to in his letter. Elisabeth also believed that Mammi somehow felt betrayed, that after sixteen years of marriage, Tata didn't trust her to handle such sad news. Elisabeth knew Tata had acted with good intent, but how could he not know his wife after so long?

Although Mammi's mood did not become

apparent to the wedding guests, Elisabeth had seen it for days. It had begun the morning after Elisabeth had confessed everything. Mammi was dressed and busying about before any of the children had awoken, and when Elisabeth looked at the clock, she saw Mammi had let them all sleep in. Over the following days, Mammi barely punished: when Rosina dropped a bowl of flour on the floor, all she had to do was clean it up. Mammi neither hit her nor demanded she kneel in the box of corn. Even when Anna forgot to feed the farm animals outside, all Mammi said was that she shouldn't forget her duties. She then gave Anna a light tap on the bum and sent her to feed the animals right away. Mammi moved through her days as though in a haze, barely noticing what was happening around her.

The music grew louder, and even usually quiet Anna and little Rosina became giddy. Margarethe-Néni smiled but otherwise remained still, as all older women did. Elisabeth wondered what went through her mind. Susi was her last child to marry off. Was her aunt happy? Sad? The marriage made her, in a way, no longer a mother.

The marching music blared through the front windows now and there was a bang on the door. Margarethe-Néni hurried over and opened it.

"We've come for the bride!" a young man

announced as the music wound down. Margarethe-Néni stepped back and welcomed the whole party in.

The parade crowded into the house, spilling into all three rooms. Rosina and Anna each picked up platters with pieces of cake and the *mandelkipfel* Elisabeth had helped bake and began passing them around to all the guests while Konrad-Bátschi passed out small servings of his homemade wine to the men. Luki, all healthy again, had arrived with the parade, too, having stayed with men from Mammi's side of the family. He looked up at Konrad-Bátschi, his eyes wide with desire, but Konrad-Bátschi shook his head.

"You're too young, yet. First, you need to become a good *skat* player!" He let out a hearty laugh, clapped Luki on the back, and continued serving the other men. Luki's face dropped in disappointment, but once Anna came around with a platter of sweet goods, it lit up again and he grabbed fistfuls of whatever desserts he could. Elisabeth saw him drop one perfectly shaped *mandelkipfel* and it broke into chunks and crumbs on the floor, only to be flattened by someone passing by. She sighed. So much for that perfectly shaped cookie.

Once everyone was served, the bride was led outside, with two young children holding her train up from the snow and slush. Everyone followed behind her. The wedding parade, careful to avoid bad luck by not following the same route twice, headed for the groom's house. Afterwards, everyone would go to the church for the religious ceremony, then to the town hall for the legal marriage, and finally they would celebrate with a party until the early hours of the morning.

"ELISABETH, ARE YOU COMING?" LUKI RAN INTO THE front room of their house and grabbed her hand. "We have to get to the *festhalle*! I think they're already dancing!" Although Luki's energy had returned from his illness, his full personality had not: he was still a little gentleman to Elisabeth.

"Yes, Luki, just hold on a moment!" she said, laughing. "If you grab my hand, I can't carry the food!"

The entire family—Mammi, Elisabeth, Anna, Luki, and Rosina—carried either a bowl or platter to take to the *festhalle* for the rest of the wedding festivities. Elisabeth's hands gripped both sides of a cake platter with her rum roll on it. Peeling it off the baking sheet had left a few rips in the cake, but buttercream icing had covered those just fine, and Elisabeth etched a few stars into it for an extra blessing. Although it was not a perfect cake, it certainly wouldn't embarrass Mammi either. Mammi carried her coffee cake, carefully balanced on top of a pot of soup; Anna carried two baskets of yeast *kipfel*, and Rosina carried some plates and cutlery.

The ceremony had been beautiful, and Elisabeth had had to wipe a few tears away herself. Susi was now married, now a woman at seventeen years of age. Next in line would come children, if God allowed, hopefully the first one before Christmas.

Luki carried everyone's dress shoes in a bag over his shoulder so they could get change into proper shoes at the *festhalle*. Mammi wouldn't dance, of course—it would be inappropriate for her to dance with another man in her husband's absence. But Elisabeth couldn't wait to see who would ask her to dance. Maybe her future husband?

"I can't wait to see all the skirts turning around on the floor!" Rosina jumped up and down in excitement and almost slipped on the packed snow.

"Careful!" Anna said with a laugh. "You won't be able to dance if your dress is soaked!"

As merry as the children were, Mammi's sadness hung like a shroud around her. Elisabeth wondered if this was what it felt like to lose someone very close to you to God. Although Mammi kept her chin up, her shoulders slumped as the family made their way through the snow to the *festhalle*. Elisabeth missed Tata, too, of course, but this time, she wondered if Mammi missed him more, especially because Konrad-Bátschi and Margarethe-Néni had already heard from him.

As they neared the hall, the music and dancing erased any concern Elisabeth had for Mammi: not because she didn't care for her, but because this was the first event she had attended since she had taken over the household, and she couldn't wait to find her friends, especially Maria.

Once inside, they carried the dinner food to the serving tables and the cakes—well-covered so no one could see them—to a table in the back corner where all the other women's fancy treats sat, waiting to be the pride or embarrassment of their creator.

Now came Elisabeth's favourite part of the whole day: when the wreath on the bride's head would be replaced by a new bonnet.

Susi's new husband, Adam, and her girlfriends and unmarried female family members, including Elisabeth and her sisters, all held hands and walked in a circle. The girls and Susi began their song:

> *Come here, come here, oh husband of mine,*
> *I want to love you until the end of time.*
> *Come here, come here, oh friends of mine,*

Let us have fun together, just one more time.

The group began to close in on Susi, with Adam breaking free and standing by his new wife's side. With the next verse, the girls stepped back and then allowed a circle of married women to come forward. As Elisabeth stepped back, she couldn't help but notice Georg standing alone in a corner of the room, far away from his wife or anyone else. But Elisabeth kept singing with the group.

> *Go away, go away, oh friends of mine,*
> *Our fun must end now, it is time.*
> *Come here, come here, oh devoted wives,*
> *Take me into your arms, into your lives.*

Gretche, the eldest sister in Susi's family, lifted the white floral wreath from her sister's head. The girls continued their song:

> *Take it off, take it off, this wreath that shines,*
> *Put on, put on, this new bonnet of mine.*

Then Konrad-Bátschi and Margarethe-Néni entered the circle for the last two lines.

> *Come here, come here, oh parents of mine,*

*I must say good-bye to you, for it is now that
time.*

Tears flowed freely down Susi's face as Margarethe-Néni pressed her hands against her daughter's cheeks and gave her one last big kiss. Elisabeth's aunt pulled a handkerchief out of her hand purse and did her best to quietly blow her nose. But her sadness overflowed so much it sounded more like a goose honk.

Elisabeth dabbed a handkerchief on her own tears. Susi was no longer one of them, no longer Schuhmacher Susi, a young girl. She was now a woman—Schubkegel Susi—and would join the world of married women and, soon, of mothers.

ELISABETH SQUEEZED OUT OF THE THRONG OF WELL-wishers once Susi had received her *haube* and headed straight for Georg, whose eyes were fixed on his youngest sister.

"Are you all right?"

He nodded, not taking his eyes off Susi.

"You look scared," she said.

"I don't want her to die."

Elisabeth glanced in Susi's direction and then back at Georg. Susi was dancing so merrily that it was hard to think of the day her life would end. What could Elisabeth say to help Georg feel better?

"She's happy now. She's alive and married. Shouldn't you be happy for her?"

Georg's eyes didn't move as he answered her. "But she doesn't deserve to die."

Those were hardly the words of a shameful person; they were the words of someone who cared for his family and was—for reasons Elisabeth didn't understand—very frightened. But Elisabeth couldn't figure out where his mind was: Was he thinking about the war? Or about his first wife and child? Nobody deserved to die, not anyone here in Semlak, or across the world in Pennsylvania where Tata was. And Jesus certainly did not deserve to die.

Jesus...Elisabeth thought back to what she'd read in Genesis and tried again to reach her cousin.

"When Jesus died, He went up to the stars and now looks down on us. I think we do the same. We'll all die someday, Georg, and then angels will take us to Him, up to the stars where we can look down on those we leave behind."

He turned his head towards her. "Do you really believe that?"

She nodded.

"Then why did I watch my best friend die? If Jesus is looking down on us, why did He take him?"

Georg looked at her for a moment, though Elisabeth couldn't tell if he actually saw her; it was as though his eyes were looking through her instead of at her. Then he returned his gaze to his sister.

Elisabeth thought for a minute before answering. "Maybe the person who killed him had lost Jesus for that moment. Maybe he didn't hear Jesus tell him to stop shooting. Or maybe his commander didn't hear Jesus and told him to shoot, otherwise he'd be shot and would never see his family again."

In truth, Elisabeth didn't know what the answer was —Luki had seemed close to death and he had lived when other children had died. But other than Georg, Elisabeth knew of no one who became seriously ill and was healed only to turn into a very different person. As far as she could tell, war did something different to some people. Not all—Tata seemed fine—but to some.

"I'd never thought of it like that," Georg said and he seemed to mull over Elisabeth's words in his mind for another few minutes. The waltz the band was playing finished and a polka followed.

"Will you dance with me?" Georg asked, his face still showing no expression. Elisabeth smiled and accepted.

It was Saturday, the last weekend before the end of Christmas break. Juliana was sitting on the couch in the living room, studying the drawing of the young woman who'd just been married. She couldn't believe the details her great-grandmother could draw at such a young age. The bride, tears streaming down her cheeks, looked both sad and happy.

Did she not want to get married? Had she been forced into this? Or did this drawing suggest what her great-grandmother had thought about marriage herself? Juliana knew from the times she had choreographed her own combinations in dance that her dances reflected more what she was feeling and less what she thought an audience might want to see. Did her great-grandmother draw the same way?

The stairs from the basement creaked, and judging by their heaviness and slowness, Juliana guessed it was Opa. A minute later proved she was right. She looked up at him. "Opa, can I ask you something?"

He sat down next to her, taking the book of drawings from Juliana. "Mammi's book of drawings," he said, studying the wedding scene. "Ah, this is the picture you showed your friend on the computer. I remember more about it now: the bride was one of Mammi's cousins." His crooked finger floated above the page as he inspected every corner of it. He stopped in front of the face of a man standing in a corner, singled out from all the festivities. "He's the one who had a bird in his head."

Huh? What on earth was that supposed to mean?

Upon seeing Juliana's confused face, Opa laughed. "I'm sorry—that was German. When someone's crazy, we say he has a bird in his head. This is Georg."

Juliana had read more about PTSD online, for example, that people reminded others to be mindful when celebrating with fireworks if soldiers lived nearby because it could really disturb them. To Juliana's disgust, insensitive remarks often followed such posts. Opa's seeming lack of sensitivity similarly bothered her.

"Georg had PTSD," Juliana said.

"That fancy word of yours again."

"Post-traumatic stress disorder, Opa. It happens to soldiers all the time. They can't cope with normal, everyday life when they come back from war."

Opa looked lost in thought for a moment and then shrugged. "I don't know—lots of men coped just fine, Mammi said. Even Ota." Then he shook his head. "No. If you can't look after your family, then you're not a man."

He looked back at the drawing and pointed to a young girl. "That's Anna-Néni when she was a girl. She was very good to me. Your Aunt Anne was named after her. Actually..." he paused, again seeming to be lost in thought. "I think Mammi said Anna-Néni couldn't wear her mittens when Georg was around, otherwise he'd get the shakes. But that's less important than the wedding. A wedding for a woman meant a new life, and that's why she got a *haube*."

Juliana thought Opa's last statement a little callous. How could a soldier suffering from PTSD be less important than a wedding? But a gut feeling told Juliana now was not the time to ask.

"You told me about the...how-ba when you met Rachel on my computer."

Opa nodded, signalling he remembered. "A bonnet. Mammi couldn't wait to have one herself. She wanted to marry and have a family." Then he looked directly at Juliana. "And when are you going to have a family?"

Juliana laughed out loud. "Me? A family? You're joking, right, Opa?"

The side door to the house opened and a draft of cold air shot through the main floor.

"You're fourteen. You should start thinking about it," Opa said.

"Opa, I've only started high school!"

"What's all the ruckus about?" Dad smiled at them as he passed by to carry his coat to the back hallway.

"Opa just asked me when I was going to get married," Juliana said.

Dad smiled. "I'm sure he's joking."

But Opa shook his head. "She's fourteen, Paul. She needs to start thinking about it, and you and Katy need to start finding her a husband."

Dad stopped for a moment, and Juliana watched his face go from happy to concerned. "Peter, where are we?"

"You don't know? In Semlak."

Judging by the look on Dad's face, Juliana knew her father was now worried.

"Peter, you haven't lived in Semlak for decades. You live in Kitchener. You left Semlak in your twenties, when your cousin arranged for you and everyone else to go to Pennsylvania, and you came here a year later."

Opa's eyes blinked a few times and then he laughed.

But it was an unnatural laugh, the kind any of Juliana's friends would use to cover up something really embarrassing, like leaking through a tampon.

"I'm just joking, Paul, you know that!" He forced his laugh some more and then got up. "Better go get some water from that well!" He slapped his knee and laughed all the way to the basement door. Standing by the doorway to the stairs, he turned around. "You know what? I'm pretty sure Mammi was fourteen when she started that book." He then faked his laugh again. "I had you there for a moment," he said, and then disappeared.

Juliana looked at Dad. "What was that all about?"

Dad's eyes grew sad. "His dementia might be further along than we thought. I think for a moment there he actually believed he was back home."

Juliana had read that people with dementia could do that and that some homes for them actually had "sets" of buildings from their younger years, like what you'd find on a Hollywood soundstage, to help keep dementia patients alert and engaged. Still others had windows painted on the backs of doors to the patients' rooms to make them think it was actually a window and not a door so they wouldn't wander away.

But she'd only really met her grandfather when they moved here. Before that, their only contact had been the odd stilted phone call and kitschy greeting cards. He really cared about her, and even if she didn't agree with everything he said, he had a lifetime of information about her family's past. How would she learn it all before his dementia took over completely?

"What's that?" Dad pointed to the book, sat down, and picked it up.

"It's what I found in the basement," Juliana said. She hadn't shown it to Dad or Mom yet, and apparently Opa hadn't said anything either. "They're from Opa's mom. So far as I know, she drew these pictures based on what was happening in her life. Don't touch the drawings, though. Opa says they'll smudge."

Dad gently flipped through the pages and stopped at one about halfway through: a man was lying down on some kind of simple, open coffin, his hands folded over his chest, his eyes closed. Nine people stood behind the coffin, their hands folded in prayer, looking solemnly in the artist's direction.

"Is he dead?" Dad asked.

Juliana studied the drawing more closely. "I think so. Man, that's creepy, eh?"

"You know, I think your mom mentioned once that they used to take pictures like this so they could send copies to any family abroad." He shuddered, and so did Juliana. Then they both laughed.

"But wait, Dad, look," and Juliana pointed to a few watermarks on the page. "Are those tears?"

Dad held the book a little closer to his face. "I think you're right. Wow." And both sat in silence for a moment. Juliana could even sense that rope that connected them returning.

Dad continued. "I love your mom, but her ancestors...they could sometimes be really strange. Let's turn to another page. What's the drawing you were looking at?"

Juliana flipped back to the picture of the wedding and explained to Dad what she knew.

"And they apparently do this ritual where she says good-bye to her friends, because she'll no longer hang out with them because she's now a wife. Isn't that horrible?"

Dad thought for a moment. "I'm sure she wouldn't stop hanging out with them, but I can understand if she spent more time with other wives than her unmarried friends. I think it depends on how you look at it. Maybe it's backwards by our standards, but it's not much different from the party Miss Kasia threw you in Calgary. You weren't getting married, but you were starting a new life and saying goodbye to your friends. Farewell parties are one ritual we have and it's kind of the same. Your high school graduation will be like that, too."

Juliana had to admit that Dad had a point. But she wasn't going to let him win the entire argument.

"But check out this guy." She pointed to Georg and told Dad what Opa had said about him. "Opa wouldn't change his mind once I explained things to him: he still believes Georg didn't care for his family. I don't get it."

The expression on Dad's face changed abruptly, and Juliana couldn't tell why. He set the book down on the coffee table, walked over to the bay window, and looked out to the street. The only sound Juliana could hear was him breathing.

"Dad?"

He shook his head. "People don't get what war can do to a man—or a woman, of course, but in your Opa's time, only men would've been accused of being lazy, shameful, all that crap. He doesn't know what it's like to grow up with a father who..." He lifted a hand to his face, and through his reflection in the window, Juliana could see him wipe away tears. Had Dad's father suffered from PTSD? She had no idea Dad's childhood had been so difficult. Juliana regretted all the things she'd accused Dad of recently. She needed to say something, but what?

"I'm...um...well..." Nothing intelligent came out of her mouth.

He sniffled and dried his eyes. "I know, you don't like mushy stuff," he said, as though he'd read her thoughts. He turned around to face her, and his eyes were red. "But you're my daughter. I don't know if you'll have a family someday or not, but I hope to God you'll never have to lose anyone to war." Dad pulled a Kleenex from his pocket and wiped his nose. "I'd better pack. After I drop you off at school on Monday, I head out of town on my first trip."

Juliana's heart sank. She and Dad argued a lot, but something good had clicked during the holidays. Why did he have to leave now? Maybe the reason they didn't argue as much was because he was actually around. Would it be more peaceful at home if he didn't have to leave so often?

"How long is this one?"

"I'm driving down to Florida. I'll be gone about five days." He patted Juliana on the shoulder. "Don't worry, I won't hug you. But you do need to know that both your mom and I love you, and that we're doing all of this for you." He didn't wait for a response, which relieved Juliana because she had none, and he headed to his bedroom. But before he disappeared down the hallway, he said, "And please don't think about marriage. Heck, don't even think about dating!"

With the wedding several days before and the first week of February now coming to an end, Elisabeth hoped she could finally rest—at least she wouldn't have to add all those wedding responsibilities to her already busy days. But alas, now she lay in bed with a fever and a cough.

And so did Anna.

And so did Rosina.

The front room was never quiet—someone was always coughing—which made it hard for anyone to sleep. Mammi ran faster than a galloping horse between the workshop and her children, getting them tea, broths—anything they needed—and finishing a customer's pair of shoes.

Surprisingly, eight-year-old Luki took on the role of

caregiver in the family whenever Mammi wasn't in the house. Although he was too young to boil water, he set out dried teas, sliced very wide, uneven pieces of bread for the girls, and otherwise tended to them.

The house door opened with a bang and Mammi came running in.

"We're fine, Mammi," Elisabeth said, assuming Mammi was assuming the worst. She coughed. "Luki's looking after us."

But Mammi had something in her hand: a letter.

"Your father has finally written us," she said, her eyes moist with happiness. "He writes that he has found work in a cigar factory. It stinks and he has to ask the people he's staying with to not smoke while he's home —the smell makes him sick—but it is a good job." Mammi smiled and then looked at her four children. "Your father is a good man." She continued reporting on the letter. "He is tired after very long days working in the factory but sometimes he still makes shoes in the evenings. And so long as God gives him strength, he'll keep working. He wants to earn money for land and a shingle roof for us, and also to help Elisabeth marry well. That will save money for the two of you." She nodded at Anna and Rosina, and then sniffled and wiped her nose with a handkerchief. "He hopes to be back before it's time for Elisabeth to marry."

Rosina coughed, followed by Anna, and then Elisabeth. They looked up at Mammi, who said nothing more.

"Is that it?" Elisabeth asked. "Is that all he wrote?"

Mammi nodded. "It is very little, but I have his address now so we may write him. Jesus has watched over our family and protected Tata. We must be thankful and continue to work hard."

Luki jumped up and down. "Daddy's alive!"

Mammi nodded, a small smile on her face. "Luki, it's time you began to learn your father's trade. Get your coat and follow me."

"No," he said, his old personality having finally returned.

Mammi's eyes flared. "What did you say?" Mammi's personality had also been restored.

"I said, no! Tata will teach me!"

Mammi would not have it. She grabbed her son by the arm, and his little body was no match for hers. "Your Tata is not here," she said through gritted teeth. "Now let's get your boots and coat." She pinched Luki by the ear and pulled him into the back room.

DAY FIVE AND ELISABETH'S FEVER HAD FINALLY BROKEN and her strength was beginning to return. She gave Jesus a prayer of thanks for her fast recovery. Mammi had taken over these past few days, cooking and shoe-making, but said she would leave the cleaning and laundry to Elisabeth once she got well. Elisabeth noticed that Mammi didn't look well herself during those days, but as always, Mammi made nothing of it and kept pushing on. Elisabeth could only hope she wouldn't have to care for her mother, not yet, anyway. Mammi was still too young for that.

Elisabeth sat propped up in her bed, her knees bent and her drawing book in her lap. She was shading in Susi's face. So far as she knew, her cousin had been happy to be married, but Elisabeth couldn't help but wonder if she was also sad to leave her parents' home and her life as she knew it. No young woman knew what moving in with her new husband would be like, and Elisabeth had heard rumours that it wasn't always nice. But to be seen as a woman and respected as one must be exhilarating, too.

She held the book away from her and studied her work. "I do draw well," she whispered to herself. "It's too bad I can't earn money from this."

She set the book back on her lap and turned to the previous drawing of Georg's hands trying to pull off Anna's mittens.

"I don't know how to draw fear into his hands," she said. "Not yet, anyway." She studied her drawing some more. "But these hands are too clean, like those of a city shopkeeper, perhaps." And she shaded in some black stains to better show his blacksmithing work.

She thought about Georg and looked up at Jesus on the crucifix. "How come he gets to earn money by creating and I don't?" Elisabeth knew that almost all Lutheran Semlakers were farmers. It wasn't so much that she was questioning that but more wondering why Georg could be paid to hammer out physical pictures—that's what blacksmithing looked like to her—but she could not earn money drawing pictures on paper. Then she shook her head.

"Elisabeth, what a silly question. How does drawing help people survive? I'm only doing this because I enjoy it and so that Tata can see what happened while he is away."

She flipped back to the wedding and began to draw Georg in the corner, watching the crowd but fearing it at the same time. As she drew his face, she couldn't imagine how Eva could be happy in a marriage to Georg. Secure, most likely, but happy?

But then, marriages were blessed by Jesus, and if Jesus was indeed looking down upon everyone, He obviously allowed unhappy marriages to happen. And Jesus was never wrong, according to Pastor Fröhlich's teachings. Elisabeth had to conclude that happiness in a marriage really didn't matter.

A knock at the house door got Elisabeth out of bed.

Anna and Rosina were sleeping—they were healing well but not as quickly as Elisabeth—so she closed the door to the front room behind her and then opened the house door in the kitchen.

"Maria!"

Her friend entered, again holding a pot of soup. "I came down with a fever a few days before you did. But I'd heard from Meier Josef that you weren't healthy yet, so here I am again!"

"Your family has been so good to us," Elisabeth said. "Once this sickness is over, we'll have you over to say thank you." Elisabeth coughed.

"Don't worry about any of that," Maria said. "You sit down and I'll serve you."

Elisabeth didn't object.

"But I also have some news to share with you."

"Oh?"

"Herr Blum is sick now: he had to send all the children home today."

Herr Blum was the teacher for the one-room school that held grades three to six. This meant he would be off for close to a week, maybe more.

And that meant Elisabeth would have to look after all her siblings by herself until Herr Blum returned to school. Suddenly, looking after one sick child seemed as easy as cooking goulash.

CHAPTER SEVENTEEN

uliana wiped the sweat off her brow while she sat on the thick carpet, stretching to cool down. School—and her new weekly schedule—started tomorrow. Although she finally knew most of the tap routine, she'd start learning the jazz number this week, on top of having to study for exams. Jasmine had also given her a few good tips on how to improve her balance on her pirouettes, and they were working! She pushed the tap board under the couch and headed upstairs. She stopped when she heard Dad say, "We just started to connect."

"And now you're leaving again," Mom said.

There was a pause followed by one of Dad's sighs. "The distance really is ruining my relationship with her," he said, "and with your work hours...I don't know.

I'm worried she'll be the one left looking after your father."

Another pause.

"Maybe we didn't think this through enough," Mom said. "It seemed like a good idea at the time."

Another sigh. But inside Juliana, panic broke out. She was just getting used to being here! She finally had everything organized and had already learned one competition routine out of five! Go back to Calgary? Juliana had to admit she didn't know what she'd prefer right now.

"But we're here," Dad said. "We can't go back. Your family is depending on us to care for your dad, and your sister is still far too busy to step in." Juliana relaxed. "And if there's one thing you've always said it's that you'd always come back here someday, just like your Oma eventually returned to Semlak with your father. We're here. Let's go ahead with everything we have planned, but maybe it's time I finally start looking into another kind of job; something that will let me stay home more often, maybe let me have a regular schedule. Our expenses are a lot lower now, so we can afford my starting fresh."

"But honey, you can't start with a new employer and then just quit."

"I know, and I won't. But starting a new career takes

time, and maybe there's, I don't know, courses or something I can take while I'm on the road."

"But school was never your strong point."

Another sigh and then a light laugh. "Maybe Juliana can help me with that."

A pause. And then a noisy kiss. Juliana recoiled in horror. Parents weren't supposed to kiss: that was just gross.

But the conversation was over. Juliana showered in the basement so her parents wouldn't know she'd been eavesdropping and then made herself a snack in the kitchen. Back in her room, she began packing her backpack for school. She started at her new school, Eby Heights, tomorrow. If it hadn't been for her dance practice sessions, she knew she'd be jumping up and down like popcorn right now, full of nervous energy. Instead, her exhaustion made her feel more like melted butter.

A familiar ring sounded on her phone and laptop. Juliana stuck in her earbuds and answered the call.

"Rachel!"

"Jules! I haven't heard from you in a few days! Thought I'd check in! See if you've decided what to do with your life!"

Juliana laughed: Rachel could always be counted on to get her smiling. She told her about her conversations with Dad and Opa but said nothing about the new studio or Jasmine. She had spent hours practicing, more than she would have at home in fact, just to begin to catch up. She saw the difference already, and she'd be lying to herself if she didn't admit that it did feel good. Maybe this studio would be better than Miss Kasia's back in Calgary.

"No way..." Rachel said, in response to Juliana's story about Dad's parents. "Your dad's gone through a lot, sure, but he's pretty normal as far as dads go."

"I know. He's almost boring." She giggled kindly. "But you know what? We actually connected. I know I'm not supposed to say this—he's my dad and I'm his teenager—but I kind of liked it. I had no idea about his family, and I think it really hurts him to talk about them."

"Wow. Who knew?"

"And then there's school," Juliana said, wanting to change the topic before Rachel asked about her studio. "It's a really old building with a huge addition on the back and a ton of portables. The winter is going to be brutal in those. This wet cold gets into your bones."

Rachel mimicked a shiver. "That sounds awful! And what about your exams? How's that going to work?"

Juliana rested her elbows on her desk and explained what she knew.

There was a knock on the door and Dad entered. He waved at Rachel and Juliana pulled the earbud jack out of her laptop so her father and best friend could talk.

"Hi, Rachel," he said. "How are you?"

"I'm fine, thank you."

"Good to hear. Listen, I need to talk to Juliana about a few things. Can she call you back?"

"Sure!"

Both best friends gave each other a look that confirmed Rachel would be waiting by her computer, and then they hung up.

"Sorry to interrupt you, but Mom and I will be heading out to the mall shortly for some last-minute shopping before it closes. I wanted to see if you needed anything for tomorrow."

Juliana pulled out her agenda and opened it to a page of notes. "I haven't checked everything off yet, but..." She ran through her packing list, rummaged around in her backpack a bit, and then closed the book. "I think I've got everything."

"Paul! Are you coming?" Mom called from the kitchen.

"Be right there!" he replied. "Listen. Neither your mom nor I expected this move to be easy, but that doesn't mean it has to be hard. You have my cell phone, and I'll have my earpiece in while I'm on the road. You call me if you need me, okay? Any time. Day or night."

Juliana nodded, signalling she'd heard him.

"And we'll be getting take-out for supper. Sushi?"

Juliana's nod turned into an enthusiastic yes.

"I'll see you later," Dad said and left.

Juliana immediately called Rachel back.

"And?"

"Man, I wish he weren't leaving again so soon."

"Jules, if there's one thing I learned about my parents' divorce, it's that sometimes it's easiest to just accept things as they are."

Juliana nodded in resignation. When Rachel was right, she was right.

The two kept talking and talking...about school, parents, their favourite cheesy Christmas TV movies, and about missing each other. Juliana didn't talk about her new studio, and to her surprise, Rachel didn't ask about it. Was she also scared that something would split them apart?

Eventually Rachel asked that very question a good hour into the conversation. "Nothing will come between us, right, Jules?"

Just then, Juliana's phone vibrated and a notification came up on her laptop screen.

It's Jasmine. Practice at my place this aft? Turns out we live close to each other.

"What was that?" Rachel asked.

"Uh, nothing." But Jasmine's request hung in Juliana's mind. It would be nice to have a new friend here in town, and especially so soon after moving here.

"Juliana?"

"Um, I should get going. I've got lots to prep for school tomorrow."

Rachel looked crestfallen. "Oh. Okay."

"You're my best friend, Rachel. I promise to call you tomorrow night, okay? After supper my time, after school your time?"

Rachel nodded. They said their goodbyes and hung up.

Juliana replied to Jasmine.

Sorry—on the phone. Sounds good! What time?

1 hour?

Sure!

Jasmine sent through her address.

Juliana then reached for her book of goals and opened it.

✓ *Make 5 new friends in January and keep them*

Would Jasmine be the first one? Juliana hoped so.

SETTING THE RECORD STRAIGHT

Between Worlds is historical fiction: the story is the backbone of a historical fiction book, but it's based on actual historical events. To learn more about some of the historical aspects of the story, read below. (You'll also find more information in the other books in the series.)

NAMES

Naming conventions in Semlak and other German towns in Eastern Europe were actually quite complex because so many people shared the same names. For example, in the roughly 2,700 families that made up the Lutheran congregation from 1819-2000, 1,000 of them shared just 10 last names. During that same time period, 411 boys were named Adam, 334 Heinrich, 421

Martin, and 534 Andreas. On the girls' side, 783 were named Elisabeth, 530 Susanna, and 196 Anna. (As a side note, "Lukas" was not a name listed in the Lutheran church books. I wanted a Biblical name and then made up the short form "Luki.")

To reduce confusion, these cultures developed patterns to name everyone more clearly. Some examples of naming patterns given in the book *Semlak*, edited by Georg Schmidt, include the following:

- *Arva-Schuster:* His last name was Arva and he was a shoemaker. ("Shoemaker" is both "Schuhmacher" and "Schuster" in German, depending on the region.)
- *Stielche-Schuster:* This is something that wouldn't happen today. He was a shoemaker but required a small chair to get around (i.e., like a walker). "Stielche" is a word in the Semlak Lutheran dialect that means "little chair."
- *Paprika-Rosza:* A gardener who planted peppers.
- *Eck-Néni:* Literally, Aunt Corner. The woman's name was actually Elisabeth Tichy, but her house was on a corner.

"Néni" and "Bátschi," though Hungarian for "aunt"

and "uncle," were also used as forms of address for anyone within one's familiar circles.

In chapter 10, Elisabeth is thinking about naming conventions in her family: Anna was born a twin, but Rosina died, and so Mammi gave the name to the next live birth that was a girl. I have an ancestor named Elisabeth, and she gave birth to four daughters, each named Elisabeth. Sadly, none survived, which is why I chose Elisabeth for the name of the historical protagonist.

SICKNESS

Sickness was dealt with differently in Elisabeth's culture than today in North America. For example, even if someone was already burning up, they may have still been covered up so they could sweat it out. As you likely know, this is not the way to go these days: if you have a fever, you might actually take medicine to bring it down, and if your fever is high, you may even go to the hospital. If your fever can be managed at home, your parents or doctor may also suggest that you wear only thin layers, like a summer PJ, so you don't heat up anymore: a high fever can lead to complications, and in Elisabeth's day, this happened often and could result in death.

TRANSLATION

It's easy to think that translation is about just finding the single word you're looking for. For example, when you learn French, you learn that "Comment ça va?" means "How are you?" in English. But if you look at it closely, it actually says, "How it goes?" German is similar: "Wie geht's?" literally means "How goes it?" The intent of the question is to ask after your well-being, and so what you learn in foreign language classes is a phrase that functions in the same way in English, even if the words are actually a little different.

The song the wedding guests sing in chapter 14 is this, taken from the book *Semlak*:

> *Trete bei, trete bei mein Ehemann,*
> *Dich will ich lieben mein Leben lang.*
> *Tretet bei, tretet bei ihr Kameraden mein,*
> *Mit euch will ich noch einmal lustig sein.*
>
> *Tretet ab, tretet ab ihr Kameraden mein,*
> *Mit euch kann ich nicht mehr lustig sein.*
> *Tretet bei, tretet bei ihr Weiberlein,*
> *Schließt mich in eure Gesellschaft ein.*
>
> *Nehmet ab, nehmet ab das Kränzelein,*
> *Setzet auf, setzet auf das Häubelein.*

Tretet bei, tretet bei, liebe Eltern mein,
Von Euch muss ich jetzt geschieden sein.

If I were to translate that word for word, it could look something like this:

Step next to me, step next to me, my
  husband,
I want to love you my whole life long.
Step next to me, step next to me, my
  comrades,
I want to be funny with you one more time.

Step away, step away, you comrades of
  mine,
I can no longer be funny with you.
Step next to me, step next to me, you little
  wives,
And lock me into your society.

Take away, take away this little wreath,
Put on, put on the little bonnet.
Step next to me, step next to me, my dear
  parents,
I must now be split from you.

It doesn't work well, does it? It's because I didn't use any context to do the translation; I simply picked English translations that were often taught in textbooks. If you know German, you may even suggest other translations instead of what I've written here. For example, the last line, "Von Euch muss ich jetzt geschieden sein," could mean, "From you [plural] I must now be divorced," because "geschieden" can be used as an adjective to say someone is divorced. However, I think you'd agree with me that, within the context of this ritual, "divorced" is the wrong word.

I settled for an interpretation of this song in such a way that you would read it as a song and understand a ritual that marked a single woman's transition into marriage.

To see how much translation can change the meaning, feel free to run part of the poem or all of it through an online translator and see what happens. And if you'd like to share your findings, you can post them on my Facebook page (www.facebook.com/loriwolfheffner) or ping me on your tweet (@ltmStraus).

(And for some extra fun, visit Translator Fails on Youtube. She runs well-known songs several times through Google Translate and then sings them.)

ACKNOWLEDGEMENTS

First off, thank you to all who purchased the first book in this series, *Between Worlds I: The Move*. Hearing your feedback helped shape this book.

Next, I'd like to thank the following people for their help and support:

Mom & Dad; Kristin; Deardra King-Leslie; Heather Wright, my consulting editor and writing coach; Susan Fish, my editor; Michelle Fairbanks of Fresh Design, my graphics designer; the Heimatortsgemeinschaft Semlak; Kyle Bergum; Ali MacGee; Donauschwaben Villages Helping Hands; Nick Tullius; Tom Harding and Helena Calogeridis from the Dana Porter Library at the University of Waterloo; and finally, my husband, Corey; and two sons, Khristopher and Jonnathan.

Contrary to popular belief and mythology, books don't get written alone, and without the help of the above people and organizations, this book may have remained little more than an idea in the back of my mind. Thank you for being a part of my journey.

BETWEEN WORLDS 3

THE FIRST STEP

Copyright

© 2019 Lori Wolf-Heffner

All rights reserved. This book or any portion thereof may not be reproduced or used in any manner whatsoever without the express written permission of the publisher except for the use of brief quotations in a book review.

ISBN 978-0-989465-00-4 (Paperback Edition)

ISBN 978-0-989465-01-1 (Ebook Edition)

ISBN 978-0-989465-02-8 (Large Print Edition)

Consulting editing by Heather Wright

Editing by Susan Fish

Cover design by Fresh Design

All photographs from Shutterstock

Head in the Ground Publishing

Waterloo, Ontario, Canada

www.headintheground.com

 Created with Vellum

Dedicated to Peter Tork (1942-2019), who's now stomping his hands and clapping his feet with Davy.

Juliana shook her head as she looked out the window. All that snow from two weeks ago had melted and the dead appearance of winter showed itself everywhere. She checked the weather on her phone: six degrees Celsius.

"I don't know how people here can live like this," she said to herself. "What on earth am I supposed to wear today?"

She looked at the time on her phone, wishing she could call Rachel. But Rachel, back in Calgary, would be asleep.

Juliana turned on some music to lift her mood and to get rid of some of her nervousness: today was her first day of high school in Kitchener. She began shaking out her limbs, the old bungalow's floor creaking beneath her. As the music's energy built up inside her, Juliana danced around her tiny room, calming herself down.

But she couldn't dance in her pyjamas all day. Quickly, she pulled on a pair of jean leggings and a loose, bulky, cream-coloured sweater that reached mid-thigh. She slid in dangling earrings and hung a Fair-trade necklace with large, colourful beads on her neck.

Now for her hair. But would it hold in this weather? Or should she just tie it up? She did a quick French twist across the front and tucked the tail of the twist behind her ear.

"No, that's too formal."

Juliana wrapped her hair into a bun and held it in place with her hand. "No. I already have to wear this for ballet."

She could search for ideas online, but another look at her phone told her she wouldn't have time to learn a new style.

"Maybe I should braid it." Juliana glanced over at the old leather notebook that lay on her night table. It was a collection of drawings Omama—her great-grand-mother—had made almost one hundred years before. In those days, women covered their hair with a *haube*—a white bonnet that fit close to the head—or a head-scarf or both. Girls usually wore their hair uncovered but always braided. "Nope. I don't want to look like I'm a hundred years old either."

She glanced at her phone again. "Rachel, can't you wake up early?"

"Juliana!" Mom called from the kitchen. "Breakfast!"

Only now did Juliana notice her favourite breakfast smell: bacon, hash browns, and eggs.

"Coming!" Juliana turned off her phone, studied her look in the mirror, and whipped her hair up into a ponytail. She could worry about a better hairstyle tomorrow: the day was going to happen whether she wanted it to or not. Miss Kasia, her former dance teacher in Calgary, had always said to just go out and have fun, no matter what.

"I'll certainly try," she said to herself as she headed to the kitchen.

"READY FOR TODAY?" DAD ASKED AS HE HANDED JULIANA her plate: half a grapefruit, four strips of bacon, two hash browns, and a generous helping of scrambled eggs. "Trucker's food," he said with a grin.

When she was young, Juliana would sometimes spend PD days in Dad's truck on short-haul trips. Now that she was fourteen, schoolwork and dance had replaced those days. She also rarely ate truck-stop food anymore: as a competitive dancer, she couldn't afford to eat anything that sapped her of her energy. Dad sometimes brought home some of the wonderfully greasy food anyway, almost like an apology for being away so often. This morning, though, Juliana couldn't tell if Dad was apologizing in advance of his first drive since the family's move across the country, or if he was wishing her good luck for her first day at her new school.

Whatever it was, Juliana wasn't sure her nerves would let her eat. She stared at her plate, though the smells and memories were urging her to shovel it in as fast as possible.

"You have to eat, sweetie," Mom said. "You'll have a hard time getting through the day if you don't." She carried her dishes to the sink.

Today was Mom's first full day at her new job, too. She was a grocery store manager, and although this had been her career for as long as Juliana could remember, it was a new store for her. Was Mom nervous, too? Before Juliana could ask, Mom had already disappeared into the bathroom to finish getting ready.

Once Juliana got the first bite of hash browns down her throat, her stomach settled and she wolfed down the delicious comfort food.

Footsteps coming up the creaky stairs signalled Opa's arrival in the kitchen.

"Oh my," he said. "My kitchen hasn't smelled this wonderful in years!"

"Here you go, Peter," Dad said as he passed Opa a plate.

Opa sat at the spot Mom had just vacated. "Today is your first day of school, right?"

Juliana had stuffed her mouth fuller than a chipmunk's, so she could only nod.

"Are you excited?"

Before Juliana could answer, Mom came rushing back into the kitchen, her coat now in hand.

"I've gotta go," she said. "I don't want to be late." She kissed Juliana on the cheek and Juliana immediately wiped that spot with her sleeve.

"Mom! I'm fourteen!"

"Young girls don't like that," Opa said to his daughter. "Your mom never did that to your sister's kids."

Mom shot them both a look. "Sometimes a mother's love is overflowing. Anyways," she continued to Juliana, "good luck with today. I won't be home until tonight. Anne will be by to cook, okay? But I'll be home in time to take you to dance this evening."

Juliana nodded, and Mom rushed to the landing by the side door and slipped into her boots. "Bye, everyone!" She closed the door behind her.

"I remember my first day of school," Opa said. "I was seven."

Dad, who had been eating at the stove this entire time, said, "Sorry, Peter, but we've got to hurry, too. I have to visit the principal with Juliana, and he asked that we come in before the bell. And since Katy has the car, we're walking."

"Oh, of course," Opa said. His face looked momentarily sad, but he seemed to shake it off. "I'll save the story for later," he said and continued eating.

After breakfast, Juliana brushed her teeth, inspected her school bag to make sure everything was packed neatly in its place, and headed out with Dad.

FIRST PERIOD WAS HALFWAY THROUGH BY THE TIME Juliana and Dad had finished in the principal's office. Mr. B.—that's what he said everyone called him because no one could remember his last name—had reviewed Juliana's next few weeks. Her old school was on a term system, with eight classes for most of the year, but her new one was on a semester system. This created a bit of a bind for Juliana. She would have to study exceptionally hard over the next few weeks so that she could write three exams: physical education & health, French, and art. And to catch up to her classmates who would be writing four exams, Juliana would have to take a class in the summer.

Way to ruin my first summer here, she thought.

Dad left to take a cab to his new trucking company,

and Juliana walked alone to her health class. When she found the right classroom, she stopped outside the door, nervous to the moon and back. *I can't shake it out, I'll look stupid*, she thought, though not being able to move added to her stress. She knew everyone would be staring at her when she entered and that she would have to sit wherever there was an empty desk, meaning there was a good chance she wouldn't be able to hide in the back. She stared at her boots. In her mind, she could hear Rachel encouraging her to just knock and go in. "Sometimes you've just got to deal with it," Rachel would say. "You'll be fine. Don't worry!"

Juliana took a deep breath, knocked, and saw heads turn toward her. She opened the door and stepped inside.

"Juliana?" the teacher asked. "Welcome! I'm Ms. Haseltine."

Juliana couldn't quite tell if Ms. Haseltine was the gym teacher or a young assistant: She didn't look much older than Juliana's cousin Rebecca, and she wore loose-fitting khakis, hiking shoes, a baggy t-shirt, and had her hair pulled up in a ponytail.

Juliana saw the full sea of expressionless faces staring at her. *Crap. Something's wrong with me. My hair?* she thought.

"The class is pretty full, so we just have this one

empty desk." Ms. Haseltine pointed to a desk in the front corner.

"Everyone, this is Juliana Roth. She just moved here from Calgary. Can we give her a big welcome?" Ms. Haseltine could've jumped out of one of those movies about an inspirational teacher who by the end triumphantly reaches even the most delinquent students. But Juliana wasn't at the end of that movie yet—so far the teacher's enthusiasm only made things more awkward.

The class responded with a monotone "hi."

"That wasn't a big hello!" Ms. Haseltine said, the energy in her voice trying to make up for the lack of joy in the class.

"Hi," Juliana said quickly to avoid forcing the class to fake another greeting. She walked across the room to her desk.

"Exam time," Ms. Haseltine said apologetically.

Maybe you're just weird, Juliana thought as Ms. Haseltine returned to her lesson.

Juliana pulled a notebook and pen out of her bag, opened it, and began to take notes. The topics for review today focused on safety and fitness. She hadn't learned much of the content in her health class at her old school, so she scribbled like mad to keep up.

Juliana walked home with her winter jacket open. The wet cold that marked winters in Southern Ontario was uncomfortable, but she had dressed too warmly for today's weather. At least, though, her fingers wouldn't freeze while she talked to Dad.

"I sat alone at lunch," she told him.

"That's normal," Dad replied, his voice tinny on the speaker phone in his truck.

"But couldn't they at least have some kind of student buddy for the day? That's what we always did in Calgary."

She turned down a street. Her school was only a fifteen-minute walk from home, and she was already halfway there.

"So you could be stuck with someone you can't stand? Remember when that happened to Rachel in grade seven?"

Dad had a point. "I guess. But if it was the right person, then I would've had a new friend already."

"Stop worrying about it—this will pass. You're a bright, beautiful, and friendly young lady. You'll find your friends."

"How do you know? You're not a teen."

"Are we starting that again? You act as though your mother and I have forgotten what it was like to be your age."

"It was different back then. You had no Internet."

"We didn't grow up in the Dark Ages, either. We were still teens attending high school. And for the record, I got Internet access when I was sixteen. So, how was the rest of your day?"

"I don't know," she said. "I have so much to learn in only a few weeks." She explained that she had spent the fourth period in what Mr. B. called "credit recovery," where she had to learn whatever she hadn't learned in Calgary in French and art.

"I know you, sweetheart," Dad said. "You'll get through it."

Juliana didn't want to talk about it anymore if all she was going to get was lame attempts at motivation. "Where are you now?" she asked, trying to change the subject.

"Buffalo."

"How far away is that?"

"Just over the border, not quite three hours away. Listen, sweetie, your mom and I care a lot about you. This is just one day out of the next three-and-a-half years. Trust me. You'll find new friends faster than you think."

There was another quiet pause. Juliana hated her dad's job: it kept him away from his family for far too long. This time, he'd be gone for five days.

"I've gotta get going," Dad said. "The traffic is really starting to pile up here. I need to stay focused. But you can call me later, okay? If I can't answer, leave me a message and I'll call you back. Got it?"

"Sure thing," Juliana said.

Dad hung up just as she reached the front door. Day one of her new life was only halfway over. Despite its less-than-stellar beginning, she at least had her evening at the dance studio to look forward to.

CHAPTER TWO

*N*ine-year old Anna stood in the doorway between the kitchen and the front room. "I've scrubbed the potatoes," she said. "Now what?"

Elisabeth rolled her eyes, her back fortunately turned to her sister. She puffed out a sheet over Luki's bed and let it float on to the mattress.

"Peel them," she said, trying hard to sound calm. *Even Jesus couldn't have had this much patience*, she thought.

"And where do I put the peel?"

Elisabeth stamped her foot and turned around, only to catch an evil grin on Anna's face. Her sister, often shy around strangers, and usually preferring a logical answer over an emotional one, was far from a saint when she didn't want to do what she was supposed to do.

Which right now was to make a chicken and vegetable soup for lunch.

"You know *exactly* where to put the peel, and you can take the slop pail out to the animals when you're done. Jesus spared our lives last week. You could at least pretend to be grateful for it!"

Anna assumed a smug look and then sauntered back into the kitchen to continue her work. The year 1920 had had a difficult start for the Schuhmachers: the family had just survived the influenza that was travelling through their Romanian village, though some families were not so lucky and had lost someone, often a young child. Other families were still sick, and there might possibly be still more deaths to come.

After days of washing and scrubbing all the linens by hand, Elisabeth could finally put fresh sheets on their beds in the front room, one of three rooms in their home. In the middle was the kitchen, and on its other side was the back room, the formal room in the house. Built onto the rear of the house was an above-ground cold-storage cellar, followed by the summer kitchen, which had been divided to make room for the family's shoemaking workshop. Behind that were the stalls for the horses and cows, and then came the outhouse.

After she tucked in the sheet on Luki's bed, Elisabeth turned around and caught sight of the figure of Jesus on the crucifix over the door.

"I'm sorry for my anger," she whispered to Jesus. "Thank you for helping us through these tough times."

The house door in the kitchen flew open, letting in a wintry breeze, before slamming shut.

"Elisabeth!" Luki yelled.

Already forgetting her desire to show her siblings more patience, Elisabeth let out an exasperated "What?"

Her young brother stayed standing at the door, remembering not to come in where the snow on his boots would melt into the dirt-and-chaff floor. With their father gone to America to earn money, eight-year-old Luki now spent time every day with Mammi in the workshop, learning how to make shoes.

"Mammi needs food," Luki said. "But just a little."

"Rosina, can you please help Luki? I'm still making the beds."

From where she sat at the table in the front room, trying to knit, Rosina said, "No!" The youngest in the family at only six, she didn't hesitate to refuse her sister's orders. Unlike Anna, who dragged her disobedience out, Rosina simply got straight to the point.

"You've been allowed to knit for the past hour," Elisabeth said. "Now please help your family."

Rosina sighed, threw her single row of knitting onto the table, and stomped into the kitchen.

Elisabeth groaned inwardly at Rosina's reaction as she spread a crocheted blanket and then a down-filled comforter on Luki's bed. She moved to the next bed, reached into an open seam in the mattress, and pushed the straw around to even it out.

Because Herr Blum—Luki and Anna's school teacher—had caught the flu himself this week, Elisabeth would have to manage with all her siblings all day for the week, and it was only Monday morning.

She glanced up again at Jesus. "You will help me, won't You?"

Elisabeth stood at the ceramic washing bowl in the kitchen.

"Just one more trip, please, Anna," she said as she handed Anna the slop pail filled with dirty, soapy water. Anna needed to dump the pail in the pigs' trough and then refill the washing bowl from the well in the yard. "We've only got a few plates left, but the water is too dirty for me to finish them."

Anna dragged her feet over to the door.

"The longer you take, the less time you'll have to do your embroidery."

Anna leaned to one side to compensate for the pail's weight. "Maybe I don't want to do embroidery today!"

Elisabeth rolled her eyes. "Then do something else! But I have to teach you how to iron this afternoon, and then we need to prepare supper. If you want a short break, hurry up!"

Not heeding what Elisabeth said, Anna moved at a snail's pace.

"God will strike you dead by the time you reach the well!" Elisabeth said.

"Anna's going to die?" Rosina cried out from the front room. She burst into tears.

Elisabeth rushed over to her sister and stroked her head. "No, she won't. It's just an expression. Anna will be fine." Then she glowered at Anna, who still stood at the door, wearing a satisfied grin.

Anna finally did move her feet faster, and by the time she returned, Elisabeth had managed to calm Rosina down and to explain that she'd meant Anna would get old and die if she took too long. But judging by the look on her sister's face, Rosina still didn't understand. To distract her instead, Elisabeth asked Rosina to help with the last few dishes.

Elisabeth picked up the bar of soap she had made several weeks before, rubbed it on her washcloth, and washed another plate. She dipped the plate several times to rinse it, trying to keep her hand out of the cold water, and handed it to Anna to dry, who then handed it to Rosina to put away. Within ten minutes, the girls had the remaining dishes finished.

"You can go and do what you choose," Elisabeth said. Their moods instantly changed and they ran into the front room.

Elisabeth dumped the water into the now empty slop pail and washed out the washing bowl with her cloth. Satisfied that everything was in place, she took a short break herself and joined her sisters. Now that she was finally getting used to running the household while Mammi took care of Tata's shoemaking business, Elisabeth could afford to sit down for a few minutes throughout the day and still complete her chores before bedtime.

Rosina had returned to her knitting and Anna had taken up some embroidery. Elisabeth pulled out Tata's letter, which had arrived the week before. The family had waited for almost two months for word of his arrival in America when this letter finally came. Anna asked immediately if Elisabeth could read the letter to them again. Both sisters stopped their handiwork and looked at Elisabeth as she read:

Dear Lissa, Lissika, Anna, Luki, and Rosina,
I have arrived safely in Harrisburg, Pennsylvania. I

have found work in a cigar factory. It stinks so much that I ask the other men I live with to not smoke when I'm home. It's embarrassing to have to make such a request. But the job is a good one and will allow me to save up money for our new roof and, I hope, a dowry for Elisabeth. The days are long, and I'm tired when my shift is over, but I still make and repair shoes. Sometimes it is in exchange for food, but food is also pay, isn't it? I hope to return within a year, as I said before I left. But if that is not possible, then before Elisabeth marries.

May God bless you all,

Your Tata

ROSINA AND ANNA'S EYES WELLED UP. ELISABETH SMILED at them, placed the letter in a special box she kept atop the large cabinet in the front room, and then opened her arms, inviting her sisters into an embrace.

"Tata will be back," she said. "But in the meantime, we must help Mammi as much as we can."

The sisters pulled back, nodded, wiped their eyes, and returned to their activities.

"Rosina, I need the scissors!" Anna shouted at her sister not a minute later.

"I need them! My end is too long and it's bothering me!"

Elisabeth sighed.

"THAT'S RIGHT," ELISABETH SAID TO ANNA AS SHE watched her sister gently push the iron up and down a pair of Luki's pants. "Now, keep that crease flat." Luki's pants, like all men's pants, were made from two widths of linen that had been spun and woven at home. The pants therefore needed several pleats to make them narrower, and it was Elisabeth's job to ensure their creases were clean and crisp.

Someone knocked at the house door and Anna immediately left the iron on the fabric and ran to answer it. Elisabeth sighed as she picked up the iron and placed it on the stove for safety.

Into the kitchen walked Omama, Mammi's mother, and Peter-Bátschi, Mammi's brother.

"Anna, fetch Luki and Mammi," Elisabeth said, and Anna said hello to her grandmother and uncle, slipped on some boots, and ran around the back of the house to the workshop without a complaint.

Of course she does what I ask when an adult is here, Elisabeth thought.

Rosina hid behind Elisabeth's skirt, and peeked out at her grandmother.

Omama was a short, stocky woman. She was among the oldest in the village—in her sixties—a position that was confirmed by her sitting at the front of church every Sunday with other elders. She wore a dress with dark blue fabric covered with a patterned print of tiny ovals. The dress buttoned up the bodice and closed at the base of Omama's neck, and a black apron covered the bottom half. Over her hair she wore a headscarf that tied under her chin, with the edge of her white *haube* just peeking out from underneath.

Elisabeth pulled out a chair for her grandmother to sit on while she removed her boots and put on her house shoes.

The house door opened again as Luki and Mammi entered.

"Where is my little man of the house?" Omama asked.

Luki ran into her open arms.

"I hope you are looking after your family?"

Actually, I *am*, Elisabeth thought.

Luki nodded eagerly. "Mammi's showing me how to make shoes!"

Omama nodded in approval. "You will be a man someday, Luki. It's a shame your father has left at such a time."

Luki frowned.

Was that comment really necessary? Elisabeth thought.

"Modr," Mammi said as she kissed her mother on each cheek. "Peter. What brings you here?"

Only now did Elisabeth notice how embarrassed Peter-Bátschi looked: his cheeks were flushed and aside from quick hellos, he kept his eyes focused on the ground.

"I am tired of picking up after my son and his wife," Omama began. Omama lived with Peter-Bátschi and his family. Her mouth turned upside down and her eyes narrowed into slits as she glared up at her son. "He was at Tiny Hay's on Friday afternoon again and didn't come home until after *I* had fed the animals."

Tiny Hay was the nickname for Hay Heinrich, whose great-grandfather had been a very short man. Hay Heinrich actually had a fairly average build for a farmer, but once a person had been given a nickname by the community, that name would be passed down through the family.

Elisabeth's uncle looked up, though he showed very little confidence. "Tiny Hay was talking about his cousin, one of the two prisoners of war who had just arrived from Russia." Elisabeth had seen the men at church yesterday and had witnessed the tight embraces and numerous kisses they had received before the service. The men looked familiar to her, but she couldn't remember their names. One was missing three-quarters of an arm. Mammi had discreetly slapped Elisabeth on the leg to stop her from staring. The other man had looked healthy. *That must be who*

Peter-Bátschi's talking about, she thought and regretted that she had spent so much time at home that she didn't know what was happening in the village.

Peter-Bátschi's attempt to defend himself was in vain. "You always have an excuse," Omama said. "Last week it was about those whatever-they're-called in Russia."

"Bolsheviks," Peter-Bátschi said.

"What do they have to do with your life?"

"Well, nothing, I suppose, but—"

To Elisabeth's dismay, Omama wouldn't let her son get a word in edgewise. One thing Elisabeth missed about her father's absence was the men's conversations, and it looked like this was as close to one as she was going to get.

"Leave Russia alone, and leave the war alone. I don't need to hear that kind of talk in my house," Omama said.

For a moment, Elisabeth felt pity for her grandmother: Adam-Bátschi and Andreas-Bátschi, two of Mammi's brothers, had died in the war. *I wouldn't want to talk about the war every day either*, Elisabeth thought.

But Omama charged on with her accusations against her son's family. "And your wife? She hasn't cleaned her floor in weeks, won't discipline her children, and insists she's too tired to keep on top of everything." To emphasize her point, Omama let out a quiet grunt.

Peter-Bátschi returned his gaze to the floor.

Omama shook her head. "I have tried and tried to make the children do what I say but no amount of punishment would work with them. And with school cancelled for two of the children, the other two refuse to go, too. It's horrible in that house. There is no respect in that family for the elders!"

Omama's story didn't surprise Elisabeth. She knew her uncle preferred to play *skat*, a card game, and to drink with other men whenever he was home. Over the winter, that was often. She also knew her five cousins to be an unruly bunch. Mammi complained it was because Sophie-Néni didn't discipline them enough and had therefore let the Devil in.

Mammi didn't bat an eyelash. "Make them kneel in the corn," she said matter-of-factly. "Not even Elisabeth's too old for that. She had fallen asleep while looking after the children and then dared speak back at me for demanding too much of her." She nodded in approval at her own decision. "Elisabeth hasn't fallen asleep or spoken back to me since."

Elisabeth's face grew hot. She had been working very hard at that time: helping with wedding preparations for her cousin, guiding her sisters in their chores, caring for Luki while he was sick. She was certain that even Jesus needed rest once in a while.

"That's what I said," Omama said. "I said that my daughter, Lissa, knows how to discipline." She threw an angry glance in her son's direction. "My oldest son—my *only* son now—doesn't and is embarrassing the family." She stood up and hobbled to the kitchen table. "Bring it here," she commanded him.

Peter-Bátschi reached behind the chair and pulled out a small suitcase Elisabeth hadn't noticed. Omama directed him to carry it to the back room, and he obliged.

"I am staying here until that house is cleaned and Peter learns to look after his chores," Omama declared.

Anna and Rosina all stared in fear, something Elisabeth would also have done were it not for her role as their caregiver now. Mammi's face showed little emotion, and Elisabeth tried to copy her. After what Omama had just said, she had to look like she was in control of everyone. Otherwise, she knew, there would be consequences.

CHAPTER THREE

uliana looked at the time on her computer: 5:02. Which meant it was 3:02 in Calgary. Rachel wouldn't be home from school yet.

She stared at her notes. How was she going to get all this information into her head? Her new class had spent the entire month of November learning a mental health unit while she only had two weeks to learn it before the exam.

"This couldn't be more unfair," she said to herself as she began to make study notes from her class notes. Her only other option would be to take two courses during the summer but having to take one was already bad enough.

Juliana opened her great-grandmother's book and

flipped through the drawings. *If only I could dance like she could draw*, Juliana thought. She turned to a drawing near the front again, a picture of the back of an envelope about to be opened. She wondered what could be so important about an envelope that had compelled Omama to draw it.

Slow footsteps down the hallway interrupted her thoughts: Opa was coming. Unlike Mom and Dad, he never knocked before entering her room, but his footsteps always announced his presence.

He poked his head into her room. "Yulika," he said, using his nickname for her. "Annie won't be coming for supper tonight. Sophie and little Scott are both sick. Stomach flu."

Annie was Mom's sister, Aunt Anne to Juliana. Of the three Schuhmacher siblings, she was the one with the big family: six kids.

"That's too bad." Secretly, Juliana half-wished they'd come over so she could catch their bug and have an excuse to not study all this material.

As Opa shuffled back down the hall, Juliana realized that this meant Aunt Anne would not be cooking supper. With Dad away and Mom at work, that left Juliana to prepare the meal. However, of all the tasks Juliana was ever asked to do in the house, the absolute worst was anything in the kitchen. *Or I could study*, she thought.

She stuck her head into the hall. "Opa, I'll cook us something."

Opa turned around and shook his head. "It's all right. I know you have to study. We've got cereal and milk. We'll be fine."

But Juliana knew that one of the reasons the Roths had moved to Kitchener in the first place was that unless Aunt Anne came to cook, Opa would eat only cereal and milk, or summer sausage sandwiches. He had never learned how to cook, not even after Oma had died, and any attempts to hire a meal delivery service had been met with a stubborn refusal. Or so Mom had said. But as soon as they had moved in, Mom had insisted on the service. Aunt Anne offered to continue cooking for another two weeks, allowing Juliana's parents to adjust to their new lives and Opa to adjust to his new cooks. After that, she could focus on her family again.

That didn't help with tonight, though, and Juliana needed something more nutritious than cereal before dance. She closed her laptop and followed Opa out to the kitchen.

"It's time for a break for me, anyway."

"All right. I'll just be downstairs," he said. "I don't want to miss the six o'clock news."

"But Opa, it's just past five."

"All the more reason to hurry. There's this big story

in the newspaper about rubber workers and I don't want to miss it," he said and headed to his room in the basement, leaving Juliana confused. What did the newspaper have to do with missing the news on TV? Or was that just a slip of the tongue? But if it was, was he always this worried about being late for something? Because she didn't know her grandfather well, she had a hard time telling what was dementia and what was just his personality.

Juliana opened the fridge and surveyed her possible ingredients and then checked the freezer, where she found a frozen apple core. Had Opa left it there?

"Now you're being paranoid," she said to herself as she took it out and threw in the green bin. "You've put a box of cereal in the fridge before." But deep down, she wasn't so sure.

BACK FROM DANCE THAT NIGHT, JULIANA AND MOM TOOK their boots off at the landing by the side door.

"I'm sorry," Mom said. "Your first day of school and then you're left to cook on top of that. We should figure out another plan."

"It was just this one evening, no big deal. We had tons of food, so I found something for us." She grabbed an apple and a handful of almonds and sat down at the table. Mom followed suit.

"Listen, Juliana," she said, "I'm afraid much of this week is going to look like today. I'll be home to drive you, but I think I'll be working at least sixty hours this week."

Juliana's shoulders drooped. "Seriously? Your first week on the job and you can't work even just, you know, like regular people?"

Mom put her apple on the table. "The place is an absolute mess. I've got workers who don't care an ounce about their jobs, there was mouldy produce almost everywhere I looked, the floors are dirty because the cleaning company rarely shows up with a full complement of staff, and I found a whole pallet of flour sitting outside. Thankfully, that company knew how to package it so bugs couldn't get in, but no one wanted to move it. So, yes, it's going to be like that."

"Great. So I'm cooking all week? When I have to get ready for exams? I've got so much to learn, I don't know how I'm going to get it all done."

Mom shook her head. "No, of course you're not cooking all week. Stop being so dramatic. I'll use my lunch break tomorrow to bring home some food you can just throw in the oven if Anne can't make it tomorrow or Wednesday. I'm off Thursday, and your dad's back on Friday."

But Juliana knew it wouldn't happen that way. Every time her parents said it would be fine, it wasn't. Too tired to debate it further, though, she grabbed her snack and bag and dragged her tired feet to her room.

"Good night," Mom called after her.

"Yeah," Juliana replied and closed her bedroom door behind her. She looked at herself in her full-length mirror. "I have to go to school, study, dance, and practice. And guess who's also going to have to cook?"

Just then, her phone beeped. She picked it up and let out a little squeal. Rachel!

You forgot to call, Rachel wrote, referring to Juliana's promise from a few days ago.

Sorry! Not my fault. Cousins sick, aunt couldn't cook. Had to make supper for me and Opa. Then dance. Just got home now.

Juliana watched the three dots fade in and out as Rachel typed.

Makes sense. Can you talk now?

No—Mom'll hear me. But I can text.

Kk. How was school?

That was all Juliana needed to unleash a flurry of words to describe in detail how lost she felt.

And it's only day 1 😔

But then Rachel texted exactly what Juliana needed to hear.

Head's up. You've got this.

The two kept texting for almost two hours. By the time they had finished, Juliana felt both better and worse: better because Rachel knew just how to talk to her to make her feel better, and worse because Rachel wasn't in Kitchener. Juliana finally dropped into a deep sleep after midnight, still in her clothes.

ON ONLY SIX HOURS OF SLEEP, JULIANA DIDN'T KNOW IF she was going to make it through the day. As she sat in health class, Ms. Haseltine droning on and on about how to stay safe when practicing sports, Juliana's eyes began to close. The girl next to her kept shifting in her chair, as though she was the princess and the pea was under one of the chair's legs. As annoying as it was to see, the girl's jitters kept Juliana awake, but just barely.

Juliana began doodling in her notebook, unable to focus on the material Ms. Haseltine was teaching.

I am definitely not an artist, she thought as she stared at the grade-two-level stick figure she'd drawn. *That gene did not get passed down to me.* She tried to draw a basic envelope, but her rendition of it looked more like a collection of misshapen triangles instead. Juliana attempted to shade in her lop-sided creation, like Omama had, but nothing she tried could come even close to the envelope depicted in the old book. As her mind drifted off to wondering more about her great-grandmother's life, her head sank onto her arms, the sound of Ms. Haseltine's voice disappearing into the background.

A gentle shaking awoke Juliana, and she lifted her head. The girl sitting next to her smiled.

"Tired?" she whispered.

Juliana looked around. No one was staring at her, but maybe they had already done that. She sat up and then noticed in horror at the little mark of drool on her notebook. She tried to discreetly cover it up, but the girl next to her had probably noticed it. However, the expression on her face told Juliana she wouldn't tell anyone.

Juliana returned to her doodling and head nodding as her brain tried to drag her back to sleep. Today was going to be absolute torture.

Juliana unlocked the door to her home and entered. She couldn't wait to fall into her bed for a nap. She left her boots by the landing and headed up into the kitchen to hang her jacket in the hallway closet.

"Yulika?" Opa called from the basement.

"Yeah?" she replied, hoping Opa wouldn't launch into a long story.

As Opa walked up the stairs, Juliana grabbed herself a tangerine and began to peel it. Opa appeared, a huge smile on his face.

"How was school?"

"Good," she replied, not really wanting to say much else.

"Better than yesterday?"

Juliana shrugged. "Someone smiled at me, so I guess, yeah." She turned around and noticed that Opa's buttons weren't matched to the proper buttonholes, with several holes skipped altogether.

Juliana wasn't sure if she should say something. She didn't want to embarrass Opa, and so long as he wasn't leaving the house, he'd probably be fine. Or would he be embarrassed later after realizing it himself and wondering how long his shirt had been like that? Opa followed her gaze before she could decide what to say.

"Oh, my," he said, somewhat embarrassed, and Juliana blushed, too. "Looks like I had a problem today." He laughed, but it was a laugh Juliana now associated with Opa pretending as though nothing was wrong. She smiled back because she didn't know what else to do.

To her surprise, Opa unbuttoned his shirt right in front of her, revealing his white undershirt. Juliana looked away, unsure if this was part of his dementia or whether he'd just gotten used to dressing anywhere in the house because he had lived alone for so long.

Although she hadn't seen him do this before, it had only been three weeks since the Roths had moved in.

"I'm pretty tired," she said, facing her tangerine. "I had a late night."

"But you haven't told me everything about your day yet. It's nice to hear that someone smiled at you!"

Juliana turned to face Opa again, and this time, his buttons matched up. "Maybe at supper?" she asked. "Please? I really need to sleep."

Opa nodded and Juliana headed back to her room, happy to get out of the awkward situation. Her phone beeped, so she pulled it out of her backpack.

How was today? It was Mom.

Fine, Juliana texted back.

Anything important happen?

Juliana debated whether she should tell Mom about Opa's shirt, but her bed looked so inviting. Even her thumbs felt like five-kilogram weights.

Lots to do. Gotta go.

There was a pause, and them Mom texted, *Ok.*

Juliana set her alarm and tucked herself in.

CHAPTER FOUR

he following morning, Mammi said she didn't need Luki. Elisabeth couldn't very well have him do household chores, but she didn't want him playing while she and her sisters cleaned. If the senior school—the one responsible for grades three to six—was closed for the week, then Elisabeth would have to step in as her siblings' teacher. That would help keep them occupied, sitting at one table for a good hour or two.

"'But when the morning was now come,'" Elisabeth read from the Bible to her siblings in the front room, "'Jesus stood on the shore: but the disciples knew not that it was Jesus.'"

"This is boring," Luki said.

"Would you say that to Herr Blum?" Elisabeth asked.

"You're not Herr Blum," Anna answered. "You're not a teacher. This is boring. I want to embroider."

"I want to knit!" Rosina added.

Elisabeth took a deep breath and let it out slowly while she prayed to Jesus for patience. How was she ever going to make it through this week? "But you need to continue with your schooling. How else are you going to learn to read and do math?"

Omama hobbled out of the back room, dressed in a dark dress with a dainty floral pattern on it, her hair covered by her *haube* and a dark headscarf. She pulled up a chair in the front room and sat down. Shivers ran down Elisabeth's spine.

"Elisabeth," Omama said, "my dress from yesterday needs washing. It's in the back room."

"Yes, Omama. I'll add it my laundry work." Elisabeth turned her attention back to the children. "We're going to continue. This is an important story from the Bible. 'Then Jesus saith unto them, Children, have ye any meat? And they answer him, No.'" Omama's frown had apparently stayed on from last night. Not sure if Omama was displeased with something in particular or everything in general, and too scared to ask lest she was expected to know the answer, Elisabeth continued. "'And he said unto—'"

"I should be helping Mammi," Luki said, his mouth also in a deep frown.

"I need to learn how to knit," Rosina said, her arms crossed.

"And how am I going to be a good wife if I can't embroider?" Anna asked.

Was it just Elisabeth, or were her siblings trying to get out of reading by saying things they knew Omama would like to hear? Elisabeth took another deep breath. Omama was here because of how horrible it was to live at Peter-Bátschi's house, and Elisabeth didn't want to embarrass Mammi by allowing her siblings to be disobedient. She had to keep them under control.

"This story is important," she explained to Anna. "It's about having faith in the Lord."

"But I already have faith," Anna stated.

Luki stood up. "Mammi doesn't read in the workshop, so why do I need to sit here?"

"Because Mammi asked you to," Elisabeth reminded him.

"She didn't say I had to read." He crossed his arms over his chest and turned his lips upside down into a pout.

Omama wagged a finger at Luki. "You listen to your sister."

Elisabeth was shocked. Omama was actually

supporting her decision to make the children sit and learn?

"No!" Luki replied.

Omama's face turned red faster than God struck down people. "Your sister has many faults, but she is in charge of the household."

"I am the man of the house," Luki said. "You even said so yesterday!"

"The man of the house knows when to listen to his wife. You don't have one, and your mother is working, so that person is your sister."

It wasn't about reading, Elisabeth now realized. It was about listening to her.

Impatient and now angry, Luki dashed for the kitchen but came too close to Omama. She grabbed him by the arm and gave him a strong wallop on the bottom. Luki immediately began to cry.

"That is how you make your siblings behave," Omama instructed Elisabeth.

Tears streaming down his face, Luki slumped back into his chair. Elisabeth reached out to him, but Omama tapped the table to get her attention.

"You are in charge of this household," she said. "You are not his friend. Now, continue with your reading."

Elisabeth glanced at Anna and Rosina, who both looked scared. Elisabeth hoped they knew she would never do that to them, just like she could never spank

Luki, no matter how disobedient he was. Something inside her told her that Jesus wouldn't do that, either.

THE REST OF THE MORNING PASSED WITH HARDLY A word exchanged between the children for fear of any kind of reprisal from Omama. Elisabeth had finished teaching their lessons and even had time to show Luki how to polish shoes, though she had to make it very clear that he only had to do this when he finished making them, and not when the family prepared to leave the house. That was a woman's job. She also helped Rosina with her knitting and explained a new embroidery stitch to Anna.

After lunch, Omama retreated to the back room to lie down on the guest bed for a rest. Luki had gone out in the workshop with Mammi, who had worked through lunch to keep up with her orders. Anna stood at the washing bowl to wash the dishes while Rosina dried them. Elisabeth wrapped cloths around a plate of hot food to keep Mammi's lunch warm. She knew Mammi would ask how the animals were so before she took the food to Mammi, she stopped to check on them first.

Elisabeth started with the poultry yard beside the

house, which included coops for chickens, geese, and ducks. One of the ducks looked nicely fattened.

"I'll be out for you later," she said to it.

She passed the wagon shed and *hambar*, a structure that was used to store dried corn, to reach the pigpen. As she turned to leave for the horse and cow stalls, a glint of something caught her eye.

"What's that?" she asked herself and looked closer. Several nails lay on the ground in the pigpen, where the pigs could step or roll on them. Elisabeth slid her arm between the boards, but she couldn't quite reach the nails. She pushed her hand in farther, lost her balance, and fell into the boards. A creak and then a light snap told her something wooden had broken.

"Oh no!"

She reached the nails, pulled her arm back, and saw that the wood on the rail had splintered and that a long, deep crack now travelled down the board. Further inspecting the damage, she discovered where the nails had come from. She tried to check all six pigs, looking for any wounds. To her relief, she found none.

"If that isn't repaired soon, the pigs could break out," she said aloud, looking at the damaged boards.

A pig oinked in response.

She quickly checked the horse and cow stalls in the main barn, adding water to the trough, throwing hay into the horses' and cows' enclosures. She hurried back and picked up Mammi's lunch and then carried it into Tata's workshop. Luki looked up when she entered.

"How are the animals?" Mammi asked, not looking up from her work. Her voice sounded unusually tired. Was Omama's stay already too much for her? Elisabeth could certainly understand that.

"Fine," Elisabeth blurted out as she set the plate down. "But we have a problem."

"Oh?" Mammi still didn't look up.

Elisabeth told her what had happened.

"I'm sorry," Elisabeth finished. "I didn't want to waste time getting those nails out, so I reached in, and that's when I stumbled and broke the boards."

Mammi waved a hand at Elisabeth. "Yes, you need to be more careful, but Elisabeth, there is no way your stumbling would have damaged them so much unless they were already nearly broken."

Elisabeth breathed a sigh of relief. For once something wasn't her fault.

"But we need someone to repair them," Mammi declared.

"I can't fix it," Luki said, "because Tata never showed me how to do that."

The tone in her brother's voice angered Elisabeth: Luki was using Tata's absence as an excuse to not help out. Mammi heard it too, judging by the look on her face. She stood up from her chair at the workbench, grabbed a scrub brush, dunked it in a small pail of water she kept in the workshop, and pushed it into his hand.

"Then make yourself useful and clean up the workbench," she said. "I want this spotless by the time I return."

Luki's eyes widened in surprise and he immediately set to work while Mammi followed Elisabeth out to the stalls to take a look.

ELISABETH CARRIED A BOWL OF BOILED POTATOES TO THE kitchen table, where Omama, Mammi, and Luki already sat waiting for supper. Anna set the table and then took her seat, rocking her chair as she waited, while Rosina carried over cheese, bread, and butter before kneeling on her chair. All that was needed was the duck, which Elisabeth now pulled out of the oven and set on some tea towels in the middle of the table.

"Elisabeth, get me some water," Omama said, and Elisabeth obliged.

Just as Elisabeth was about to sit down, Mammi instructed her to carve the duck and serve everyone.

"But you're the head of our household," Elisabeth said, confused.

"And I've worked hard enough outside. Or are you

suggesting that you work harder in here?" Mammi's accusation took Elisabeth aback. She had meant no such thing: she was just confused by the change of routine. But without saying another word, she carved the duck, placed a slice on each person's plate, and helped her siblings cut their portions.

"Mammi, I want school to start again," Anna said, rocking on her chair.

"Psht!" Mammi said. "You do not speak at the table! And sit like a woman."

Anna looked down at her plate of food. Elisabeth began slicing her own duck. Then Luki spilled his glass of water. Elisabeth raced to the back room to get tea towels and returned to find Anna rocking again.

"Anna, stop it." Why wasn't she listening? There were adults in the room. Or was she trying to get her older sister in trouble?

"It's your job to discipline her," Omama said. "You are in charge."

Elisabeth prayed that Anna would listen to her and avoid forcing an uncomfortable confrontation between Elisabeth and their grandmother. She dried Luki's spill and sat down, hoping to finally start eating, only to catch Rosina trying to pour water from the water jug. Fearing another accident, Elisabeth helped her.

"Aaahhh!" Anna screamed as her chair tipped back.

Anna's head hit the ground, and Elisabeth immediately rushed to help her sister up.

"If you had sat like a woman," Mammi said, "this wouldn't have happened."

Omama nodded in agreement. "You should have listened to your mother." Neither got up to help, and Elisabeth wondered how their words helped at all. She didn't know the Bible off by heart, of course, but she could not think of a single passage where Jesus spoke that way. And was it not a Christian's duty to be like Him?

So far as Elisabeth could tell, though, Anna hadn't heard a word of it: she was wailing.

"Shh," Elisabeth said to her sister as she helped her up. "Eat the rest of your food. You'll feel better soon."

Still sniffling, Anna nodded while Elisabeth placed her chair back at the table. Anna sat down and picked at her food.

"That is no way to teach her," Omama said. "She'll only do it again."

Elisabeth's shoulders tensed. Why on earth would Anna rock her chair again after such a fall? Even if she did, a gentle reminder about her fall should be enough to deter her the next time. Elisabeth sometimes wondered if adults really did understand children the way they said they did.

Another string of requests from everyone, though,

meant that by the time Elisabeth finally sat down to eat, everyone else had finished their meal. Elisabeth often counted on her meals as breaks from her endless list of chores. Hopefully Omama and Mammi would give her enough time to eat.

"Anna, Rosina, go into the front room and work on your projects. Luki, try not to be a nuisance," Mammi instructed.

"He can practice polishing shoes," Elisabeth offered.

Mammi raised her eyebrows. "A very good idea, Lissika. Luki, continue with your practice."

Luki sulked, but one look from Omama wiped it off his face. The three younger siblings disappeared into the warm room of the house and Mammi closed the door behind them.

Elisabeth's heart started to race. Had she done something wrong? Said something to embarrass her mother? Insulted Omama in some way?

Mammi stood with her back to the door and looked Omama in the eye. Elisabeth didn't think her heart could race any faster.

"We need to talk about your future," Mammi began. Elisabeth kept eating. "You turn fifteen this summer. It's time we start finding you a husband."

Elisabeth's hand with its forkful of duck froze halfway along its path to her mouth. *A husband? Am I ready for one already?*

"You still have much work to do," said Omama. "You need to stop speaking up like you do, especially the way you did at church on Christmas Eve. The Bible says, 'Let your women keep silence in the churches: for it is not permitted unto them to speak; but they are commanded to be under obedience, as also saith the law.'"

Upon hearing that verse, Elisabeth bristled. "But Krehling Maria and Wagner Anna were speaking up at a time when it was wrong to do so."

Omama wagged her crooked finger at Elisabeth. "That is for Jesus to judge, not you."

But Mammi had approved Elisabeth's speaking up: the other women had been criticizing Pastor Fröhlich's preference for Hungarian as the language of worship in the church and of instruction in the schools, though the children currently learned in Romanian as the new laws dictated. Christmas Eve was an inappropriate time to discuss such topics. Was Elisabeth supposed to stay silent and let those women disturb the sanctity of the church with a political discussion?

"Modr, Elisabeth still has much to learn," Mammi said, clearly not taking either side, at least not in front of her mother. "She has at least two years to find someone, and I will help her learn what she still needs to know."

Omama nodded and broke off a piece of bread from

the loaf that still sat on the table. "Does that mean she'll learn to stop smiling so much?"

Omama's question angered Elisabeth, but she swallowed her words. Her mother had told her in the past to smile less, because otherwise people would think she looked stupid. *But smiling means someone is happy and enjoying what Jesus has blessed them with. Why should I not show that?*

"You must always be on your best behaviour," Omama said. "Just like your husband must respect you, you must respect him, and that means learning your role in the family."

Elisabeth smiled at Omama, who scowled back. Even Mammi shot her oldest child a look of mild scorn.

"Now," Mammi said, "we've invited someone to tea tomorrow to discuss the pigpens. I expect you to be polite to him."

Maybe Mammi meant it would be a young man. Elisabeth nodded.

"Good. Get your sisters and begin cleaning up the kitchen," Mammi commanded. "Luki and I will head back to the workshop."

Mammi believed Elisabeth was ready to marry and receive her *haube*, and to have a family. Elisabeth smiled, jumped up from her chair, and called her siblings. Excitement filling her soul, she ignored Omama's comments about smiling.

CHAPTER FIVE

uliana wiped the sweat from her brow as she and the rest of her tap group headed to the change room after a particularly intense practice.

"You all right?" Jasmine asked Juliana. "You were completely distracted in class there."

Juliana couldn't argue with her: she had forgotten parts of the choreography she and Jasmine had practiced last weekend, before school had started, and Miss Denise had had to repeat herself several times during the past two hours. Juliana knew she had a long road ahead of her to catch up to the calibre of her new team, but she was failing miserably at it today.

"Life's just really crappy right now," she confessed. "My grandfather's acting weird and my dad's on the road until Friday. My aunt was supposed to cook for us last night but she couldn't, so I had to, and Mom's hardly home right now, too, and to top it all off, I've got to catch up on half a year's work within a couple of weeks."

When the entire group grabbed water and snacks and headed to the homework room, Jasmine held Juliana back.

"Listen. It sounds like you've got a lot going on, but the more energy you waste brooding about it, the worse it's going to get."

Jasmine's comment took Juliana aback. "I'm not brooding," she insisted. "We moved in with my grandfather to look after him, and I'm scared I'm the one who's actually going to be stuck with that job. I've never had this much schoolwork before, I'm the worst dancer on the team—don't try and tell me otherwise —and I feel like I'm completely alone here in all of this."

"What does complaining do about it?" Jasmine asked. "Either get help and fix it or stop brooding. You're not going to get through this if you complain all the time."

Now Jasmine thoroughly confused Juliana. She could be super-friendly one moment, and mean the next. Couldn't she show at least a little understanding?

"Well, it's tough and I need to talk about it to someone," Juliana said, defending her position. "I feel like I'm going to explode."

Jasmine picked up her snack, water, and schoolbooks and opened the door. "Then you'd better find a way to deal with it, because you've only got only a few weeks to do all that studying and if you explode before then, you'll fail on all fronts." She left. Juliana stood frozen to the floor in astonishment.

"Something wrong?" Mom asked as Juliana silently slipped into the car.

Juliana threw her bag into the back and strapped on her seatbelt without speaking.

"Well?" Mom said, looking over her shoulder as she backed out.

"It's nothing."

Mom shot her a concerned look before pulling out of the parking lot. "I know that tone of voice. It's not nothing."

Dance had felt particularly punishing, leaving Juliana with little energy to even begin to tell Mom about everything going wrong in her life. Add to that Jasmine's comments, and Juliana really wasn't in the mood for talking.

When they stopped at the intersection at the end of

the short street, Mom studied Juliana. Once the road was clear, she turned out onto the main street. "I can tell something's bothering you. I know I've been really busy with work, but I've got time now. What's up?" Mom turned on her blinker, checked her rearview mirror, and pulled into the left-hand lane. "Is it school? Dance? Tata?"

"How about all of the above?" The words fell out of Juliana's mouth before she could clamp it shut. *Great. Now she's going to dig*, Juliana thought.

"I see. Okay, let's start with school. What's wrong there?"

Juliana adjusted her position in her seat. The tone in Mom's voice suggested she wasn't taking her seriously, but now that the conversation had started and Juliana was stuck in the car with her, she might as well say something.

"I don't know if I can handle all the work."

Mom stopped at a red light and faced Juliana. "You know how to organize yourself, so that's just what you'll have to do. You'll be fine."

"What if I don't know everything?"

"How can you know everything? Your father and I knew these three weeks weren't going to be easy, but we also knew you would pull through. If your marks drop a bit, it's fine. I promise we won't be angry with you."

Juliana had always maintained a ninety-percent

average since percentages had first appeared on her report cards. She wasn't going to let this move hold her back from keeping that streak. How could Mom not understand how important this was to her? "Couldn't we have waited to move until I started grade ten?"

The light turned green.

"This job opened up for January, not July. And the pay is really good. We didn't know if another opportunity like this would come up again."

"Did you plan on leaving me alone at home a lot?"

Mom's voice got tense. "That's not fair. I knew the situation at the store was bad, but I didn't know how bad it was. We need to earn money, and if I don't turn things around, I won't have a job. Unlike school, where you can fail and still move forward, if you fail at your job, you get fired."

What was that supposed to mean? Just because Juliana would still go to grade ten regardless of her marks didn't mean her life was somehow easier. And why was money so important? What happened to all the money they would've gotten from selling everything? Surely her parents must have a stash of it in the bank now.

"But you sold our house and Dad's truck back home! Where did that money go? That was over half a million at least!"

Another red light. Mom hit the brakes hard, and both she and Juliana lurched forward.

"Just because you're fourteen doesn't mean you know everything," Mom seethed. "That includes our financial situation. Do you know how much of our mortgage we still had to pay off?"

Juliana had seen the price of the house online, and although she didn't know how much her father's truck sold for, she knew it wasn't pennies. But she hadn't thought about debt.

"No," she said meekly.

"Your father and I bought that house as an investment and we owed about two-thirds of its value when we sold. So that went to the bank. And then there's putting money away for Tata's care, because his employer went bankrupt when you were still young, so all three of us are contributing what we can, because we know the day will come when he needs more help than we can give him. And then we're also saving for university for you. Ontario is more expensive than any other province, and your education is going to cost us a lot. Then there's your dance lessons, income taxes, utilities, food, the cleaners...need I go on?"

Juliana sank down in her seat as far as her seatbelt would allow. "No."

"Good." The light turned green. "And before you make another accusation like that at me, *think* first!"

It would have helped if you'd told me all this earlier, Juliana thought.

THE NEXT DAY OF SCHOOL WASN'T MUCH OF AN improvement, and Juliana's new knowledge about her family's financial situation weighed heavily on her. But by the time she got home, she admitted to herself that she was tired of every day dragging down her spirits. Miss Kasia's words came back to her: *Just go out and have fun, no matter what.*

"To which Rachel would tell me now to just listen to Miss Kasia," Juliana said out loud. She smacked herself in the forehead. "Great. Now I'm having conversations with myself." But maybe lightening up a little would help her. She unlocked the side door to Opa's house, vowing to leave her stress on the driveway.

"I'm home, Opa!" she called down the stairs as she took off her boots. The door to his bedroom squeaked open and he appeared at the bottom, properly dressed. He walked upstairs as Juliana headed into the kitchen. He had had no problems conversing that morning, had put everything in its spot, and had even avoided starting any long stories while the rest of the family was in a hurry to get out the door. And now, Juliana couldn't see any signs that he was having any difficulties. If those issues before were just memory blips, then they couldn't have been serious ones. *And maybe that's just what he's like*, she thought.

She tossed her bag into her room before coming back for a snack. She poured a glass of water, found a tangerine, and sat down.

"How was today?" he asked.

"The best day so far," she said and then took a sip. "Still no one to eat with. My phys ed teacher is a bit weird, but I think I'm getting used to her. How about you?"

"Mine was *besser als sonst*," he replied. After seeing the look of confusion on her face, he said, "Sorry. Sometimes it just slips out. Your mother's used to it." Was mixing languages another sign of his dementia? "And before you think it's because of my brain, it's not," he said, as though he could read her mind. "If you came out to the German club, you'd hear all of us older folks talking Denglish."

"Talking what?" Now he was making up words?

"Denglish. *Deutsch* plus English. Denglish."

Juliana nodded. It sounded plausible, though a bit strange. "So, what did you say?" she asked and took another sip of water.

"My day was better than usual. Doctor called today and said my urine test came out fine again."

Juliana choked on her water, and Opa's expression turned to one of concern.

"Are you all right?" He patted her on the back, and she waved her hand, signalling she didn't need the assistance.

"I'm fine, Opa. That's, um, just not the kind of thing you talk about with grandkids."

Opa patted her on the back again, but this time in a friendly manner instead of a lifesaving one. "You'll realize when you get old that there are some things you don't care about anymore, like table manners, and some things you do, like getting tested for diseases that old people get."

Juliana couldn't help but smile. "But I still care about table manners, Opa."

After her snack and a little more chitchat with her grandfather, Juliana returned to her room, feeling a bit happier. She pulled out her French books, but as she studied her irregular verbs, her mind kept wandering back to Opa and the symptoms she'd witnessed over the past few weeks. For example, he sometimes abruptly ended their conversation because he remembered something. And there was that one time he thought he was back in Semlak and told Juliana she needed to start looking for a husband because she was fourteen. Now the shirt and the apple core...Juliana's concerns distracted her enough that she eventually went online to look up Opa's symptoms. The more she read, the more concerned she became.

"This can't be right," she said to herself. "I have half the symptoms myself: forgetting, having a hard time learning stuff..." She looked at the clock on her laptop screen. "Heck, I can't even concentrate to learn the new stuff and remember it, and I know I've misplaced things. How is that any different from Opa?"

A knock at the side door to the house interrupted her thoughts and her attempt at studying. As she stepped out of her room, she heard Opa greeting Aunt Anne, Dean, and Charlie. Dean was exactly Juliana's age, but they had very little if anything in common, and Charlie was three years older and almost finished high school.

Juliana was shocked to see Charlie wearing a sleeveless basketball jersey.

"Aren't you cold?" she asked.

"No," he replied and traipsed into the kitchen. The weather was certainly warmer winter weather than Juliana was used to, but even she wore long sleeves or a sweater.

"Stomach bug over," Aunt Anne announced. "Rebecca's cooking for Tony and Scott, and the three of us are tonight's cooking brigade!"

Juliana was relieved to not have to cook or eat the packaged junk Mom had brought home.

"Where's Sophie?" she asked.

Aunt Anne handed Juliana her coat. "At climbing lessons. There's no snow outside, so she can't go skiing."

"There's nowhere to ski here, snow or no snow," Juliana said.

"There's Chicopee," Aunt Anne replied.

"The garbage dump Mom told me about?"

Aunt Anne laughed. "No, but everyone thinks that. The garbage dump is where Tata used to take us to go sledding: Mount Trashmore. Remember that, Tata?"

"What was that?" he asked.

"Mount Trashmore," Aunt Anne said.

Opa still looked confused.

Semlak had about five thousand people living in its streets: Romanians, Germans, Slovaks, Jews, Gypsies, Serbians, and a few other groups. From those, the Christian population worshipped at one of five churches: Greek Catholic, Roman Catholic, Orthodox, Calvinist, and Lutheran, the latter two being dominated by the Germans in the village. The Lutheran church had over a thousand congregants, and the Calvinist church several hundred. Everyone usually stayed with their own kind, meaning everyone in the church knew almost everyone else in the church.

And so it happened that Sophie-Néni's brother, Hagel Samuel, and his son, Konrad, appeared at the Schuhmacher door, offering to fix the pigpen for them. Hagel Samuel, whose first wife had died not long before

Christmas after falling through the ice that covered the Marosch River, had recently married a war widow, Kaiser Theresia. The Hagel household had several daughters and had lost two sons to the war. Konrad was the only son left now.

As Elisabeth looked at Konrad, she remembered her conversation with Mammi and Omama. *It's time we start finding you a husband*, Mammi had said. Judging by the giddy looks on her siblings' faces, Elisabeth wondered if they had overheard the conversation yesterday.

Konrad had almost-black hair and deep, brown eyes. He was like any other boy: he hung out with his group of friends and was teased by the older boys when he was young, teased the younger boys when he was older, and eventually had begun learning his father's trade: carpentry. Elisabeth knew that marrying a carpenter, or even a wainwright, would ultimately mean less work for her. On the other hand, because Konrad was the only son in the family now, marrying him would mean moving in with his parents after the ceremony. However, that also meant they would inherit the home when her in-laws passed away. As she weighed her options with Konrad, she decided he was certainly worth getting to know more.

"Welcome, Herr Hagel," Elisabeth said, "and Konrad. Please, come in." She smiled at them gently, in part because she believed Jesus would want it, and in part because Omama was sitting in the front room with the rest of the family and couldn't see her face.

The father and son removed their hats and stamped the snow off their boots. Elisabeth offered them rags to dry them.

"Thank you," Herr Hagel replied. Konrad also thanked her and smiled at Elisabeth, leaving her with a good first impression. Both men followed Elisabeth in to the front room where everyone else was sitting. The table was decked out in a linen tablecloth Elisabeth had woven a couple of years before, covered by a crocheted runner that had been passed down through Mammi's family. Elisabeth had baked cookies earlier that day—Mammi and Omama had agreed today's visit was a good reason to do so—and they were arranged decoratively on a silver platter, while hot tea steeped in the porcelain teapot. Although the butter cookies were simple circles, Elisabeth had iced them with exquisite floral designs.

"Thank you for coming," Mammi said as the cookies and tea were passed around. "Without my husband here, and with no older boys, managing some of the duties around the house has become hard."

Herr Hagel took a sip of tea. "We're happy to help. Anything you need done, Frau Schuhmacher, please just let us know. Women shouldn't have to take on their husband's work. If you can make some of your goulash while we're here, that will be more than enough payment."

Mammi looked at Elisabeth when she answered. "Because I now look after my husband's shoemaking business, Elisabeth is in charge of the household. It'll be her goulash you'll be tasting."

Konrad made eye contact with Elisabeth, and she smiled back. She offered him the platter of cookies, and he put several on his plate.

"I'll fix your pigpen for you," he said, raising his chest a little.

"Thank you." Elisabeth took a sip of her tea and watched as Konrad threw a cookie into his mouth without so much as noticing her work. "I made the cookies, too," she added.

"They're tasty," Konrad replied, and threw another one into his mouth. His mouth full, he asked, "Have you heard from your father?"

Elisabeth nodded. "He had to find work in a cigar factory, but he said the job is good."

Konrad swallowed. "That must be terrible, being cooped up inside all day like that. No sunlight, no fresh air."

Elisabeth's spirits dropped. She hadn't thought of that. Tata had written about the smell of cigars, but nothing about the work conditions otherwise. No matter the weather, Tata always left the door to his small workshop open to let in fresh air. During harvest season, he helped outside like almost everyone else, and he would get out of his workshop during the day to join the family for meals. Even when Elisabeth's own days were filled, she still had opportunity to go outside. The warmth of the sun on her face would almost feel as though Jesus were talking to her, while the cold chill of the wind helped her focus again on her duties.

"He's doing it to help his family," Elisabeth said.

"Something all men should do," Konrad replied.

Elisabeth took another sip of her tea. "It's something I appreciate."

Konrad smiled at her.

Anna snickered.

Luki kicked Elisabeth's leg.

Rosina ate a cookie as her eyes darted questioningly between her sister and Konrad.

Ignoring her siblings, Elisabeth smiled back.

THE BLOWING SNOW OUTSIDE THAT EVENING MADE Elisabeth shiver, even though she and her family were sitting inside, sharing the warmth that came from the back side of the stove in the front room.

"No, Anna. Pull out the thread and do that stitch again. It's uneven," Omama said. Anna slouched as she unthreaded her needle and pulled the stitch from her embroidery. Elisabeth looked on with a twinge of jealousy: Anna was constantly praised by Herr Blum for her attentiveness in school. All the adults she encountered remarked at how obedient she was and gently laughed at the simple logic with which she sometimes answered questions. But if Elisabeth asked her to do something and no adults were around, there was a good chance Anna would defy her.

"Let me try!" Rosina insisted as she pulled her knitting back from Elisabeth's hands. Unlike Anna, Rosina didn't pay attention to who was in the room: if she didn't like something or wanted something that she was refused, she said so, and loudly.

Ignoring Omama's warning look, Elisabeth answered her sister, "I'm only trying to help. If you insist on doing it yourself, then fine, but it'll take you longer."

"I want to do it myself!"

Elisabeth shook her head in surrender.

"Rosina," Omama said in a warning tone.

"Please," Rosina replied, and Omama nodded in approval.

"Elisabeth, they will not respect you if you allow that kind of talk," Omama said.

Aware of Mammi's watchful gaze, Elisabeth had to

think quickly of what to say. She disagreed with Omama, but she did not want to insult her either.

"I guess I'm too tired this evening," Elisabeth replied, and watched both Omama's and Mammi's faces turn upside down.

"A wife works from the moment she opens her eyes in the morning to the moment she closes them at night," Omama said. "Without a strong wife, a family is nothing. Just look at what my son's family has become." Thankfully, Anna had done something that now impressed Omama, for Omama returned her attention to her. "Yes, beautiful, Anna. Do another stitch just like that one." Anna flicked Elisabeth a smug smile and Elisabeth rolled her eyes. Mammi returned to her knitting, seemingly oblivious to the exchange.

With everyone occupied—Luki was sitting near the stove, using a rubber ball to knock down a group of dried corn cobs that had been cut in half—Elisabeth retrieved a few sheets of paper and a pencil to write a letter to Tata. The straw of her mattress crunched as she sat on her bed, away from the prying eyes of her family. Although the light from the lanterns on the table was thin, she could see enough to write.

February 18, 1920

Dear Tata,

Omama is staying with us. She says it's because Peter-Bátschi's family doesn't show her any respect.

I have been having problems with the others: Herr Blum is ill this week, so school is closed. Monday was horrible. They wouldn't listen to me. I think the only reason they listen to me sometimes now is because of Omama. She spanked Luki, and since then, I've had fewer problems with the others whenever she is around.

All of us, except Mammi, had the flu a few weeks ago. God took several children to Him through it, but He let us live this time. We also recently learned that two POWs returned from Russia. The war has been over for more than a year now. How many more POWs can there still be?

Cousin Susi is married, so Margarethe-Néni and Konrad-Bátschi now live at home with only Georg and Eva.

Some boards in the animal stalls have begun to splinter and loosen. Omama told Mammi to ask Hagel Samuel and his son, Konrad, to help. Omama and Mammi want to start finding me a husband—they said so! I'm excited and scared. Scared, because I don't know what my future will be. Excited because I will be able to start my own family and also because the earlier I marry, the sooner you will come home.

I have a question to ask you, Tata, but I'm scared of the answer. You wrote about how bad the smell in the *cigar factory is, but Hagel Konrad said you also don't have any fresh air or sunlight. Is that true? Does that mean your work days are very hard? If they are, then I will pray even harder to Jesus that your job becomes easier for you.*

I have only drawn a few pictures in the sketchbook you bought me: I am so busy here that I hardly have time to draw at all. But I am trying to find time to at least draw the most important things in it.

I miss you, and I hope you stay safe.

Love,

Your Golden One

Elisabeth reread her letter and, satisfied with it, folded it up. Luki's little ball rolled across the floor to her. As she bent over to pick it up, the letter dropped out of her lap. Luki snatched it up.

"Give that back!" Elisabeth said.

"What does it say?" He unfolded it and cocked his head to the side as he tried to decipher the words. "I can't read it."

"If you would pay more attention in class and to me, you might be able to. Now, give it back."

"No!"

Dismayed, Elisabeth stood up and Luki shot into the kitchen.

"Luki!" Omama shouted and banged the table. "Return that letter to your sister at once!"

Luki froze and turned around, fear in his eyes.

"At once, I said," Omama repeated, her voice stern. As Luki walked slowly back to the front room, Omama said to Elisabeth, "*That* is why you spank them."

Elisabeth sighed. She almost wished Luki hadn't listened to their grandmother.

CHAPTER SEVEN

It was Friday morning, the last day of her first week at Eby Heights, and Juliana couldn't be happier. It was first period, enough to make any student complain, but she had figured out a way to schedule her studying for the next couple of weeks so she could cover everything she needed to learn. She had to admit that Jasmine was right again: once she stopped focusing on everything going wrong, Juliana could move ahead in her plans. Unfortunately, it meant she couldn't spend as much time practicing, but for now she didn't have a choice. Competition season didn't start until late February for her new studio, so Juliana would have lots of time to practice afterwards. She just needed to get through this month.

Ms. Haseltine asked everyone to partner up, leaving

Juliana in the awkward position of having to wait for someone to choose her. She soon realized that the class had an odd number of students, leaving her with no partner at all. To her relief, the girl beside her, whose name Juliana had finally learned, invited her to join in.

"It's gotta suck not knowing anyone," Meghan said.

"Yeah, pretty much," Juliana replied.

"This is Shawna." Meghan indicated a girl with brown hair and green eyes sitting next to her.

"Hi," Juliana said, happy to finally *meet* people. Shawna looked at her without speaking.

Meghan flipped her pencil through her fingers. "Don't worry about her. She's just quiet."

Ms. Haseltine assigned each group a subject in health studies and asked them to create a list of questions that could be on the exam.

A boy in the next group scoffed. "She probably wants us to come up with the questions for her."

"No, Bradley," the teacher said. "The exam's already been written. I want you to put yourselves in my shoes and figure out the questions. We'll compile a list at the end of class and then you'll all have something to study from."

Another student objected to the exercise and Juliana became impatient. She just wanted to start working: her study schedule had very little wiggle room if she was going to cover everything, and every minute she could use in class was one minute extra at home she could devote to reviewing something else. If her group actually finished their questions early, she could even begin answering the ones she knew the answers to.

Juliana's group was asked to prepare questions on social factors for substance abuse. Juliana opened her binder, which was filled with handouts Ms. Haseltine had given her earlier in the week, and began searching for the topic.

"I'm going to go sharpen my pencil," Meghan said and got up.

"Um, where should we start?" Juliana asked Shawna.

"Doesn't matter," Shawna replied as she began to write down one question after another.

"Do you have this material already memorized?" Juliana asked.

Shawna's only response was a shrug, but as Juliana watched Shawna, she got her answer: yes. By the time Meghan returned, Shawna had already written down five questions. Meghan didn't give Shawna's work a glance, but instead sat down, licked the tip of her pencil, and opened her binder, only to have a chunk of papers slide out and onto the floor.

Juliana was helping Meghan pick up the papers when an idea came to her out of nowhere. "War," she said. "War could be a factor in substance abuse."

"That's not in the material," Shawna said matter-of-factly.

"It's still a social situation. I think, anyway. Just think of what someone sees if they go to war: dead people, people being killed. It can't be easy to come back."

"No different than watching TV," Meghan said.

"No, I think it's pretty different. You can shut off the TV and get back to your normal life. Soldiers can't turn off the war." Juliana raised her hand and asked Ms. Haseltine if war was a possible social cause for substance abuse.

"You know what? I'd really never thought of that before. What made you think of it?"

"I don't know." Juliana paused for a moment. "I guess my grandfather. He told me about a cousin of his who fought in World War I and had what I think would now be called PTSD. I don't know if he drank or took drugs or anything, but apparently everyone made fun of him. That makes it a social situation, doesn't it? I can see it being a problem when thousands of soldiers come back from war and can't cope."

"That's great thinking," Ms. Haseltine said, "but because we didn't cover it in class, it may not help you with the exam."

Juliana felt dejected. She finally thought she knew something. However, Ms. Haseltine had said "may not..." not wouldn't.

Ms. Haseltine walked over to another pair to answer their question.

"War should be an answer," Juliana said.

"I also think I should be the one to win the OFSSA one-hundred-metre swim," Meghan said, "but I won't if I don't do exactly as my coach tells me to."

She had a point. "What questions do you suggest?" Juliana asked.

By now, Shawna had at least fifteen written down, but she didn't look inclined to share them with the group.

"How do friends make you take drugs or drink?" Meghan offered.

"Sounds good."

"Where are you from again?" Meghan asked as they wrote it down.

"Calgary."

Meghan looked up, excited. "Oooh...I'd love to live out there. Those mountains are so awesome. My dream is to swim in a glacier lake at some point."

"Those are cold, you know."

"Yeah, but that's the cool part, no pun intended. I've always imagined that swimming in that clear mountain water has got to be the most amazing experience."

"Meghan," Ms. Haseltine called. "Focus, please."

"Okay," Juliana said. "How about...What do you do when your friend is drunk?"

Meghan and Juliana both wrote it down.

"So what was it like moving here?" Meghan asked.

"Honestly, it's kind of depressing. It's so flat, and there are so many trees, you can't see the horizon. And it's so brown and gray."

"Yeah—we got our snow in November, Christmas had a dusting, then that snowstorm a few days later, and now this. That's normal for us, though this year seems to be a bit on the no-snow extreme side so far."

"But it's less shovelling," Shawna said out of the blue, not taking her eyes off her work.

"Well, we don't have to always shovel tons of snow in Calgary, but when the snow falls, it stays. I can't adjust to this snow-and-thaw thing," Juliana said.

Shawna didn't respond.

"My parents have a snow removal service," Meghan said. "So I wouldn't know."

"Girls," Ms. Haseltine said. "I know it's exciting to have a new class member but you need to get your questions written down."

"Lunch?" Meghan asked.

"Sure." Juliana smiled. Finally!

JULIANA WAS SITTING IN HER BEDROOM, ANSWERING THE questions from health class when she heard the side door to the house open. Her heart skipped a beat as she bolted out of her room to see Dad come into the kitchen. She gave him a huge hug.

"Whoa!" Dad said and chuckled. "Exactly what I was hoping for. I missed you, too."

When Juliana finally let go, he took off his coat and put it in the hallway closet.

"I finally met some girls in school today!"

Dad grinned. "See? I told you that you would. Tell me about them." He put two slices of bread into the toaster and pulled out the peanut butter and strawberry jam.

"Well, one girl's Meghan. She's really nice, but she talks a lot. Our phys ed teacher had to keep telling us to stop talking."

"I hope you listened?"

Juliana looked at the ground. "Well, sort of. I tried."

"Juliana, you need to listen to your teachers."

"I know, I know, but I've spent all week by myself."

The toast popped out of the toaster and Dad put it on his plate.

"Anyways," Juliana continued. "I met one of her friends. Shawna was in phys ed class with us. She's really quiet."

"So she listened to the teacher?" Dad scraped the peanut butter along the toast with his knife.

"Dad, seriously! You told me to tell you about my day."

"I'm also your parent and need to make sure I tell you how to behave in school."

"Can I just talk? Or are you going to constantly interrupt me?"

Dad raised his hands in a fake surrender. "Keep going." He spread the jam on his toast and carried his plate to the table.

"Well, actually, that was it. I mean, I actually ate lunch with someone today, well, two people, so that was pretty cool. And I'm catching up on French pretty easily."

"Good to hear. Keep studying." Dad swallowed a bite of toast. "And how's Opa doing?"

Juliana tucked a piece of hair behind her ear. "I don't know. I thought he was having problems this week, but then he looked like he wasn't. I can't figure out if he's okay or not." She told him about the shirt incident and the apple core.

Dad swallowed again and looked at her, his face serious. "Listen, Jules. If and when things become serious with your Opa, we'll get help. Your mom and her siblings are setting money aside for that. But right now, he's only in the early stages of dementia. There will be blips."

"Okay," she said, somewhat hesitantly. "But one

time he said some German words in the middle of his English ones. Is that normal? I couldn't find anything online about that being part of dementia."

Dad smiled. "He's been doing that since I met him. I'm surprised he's actually been able to keep both languages separate until now."

"So you think he's okay?"

Dad nodded. "Things will come and go with him. If you're ever really scared, you can call Mom, me, Aunt Anne, or even Uncle Peter. If he's in town, I'm sure he'll be able to help."

Dad and Juliana talked for a few more minutes, and then Dad lay down for a short nap.

Juliana went to her room to study. She sat at her desk, trying to answer the questions from health class, but after fifteen minutes, she gave up: she couldn't concentrate. When she was first moving in, she was worried Opa would do embarrassing things like drool or eat with his mouth wide open...things she'd heard that old people did. But that hadn't been the case, and the more she tried to figure things out for herself, the more she had begun to worry about him. She opened up the dementia website she had visited the other day and kept reading.

She read about symptoms of dementia in the advanced stages: wandering, emotional outbursts, anger. *Sometimes I wish I couldn't read*, she thought. Would she be able to tell the difference between a normal expression of anger and one caused by his dementia? She hated it when people assumed her behaviour stemmed from her being "just a teen," and so she tried really hard to not see Opa as "just an old man with dementia." But the more she read, the more she realized that dementia could become really serious. How would she know when he had crossed over from these early stages to the more advanced ones? As she read, she learned that dementia could take years to fully develop. But what if Opa was farther along than everyone actually thought? Hadn't Dad suspected that just last week?

She pulled out the book of drawings from her great-grandmother and passed her hand over the stiff, brown leather. How was she going to learn what all these drawings meant before Opa's memory faded forever? In the few weeks she had been living with him, she'd learned from him that his mother had grown up in a house without electricity or a phone, and that it had had a dirt floor. She had taken tours of pioneer homes back in Calgary, and even they had floor boards. No electricity, of course, but at least they weren't walking on dirt, and those homes had been built easily fifty years before the one drawn in this book, maybe even a hundred.

Juliana turned page after page, glancing at each

pencil sketch as she went, realizing how little they meant to her. She then paged backwards and eventually stopped at the image of the envelope being opened. Why had it been so special to her great-grandmother? Was she just happy they had mail at all, since they didn't have a telephone? Or had the letter said something important?

She closed her study notes, calculated how much study time she'd lost, and wrote it down so she could try to reschedule it. She then headed downstairs to the basement. If she couldn't concentrate, she might as well get a few questions answered. She knocked on Opa's bedroom door.

"*Ja?*" Opa said.

"Can I come in?" Juliana asked.

"Of course!"

Juliana opened the door and entered. She had only been inside her grandfather's bedroom once before—to get a better look at her great-grandmother's book after she had discovered it—and at that time it had been clean. This time, though, his clothes were all over his bed, the floor, his night table, and chair. "It's easier to find clothes when they're out here," Opa explained when he saw her look.

She held up her great-grandmother's book. "Can I ask you about this?"

Opa looked confused for a moment, as though he didn't recognize it.

"It's your mom's book of drawings," Juliana said.

Opa's eyes lit up. "Of course! I couldn't quite tell without my glasses." He found his glasses on top of the clothing on his night table and set them on his nose. He pushed aside some of the piles on his bed and made room for Juliana. She sat down beside him and opened the book up to the drawing of a hand opening an envelope.

"I'm trying to figure out why Omama would put this in here. Do you have any idea what's so important about an envelope?"

Opa scratched his balding head as he studied the image. He flipped a few pages ahead and then all the way to the front.

"That's the kitchen...I don't remember what those mittens are about...that's Susi's wedding..." He lost himself in thought for a few moments. "I don't remember when Susi got married. But the envelope... Mammi's father worked in America for some time, so I wonder if this envelope is about something either he wrote or she wrote."

"Were her parents divorced?"

Opa laughed. "No, Yulika, no one divorced back then. You would've shamed your family if you had. He moved to Pennsylvania for..." Opa thought for a moment. "I don't remember how long."

"But didn't you know him?"

Opa shook his head. "He died before I was born. But she loved him and told me about him all the time. No, I think this envelope is about writing to him."

The phone upstairs rang. It was an old phone with a shrill, clanging sound that could be heard throughout the entire house. Opa jumped up to answer it without a word. Was this his dementia or the same eagerness she felt when Rachel texted her?

Still not wanting to study, she walked into the rec room, sat on the thick carpet, and began to stretch. She was still in her day clothes, but she made do and settled into a deep lunge. She couldn't help but wonder what it must have felt like to have a father living all the way across the world and only have letters to communicate with. Maybe Dad's travel wasn't so bad after all.

CHAPTER EIGHT

*L*uki was sitting at the table in the front room, polishing a pair of shoes Mammi had finished. Mammi had again sent Luki inside, which puzzled Elisabeth, because their mother didn't like shoemaking messing up the house. *She's spending a lot of time alone,* Elisabeth thought. *Perhaps she's still sad about Tata.* Whatever the reason, Luki was at least occupied for the time being. In fact, all of Elisabeth's family, save for Mammi, was quietly occupied with one activity or another in the front room: Rosina with her knitting, Anna with her embroidery, and Omama with exquisite crocheting. As fearsome as Omama was, Elisabeth had to admit that the forced quiet she brought with her was a nice blessing. At the very least, it allowed Elisabeth to start working on a pot of goulash for lunch instead of wasting time yelling at her sisters.

Konrad entered the house, letting in a blast of cold air. He and his father had been outside for several hours already, inspecting and repairing the pen. He rubbed his hands together, smiling at Elisabeth as he did so. She smiled back.

"It's nice to have a minute to warm up," he said. "It turns out you have a lot of weakened boards out there."

"Oh? Well, thank you for taking the time to look."

"Of course. We'll get them all fixed for you, and properly."

"If we need to pay for supplies, please let me know."

Konrad nodded. "Where's Luki? I came in to get him: we have some tasks he can help us with."

Elisabeth pointed in the front room. "He's polishing some shoes for Mammi. Luki? It's time to set those down and go out and help Konrad and Herr Hagel."

"I'm not done," Luki said.

Please, Luki, not in front of Konrad and Omama, Elisabeth thought. "I can finish those up for you. It's time for you to go outside and help."

"Luki," Omama said, a threatening tone in her voice. "You are the man of the house. You must help those who have come to help you."

Luki paused for a moment as his gaze moved from

Omama to Elisabeth to Konrad, giving Elisabeth hope that he might stop his fight before it got worse. She even prayed to Jesus for a bit of extra help.

"No," Luki said with the confidence of a grown man. "It's cold outside."

Elisabeth shot an apologetic look to Konrad, wiped her hands on her apron, and walked into the front room. Jesus must have been busy with another family right now or He was angry at Elisabeth for something. She would have to settle this on her own.

"Luki, now. Please."

"No!"

Between clenched teeth, Elisabeth said, "You're embarrassing your family. Stop this *now*."

Almost tauntingly, Luki glared at Elisabeth. "I'm *not* going outside."

Omama stood up. "This is enough," she declared. "Luki, either you go with Konrad and help, or you can kneel in the box of corn."

Jesus, what do I do? Elisabeth prayed. Unfortunately, the answer came from Omama instead.

"Lissika," she said, "you must discipline him."

Elisabeth couldn't do it. There had to be a kinder way of forcing Luki to do what was needed. Her brother certainly wasn't Jesus—Jesus hadn't thrown tantrums when He was a child—but he was human, like Jesus.

Making Luki kneel in corn seemed almost as painful as placing a crown of thorns on Jesus' head.

Konrad stayed where he was, by the front door, and watched the entire event in silence.

"Luki," Elisabeth said, "you'll be a man someday. You have to learn this."

"No!"

Elisabeth looked up at everyone. She saw nothing but disapproval from Omama. Anna and Rosina, though, looked worried.

"It's cold outside!" Luki protested. "I'm not going! It's not fair that everyone else gets to stay inside."

"That is it," Omama declared. She hobbled as fast as she could into the kitchen, pulled out the box of dried corn kernels, and carried it into the front room. "Luki, roll up your pants!" she commanded.

"No!"

Omama's face turned so angry, Elisabeth almost wondered if the Devil had gotten hold of her. Omama hobbled back to Luki and grabbed him by the ear. His shouts of protest now turned into cries of pain. Elisabeth didn't know what to do: she wanted to protect her brother, but she knew she had to listen to her grandmother or she would be next in line after him and their family would become the gossip of the congregation alongside Peter-Bátschi's family.

Jesus, why can't You help me? she prayed silently.

"Roll up your pants!" Omama repeated.

An idea came to Elisabeth. "Omama, please, let me," she said. Omama looked doubtful. "I know what to do," Elisabeth insisted. Omama let go.

Luki tried to dart away, but Elisabeth grabbed him by the arm. "Stay here." Luki tried to pull free of his sister's grip, but Elisabeth held tight. "When I let go of you, go get your coat on. I know how to keep you warm."

Luki's normally sweet face had by now turned ugly with defiance, but before he could say another word, Elisabeth explained. "I promise. You must help outside, but I can make it a little easier for you. Now, get your mittens on, the black ones that Mammi made especially for you for Christmas, and get on your coat."

Elisabeth let go but prepared herself in case Luki attempted to escape again. To her relief, he didn't move, and Elisabeth sent a silent thank you to Jesus. Maybe He was keeping an eye on her after all.

"When Tata comes home and sees the new pigpen, you'll be able to tell him you helped," Elisabeth said. "Now, go get dressed." He finally listened.

While Luki put on his coat, Elisabeth found rags in the front room, opened the oven, and reached inside with a pair of tongs to pull out a few pieces of coal. She wrapped them up tightly and by the time Luki had emerged from the back room, ready to put on his boots, she had little bundles of warmth prepared for him. She placed one in each pant and coat pocket, four in total. "If your fingers get cold, warm them up in your pockets," she instructed.

Elisabeth caught a frown on Konrad's face, which disturbed her. Did he really expect her to send her brother out in the frigid winter without a source of heat for his small, skinny body? It was not the same as when Luki ran about with his friends after school, coming home all sweaty even in the winter. Instead, he would be standing outside by the pigpens, without any sunlight to warm him, and with cold winds blowing around.

A smile appeared on her brother's face and Elisabeth tapped him on the back of his shoulder. "Now, get out there and help Herr Hagel and Konrad with the repairs. I'll even add a little note to my letter to Tata that you helped." At that last suggestion, Luki's chest lifted. "I have to go see the postman in a bit to mail my letter," Elisabeth continued. "When I return, we'll see how you're doing, all right? If Herr Hagel and Konrad approve, you can come inside and do some reading."

Luki's chest fell. "I hate reading," Luki said.

"You need to read for school," Elisabeth said gently.

Omama scowled. "Nonsense," she said. "A man who can maintain his house and farmland is more useful than a man who can read. The Hagels are here now and can teach Luki what a man needs to know. He can read again when he returns to school."

Konrad spoke up. "Father told me not to worry about reading. Luki, one day, you'll marry, and providing for your family will be your purpose. I've barely read a thing since I finished school. Let's work on the pigpens and make your father proud."

Elisabeth was dumbfounded. What she had meant as a way of encouraging Luki to go outside had turned into Konrad discouraging her brother from reading. She didn't know what to say next, but it didn't matter. Konrad put his arm around Luki and ushered him out to the pigpens.

"As it should be," Omama muttered. "Now, everyone, back to work."

How can someone hate reading? Elisabeth thought as she retrieved her letter to add a note about Luki. Her father's encyclopedia, for example, helped her see where he now lived. She knew it was far away, but to see it on a map and read about the country comforted her a little. When Elisabeth had read Tata's letter again to her sisters the other day, hearing Tata's own words had awoken in them their love for him. Today she would mail him her reply. She missed him dearly, but she knew where he was and that he was safe because of his letter. Reading gave Elisabeth almost as much comfort as her faith in Jesus.

How could Konrad hate reading? Elisabeth finished her note in the letter, put it back in its envelope, sealed it shut, and continued preparing her goulash, unable to answer the question.

CHAPTER NINE

"Ugh, I don't want to see another book! I can barely think anymore!" Juliana complained as she entered the kitchen that morning, her hands pressing against her head as though she was trying to squeeze juice out of it. Two weeks had passed, and she had one exam behind her, with two more to go. Today was phys ed and health. Tomorrow was French. She had tied her hair up in a loose bun so it wouldn't bother her and had put on her most comfortable leggings and sweater, but despite her morning shower, she felt exhausted and half-asleep, even though she had actually slept eight hours.

"*Guten morgen,*" Opa said as he sat at the table eating breakfast.

Juliana ignored him, her nerves forcing her to focus,

and she began reciting what she'd studied. "Religion and socio-economic status can affect someone's ability to buy healthy food. Environmental factors that affect healthy food choices include transportation systems, packaging, and...and...food production. Age is also a factor that can affect someone's ability to buy healthy food. What's the best choice to reduce my carbon footprint? Buying local food."

"You'll do fine," Mom said as she handed Juliana a bowl of oatmeal with cut-up apples and a sprinkle of cinnamon.

"What?" Opa asked.

"It can be hard to ship healthy food to the far north of Ontario. Someone might be interested in learning about traditional foods their ancestors ate."

"Nothing, Tata," Mom said over Juliana's recitations. "She's just reviewing her material. It means she's stressed and she needs to be left alone. She started this in grade six out of nowhere. It's not going to make any sense to you, but it's how she calms herself."

"Oh!" Opa held a finger to his lips, indicating that he would stop talking.

Juliana continued reciting one fact after another for her exam, and when she had food in her mouth, she recited the facts silently in her head. She hated studying, but if she was going to maintain her ninety percent average, she had to do it.

"I should be home in time to cook tonight," Mom said, and Juliana nodded in acknowledgement.

"Mental health issues can cause someone to withdraw from relationships."

"Dad texted me to wish you luck on your exam today. He didn't want to risk disturbing your studies by sending you a message."

"Talking about suicide may be a call for help."

"What?" Opa asked, visibly alarmed. "This is what they learn in school?"

"Tata, not now," Mom said to him. Then to Juliana, "You'll do fine. Just this one and French tomorrow, and then you're free for the rest of the week!" Mom grabbed her keys and headed out. "Good luck!" she said as she closed the door behind her.

"Good friends help their friends get help. Help can include community elders, therapists...crap. What else?"

"Family?" Opa offered.

"Yes! Family! And community health service providers, telephone help lines..."

Opa carried his bowl to the sink. "I have a doctor's appointment today," he said, interrupting Juliana's list. "But I'll be home before you get here. Annie is driving me."

"Okay," she said, only half-registering what Opa had said. "When do you call 911? Life-threatening emergencies. What are examples of life-threatening emergencies? Heart attack, choking, stroke—"

"And make sure you put on warm clothes today, Yulika. The windchill out there is -25 or something like that."

Opa's statement derailed Juliana's chaotic train of thought. "What?"

"They said it's going to get really cold. So put on warm clothes."

Juliana stared down at her thin leggings and sweater. The temperatures had dipped back down to below zero, and there was snow on the ground again, but she didn't know it would get *that* cold that fast. "Okay, I'll figure it out." Then her train of thought got back on track. "When do else do you call 911? Frostbite, heat stroke—"

"I'm going to shower."

"Stop interrupting me," Juliana said as she continued to spit out first-aid facts.

"Yulika, you will do fine," Opa said. "Have a good day. I'll see you later. Good luck!"

Juliana nodded. "When else do you call 911? Broken leg, sprained ankle, dislocated hip, slipping..." A sudden fear overcame Juliana: what if Opa fell in the shower and he broke his leg or split his head open? There'd be no one here to help him. She ran to the top of the stairs. "Opa, why don't you wait until someone's home? You know, just to make sure you're safe?"

Disappointment flashed across Opa's face. "Don't tell me you're thinking like that, too," he said.

That wasn't a reaction she had anticipated. "Oh, no, Opa, it's just that, well..." Juliana didn't know what to say.

"I'm fine. I forget a few things now and then, but I can shower by myself. I'm not stupid," he said and stomped down the stairs.

Juliana froze. She hadn't meant to insult him. But if he did slip on the wet floor, there'd be no one home to help him, and he didn't even have a cordless phone in the house to take with him should he need to call for help. Should she run after him to ask him to wait again? Or should she apologize?

One look at the clock told her she had to boot it to school. She needed to be there at least thirty minutes beforehand so she could start reciting facts there in the hopes of making use of the environment to help her remember things during the exam. It was a tip she'd read online.

"Opa, I'm really sorry!" she shouted downstairs one last time before grabbing her things and running out the door.

Juliana watched the clock on the classroom wall ticking away, each second gone once the second hand had passed it. *And that's one more second you've missed and will never get back*, she thought as she returned her attention to her exam. The next question read "Explain a social situation where you might be pressured to drink. How would you get out of it?"

Juliana described being at a party where people were drinking. After a few minutes of writing, she re-read her answer. Satisfied with it, she moved on to the next question: "List five situations in which you might call 911 and then write down what you would say to the operator."

Ha! I know this! she thought, but before she could command her hand to start writing, she remembered her worries about Opa. Was he okay? What if he had fallen in the shower? The second hand kept ticking away and she made herself begin writing.

1. Heart attack. Address, the person's age, sex, name if known, not breathing, suspected heart attack.

Then Juliana remembered that Aunt Anne was picking up Opa, and she immediately felt relieved.

2. Heat stroke. Address, age, sex, name. Breathing pattern, flushed.

But what if Aunt Anne had found Opa on the floor and now they were at the hospital? No, that would be okay, right? He was at least getting care. But what if he'd died and Juliana could've prevented it by calling someone?

Get a grip! she admonished herself. *It's just dementia! He's fine!* She wrote down, *3. Drowning.*

But I really didn't mean to make him angry, she thought. *I hope I didn't ruin his day or something. Will he tell Mom?*

She paged through the entire exam and then looked up at the clock. She still had fifty-five minutes, and there was one short essay question at the end she had to budget time for.

You can do this, she thought to herself, but then her mind drifted again to Opa.

JULIANA DRAGGED HERSELF INTO THE HOUSE AFTER HER exam.

"Hi," Opa said cheerfully from the kitchen table. He was dressed neatly in a turtleneck with a knitted vest over it, reminding Juliana of ads for retirement homes and dentures. "How was your exam?"

"I think I aced it," she said. At his confused look, she explained, "I did really well."

"That's wonderful!"

Juliana remembered Opa's appointment and asked

him about it, but Opa waved his hand, dismissing the question. "Nothing important," he said.

His reaction puzzled her. The other day, he had been thrilled because his pee was fine, but now he wasn't happy. Juliana guessed that something had happened. Given how he'd reacted this morning, though, she wasn't sure if she should ask him. "Well, if you want to talk about it…"

"No, I'm fine," he said. "There's nothing wrong with me and I wish everyone would stop acting like there was. I can look after myself, and I certainly don't need your family here to babysit me."

Juliana stood still. What was she supposed to say to that?

Opa took a stack of neatly folded tea towels from under the sink and walked to the stairs.

"What do you need those for?" Juliana asked. "Did something spill?"

Opa's mood changed again, and he said in a tone that suggested the answer was obvious, "They're dirty and they need cleaning. I can look after myself, Yulika."

He disappeared into the basement and Juliana stared after him. There was no need for him to wash those tea towels.

"*Verdammt nochamol!*" she heard from downstairs.

Part of Juliana wanted to rush downstairs and see if he needed help, but part of her was scared he would get angry at her again. She continued to listen to hear whether she was needed. A metallic bang startled her, but just as she was about to head down, she heard Opa grumbling to himself as he shuffled to his room and closed the door behind him. She could hear that he had turned on his television so she tiptoed down and into the laundry room. The stack of tea towels was all over the floor. Was he angry because he'd dropped them? She inspected the washing machine to make sure it wasn't damaged and then noticed a more likely cause of Opa's frustration: a small light glowed on the machine, and next to it were the words "child lock."

A child lock for a grown man. That would make Juliana angry, too.

CHAPTER TEN

"Let's go!" Elisabeth urged her sisters as she pushed the pot of goulash into the oven. The mailman only showed up once a week to take mail and deliver the week's news, and she finally had an opportunity to listen to what he had to say. She waited impatiently by the house door as her sisters finished tying their boots.

"Hurry!" she said. "I don't want to miss the news!"

"But I want to stay home," Rosina pouted.

Elisabeth bent down to Rosina's height and whispered, "And stay alone with Omama?"

Rosina's mood changed in the blink of an eye. Anna must have heard, too, for she also stepped up her pace. Elisabeth tiptoed into the back room, where Omama was snoring soundly, to get their shawls, headscarves, and mittens. Each girl dressed herself, and Elisabeth pulled her dress sleeves down extra hard: she hated it when cold air travelled up them.

The sky was gray, and outside, the temperature must have been around minus ten Celsius. Each girl had several shawls pulled tightly around her, and all three scurried along the side of the house to the front gate and out into the street, when Elisabeth suddenly stopped.

"What are we waiting for?" Anna asked.

"*Shh...*"

Her sisters stared at her, puzzled, but then she heard it: a laugh from Luki. It meant that, for now, he was listening and hopefully eagerly helping the Hagels. Satisfied, Elisabeth led her sisters to the town hall, which lay about three blocks west of their home.

"Were you listening for Konrad?" Anna asked, a mischievous smile on her face.

Elisabeth shook her head.

"Are you going to marry him?" Rosina asked.

"It's too early to tell," Elisabeth said.

"But he likes you," Anna followed up. "I can tell."

"Oh, really?" Elisabeth asked. "And just what did you see?"

"He smiled at you." Anna made kissing noises.

"Stop that!" Elisabeth said.

"Would he be a good husband?" Anna continued.

"I think so," Elisabeth said, but no sooner had she answered Anna's question than she doubted her answer's truthfulness. "He's learning how to be a carpenter from his father, and their family farm uses day-labourers on their land. It means I wouldn't have to work as hard as Mammi does." That did sound like a good match, didn't it?

The postman began drumming in the distance to announce his arrival to anyone nearby. The sound distracted her from any further thoughts on the matter as she picked up her pace even more.

"Like Eva?" Anna asked as she tried to keep up.

"Sort of. She and Georg will have their house passed down to them and they won't have to pay for it. So that makes things easier for them, and that would happen to me, too, if I married Konrad. However, Eva and Georg don't have any day-labourers on their farm like the Hagels do." She then thought about her cousin Georg's shaking episodes and wondered how those would affect his ability to look after his land. "But maybe they will hire help one day," she added.

"Wait for me!" Rosina called from a few steps behind them. Elisabeth turned around, smiled at her youngest sister, and beckoned her to hurry.

"Does Konrad have the shakes like Georg?" Anna asked, worried. Elisabeth thought back to the day when she and Anna had been helping with wedding preparations at their aunt and uncle's house. After seeing Anna's red mittens, Georg had erupted into an inexplicable panic and collapsed in a fit. That episode had troubled Anna greatly.

Elisabeth placed a hand on her sister's shoulder. "No, he doesn't. He didn't fight in the war, and that affliction only affects soldiers. Well, some of them, anyway."

Anna breathed a sigh of relief.

"But if you marry him," Rosina said, "that means you'll move out of our house and in with the Hagels. Tata's already gone. I don't want you to leave."

Elisabeth smiled at her youngest sister. "Rosina, even if I did marry him, it wouldn't be for at least another year: Tata said he would be home before I marry but he also wanted to stay away for a year. Besides, I'd have to get to know Konrad a little better first." She patted Rosina on the back.

The drumming got louder and faster, and Elisabeth hurried, now leaving her sisters behind. She waved at people she knew, including her best friend, Maria, but as much as she longed to stop to talk with them, she needed to make sure she mailed her letter to Tata and heard the week's news. It was the next best thing to listening in on visits from the men in the village.

She arrived to find the usual crowd of people surrounding the postman, who was still drumming away to call attention to anyone near the town hall. As Elisabeth tried to push her way through the crowd to get closer to the front, her sisters ran to catch up, bumping into her before they could stop. She stumbled into a man standing in front of her.

"I'm sorry," she said to him, and before she could scold her sisters, the man turned around. Elisabeth found herself looking up at Georg. Anna immediately hid herself behind Elisabeth and tucked her red-mittened hands under her armpits. Rosina just stared at him. His hulking stature and expressionless face often frightened people, and his sudden outbursts fed the gossip circles weekly, embarrassing not only his wife but his entire family. Many in the village called him "crazy" and "weak." Although Elisabeth had never particularly liked him growing up, in her eyes now he had become a sad ghost: his body was there, but she could tell his mind was often not, as though it was travelling somewhere between Earth and Heaven. She pitied him now. His life was in shambles all because a few people they didn't know had chosen to fight each other and to drag their countries into a conflict that had killed millions, mostly men.

Next to Georg stood one of the two prisoners of war, the POWs she had seen in church and whom Peter-Bátschi had talked about, including the one with the missing arm. Elisabeth's eyes fixated on his stump, making her forget her manners. The man stood at about the same height as Georg, but he was very thin, about a third of the size of Georg's large frame. His brown hair stuck out in different directions from under his cap, suggesting it was a little longer than usual for men in the village. He was definitely older than Elisabeth, but he looked younger than Georg.

"Will it grow back?" Rosina asked in wonder. "His arm?"

"Rosina!" Elisabeth scolded. Her cheeks burned, both because of her own reaction to the missing limb and that of her sister's. But she did notice the corners of Georg's mouth turning up just a little.

The man tipped his hat, a charming smile on his face. "I'm Stefan Schäfer."

Elisabeth came to her senses. "I'm sorry," she said, now flustered.

"It's all right," Stefan said. "It's not a usual sight."

"Oh, no, it's not that!" Elisabeth replied, trying to cover up her behaviour. Of course, it was exactly his missing arm that flustered her so much, but she couldn't say that. That would have been impolite.

"These are my cousins," Georg said, relieving her of any further awkwardness, and introducing each of the sisters by name. "You may have met Lukas-Bátschi when we were younger. The shoemaker?"

"I think so," Stefan said to the sisters. "I'm sorry, I tried so hard to hold on to memories of Semlak, but—"

"They don't need to hear about it," Georg said gently.

Stefan didn't continue with his explanation, but Elisabeth longed to hear it. If anything, it would have opened the door a little more to understanding Georg's mind and maybe could help her assist him somehow. She glanced quickly at Anna and thanked Jesus that her sister still hid her mittens. What if they upset Stefan, too?

Georg continued with the introductions. "Stefan is cousins with Tiny Hay, and he's a friend of mine and Samuel's." Georg was referring to his brother, of course, and not Hagel Samuel.

"Oh, yes?" Elisabeth said. Stefan looked familiar to her, but whether it was because she had known him fleetingly from her childhood or because he looked like someone else, she couldn't tell. Then again, everyone in their congregation looked familiar, because almost everyone followed the same dress code and saw each other every Sunday at church, as well as sometimes Tuesdays or Thursdays during the winter at weddings, and on any day at christenings and funerals and dances.

The postman's drumming stopped. Both men and the three sisters turned to face him as he announced the week's headlines.

"Arad under threat to be left without charcoal!"

"No charcoal in Arad?" someone interrupted.

"None," the postman confirmed. "The central directorship of the Romanian Railway in Cluj has stopped supplying Arad with charcoal as of Tuesday. It proposed that the electrical plant be transformed so that wood can be used instead of charcoal."

"What is the city doing about it in the meantime?" someone else asked.

"Mayor Robu asked that General Leca intervene. The newspapers say that progress was made by appealing to the Transylvanian troop commanders."

A few murmurs travelled through the crowd, but the postman continued.

"Butchers and sausage-makers of Arad ask the price supervisory committee to increase their prices!

"A reminder: the chief physician of the city of Arad asks all practitioners to report to him all cases of the Spanish flu and other cases of contagious diseases!

"Victorious Romania pulls more soldiers out of Budapest!"

Elisabeth didn't like hearing about the Hungarian-Romanian war that had begun immediately after the end of the bigger war that had seemed to pull in the whole world and that had caused so much suffering. It was hard enough to live now in a country that had been her homeland's enemy. Although Tata had said that many of the people who lived in the Banat, the large region Semlak was in, had voted to join Romania, Elisabeth still could not wrap her mind around the simple fact that her home was now part of what she had always thought of as enemy territory. Immediately after that great war had finished, Romania had declared war on Hungary, and although that war had ended last summer, she had heard that Romanian troops continued to occupy Budapest this entire time. She shook her head at the futility of so much war and stared again at Stefan's missing arm.

"Now for your mail," the postman announced, interrupting her thoughts.

"That's a concern about the charcoal, isn't it, Georg?" Stefan said as the postman began handing out packages. "Hopefully the shortage doesn't affect blacksmiths."

Georg, who was a blacksmith, only grunted.

Elisabeth waited in the short line to hand the postman her letter. He inspected the stamp, tipped his hat to her, and tucked the letter inside his bag. By the time she turned around with her siblings to return home, Georg and Stefan were already on their way back to Georg's home. Anna could finally shake out her mittened hands.

"Anna, Rosina, I need to ask for a big promise from both of you," Elisabeth said as they returned home. Elisabeth's sisters looked up at her. "I know you don't like to listen to me, but so long as Omama is staying in our home, can you please do as I say? I promise I won't make you do anything you shouldn't normally do, but if you yell at me, Omama will yell at all of us and may discipline us like she has Luki."

Anna looked suspicious, while Rosina said defiantly, "Then I'll run away from her."

"And do what?" Elisabeth asked. "Sleep out in the stalls with the cows and horses at night? She will catch you at some point. The problem is that I want to look after all of you, but I don't want to embarrass Mammi."

"What do we get in return?" Anna asked.

"Pardon me?" Elisabeth said. "What do you get in return? I'm asking you, my sisters, to help me here. I'd rather you listened to me all the time—Mammi has put me in charge of the household—but all I'm asking is that, so long as Omama is here, you do your best to behave."

They walked a little farther while her sisters seemed to deliberate her request. Before they answered, Rosina squinted her eyes in concentration and asked, "What's that noise?"

The other two stopped and listened.

"Just someone's animals," Elisabeth replied and

continued walking. But as they neared their street, "just someone's animals" turned into panicked squealing, clucking, quacking, and honking, and once they turned onto their street, Elisabeth could see pigs on the road in front of their home. She lifted the front of her skirt and began to run.

"Wait for me!" Rosina cried.

"I can't!" Elisabeth yelled back. "I think it's *our* animals!"

When she arrived at the front gate, Elisabeth shrieked: their pigs had gotten loose, with several on the road and the rest in the front yard, dangerously near the open gate. All the birds were flapping madly about in their coops as they sounded the alarm. Omama was standing underneath the overhang, shaking her fist at the Hagels, and Mammi had an arm wrapped across her waist as she shouted at them.

Luki was nowhere to be seen.

Juliana practically skipped all the way home, the frigid air stinging her lungs. Today's windchill had apparently hit minus thirty Celsius, and rumour had it that exams had almost been postponed because of it. She still couldn't figure out how people here could live when temperatures could fluctuate by more than thirty degrees in a week, but it didn't matter! She was done! Although she had only had three exams, she had spent so much time studying the material that her brain felt like a plate of ground beef.

"Which can be a good source of iron," she said aloud. "Stop it! You're done!" She came up to a patch of ice and slid across it, shouting, "You're done!" She couldn't wait to begin practicing again: now that she had caught up on her schoolwork, she could focus again on catching up on her dancing.

The energy in her threatened to spill over into a tight bear hug with the first person she saw when she arrived home. At the door, she searched for her keys in her backpack. Her excitement coursing through her entire body, she couldn't keep her fingers still enough to pull her key out in one try. Getting the key into the lock required as much concentration as trying a double pirouette *en pointe*.

The lock finally turned and she threw the door open.

"I'm home and I'm done!" she shouted. She slammed the door behind her out of exuberance, kicked off her boots, and leaped over the two stairs to the kitchen. "Opa! I'm home!" She ran into her bedroom, threw her backpack onto her bed, only to watch it topple and crash onto the floor.

"And you know what?" she said into the air. "I don't care! I'm done! I did it!"

She ran back into the kitchen. "Opa?" she called out again. She paused for a moment to listen for the familiar creaks in the house. After a few seconds of silence, she ran downstairs, panicking that something had happened. She peeked into Opa's room, the rec room, the bathroom, the laundry room, and even the fruit cellar, where she had found Omama's book, but he wasn't there.

She ran back up into the kitchen and was about to call her aunt when she saw an entry on his calendar: "Deutsch Klub 2:30."

"Oh." Juliana's excitement deflated faster than a balloon. She grabbed her usual snack and water and dropped into a chair at the table. A moment ago she had been brimming with joy, and now sitting in the small, empty house, with no one to welcome her home on the day when she had actually triumphed, that joy churned inside her stomach, transforming into uncomfortable feelings she tried to push away.

"No," she said, "this can't be happening to me. I've made it through this month, and there's no one to tell?" Now anger began to seep in. "How can there be no one here?" Her mother was one of three, her aunt had six kids and lived nearby, Opa was usually home, and despite all that, there was no one else in the house.

She returned to her room, shut the door, and stared at herself in the mirror.

"You're the only one here to celebrate with," she said to herself. "Rachel's in Calgary, and Jasmine, Meghan, and Shawna have their regular friends." Tears began to well up in her eyes. "Dad's in Florida again, Mom's at work, and Opa's with his friends. And you're here alone."

The tears flowed stronger now. Whenever she and her old dance team had won a big award, Miss Kasia had ordered in pizza. And whenever she and Rachel wanted to celebrate anything, whether it was an award at a dance competition, or someone's birthday, or passing a major test at school, they had a sleepover and watched movies all night.

"This isn't fair," she said. "Why am I being left behind?"

Juliana's loneliness weighed on her so much that she didn't even have the heart to dance. She collapsed into her bed and fell asleep.

JULIANA SQUINTED AT THE SUDDEN BRIGHT LIGHT AND SHE heard someone call her name. She shielded her eyes as she sat up and saw Sophie. What was Sophie doing in her bedroom?

"Hey," Juliana said, her voice groggy. "Is everything okay?"

The confused expression on her cousin's face told Juliana she'd asked the wrong question.

"Is everything okay with *you*?" Sophie asked.

Juliana at first nodded and then remembered Sophie might not have seen her reaction: her cousin was losing her sight at the centre of her vision. "Yeah, I'm fine. Why?"

"We were worried," Sophie replied. "We tried calling you, but you didn't answer your phone or the house phone."

Had Juliana really slept that deeply that she hadn't heard the house phone's shrill ring? And how could she not have heard her cell? But one glance at her backpack on the floor suggested her phone had gotten buried in the fall.

"We were going to take you and Opa out for supper instead of cooking tonight," Sophie continued, "but then you didn't pick up."

"Yulika?" Opa called from the hallway.

"She's in her room, Opa," Sophie called back. Juliana heard Opa's familiar steps.

"Are you sure you're okay?" Sophie asked.

"Yeah," Juliana replied, though her voice sounded more like a frog's croak.

She rubbed her eyes and stood up just as Opa entered. He stared at her face for a moment. "Your eyes are puffy. Were you crying?"

Juliana shook her head, but Opa insisted. Just then, another set of footsteps travelled down the hallway and Juliana looked over Opa's shoulder to see Aunt Anne.

"Juliana?"

By now, Juliana was frustrated and embarrassed.

When she wanted someone home to celebrate with, there was no one. When she wanted privacy, everyone showed up.

"She's been crying, Anne," Opa said.

And now they're talking about me like I'm not even here, she thought.

"What's wrong?" Aunt Anne asked.

"Nothing," Juliana said, frustration creeping in to replace the tiredness in her voice.

"Tata, Sophie, can you leave us alone for a minute?"

Great. Now I get "a talk," Juliana thought as her cousin and grandfather returned to the kitchen.

"I know we hardly know each other, but I can tell you're upset," Aunt Anne said. Her voice was gentle, but the last thing Juliana wanted to do right now was talk.

"I'm fine, just tired," Juliana replied. She dug her phone out of her bag and glanced at its clock: it was late enough that Rachel might be available now. *Crap—she's at the studio all evening,* she remembered. *Still no one to talk to.* "Really, I'm okay. Just exhausted from the past few weeks."

Aunt Anne studied her. "You had your last exam today, didn't you?"

Juliana nodded.

"And no one was here to celebrate with you."

Juliana could feel her tears returning, and she closed her eyes to try and push them back. Aunt Anne immediately pulled her phone out of her jacket pocket. She tapped it a few times and then held it up to her ear. "I'm trying your mom."

Juliana sighed. If she'd been allowed to just sleep a little longer and then refresh herself—in private—no one would have noticed and she could just move on. Her parents had made it clear to her that they had to work, so what was the point in trying to get a hold of them? As if confirming her thoughts, Aunt Anne shook her head.

"She's not answering. Well, it is student discount night. Maybe they're swamped. I'll try your dad." Moments later, Aunt Anne shook her head. "Nope, he's not answering either. What did you do after exams back in Calgary?"

"Hung out with Rachel and my other friends usually."

"And you don't know anyone well enough here yet." Aunt Anne tapped her phone a few times and then started texting. "We're going out as planned and we're going to celebrate your last day of exams." She looked up from her phone at Juliana, who knew she had to nod, because anything else would've been rude. Aunt Anne continued tapping on her phone. "I'm just letting your parents know."

"I have dance tonight."

"That's fine. Pack your stuff. If Katy isn't able to get

away from work in time, we'll just take you after we finish eating. I'll wait for you in the kitchen."

As Juliana packed her dance bag, she had to admit that she felt a little relieved. She didn't want the attention, but her aunt trying to make her feel better was, well, nice. And once she was at the studio, she'd at least be able to talk to Jasmine.

She'll probably tell me to stop brooding, Juliana thought. But then she realized that maybe that was exactly what she needed right now.

CHAPTER TWELVE

"*I* told you not to pull down both boards!" Hagel Samuel shouted at his son.

"You did not!" Konrad replied.

"Yes, I did tell you!"

"Well, if Luki hadn't been in the way, I would've done my job right!"

"If you had closed the gates behind you when you came back with those boards, the animals wouldn't be on the road now!"

The father and son argued back and forth, blaming each other and Elisabeth's brother without solving anything while the family's pigs kept roaming freely all over the road and front yard, and the ducks, geese, and chickens made more noise than three bad bands at a wedding. Elisabeth knew she and her sisters had to act quickly but also that the unpredictable animals in the yard were too dangerous for Rosina, so she instructed her youngest sister to go inside and find Luki. Elisabeth immediately closed the gate to keep the remaining pigs from escaping.

"Mammi! Can you help?" Elisabeth called. Mammi shook her head, her hand still over her stomach, which now worried Elisabeth: was Mammi sick? But she had no time to think about that right now.

"Anna, it's up to us," she said. Anna swallowed and clung to Elisabeth. "Stay calm," she said. "I know this looks scary, but if we panic, it will make things worse, understand?" Anna nodded, though she didn't show any signs of calming down. "Keep an eye on the pigs on the road and yell to me if they run. I'll be back shortly with corn," Elisabeth reassured her. Anna nodded again and then turned around to perform her duty. For now, the pigs on the road seemed calm, happy to roam and search for food, and Elisabeth hoped they would stay that way.

Elisabeth walked through the front yard as calmly as she could, doing her best to avoid the running pigs, and entered the poultry yard. The Hagels were still yelling at each other, ignoring the agitated animals.

"Herr Hagel," she said, "please repair the pigpen."

"My son must fix his mistake!" he insisted and continued arguing with Konrad.

Elisabeth shook her head in disbelief as she tried to think of what to say next.

"Elisabeth!" Anna yelled. But it was not the pigs Elisabeth saw when she turned around. Instead she saw Georg and Stefan standing outside the front yard and Anna tucking her mittened hands into her armpits again.

"Do you need help?" shouted Stefan. Georg remained still but waiting. With their family home not too far away, they must have heard the noise. Elisabeth smiled when she saw Anna urgently nod in answer to the question. Elisabeth beckoned for them to enter.

She turned back to face Konrad's father. "If we're to get the pigs back into their pen, we need those boards up immediately, Herr Hagel. It doesn't matter who's at fault: all that matters in Jesus' eyes is that we help each other. So please, both of you, just repair it."

The Hagels looked stunned, and Elisabeth could tell by the look on Konrad's face that he did not approve of Elisabeth telling him what to do. But Elisabeth could not care less: the pigs had escaped their pen and the birds flapped and squawked frantically. If the yard was not brought back to order, the animals could begin hurting each other. Elisabeth implored the Hagels one more time, and only then did they return to the pigpen to finish the repair.

Stefan and Georg by now had reached Elisabeth.

"Let's get the birds calmed first," Stefan said. "That noise sounds worse than a volley of gunshots." He covered one ear with his hand, but his stump also lifted, as though he still had his other hand with which he could cover his other ear.

Doing her best to ignore the odd sight, Elisabeth shook her head. "We need the animals brought back into the poultry yard first. Then we calm the birds down while the Hagels finish the repair," she said above the oinking, quacking, and squawking.

"One pig's wandering away!" Anna yelled at the top of her lungs from the road. Elisabeth signalled that she had heard.

Georg turned to Stefan. "This is Elisabeth's house. We should do as she wishes," he said, surprising Elisabeth. Stefan nodded and Elisabeth proceeded to direct them.

The two men headed for the wagon shed and each retrieved a sheet of wood to herd the animals off the road. Elisabeth grabbed a pail that hung outside the chicken coop and filled it with cobs of corn from the *hambar*. When she dropped several cobs on the ground in the front yard, the pigs there calmed down at the sight of easy-to-reach food.

Anna pulled her hand out of her mitten and opened the gate for Georg, Stefan, and Elisabeth. Step by step, the two men used the boards to help coax the animals into the front yard while Elisabeth tempted the pigs to follow her by dangling corn in front of their snouts. Once the last pig had been corralled back in, Anna closed the gate and slid her mitten back on.

"Tata has some tools in the wagon shed," Elisabeth said to the two men. "Help the Hagels finish the repairs. The pigs are fine for now."

The cousins nodded and did as instructed. Meanwhile, the girls filled their pails with dried corn kernels and began dropping small handfuls of the feed on the ground near the enclosures. The chickens, ducks, and geese began to quiet down.

Herr Hagel came running out, his face red with anger.

"I will *not* work with that crazy man!" he insisted.

Elisabeth had had enough. "Herr Hagel, that man is my cousin. He fought in the war. And whatever you may think of him, I know for one thing that he would not create a mess such as you and your son have. We need that pen fixed *now,* and since you and your son have done little to help, you must accept Georg's help."

"I *lost* two sons in that war, Elisabeth, and I know many in our village—including your fine father—who do not have problems. How do I know your crazy cousin won't swing a hammer at me and my last son and try to kill us?"

Elisabeth was dumb-founded. Were people that

frightened of Georg? Was that what they were saying about him? The look of triumph on Herr Hagel's face at Elisabeth's silence fed her anger, and she found her words again.

"Let me put it to you this way, Herr Hagel. You and your son promised my family that you would repair our pen. Either you complete your promise or the village will know that you are not a man of your word."

"I did not say I would repair it *with a crazy man*."

"You did not say without one either," Elisabeth replied. "It is your choice. Either you fulfill your promise and receive Jesus' blessing, or you do not and must go home, with Konrad, and confess your sins to our Lord."

With that, Elisabeth turned her back on Herr Hagel and focused her attention again on tempting the pigs into the poultry yard.

ELISABETH COULDN'T WAIT FOR THE EVENING TO BE over. Throughout cleanup, cooking, and dinner, she kept looking up at the crucifix, begging Jesus for one more moment of patience. Not only did she have to help herd the pigs back in to their pen and calm all the birds, but she and Anna had needed to change before starting supper because of how dirty and smelly their clothing had become. Elisabeth knew this meant there would be more laundry. Anna had a scowl on her face, because she, too, knew the extra work she would now have to help with.

Elisabeth had managed to hold in her anger all evening but she did not smile. The Hagels now stood at the door, after they had consumed a great deal of food, and continued to blame one another for the mess. If they didn't leave within two minutes, Elisabeth was certain she would have to pull the crucifix down from the wall and hold on to it to push down what she really wanted to tell this father and son.

Rosina had found Luki hiding under his bed, crying. "He kept saying it wasn't his fault," Rosina had told her sisters. Hearing that made Elisabeth's heart bleed for her young brother.

Konrad smiled at Elisabeth when she handed him his coat. But she did not return the smile.

"Thank you, Herr Hagel, for helping with the repairs," Mammi said, her voice tense and unnaturally polite.

Herr Hagel nodded in a way that said he was pleased with himself. "It was our honour, Frau Schuh-macher," he replied. "Had Konrad done his job better, of course, we would not have had the, um, difficulties that we did today."

"That was not my fault!" Konrad replied as he put his coat on.

"Do you always fight?" Rosina asked. Elisabeth couldn't scold Rosina for her question: she was fighting back an urge to chuckle herself.

"Children must obey their parents," Herr Hagel told her. He then looked down at Luki. "This young lad needs to learn to obey better, Frau Schuhmacher."

Elisabeth's anger began to push against her throat. *Please help me stay quiet, Jesus*, she prayed to herself.

Mammi replied. "He can be difficult, but boys will be boys, Herr Hagel. I'm certain you were no better."

"And I was disciplined accordingly," Herr Hagel replied, "as Konrad has been."

Elisabeth could no longer control her anger. "Herr Hagel, how dare you insult my mother! She has raised us well and continues to do so! It doesn't matter whose fault it was out there. What matters is that it was dealt with quickly. Need I remind you that *I* led the herding? If your son was raised so well, why did he not take charge so you could finish the work?"

Herr Hagel's mouth dropped open and he needed a moment to compose himself. "That is no way to speak to a man, Elisabeth."

"It is when he insults my family," she replied. After an uncomfortable pause, she changed her tone. "I really must start cleaning up the dishes now. Thank you again for your help. I'm sure we will see you at church on Sunday."

No sooner had the door closed behind the Hagels a few moments later when Mammi and Omama said in unison, "You're not marrying him." Elisabeth breathed a sigh of relief. Omama hobbled back to the kitchen table and sat down, while Mammi began rinsing dishes in the washing bowl and Elisabeth carried the remaining dishes from the table to Mammi.

"A good man looks after and protects his family," Mammi said. "You remember that, Luki."

Elisabeth's brother nodded.

"And he apologizes when he's made an error," Omama replied, as though what Elisabeth had just done had never happened. "No. He was a bad choice. We will find you someone else."

As happy as she was with this news, Elisabeth wondered if she was better off finding the right man herself. If Hagel Konrad was any sign of what Mammi and Omama thought would be a good match for Elisabeth, she might need to take matters into her own hands.

WHEN ALL HER SIBLINGS WERE TUCKED IN BED AND Omama was snoring in the guest bed in the back room,

Elisabeth sat down at the kitchen table with her drawing book, a lantern, a slice of bread and butter, and a cup of tea. She wanted to draw the chaos that had transpired outside today, but if Tata wanted this book to show him everything that had happened in his absence, she wanted it to be filled with important memories.

Mammi emerged from the front room in her sleeping gown, her *haube* on, and her hair in a single braid down her back. Elisabeth placed her drawing pencil in her book and closed it.

"Would you like some bread?" she asked. "You hardly ate at supper tonight."

Mammi waved away the comment. "Today was more stress than planning my wedding was," she said. "Those Hagels will not be helping us in the future."

This time, Elisabeth didn't stifle her chuckle.

"It isn't funny, Elisabeth," Mammi admonished her, and Elisabeth dropped her smile right away. "You need a man who puts his family first. Hagel Samuel puts himself first, and his son is no different. A good man is in charge of his family, which is his source of pride. I knew Hagel Samuel was a proud man, but I did not know he would throw his own son under a horse's hooves to protect his pride. Konrad will follow in his footsteps." She shook her head. "No, he is not for you."

Mammi saw Elisabeth's book of drawings, pulled it toward her, and opened it up. She turned the first few pages and saw Elisabeth's drawings of the kitchen, Georg's hands pulling at Anna's mittens, and the wedding. She shook her head again as she closed it and stood up.

"Such a beautiful but useless gift," she muttered, and returned to the front room.

Elisabeth also didn't know why she felt compelled to draw. "What good is it?" she asked Jesus as she bit into her slice of bread and began sketching the back side of an envelope.

CHAPTER THIRTEEN

Juliana sat in the change room, disappointed again. Supper had gone well, but after Aunt Anne offered to take Juliana to dance, Mom had accepted because she apparently had too much to do at work. *What's the point of being a manager if you can't leave when you want to?* Juliana wondered in anger. Moreover, Juliana had hoped to catch Jasmine before class, but one of the teachers had called in sick, and since Jasmine was in the studio's apprentice program, she'd been asked to supply.

"Today just sucks," she said to herself. She slid on her ballet shoes, pulled her leg warmers all the way up, and slipped into a tight-fitting ballet sweater. Miss Ambrosia, the ballet teacher, allowed students to wear warm-up clothing, but after barre, it all had to be removed.

Juliana walked out of the change room and almost got run over by a group of kids. *Is class already starting?* she wondered. But none of the other classes had come out yet. Juliana shrugged and was continuing on her way to go see the dancers from her group in the homework room when she heard muffled yelling coming from one of the music rooms. Juliana looked around at the other parents calmly waiting for their kids. No one seemed to bat an eyelash, so at first Juliana ignored the yelling, too. But as she continued to the homework room, the yelling didn't stop and Juliana felt that something was wrong. Who needed to yell that much at a student? As she neared the music room, she could hear some of the words.

"...she's too young!...What were you thinking...?"

Juliana stopped at the door and peeked in the window. A woman's back was turned to the door, her arms alternating between flying everywhere and parking on her hips. Now, Juliana could hear every word she was saying.

"What right do you have to tell the kids they can't move the way they want to? They're seven! She needs to explore her imagination! Or don't you have any? My daughter just started last year and you're already expecting her to be a prima ballerina!"

Juliana craned her neck and gasped: the woman was yelling at Jasmine. Juliana's new friend stood there like a statue, fear frozen on her face. Jasmine needed help, but what could Juliana do? The other teachers were still in class. Juliana hurried back down the short corridor to the reception desk. Unfortunately, Mrs. Laing and her office assistants were occupied with other parents. The woman's voice became louder. Juliana glanced at the men and women sitting in the waiting room. A few looked in the direction of the noise, but then they returned their attention to their devices.

How can they not care enough to get up and see what's going on?

Juliana rushed back to the music room and looked inside. The woman's gestures had become more frantic. Juliana had to help, but she didn't know what to do. Should she try to intervene? Who else was going to help if she didn't?

"My daughter *loves* dance! And because of you, she didn't smile all class!"

Juliana placed her hand on the doorknob.

"I pay lots of money to have the top teachers instruct her, and tonight she's left with a teenager!"

Juliana's hand stopped. No, another teenager would make things worse: this was way out of her control. She had to get help. She bolted down the hallway, turned the corner, and continued running to the last studio, where Miss Denise was teaching the seniors. Juliana burst into the studio. The dancers stopped, but the music kept blaring over the speakers.

Miss Denise placed her hands on her hips. "Juliana, you don't interrupt—"

"Jasmine really needs your help," she said. "Some mother is screaming at her."

A look of concern crossed Miss Denise's face. She instructed one of the dancers to restart the music while she looked into things. Juliana told her what she'd over-heard as they rushed toward the music room. When they reached Jasmine, they heard the mother swearing at her. Without hesitation, Miss Denise swung the door open. Jasmine startled but then relaxed when she saw who it was.

"You do not speak to my students that way," Miss Denise said. "You talk to me. Juliana, Jasmine, you've got class shortly. Go get ready and close the door behind you."

As the two headed down the hallway to ballet, they could hear the mother yelling at Miss Denise, and Miss Denise in turn speaking firmly back to her. Heads turned and stared at the girls.

Sure, now they pay attention, Juliana thought. Once they were back in their change room, she asked Jasmine if she was all right.

Jasmine's answer came out cold, her eyes avoiding

Juliana. "Yeah, I'm fine." She quickly switched her shoes.

"How can you be fine?" Juliana asked. Jasmine usually exuded a confidence that intimidated Juliana, but watching her scratch her head, adjust her hair, fiddle with her shoes, and twice drop a leg warmer, for the first time Juliana witnessed fear and agitation in her friend instead.

Jasmine continued to avert her gaze from Juliana. "You have to move on. What good is it dwelling on someone like that?" She took a swig of water before practically running out of the change room.

Juliana followed her, keeping pace. "She swore at you!" she said through clenched teeth. "No one deserves that!"

Jasmine stopped, and Juliana almost ran into her. "But I still have to move on. I refuse to let a mother who can't control her anger interfere with my training."

Jasmine picked up her pace and Juliana followed. "But how can you not be even a little upset by that?"

"Stop it, okay?" Jasmine said. They reached the studio and this time she bore her gaze into Juliana's eyes. "I have goals in life that I'm going to achieve. That mother is an absolute witch, and everyone knows she's like that. But if I'm going to pass my ballet exams this year and keep up my high scores in competition, I need to focus. The last thing I need is for you to keep reminding me about this."

The moment Jasmine stepped over the threshold and into the studio, her mood changed, as though she had entered onstage and was about to perform in front of a panel of judges. *How does she do that?* Juliana wondered. But something inside her told her that Jasmine wasn't fine. Miss Denise came down the hallway and Juliana indicated she wanted to speak with her.

"Are you okay?" Miss Denise asked.

Juliana nodded. "But I don't know if Jasmine is. She said she was fine, but something just doesn't feel right."

Miss Denise looked past Juliana and into the ballet studio, where Jasmine was already warming up.

"Thank you. You did the right thing coming to get me. I'll talk with Jasmine when she has a moment. But I know she often prefers time alone first, and if she can spend that time dancing, that helps her a lot."

Juliana understood exactly what Miss Denise meant.

It was Saturday, the most important day of the week after Sunday. Saturday was the day the girls and women in every German home in Semlak scrubbed the house from top to bottom. Right now, all three Schuhmacher daughters were working on the very bottom: smoothing out the little dents and holes in the dirt-and-chaff floor. Anna and Rosina were in the back room, on their hands and knees, with the carpets rolled back, rubbing at the wetted floor.

"That spot must be made perfectly smooth!" Omama ordered from her bed.

"I'm trying!" Rosina said.

"Not hard enough!" Omama countered.

"She is learning, Omama, I promise. Just after

Christmas, it took us a lot longer to finish this room than it did today," Anna said in her sister's defence.

"You're not done yet."

"Almost. And we're getting faster because Rosina's getting faster."

Inwardly, Elisabeth smiled. Her sisters had been on their absolute best behaviour the last couple of days—of course, only when Omama was around. But that didn't matter. It meant that the box of dried corn kernels had stayed in the cupboard.

Elisabeth stood in the front room with the special watering can used to gently wet the floor before she could begin rubbing away at the divots and crevices that had made their way into the floor over the course of the week. The chairs had been lifted onto the table, and the blankets folded up onto the beds so she could reach underneath and get out any bugs that might have made their home in there over the past week.

Luki sat uncharacteristically quietly on his bed, tossing a rubber ball up and down while Elisabeth gently poured the water from the can onto the floor, creating the outline of a simple flower.

"You're quiet," she said to her brother, whom Mammi again had sent inside. "Is everything all right?"

Luki didn't respond. Elisabeth knelt down on the ground and began rubbing.

"Anna!" Omama reprimanded. "You missed a spot under my bed!"

Elisabeth rolled her eyes. She could only imagine what Peter-Bátschi and his family must have faced with his mother in their home.

"I'm very sorry, Omama. Let me get that one."

Elisabeth felt horrible for her sisters, but what else were they supposed to do? Mammi would be embarrassed if her children fought with her mother, and even if the siblings' wildest dream could ever come true—kicking Omama out—the entire village would talk about them and Mammi could lose her customers.

Jesus, please send Omama home, she prayed. It was the only request she believed she could make without harming her family's reputation. Then she returned her attention to her brother. "Luki, you can talk to me." She looked up at him as she rubbed at the floor, and he finally stopped playing with his ball.

"Are you going to marry Konrad?" he asked.

Elisabeth stopped. "Is that why you're so quiet? You're worried about that?"

He kept his eyes focused on his ball as he nodded. "He yells more than Omama does." Elisabeth stroked his arm and then returned to rubbing the floor. "No," she replied. "I will not."

Luki's eyes lit up. "Are you sure?"

Elisabeth smiled and nodded and Luki began

bouncing up and down on his bed and laughing, the crunching hay in the mattress sounding just as happy as he did. Elisabeth couldn't help but laugh, too. She was also happy that Konrad would not be part of her future.

Jesus had answered Elisabeth's prayer! Peter-Bátschi had come by after lunch and had said that he would pick up Omama before supper to take her home. Sophie-Néni had managed to give their house a decent cleaning, and he had apologized to his mother for the state of his family and had promised to do better.

A knock on the door made Elisabeth rush to answer it and she let her uncle in, a big grin on her face.

"It's about time he got here," Omama grumbled as she came into the kitchen from the back room.

Peter-Bátschi kissed Elisabeth and Mammi on each cheek, patted the younger girls on the head, shook Luki's hand, and then nodded to his mother. His cheeks were red, but Elisabeth was certain it wasn't because of the cold: he only lived a few houses away so he couldn't have been outside long enough for his cheeks to turn red. His face was flushed clearly because of the entire situation.

"My suitcase is in the back room," Omama

declared. Elisabeth took a step to get it, and Omama grabbed her wrist. "My son can do that," she said. Peter-Bátschi wiped his boots off well and retrieved Omama's belongings. "I must say," Omama continued, "it's easier to live in a household where the father isn't around at all than one where the father ignores his family."

Peter-Bátschi's face turned an even deeper shade of red, and although Elisabeth found her uncle's reaction a little funny, Omama's comments hurt her. If Tata had been around, none of this week's chaos would have happened, Luki would have had a father at home to show him how to be a good man, and Elisabeth would still have had her teacher. As much as Elisabeth tried to be honest with her family and friends, and as much as she appreciated when others were kind and honest with her, too, she sometimes wished some words were never said.

"But your family needs me," Omama declared to her son. "If only to make sure you spend less time with your friends and more with your family, like I raised you to do." She swatted him on the shoulder and hobbled out the door.

"She didn't even say thank you," Rosina said. "You're supposed to say thank you when someone does something nice for you."

Peter-Bátschi nodded in agreement and tipped his

hat. "But I will say thank you for your help this week." He sighed. "And I'm sorry."

Now Mammi whacked him on the shoulder. "Get your family in order and stop leaving messes for the rest of us to clean up after you." Elisabeth tried to stifle a chuckle, but Anna and Rosina failed at it. Mammi faced Elisabeth, her expression serious. "This is also the kind of man you don't want."

Peter-Bátschi's face remained red as he turned and hurried out the door.

"Peter!" Mammi shouted after him. "Modr's suitcase!"

He reappeared, grabbed it, and disappeared. After Mammi closed the door, all four children giggled.

"It's not funny," Mammi said. "He's an embarrassment to the Braun name. Who can't look after his own family?" Her steely eyes focused on Luki, and he ducked behind Elisabeth. "Yes, that's right," Mammi said. "You'll be living with me for as long as I live."

The three sisters burst out in laughter.

EVERYONE WAS IN BED, EXCEPT ELISABETH. SHE HAD promised Mammi she wouldn't stay up late but she needed some time to think. Although Mammi's face had showed she disapproved of such wasted time, she had mumbled, "If it's God's will that you have this gift, then...fine."

Elisabeth completed her sketch of an envelope in her book. She drew it to show the envelope being opened by someone, hoping to remind Tata of the anticipation they would both feel in that moment, eager to read words from someone they loved. Would she someday write in a letter the name of the man she would marry? Or would she instead tell Tata story after story of men she did not like?

With two POWs returned, the war had taken fifty-one young men from the village, leaving more girls and widows vying for the ones left. Several more soldiers were still stationed in Budapest, hopefully to return in the coming months. Was Konrad perhaps one of the better men left?

Even though finding a husband was exciting for Elisabeth, after this past week, she could sense how unsettling the prospect was for her siblings. It had never occurred to her that the fear of her leaving was so strong in their minds. Perhaps it was best to leave it alone for now? But the thought of having her own house to run as she pleased was too exciting to just let go. She also knew that once she turned twenty, she would have a harder time finding someone.

What news would Elisabeth's next letter to Tata contain?

CHAPTER FIFTEEN

The following morning, Juliana stared at her phone.

Should I or shouldn't I?

She wanted to call Jasmine and see how she was feeling, but Jasmine's retort played over and over in her mind: *The last thing I need is for you to keep reminding me about this.* But Miss Denise had said that Jasmine often needed to dance before she was ready to talk. What if Jasmine wanted a friend now the way Juliana could have used one the night before?

She's got friends from school, Juliana thought. *Probably people she's known for years. Would I want some new girl calling me up while I was talking things out with Rachel?*

On her night table was Omama's book of drawings, opened to the envelope. Juliana had asked Opa again what might have been in it, but he only repeated the same thing: that it was likely about a letter either from his grandfather to his mother or vice versa.

She draws it so realistically, I want to rip it open and find out what's inside. Juliana sighed. This book contained so many mysteries, and she didn't know if she would ever solve even half of them.

But she would have had to wait...how long did letters take to travel back then? Juliana thought for a few moments and then searched for the answer on her phone. *A couple of weeks at least?* That was a long time to wait for someone you cared about to help you with any problems you had. She reconsidered her own dilemma. If she had met a new girl in class, and that girl had helped her, wouldn't Juliana find it nice if that girl asked how she was doing, even if the timing wasn't convenient? Moreover, Jasmine struck Juliana as someone who didn't like asking for help. What if she wanted someone to talk to right now but didn't want to say anything? That meant Juliana wasn't being a good friend by not asking.

Worst case scenario, she won't answer me and I can ask her about it tonight, Juliana thought. She wouldn't have to wait for weeks for her message to arrive and then several more weeks to get an answer.

She opened up her messaging app and stared at it for a few more moments as she wondered just what to ask. Thankfully, the right question appeared in her mind.

Did you want to practice today? I'm behind because of my exams and could use a practice partner.

She stared at her phone, hoping for a reply. Only after her hands got stiff did she realize she'd been gripping her phone tightly for several minutes. "Several minutes feels like several weeks," she said aloud. She glanced over at the old book. "How did you manage?" Then her phone beeped and she almost squealed in delight. It was Jasmine.

What time?

Juliana quickly typed back. *Any time. Now? After lunch? Your place or mine?* She waited, and soon enough, the three dots began pulsating as Jasmine typed.

Now's good. Your place.

Awesome!

Juliana quickly typed in her address, dropped her phone onto her bed and jumped up to get ready for Jasmine's visit. She looked at herself in the mirror and smiled. "The first time I'm having someone over!" she said to her happy reflection, and she jumped up and down, the nervous energy rushing into her body and needing an immediate exit. Her phone beeped again and she picked it up.

Thanks about last night. And sorry. It wasn't personal.

No worries. Let's just dance and leave the rest alone. Kk? Bring tap board.

There in 20.

Juliana responded with a thumbs-up emoji, tucked the phone into her pants pocket in case Jasmine texted again, and began double-checking her room, the kitchen, and the rec room for any unsightly messes.

JULIANA RUSHED TO OPEN THE DOOR. "HEY!" SHE SAID TO Jasmine. "Come on in!" Jasmine smiled and stepped inside with her tap board, which made it a tight squeeze for the two of them on the landing. "Here, let me take that," Juliana offered and rushed it into the basement, placing it next to hers.

"There's no hurry!" Jasmine called down.

Juliana giggled. "Sorry! It's the first time I've had a friend over. Well, here, not the first time ever! I'm a little excited!" She bounded up the stairs, yanked Jasmine's coat out of her hands, and hung it in the hallway closet. Jasmine followed Juliana into the kitchen.

"You really wear your emotions on your sleeve, don't you?" Jasmine said, a slightly bemused expression on her face.

Juliana had never thought about it before. "I just need to get my energy out, I guess. Something to drink?" Her heart still beating a million miles a minute, she grabbed a glass before Jasmine could even answer.

"Sure," Jasmine said with a laugh and pulled out a chair. "Just water, though."

"My favourite," Juliana said and poured two glasses. "I'm glad you could come over. It can get pretty lonely here."

"Your parents not home?"

"No. Mom's at work and Dad's on a drive to Georgia. Opa's here, though, but he's in his room right now, probably watching some news or talk show."

An awkward silence settled in the kitchen. Juliana wanted to ask about last night, but she didn't want to upset Jasmine either. If something was bothering Jasmine, Juliana wanted her new friend to know that she could talk about it.

"Thanks for coming over," she said to break the silence. "I'm so behind and need to catch up."

Jasmine swallowed her mouthful of water. "I know why you wanted to get together today. You asked me over to make sure I was okay."

Juliana blushed. "Am I that obvious?"

"Yup."

"Sorry."

"But I'm fine. Mrs. Orzel is one of those crazy dance moms who thinks her child is going to make it big just because she's cute." She drank the last sip of water and set her glass down. "Downstairs?"

"Yup!" Juliana finished hers and then led the way. When they were halfway down the stairs, Opa came out of his room.

"Hello," he said. "Who are you?"

"Opa, this is Jasmine. She's from my new dance school," Juliana explained. "We're going to practice."

"Hi," Jasmine said, a friendly smile on her face.

"It's nice to meet Yulika's friends. I'm Peter. Have fun!" Opa said and let the girls come down the stairs before he went up.

"Yulika?" Jasmine asked. "Is that your real name or something?"

"No," Juliana said. "It's his nickname for me. It's either that or Yuliana. He doesn't like putting the *j* sound at the front of it for some reason."

They entered the rec room. "He seems really sweet," Jasmine said. "How has he been?"

Juliana shrugged. "I think normal for where he's at. I wish my parents were home more often, though. Lately, I feel like I'm the one who's supposed to look after him. I mean, I knew Dad would be gone for long stretches, but I honestly thought Mom would be home more often."

Juliana sat on the floor in a wide straddle to stretch

her hamstrings and inner thigh muscles, and Jasmine stretched into a deep lunge.

"Sounds pretty peaceful, though," Jasmine said.

"It can be, but when both Mom and Dad are home, I've got two parents and a grandfather watching me, and then it seems like I can't do anything right."

"I know the feeling," Jasmine replied.

As they continued to warm up and chat, something in Juliana dissipated. It took her a few moments to figure out what it was and why, but then she got it: the stress of the past month had finally disappeared, and the reason was Jasmine's visit. It felt good to finally have a friend over. She couldn't wait to find a time for Meghan and Shawna, but that would have to wait until next week, when school started again. Juliana was certain she'd be sleeping and practicing a lot the rest of this week.

Juliana's ears were wide open.

"Semlak wasn't backwards," Opa insisted.

"Really?" Mom countered. "You lived on dirt floors and had an outhouse and a well in the 1950s."

"It was that bad?" Dad asked.

"You have no idea," Mom replied. "And then the"

Communists came and things got even worse. Some rural areas in Romania still don't have indoor toilets."

"But we eventually had floorboards and a range. I believe Mammi actually had a Vesta after she married."

"A what?" Juliana asked.

"Vesta was the brand name for these massive, ugly ranges that eventually replaced the brick-and-lime ovens they had," Mom answered. "Modr could never stop talking about it when I was a kid. She kept saying how much more advanced things were in Temeswar, where she grew up."

The entire family was dining out at a steakhouse in Kitchener. Mom hadn't eaten there in years, and so she had begged everyone to drive halfway through town to humour her. Opa was sharp as a whistle this Friday evening, so Juliana had asked to hear more about Semlak. She hadn't intended to unleash a debate, though.

"We eventually put floorboards in," Opa said. "And Mammi painted beautiful designs on the walls, something that became the fashion over there and never here."

"Well, I guess you have a point. Here, wallpaper became the fashion, and look where that got us."

Juliana chuckled. The fuzzy, floral wallpaper in her room certainly proved Mom's point. But her thoughts whipped back to Opa's comments. Omama did more than just draw in a notebook? But what were Communists? And if Omama had an outhouse and no running water, where did everyone shower? A thousand more questions ran through Juliana's head, jamming her train of thought and preventing her from asking even just one.

"And we had friendships that lasted years and even generations," Opa said. "You only moved out of Semlak because of war, to go to America, or to go to God. Everyone knew everyone."

"Tata, by the time you went to school there, people were leaving to move to the city."

"But not my friends."

Dad took a sip of his beer. "It does sound nice, though. Something comforting about knowing everyone."

"He's making it sound nice," Mom said. "Everyone knew everyone's business. *Everyone* knew your life and *everyone* judged you for it."

"They made sure you behaved properly," Opa insisted. "And if you needed money, your friends lent it you. You didn't have to waste money getting money from a bank."

"You had a credit union! Don't tell me no one borrowed from the credit union."

"But your friends still borrowed you money."

"'Lent,' Tata, it's 'lent' in English."

"Fine. And weddings were beautiful! Everyone brought their own dishes, all the family and close friends cooked—"

"The *women* cooked and didn't get paid."

"The men butchered the pigs!"

"And that was it!" Mom's phone beeped. "Just a sec, Tata." She pulled it out of her purse, read the message, and then began texting.

"Seriously, Mom?" Juliana said. "You won't let me text at the dinner table."

Not taking her eyes off her phone, Mom said, "You don't manage fifty people, all of them wanting your attention and relying on you to support their families. Sorry, I've got to call them. This can't wait." She left the table.

"This is the most I've heard about any of this," Dad said, apparently just as intrigued about Semlak as Juliana. "Katy rarely brings it up. You were saying, Peter?" And then his phone rang. He checked the number. "Sorry—it's my boss."

Opa raised his eyebrows. "On a Friday night?"

"Every ride I do I get paid for," Dad said. "I'm new in the company, and that means I don't get to ignore my boss when he has a trip for me." Dad answered the phone and also left the table.

Juliana watched as her parents walked out of the eating area toward the lobby.

"These phones you all have," Opa said. "They do nothing but cause trouble."

"Not entirely," Juliana said. "They do let me stay in touch with Rachel and my friends."

Opa shook his head in dismay at her parents. "This would have never happened back at home. When everyone sat down to eat, everyone talked to each other." He paused as he seemed to remember something. "Although I remember Mammi saying that when she was a child, she wasn't allowed to talk at the table."

"This conversation was nice, I have to admit," Juliana said.

Opa reached over and grabbed her hand. "Your parents do love you, a lot, Yulika. It's why they do what they do." He let go and leaned back in his chair. "But these phones...are they really necessary?"

An idea popped into Juliana's head. Her own phone was in her jacket, which was hanging over the back of her chair. Memories seemed to be crystal clear to him right now, and if his memory was indeed fading, then...

"What were you saying about Omama's painting?" Juliana said as she discreetly pulled her phone out, turned on the voice recorder, and pretended to adjust the serviette on the table while she lay the phone just next to it.

"That her painting was very beautiful. She would paint lovely flowers on our walls—it had finally become fashionable between the wars to decorate the white walls, and she continued it when we returned to Semlak when I was a child."

"Wait. You mean you weren't born there?"

"I was born there. But then Mammi moved away to Temeswar for a little." His eyes began to lose focus and he appeared to be drifting into his memories. "No, your mother is wrong," he continued. "It was a small community, and the only place Mammi felt comfortable raising her young child without his father. Yes, they gossiped about her—even I heard the rumours once I started attending school—but everyone made sure I was taken care of."

"You had no father?" Juliana leaned forward, eager to hear more.

"I'm back," Mom said, and Juliana almost jumped. Really? Now? Mom couldn't talk on the phone longer? Juliana slid the serviette over her phone and moved both items on to her lap where she could turn off the recording app. "What were you talking about?" Mom asked.

Opa thought for a moment and then shrugged. Had he really forgotten?

"What?" Mom asked. "Was it some kind of secret?" She smiled, and Juliana forced a smile back.

"I asked Opa to tell me more about Omama's paintings."

Opa's eyes lit up. "They were so beautiful, Katy. I wish you could've seen them. But is everything all right at work? I mean, for them to call you on your night off...?"

For the rest of the meal, Juliana couldn't take her thoughts away from what Opa had said. He had no father? Or had his father maybe died? If Omama returned home after choosing to move away, then something horrible must have happened, otherwise why else would she do it? *Or, maybe she just missed her family*, Juliana thought. After what had happened this past month to her, she could relate.

CHAPTER SIXTEEN

Rosina sat dutifully at the table in the front room, her tongue stuck out as though its presence would help her finish her third row of knitting. Herr Blum had returned to school, so both Anna and Luki were finally back in class.

"I'm taking food out to Mammi!" Elisabeth called to her, and Rosina nodded, not taking her eyes off her handiwork.

Elisabeth switched out her shoes for her boots and wrapped a shawl around her shoulders—the weather had warmed up a little, but not enough for her to be able to leave her shawl behind. She carried a cup of tea in one hand and a plate with buttered bread and a few slices of salami in the other.

The wind blew fiercely along the side of the house,

and Elisabeth hoped Mammi wasn't too cold in the workshop. Although Tata had built it into the summer kitchen at the back of the house so it was sheltered, they didn't have the time or money to build any kind of heat source into it. Only the few gas lamps Mammi had in there provided any warmth. Maybe Elisabeth should have brought Mammi an extra blanket, too? But when Elisabeth neared the door, a more immediate worry appeared: she could hear Mammi throwing up. Elisabeth's heart began to race. Had the Spanish flu the postman had talked about gotten its grip on their mother?

Elisabeth burst into the workshop to see her mother leaning over a bowl. "Mammi? What's wrong?"

Mammi's eyes pierced Elisabeth's. "Nothing is wrong! What are you doing here?"

Taken aback by Mammi's flash of anger, Elisabeth lost her words.

Mammi saw the food in Elisabeth's hand. "Leave that here and go."

As Elisabeth set the plate down on the workbench, her voice finally returned. "But you're sick...You need to rest."

"I'm fine. Now go and look after the day's chores."

"But..."

"Go! You have chores to do!"

Mammi's cheeks puffed out and she gestured for

Elisabeth to get out of the workshop. Just as Elisabeth closed the door, she heard Mammi get sick again.

ONCE SHE RETURNED TO THE LIVING AREA OF THE HOUSE, Elisabeth heard Rosina crying. It was only mid-morning and she was beginning to wonder what else could happen today.

"What's wrong?" she asked her sister.

Rosina slammed her knitting on the table. "I can't do it!"

Really? Elisabeth asked Jesus as He hung on His cross. *Mammi's sick and now I have to deal with my impatient little sister?* Elisabeth took a deep breath and, after putting on her house shoes, walked over to her sister and stroked her shoulder. "I keep telling you that crocheting is easier to learn when you're young. If you would listen to me, you wouldn't be so upset."

But her words had the opposite effect on Rosina. She clutched her knitting needles in her little hands again. "I'm knitting!" she shouted, and within moments her tongue was again sticking out between her lips, trying to help her get the needle with yarn wrapped around it back through the loop.

Exasperated, Elisabeth decided to move her list of chores around and do some ironing: she needed something to calm her down. Back in the kitchen, she lay two tablecloths over the table, got the iron from the kitchen cabinet and filled it with simmering coals from the oven. She grabbed a pair of Luki's pants out of the basket of dry laundry. While the iron warmed up, Elisabeth laid out the pants and carefully folded the legs lengthwise.

As the iron glided up and down the soft linen, Elisabeth's thoughts kept turning to her mother. How could she be sick but fine? All last week, Mammi had seemed fine except when the pigs got out and she had held her hand over her stomach. Then Elisabeth realized something. "She barely ate all week," Elisabeth said to Jesus on the crucifix. "She worked alone often, couldn't help with the animals on Wednesday, and she's sent Luki inside several times, even to polish shoes. Has she been sick all this time?" The more Elisabeth recalled the events of the week, the more concerned she became. She set the iron on the stove, changed her shoes once more and grabbed her shawl.

"I need to ask Mammi something!" she shouted back to Rosina.

"I'm concentrating!" Rosina shouted back, and Elisabeth took that to mean her sister had heard her.

Once outside the door to the workshop, Elisabeth stopped for a moment to listen to Mammi, who was tapping away on a shoe. Elisabeth entered, but she almost recoiled from the smell of vomit in the air.

"What is it now?" Mammi growled at her.

This time, Elisabeth stood her ground. "You're sick, Mammi. You told me—"

"I told you I was fine. Now go!"

Without another word, Mammi returned to her work, ignoring any pleas from her daughter.

ELISABETH STOOD AT THE STOVE IN THEIR EMPTY HOUSE, where she had been steeping chamomile flowers in boiling water for twenty minutes to make a concentrated tea. She didn't know what was wrong with Mammi, but she knew she was having problems with her stomach. She wanted to make Mammi a tea and hopefully convince her to at least come inside and rest for a bit. She had sent Rosina over to a neighbour's house to play. With the house now empty, Mammi could rest without anyone else in the family knowing she was ill.

Elisabeth removed the tea from the burner, sliced some bread and sprinkled it with paprika. She placed a lid on the tea and headed out back to fetch Mammi.

When she opened the door, Mammi slammed her fist on the table. "What now?!"

Elisabeth remained calm. "I've made some tea for you, some bread and paprika, and sent Rosina to the Bartolfs on the corner to play," she said, not wavering under her mother's anger this time. "You need to rest. I can scrub down the workshop for you, organize your materials if you need that done...Whatever you wanted to do this afternoon by the time everyone got home, I'll look after it as best I can. But you're sick, Mammi." Tears welled up in Elisabeth's eyes. "We can't lose you, too. You've hardly eaten this past week, and then you wouldn't help with the animals, and you looked sick but I was too busy being angry at the Hagels and forgot about it. But now I see it clearly. You need to let me help."

She wiped the tears away from her face, ashamed that she was crying at all. Mammi hadn't even cried when Tata had left.

"You worry too much about me," Mammi said. Her tone had softened. "If I were ever to get sick, I would tell you. I am not sick."

"Then at least come inside, where it's warm, and rest for a bit. Maybe we should ask Georg to build a little stove for in here. I'm certain I can offer to help him and Eva with something in return."

Mammi took a long look at her daughter, and Elisabeth stared back. She was not going to let her mother's anger push her down. Not this time, at least.

To Elisabeth's relief, Mammi nodded and stood up. "But just to warm up and eat, then I'm coming back out here," she said.

In the kitchen, Mammi stood by the oven, warming her hands, while Elisabeth set the tea and food on the table. Once both had sat down, though, Elisabeth continued pressing for an answer.

"Nobody is 'not sick' and throws up," she said. "Something is wrong with you."

Mammi glanced to the front room and then the door. Elisabeth couldn't figure out what was going on. What kind of illness could be so humiliating except for the kinds that robbed you of your memory and control?

"You're not old enough to know this yet, but, very well, I will answer you," Mammi said.

"I'm almost a woman," Elisabeth insisted.

Mammi nodded. "Yes, you are, but not yet. You *cannot* repeat this to anyone, including your sisters or brother or Maria. Is that understood?" Mammi took a tiny bite of the bread. "I am expecting a child, Elisabeth, and this one is very difficult."

The news shocked Elisabeth. A child? Why would God make Mammi a mother again when Tata wasn't home? Or was God doing this so Tata would have to return home sooner? But then the family wouldn't have a shingle roof, and Elisabeth might not be able to marry well if her dowry wasn't big enough. And what if

Mammi died when she was about to receive the baby from God?

Elisabeth remembered Mammi's words from the evening she and Omama had discussed Elisabeth's readiness for a husband: *Elisabeth still has much to learn.*

Elisabeth didn't realize until now just how true that was.

CHAPTER SEVENTEEN

Juliana was jumping up and down in jazz choreography class.

"You get excited easily, don't you?" Jasmine said.

Juliana nodded her head fast. "It's costume day!"

Jasmine raised an eyebrow. "Did you not have costumes in Calgary?"

Juliana stopped jumping. "You people really think we live in a different country out there, don't you? Of course we had costumes. But I always love trying them on for the first time."

Miss Denise entered the studio, followed by Mrs. Laing, their arms full with black costumes in plastic garment bags. They hung them on a barre, and then Mrs. Laing walked out again.

"So, what do you think?" Miss Denise asked, holding one up.

Juliana thought her body was going to explode from all the excitement. The bodice piece was black, with wispy silver accents sewn randomly around it. The broad shoulder straps flowed into a v-neck and the bottom of the bodice extended into bike shorts. Over the hanger, she saw long, black gloves.

"Each of you gets a hat," Miss Denise said as Mrs. Laing reappeared with a stack of bowler hats. "Make sure you take the elastic that's pinned to your costume tag and have your moms sew it on."

She then began calling out each student's name, and Juliana kept hopping on the spot, waiting for hers. By the time the first fifteen had left to get changed, though, Juliana worried that maybe she'd been forgotten.

Wouldn't be the first time this year, she thought dryly.

"Mackenzie...Isaac...Savannah..."

Juliana stopped hopping. Was this really happening to her on one of the best days of the year? But to her relief, once everyone had left, there was indeed one costume still hanging on the barre.

"I need to talk to you for a moment," Miss Denise said.

Maybe this wasn't going to be one of the best days of the year. Juliana's palms began to sweat.

"I'm sorry I haven't spoken to you about what happened with Jasmine earlier this week."

Juliana gulped. Was she about to get into trouble?

Miss Denise shook her head in disbelief. "I can't believe that mother had the gall to talk to one of my students that way. She insisted last year that her daughter wear pigtails on stage at the recital instead of the ponytail she was supposed to wear because she swore ponytails made her daughter's head look big." Miss Denise rolled her eyes. "The poor girl was so embarrassed that she almost didn't go on stage. Anyway, I wanted to say again thank you for getting me. You saved your friend from a very high-maintenance customer."

Juliana's elation rose so fast inside her at the compliment that she now couldn't move.

Miss Denise continued. "Every studio has parents like that, so that's nothing new. But I'm telling you this because I know you wanted to join the apprentice program this year. I'd told your mom I wanted you to get used to the studio first, and it looks like it was a good thing. Your mom tells me that January was particularly hard on you."

"You talked with my mom?"

"Of course. We've been talking on the phone each week to make sure you're doing okay. We'll continue that for this month, and then we'll see if it's needed afterwards."

Juliana wasn't sure if she should be happy that her mom was taking part in her life or creeped out that she was spying on her. She didn't have time to decide, though: Miss Denise handed Juliana her costume.

"Keep up that kind of attitude, Juliana, and I'll be more than happy to put you in the apprentice program next year."

The news excited Juliana so much that she was again speechless, but her grin reached from ear to ear. Miss Denise smiled back. "Now get going, or you're going to hold up the group."

Juliana grand-jétéd out of the studio and ran to the change room.

"So, what courses are you registered in?" Meghan asked.

Juliana's new semester had begun, and she sat at a table in the Eby Heights cafeteria with Meghan and Shawna.

"English and math in the morning, and then science and geography after lunch." Juliana bit into her hummus-and-chicken sandwich.

"What teachers?" Meghan asked.

Juliana pointed to her full mouth, then pulled out her phone and opened her calendar app.

"You have your classes entered in your calendar?" Meghan asked incredulously. Even Shawna looked surprised.

Juliana swallowed her food. "Everything's in here. See?" She turned the phone so her new friends could see her schedule. Shawna took it out of her hand, a look of surprise still on her face.

"How can you handle all this?" she asked, her voice quiet as always.

"I just do it."

"You don't get stressed?" She handed the phone to Meghan so she could see it, too.

Juliana shrugged. Sure, she had been stressed in January, but that was a one-off situation. A packed schedule was nothing new for her, and concentrating on four courses in one semester would probably even be easier to manage than the eight courses she took every day in Calgary.

"Okay, let's see," Meghan said as she scrolled through Juliana's calendar. "You've got Ms. Lee for English. I had her last semester. She made Shakespeare feel like a death sentence. Gulminska for math...she's okay, nothing special, but I don't have her. Then Mr. Schmidt for science this afternoon. Hey, so do I! I hear he's awesome. Oh, and Ms. Haseltine again, for geography. Me, too! Hey, you have her, too, don't you, Shawna?"

Shawna nodded.

"I liked her," Juliana said. "She was weird but somehow I liked her."

"She actually makes you feel welcome in class," Shawna said.

"This is awesome," Meghan said. "We've got our afternoon classes together!"

Juliana's phone buzzed. Meghan handed it back to her. "A message from Rachel…?" she said.

Rachel was supposed to be in class. Juliana quickly looked at the message.

I need to talk to you NOW.

"Um, sorry, but I'd better call her," Juliana said and texted back.

"Who's Rachel?" Meghan asked.

"My best friend from back home. Something's up, or she wouldn't be texting at this time."

"It's lunch, though," Meghan said.

"Not in Calgary. Two hour time difference?"

"Oh, yeah, right."

Juliana left her lunch at her table and sought out a quieter corner in the cafeteria. She dialled.

Rachel was sobbing as she answered.

"Rachel! What's wrong?"

"Mom was in a car accident on her way to work."

"Oh my god, I'm so sorry! How's she doing?"

Rachel couldn't stop crying.

"Deep breaths," Juliana said. "I know I'm not there in person, but I'm with you. How's she doing?"

She could hear Rachel breathing into the phone as she tried to calm down enough to speak.

"Juliana, Mom's on life support."

Juliana felt like a powerful hand had clamped itself around her heart and had begun to squeeze.

"Rachel, oh my god, oh my god, oh my god!" Juliana shook her free hand to release the jittery, horrible energy now coursing through her. She forced herself to take deep breaths now, too.

"I don't know what to do," Rachel said. "Dad's coming to pick me up right now. I probably have to stay with him, which is fine, but..." Her voice trailed off.

How on earth could Juliana help Rachel from this distance?

"Jules, I love her, and I don't know if I've ever said that to her."

If there was one thing Juliana wanted more now than anything, it was to be by Rachel's side.

Juliana thought again about her great-grandmother. If Omama's father had ever written her that he was ill, she wouldn't know until his next letter whether or not he was even alive. No phone, no email, just letters. How did she deal with situations like that? All Juliana had to do now was jump into a plane and fly to her best friend. She could be there in a matter of hours. If she was allowed, which she knew would never happen. *It's unfair to be so far away!* she thought angrily.

But her anger wouldn't help Rachel. No. Juliana couldn't share that with her best friend who needed her more now than ever. Instead, Rachel needed to hear what she always told Juliana.

"Rachel, it'll be fine. I promise we'll get through this."

But was that a promise Juliana could keep?

SETTING THE RECORD STRAIGHT

Between Worlds tells a completely fictional contemporary story together with a story that is historical fiction. In the historical part of the book, I've taken facts about life in a previous time and included them in a fictional story. In writing novels, the story always comes first (because otherwise this would be a history textbook), so this section explains any facts that may have been changed to fit the story, and adds some more background to the story. If you have any questions about what you've read in this or any of the other books in the series, ask away! My contact information is in the section "Stay in Touch!"

GETTING HELP WITH RESEARCH

The most difficult aspect of writing this series is accessing information written in Hungarian or Romanian. In addition to English, I speak and read German, but that only takes me so far. Through an online skills marketplace, I found two researchers who have helped me considerably with finding out more details about these times. This book only scratches the surface of what they found, but you will certainly read more in upcoming books.

MARRIAGE IN SEMLAK

In *Between Worlds 2: The Distance*, we followed Elisabeth as she helped a cousin with wedding preparations and were introduced to Georg and his young wife, Eva. My information for marriage in this time period comes from several sources: The book *Semlak* by Georg Schmidt, and recollections from my own great-grandparents who came from a different German settlement in a different region.

In his book, Schmidt explains that divorce was extremely exceptional in Semlak, and that young women married as early as fourteen, though sixteen was more the norm. Young men usually waited until after their required military service, although I haven't fully researched that aspect of village life yet. Schmidt further writes that engagements in Semlak were a mix of attraction and planning: young men and women were drawn to each other but then were carefully supervised; if they chose to marry, their parents had to approve.

How young couples came together in these German communities in Eastern Europe varied, and this is what I brought into the series. One of my great-grandmothers, Katharina, was born in 1910 in a village that today is located in Serbia. She told me a long time ago that she and my great-grandfather, Sebastian, were brought together by a matchmaker of sorts. She was, so far as I can remember, supposed to marry another man, but he became seriously ill, so he was no longer "in the running." In addition, Sebastian was a furrier (he worked with animal furs), which was important to Katharina because it meant she wouldn't have to work as hard as the farmers' wives did. And I still remember her light chuckle when I turned sixteen and she told me she was married by that age. (I didn't marry for another fourteen years.)

However, wars change things, as you'll see with the series. As far as marriage goes, by the time Katharina and Sebastian's daughter, Mary, married my grandfather, John, in 1950, it was definitely for love: you can see it in one of their wedding photos. In addition, my grandmother was eighteen by then, and my grandfather twenty-one. Marrying in my family happened later with each successive generation.

GETTING THE NEWS

The mailman did indeed come into town weekly, beat his drum to get attention, announce the week's headlines, and deliver the mail. Three of the four headlines used in this book were discovered by one of the researchers I hired in Romania. She had found digitized copies of *Românul*, a daily from Arad, the main city in Arad County, which Semlak belonged to. The headlines came from editions from February 10, 12, and 15, 1920. If you read Romanian, you can read the newspaper here: http://dspace.bcucluj.ro/handle/123456789/15738.

The fourth headline (about Romania being victorious and withdrawing from Hungary) is fictional, but the historical event is fact. Whereas most of us in North America celebrated the end of World War I on November 11, 1918, and have been doing so for more than a hundred years now, for many in Europe, war continued. On November 13, 1918, the Romanian army crossed into Transylvania, which was then still part of Hungary. Military events did not begin until April 1919 and they lasted until August of that year. Romanian troops occupied Budapest, Hungary's capital, until 1920.

You'll find more information about the Hungarian-Romanian war on Wikipedia.

POWS

POWs, or prisoners of war, were soldiers caught and imprisoned by their enemies. Both sides of the war took prisoners, and treatment of these prisoners varied considerably. Many POWs were repatriated (i.e., returned to their own countries) relatively soon after the end of World War I. However, Russia was undergoing a lot of turmoil: from mid-1914 until 1922, three separate governments ruled the massive country, each one with their own opinion of how POWs should be treated. In addition, a civil war raged in Russia from 1917-1920, making repatriation of these POWs even more difficult. The last POWs were sent home in 1922, three years after the war ended. You can read more about WWI POWs in Russia here: https://encyclopedia.1914-1918-online.net/article/prisoners_of_war_russian_empire

I don't know if any Semlakers were prisoners of war in WWI, but Schmidt does confirm in his book that fifty-one German men from the village died in the conflict. The war killed many sons, brothers, and fathers, and Semlak was not spared from that tragedy.

A QUICK WORD ABOUT FIRST AID

Juliana studies some first-aid facts in preparation for her exams. Regardless of when you read this book, please don't follow them. First-aid instruction changes over the years, and what's in here may no longer be accurate by the time you read this. For example, when I did my lifeguard certification in the 1990s, we were instructed to place a leg between a standing person's legs when applying abdominal thrusts to a conscious, choking victim. When I recertified for my Bronze Medallion (the first level of lifesaving in Canada) in 2009, our instructor told us too many lifesavers had been injured that way and therefore we weren't allowed to place the leg there anymore. If the person became unconscious, we had to let them fall.

ACKNOWLEDGEMENTS

The deeper I get into these books, the more information and support I need to complete them.

Thank you to Georg Schmidt and the HOG Semlak (semlak.de), Anne Dreer, and the members and organizers of Donauschwaben Villages Helping Hands for their help with making Semlak come alive to me and my readers. In addition, I'd like to express thanks to my Romanian researchers, Crenguta Nicolae and Gabriela Rat, who are helping me discover the details that demonstrate just how much change the residents of villages like Semlak had to contend with.

For Juliana's storyline, trying to figure out how she transitioned from grade nine in Alberta to grade nine in Ontario was not an easy task. Special thanks go out to high school teachers Annamae Elliott and Erika

Werner, and St. Mary's High School vice principal Deanna Wehrle for helping me solve the problem. Thank you, too, to Sara Marsh, a fellow grad student who shared with me stories of growing up with a father who drove trucks for his career. And I'm always indebted to Deardra King-Leslie, my dance teacher for almost twenty years, who influenced my life in more ways than I could ever count.

This book can't logistically come together without my publishing team: Heather Wright, my writing coach and consulting editor; Susan Fish, my editor; and Michelle Fairbanks of Fresh Design, my graphic designer. Also special thanks to Kyle Bergum for helping me evaluate the first large-print editions for this series and to Ali MacGee for her advice and mentorship.

Thank you, too, to my writing family, the Professional Writers Association of Canada, whose members support my writing and give me feedback on various aspects of these projects when asked. For this story, a shout-out to Jennifer Lewington for some help with the loose-animals scene.

And last, my family: Mom & Dad, my sister's family, and Corey, Khristopher, and Jonnathan. Thank you for continuing to encourage and support me in my writing.

Photo by Erin Watt Photography

Lori Wolf-Heffner is a former competitive dancer, dance teacher, and theatre manager. She was a member of the first Canadian National Tap Team, back in 1996, under the leadership of Bonnie Dyer, with choreographer Mathew Clark. She's written for *Dance Canada Quarterly*, *just dance!* magazine, and *The Dance Current* (all under Lori Straus).

Fluent in German, Lori lived in Germany for three years, never once realizing just how close she was to some of the villages her ancestors left to migrate to Eastern Europe in the 1700s.

Lori lives in Waterloo, Ontario, with her husband

and two sons. She is a member of the Canadian Free-
lance Guild.

facebook.com/loriwolfheffner

twitter.com/LoriWolfHeffner

instagram.com/loriwolfheffner

goodreads.com/lori_wolf-heffner

bookbub.com/author/lori-wolf-heffner

pinterest.com/loriwolfheffner

amazon.com/author/loriwolfheffner